WILD CARDS

Before Vietnam, before Watergate, before the hippies, there came the wild card virus. From it emerged a new race of metahumans with extraordinary abilities who shaped the turbulent decades to come.

In this volume, you'll meet those wild cards who ushered in the '80s and came upon a terrifying enemy from a distant world:

THE GREAT AND POWERFUL TURTLE
A reticent ace with a heart of gold and a shellful of awesome power.

THE SLEEPER
The hibernating mercenary who wakes each time with a new body and powers to match.

KID DINOSAUR
A starry-eyed teenage boy whose strange powers earned himself a place in the action.

DR. TACHYON
The diminutive alien who has vowed to protect Earth from his own kind.

FORTUNATO
Whose experience with the erotic power of Tantric magic unleashed his own dark talents.

CHRYSALIS
Though her skin is transparent, no one can see through to the mysteries she hides within.

JUBE
The walrus who peddles newspapers and, on the side, masterminds an attempt to save the human race.

WILD CARDS

WILD CARDS

VOLUME TWO

ACES HIGH

a mosaic novel
edited by
George R.R. Martin
and written by:
Lewis Shiner
Roger Zelazny
Walter Jon Williams
Melinda M. Snodgrass
Victor Milán
Pat Cadigan
John J. Miller
George R.R. Martin
Walton Simons

TITAN BOOKS
LONDON

WILD CARDS 2: ACES HIGH
ISBN 1 85286 159 2

Published by Titan Books Ltd
58 St Giles High St
London WC2H 8LH

Published by arrangement with Bantam Books, a division of Bantam Doubleday Dell
Publishing Group Inc.

First Titan edition September 1989
1 2 3 4 5 6 7 8 9 10

for Chip Wideman, Jim Moore,
Gail Gerstner-Miller, and Parris,
the secret aces without whom the
wild card might never have been played

WILD CARDS

CARDS

VOLUME TWO

ACES HIGH

1979

PENNIES FROM HELL

By Lewis Shiner

There were maybe a dozen of them. Fortunato couldn't be sure exactly because they kept moving, trying to circle behind him. Two or three had knives, the rest had sawed-off pool cues, car antennas, anything that would hurt. They were hard to tell apart. Jeans, black leather jackets, long, slicked-back hair. At least three of them matched the vague description Chrysalis had given him.

"I'm looking for somebody called Gizmo," Fortunato said. They wanted to herd him away from the bridge, but they didn't want to physically push him yet. To his left the brick path led uphill into the Cloisters. The entire park was empty, had been empty for two weeks now, since the gangs had moved in.

"Hey, Gizmo," one of them said. "What do you say to the man?"

That one, with the thin lips and bloodshot eyes. Fortunato locked eyes with the kid nearest to him. "Take off," Fortunato said. The kid backed away, uncertain. Fortunato looked at the next one. "You too. Get out of here." This one was weaker; he turned and ran.

That was all he had time for. A pool cue came slicing for his head. Fortunato slowed time and took the cue, used it to knock away the nearest knife. He breathed in and things sped up again.

Now they were all getting nervous. "Go," he said, and three more ran, including the one called Gizmo. He sprinted downhill, toward the 193rd Street entrance. Fortunato threw the pool cue at another switchblade and ran after him.

They were running downhill. Fortunato felt himself

3

getting tired, and let out a burst of energy that lifted him off the path and sent him sailing through the air. The kid fell under him and rolled, headfirst. Something crunched in the kid's spine and both his legs jerked at once. Then he was dead.

"Christ," Fortunato breathed, brushing dead October leaves from his clothes. The cops had doubled patrols around the park, though they were afraid to come in. They'd tried it once, and it had cost them two men to chase the kids away. The next day the kids were back again. But there were cops watching, and for something like this they'd be willing to run in and pick up a body.

He dumped the kid's pockets, and there it was—a copper coin the size of a fifty-cent piece, red as drying blood. For ten years he'd had Chrysalis and a few others watching for them, and last night she'd seen the kid drop one at the Crystal Palace.

There was no wallet, nothing else that had any meaning. Fortunato palmed the coin and sprinted for the subway entrance.

"Yes, I remember this," Hiram said, picking the coin up with a corner of his napkin. "It's been a while."

"It was 1969," Fortunato said. "Ten years ago." Hiram nodded and cleared his throat. Fortunato didn't need magic to know that the fat man was uncomfortable. Fortunato's open black shirt and leather jacket weren't really up to the dress code here. Aces High looked out over the city from the observation deck of the Empire State Building, and the prices were as steep as the view.

Then there was the fact that he'd brought along his latest acquisition, a dark blonde named Caroline who went for five hundred a night. She was small, not quite delicate, with a childlike face and a body that invited speculation. She wore skintight jeans and a pink silk blouse with a couple of extra buttons undone. Whenever she moved, so did Hiram. She seemed to enjoy watching him sweat.

"The thing is, that's not the coin I showed you before. It's another one."

"Remarkable. It's hard to believe that you could come across two of them in this good a condition."

"I think you could put that a little stronger. That coin came off a kid from one of those gangs that's been trashing the

Cloisters. He was carrying it loose in his pocket. The first one came off a kid that was messing with the occult."

It was still hard for him to talk about. The kid had murdered three of Fortunato's geishas, cut them up in a pentagram for some twisted reason that he still hadn't figured out. He'd gone on with his life, training his women, learning about the Tantric power the wild card virus had given him, but otherwise keeping to himself.

And, when it got to bothering him, he would spend a day or a week following one of the loose ends the killer had left behind. The coin. The last word he'd said, "TIAMAT." The residual energies from something else that had been in the dead boy's loft, a presence that Fortunato had never been able to trace.

"You're saying there's something supernatural about them," Hiram said. His eyes shifted to watch Caroline as she stretched languorously in her chair.

"I just want you to take another look."

"Well," Hiram said. Around them the luncheon crowd made small noises with their forks and glasses and talked so quietly they sounded like distant water. "As I'm sure I said before, it *appears* to be a mint 1794 American penny, stamped from a hand-cut die. They could have been stolen from a museum or a coin shop or a private . . ." His voice trailed off. "Mmmmm. Have a look at this."

He held the coin out and pointed with a fleshy little finger, not quite touching the surface. "See the bottom of this wreath, here? It should be a bow. But instead it's something sort of shapeless and awful looking."

Fortunato stared at the coin and for a half-second felt like he was falling. The leaves of the wreath turned into tentacles, the ends of the ribbon opened like a beak, the loops of the bow became shapeless flesh, full of too many eyes. Fortunato had seen it before, in a book on Sumerian mythology. The caption underneath had read "TIAMAT."

"You all right?" Caroline asked.

"I'll be okay. Go on," he said to Hiram.

"My instinct would be to say they're forgeries. But who would forge a penny? And why not take the trouble to age them, at least a little? They look like they'd been stamped out yesterday."

"They weren't, if that matters. The auras of both of them

show a lot of use. I'd say they were at least a hundred years old, probably closer to two hundred."

Hiram pushed the ends of his fingers together. "All I can do is send you to somebody who might be more help. Her name is Eileen Carter. She runs a small museum out on Long Island. We used to, um, correspond. Numismatics, you know. She's written a couple of books on occult history, local stuff." He wrote an address in a little notebook and tore out the page.

Fortunato took the paper and stood up. "I appreciate it."

"Listen, do you think . . ." He licked his lips. "Do you think it would be safe for a regular person to own one of those?"

"Like, say, a collector?" Caroline asked.

Hiram looked down. "When you're finished with them. I'd pay."

"When this is over," Fortunato said, "if we're all still around, you're welcome to them."

Eileen Carter was in her late thirties, with flecks of gray in her brown hair. She looked up at Fortunato through squared-off glasses, then glanced over at Caroline. She smiled.

Fortunato spent most of his time with women. Even as beautiful as she was, Caroline was insecure, jealous, prone to irrational dieting or makeup. Eileen was something different. She seemed no more than a little amused by Caroline's looks. And as for Fortunato—a half-Japanese black man in leather, his forehead swollen courtesy of the wild card virus—she didn't seem to find anything unusual about him at all.

"Have you got the coin with you?" she asked. She looked right into his eyes when she talked to him. He was tired of women who looked like models. This one had a crooked nose, freckles, and about a dozen extra pounds. Most of all he liked her eyes. They were incandescent green and had smile lines in the corners.

He put the penny on the counter, tails up.

She bent over to look at it, touching the bridge of her glasses with one finger. She was wearing a green flannel shirt; the freckles ran down as far as Fortunato could see. Her hair smelled clean and sweet.

"Can I ask where you got this?"

"It's kind of a long story," Fortunato said. "I'm a friend of Hiram Worchester. He'll vouch for me if that'll help."

"It's good enough. What do you want to know?"

"Hiram said it was maybe a forgery."

"Just a second." She took a book off the wall behind her. She moved in sudden bursts of energy, giving herself completely to whatever she was doing. She opened the book on the counter and flipped through the pages. "Here," she said. She studied the back of the coin intently for a few seconds, biting on her lower lip. Her lips were small and strong and mobile. He found himself wondering what it would be like to kiss her.

"That one," she said. "Yes, it's a forgery. It's called a Balsam penny. Named after 'Black John' Balsam, it says. He minted them up in the Catskills around the turn of the nineteenth century." She looked up at Fortunato. "The name rings a bell, but I can't say why."

"'Black John'?"

She shrugged, smiled again. "Can I hang on to this? Just for a few days? I might be able to find something else for you."

"All right." Fortunato could hear the ocean from where they were and it made things seem a little less dire. He gave her his business card, the one with just his name and phone number on it. On their way out she smiled and waved at Caroline, but Caroline acted like she didn't see it.

On the train back to the city Caroline said, "You want to fuck her, don't you?"

Fortunato smiled and didn't answer her.

"I swear to God," she said. Fortunato could hear Houston in her voice again. It was the first time in weeks. "An overweight, broken-down old schoolmarm."

He knew better than to say anything. He was overreacting, he knew. Part of it was probably just pheromones, some kind of sexual chemistry that he'd understood a long time before he learned the scientific basis for it. But he'd felt comfortable with her, something that hadn't happened very often since the wild card had changed him. She'd seemed to have no self-consciousness at all.

Stop it, he thought. You're acting like a teenager.

Caroline, under control again, put a hand on his thigh. "When we get home," she said, "I'm going to fuck her right out of your mind."

"Fortunato?"

He switched the phone to his left hand and looked at the clock. Nine A.M. "Uh huh."

"This is Eileen Carter. You left a coin with me last week?"

He sat up, suddenly awake. Caroline turned over and buried her head under a pillow. "I haven't forgotten. How are you doing?"

"I may be on to something. How would you feel about a trip to the country?"

She picked him up in her VW Rabbit and they drove to Shandaken, a small town in the Catskills. He'd dressed as simply as he could, Levi's and a dark shirt and an old sport coat. But he couldn't hide his ancestry or the mark the virus had left on him.

They parked in an asphalt lot in front of a white clapboard church. They were barely out of the car before the church door opened and an old woman came out. She wore a cheap navy double-knit pantsuit and a scarf over her head. She looked Fortunato up and down for a while, but finally stuck out her hand. "Amy Fairborn. You would be the people from the city."

Eileen finished the introductions and the old woman nodded. "The grave's over here," she said.

The stone was a plain marble rectangle, outside the churchyard's white picket fence and well away from the other graves. The inscription read, "John Joseph Balsam. Died 1809. May He Burn In Hell."

The wind snapped at Fortunato's coat and blew faint traces of Eileen's perfume at him. "It's a hell of a story," Amy Fairborn said. "Nobody knows anymore how much of it's true. Balsam was supposed to be a witch of some sort, lived up in the hills. First anybody heard of him was in the 1790s. Nobody knows where he came from, other than Europe somewhere. Same old story. Foreigner, lives off to himself, gets blamed for everything. Cows give sour milk or somebody has a miscarriage, they make it his fault."

Fortunato nodded. He felt like a foreigner himself, at the moment. He couldn't see anything but trees and mountains anywhere he looked, except off to the right where the church held the top of the hill like a fort. He felt exposed, vulnerable. Nature was something that should have a city around it.

"One day the sheriff's daughter over to Kingston came up missing," Fairborn said. "That would be the beginning of August, 1809. Lammastide. They broke in Balsam's house and found the girl stretched out naked on an altar." The woman showed her teeth. "That's what the story says. Balsam was got up in some kind of weird outfit and a mask. Had a knife the size of your arm. Sure as hell he was going to carve her up."

"What kind of outfit?" Fortunato asked.

"Monk's robes. And a dog mask, they say. Well, you can guess the rest. They strung him up, burnt the house, salted the ground, knocked trees over in the road that led up there."

Fortunato took out one of the pennies; Eileen still had the other one. "This is supposed to be called a Balsam penny. Does that mean anything to you?"

"I got three or four more like it at the house. They wash up out of his grave every now and again. 'What goes down must come up,' my husband used to say. He buried a good many of these folks."

"They put the pennies in his grave?" Fortuanto asked.

"All they could find. When they fired the house they turned up a keg of 'em in the root cellar. You see how red it looks? Supposed to be from a high iron content or some such. Folks at the time said he put human blood in the copper. Anyways, the coins disappeared out of the sheriff's office. Most people thought Balsam's wife and kid made off with 'em."

"He had a family?" Eileen asked.

"Nobody saw too much of either of 'em, but yeah, he had a wife and a little boy. Lit off for the big city after the hanging, at least as far as anybody knows."

As they drove back through the Catskills he got Eileen to talk a little about herself. She'd been born in Manhattan, gotten a BFA from Columbia in the late sixties, dabbled in political activism and social work and come out of it with the usual complaints. "The system never changed fast enough for me. I just sort of escaped into history. You know? When you read history you can see how it all comes out."

"Why occult history?"

"I don't believe in it, if that's what you mean. You're laughing. Why are you laughing at me?"

"In a minute. Go on."

"It's a challenge, that's all. Regular historians don't take it seriously. It's wide open, there's so much fascinating stuff that's never been properly documented. The Hashishin, the Qabalah, David Home, Crowley." She looked over at him. "Come on. Let me in on the joke."

"You never asked about me. Which was nice. But you have to know that I have the virus. The wild card."

"Yes."

"It gave me a lot of power. Astral projection, telepathy, heightened awareness. But the only way I can direct it, make it work, is through Tantric magic. It has something to do with energizing the spine—"

"Kundalini."

"Yes."

"You're talking about real Tantric magic. Intromission. Menstrual blood. The whole bit."

"That's right. That's the wild card part of it."

"There's more?"

"There's what I do for a living. I'm a procurer. A pimp. I run a string of call girls that go for as much as a thousand dollars a night. Have I got you nervous yet?"

"No. Maybe a little." She gave him another sideways glance. "This is probably a stupid thing to say. You don't fit my image of a pimp."

"I don't much like the name. But I don't run away from it either. My women aren't just hookers. My mother was Japanese and she trains them as geishas. A lot of them have PhDs. None of them are junkies and when they're tired of the Life they move into some other part of the organization."

"You make it sound very moral."

She was ready to disapprove, but Fortunato wouldn't let himself back away. "No," he said. "You've read Crowley. He had no use for ordinary morality, and neither do I. 'Do what thou wilt shall be the whole of the Law.' The more I learn, the more I realize that everything is there, in that one phrase. It's as much a threat as a promise."

"Why are you telling me this?"

"Because I like you and I'm attracted to you and that's not necessarily a good thing for you. I don't want you to get hurt."

She put both hands on the wheel and watched the road. "I can take care of myself," she said.

You should have kept your mouth shut, he told himself, but he knew that wasn't true. Better to drive her off now, before he got any more involved.

A few minutes later she broke the silence. "I don't know whether I should tell you this or not. I took that coin around to a couple of places. Occult bookstores, magic shops, that sort of thing. Just to see what I could turn up. I met a guy named Clarke at the Miskatonic Bookstore. He seemed really interested."

"What'd you tell him?"

"I said it was my father's. I said I was curious about it. He started asking me questions like was I interested in the occult, had I ever had any paranormal experiences, that kind of thing. It was pretty easy to feed him what he wanted to hear."

"And?"

"And he wants me to meet some people." A few seconds later she said, "You've gone quiet on me again."

"I don't think you should go. This stuff is dangerous. Maybe you don't believe in the occult. The thing is, the wild card changed everything. People's fantasies and beliefs can turn real now. And they can hurt you. Kill you."

She shook her head. "It's always the same story. But never any proof. You can argue with me all the way back to New York City, and it's not going to convince me. Unless I see it with my own eyes, I just can't take it seriously."

"Suit yourself," Fortunato said. He released his astral body and shot ahead of the car. He stood in the roadway and let himself become visible just as the car was on him. Through the windshield he could see Eileen's eyes go wide. Next to her his physical body sat with a mindless stare. Eileen screamed and the brakes howled and he let himself snap back into the car. They were skidding toward the trees and Fortunato reached over to steer them out of it. The car died and rolled onto the shoulder.

"What . . . what . . ."

"I'm sorry," he said. He didn't manage a lot of conviction.

"It was *you* there in the road!" Her hands still held the wheel and tremors shook her arms.

"It was just . . . a demonstration."

"A demonstration? You scared me to death!"

"It wasn't anything. You understand? Nothing. We're talking about some kind of cult that's a couple of hundred years old and makes human sacrifices. At the least. It could be worse, a hell of a lot worse. I can't be responsible for you getting involved."

She started the car and pulled onto the road. It was a quarter of an hour later, back on I–87, before she said, "You're not quite human anymore, are you? That you could scare me that badly. Even though you say you're interested in me. That's what you were trying to warn me about."

"Yes," he said. Her voice was different, more detached.

He waited for her to say something else, but instead she just nodded and put a Mozart tape in the stereo.

. ` He thought that would be the end of it. Instead, a week later, she called and asked if he could meet her for lunch at Aces High.

He was waiting at the table when she came in. She would never, he knew, look like a fashion model or like one of his geishas. But he liked the way she made the most of what she had: narrow gray flannel skirt, white cotton blouse, navy cardigan, amber beads, and a wide tortoiseshell band for her hair. No visible makeup except for mascara and a little lip gloss.

Fortunato got up to hold her chair and nearly bumped into Hiram. There was an awkward pause. Finally she held out her hand and Hiram bent over it, hesitated just a little too long, and then bowed away. Fortunato stared after him for a second or two. He wanted Eileen to say something about Hiram but she didn't take the hint. "It's good to see you," he said.

"It's good to see you too."

"In spite of . . . what happened last time?"

"What, is that an apology?" The smile again.

"No," he said. "Though I really am sorry. I'm sorry I got you into this. I'm sorry I couldn't have met you some other way. I'm sorry we have this ugly business between us every time we see each other."

. "So am I."

"And I'm afraid for you. I'm up against something like I've never seen before. There's this . . . thing, this conspiracy, this cult, whatever it is, out there. And I can't find anything out about it." A waiter brought menus and water in crystal goblets. Fortunato nodded him away.

"I've been to see Clarke," Fortunato said. "I asked him some questions, mentioned TIAMAT, and all I got were blank looks. He wasn't faking it. I looked in his brain." He took a breath. "He had no memory of you."

"That's impossible," Eileen said. She shook her head. "It's so strange to see you sitting there talking about reading his mind. There's got to be some kind of mistake, that's all. You're sure?"

Fortunato could see her aura clearly. She was telling the truth. "I'm sure," he said.

"I saw Clarke last night and I can promise you he remembered me. He took me to meet some people. They're members of the cult, or society, or whatever it is. The coins are some kind of recognition thing."

"Did you get their names, or addresses, anything like that?"

She shook her head. "I'd know them again. One of them was called Roman. Very good looking, almost too good looking, if you know what I mean. The other one was very ordinary. Harry, I think his name was."

"Does the group have a name?"

"They haven't mentioned one." She glanced at the menu as the waiter came back. "The veal medallions, I think. And a glass of the chablis."

Fortunato ordered insalata composta and a Beck's.

"But I did learn some other things," she said. "I've been trying to trace Balsam's wife and son. I mean, they are a couple of loose ends in the story. First I tried the usual detective routine, birth and death and marriage records. No dice. Then I tried to find occult connections. Do you know the *Abramelin Review*?"

"No."

"It's a sort of *Reader's Guide* to occult publications. And that's where the Balsam family turned up. There's a Marc Balsam that's published at least a dozen articles in the last few years. Most of them were in a magazine called *Nectanebus*. Does that ring any bells?"

Fortunato shook his head. "A demon or something? It sounds like I should know it, but I can't put my finger on it."

"It's a good bet he's involved with the same society that Clarke is."

"Because of the coins."

"Exactly."

"What about those kid gangs that have been running wild up at the Cloisters? I took a coin off one of those kids. Can you see any possible connection?"

"Not yet. The articles might help, but the magazine's pretty obscure. I haven't been able to turn up any copies of it."

The food arrived. Over lunch she finally mentioned Hiram. "Fifteen years ago he was more attractive than you might think. A little hefty, but very charming. Knew how to dress, what to say. And of course he always knew fantastic restaurants."

"What happened? Or is it any of my business?"

"I don't know. What ever happens between people? I think most of it was that he was too self-conscious about his weight. Now it's me that's self-conscious all the time."

"You shouldn't be, you know. You look great. You could have any man you wanted."

"You don't have to flirt with me. I mean, you have all this sexual power and charisma and everything, but I don't like the idea of your using it on me. Manipulating me."

"I'm not trying to manipulate you," Fortuanto said. "If it looks like I'm interested in you, it's because I'm interested in you."

"Are you always this intense?"

"Yeah. I guess I am. I look over at you and you're smiling all the time. It drives me crazy."

"I'll try to stop."

"Don't."

He'd come on too strong, he realized. She set her silverware neatly on her plate and dropped her folded napkin next to it. Fortuanto pushed the rest of his salad away. Suddenly something bubbled up in his mind.

"What did you say the name of the journal was? Where Balsam was publishing?"

She got a folded scrap of paper out of her purse. "*Nectanebus*. Why?"

Fortunato signaled for the check. "Listen. Can you come back to my apartment? No funny business. This is important."

"I suppose."

The waiter bowed and looked at Eileen. "Mr. Worchester is . . . unavoidably detained. But he asked me to tell you that your lunch is compliments of the house."

"Thank him for me," Eileen said. "Tell him . . . just tell him thank you."

Caroline was still asleep when they got to the apartment. She made a point of leaving the bedroom door open while she walked naked to the bathroom, then sat on the edge of the bed and slowly put her clothes on, starting with stockings and a garter belt.

Fortunato ignored her, sorting through the stacks of books that had grown to fill an entire wall of the front room. Either she'd learn to control her jealousy or she'd find another line of work.

Eileen smiled at her as she clomped out on her four-inch heels. "She's beautiful," she said.

"So are you."

"Don't start."

"You brought it up." He handed her Budge's *Egyptian Magic*. "There you go. Nectanebus."

"'. . . famous as a magician and a sage, and he was deeply learned in all the wisdom of the Egyptians.'"

"This is coming together. Remember Black John's dog mask? I'm wondering if Balsam's cult isn't the Egyptian Freemasons."

"Oh my god. Are you thinking what I'm thinking?"

"I'm thinking that the name Balsam could be an Americanization of Balsamo."

"As in Guiseppe Balsamo of Palermo," Eileen said. She sat down hard on the couch.

"Better known to the world," Fortunato said, "as Count Cagliostro."

Fortuanto pulled up a chair across from her and sat with his elbows on his knees. "The Inquistion arrested him when?"

"Around 1790, wasn't it? They put him in some kind of dungeon. But his body was never found."

"He's supposed to be connected with the Illuminati. Suppose they broke him out of jail and smuggled him to America."

"Where he shows up as Black John Balsam, the local weirdo. But what was he up to? Why the coins? And the human sacrifice? Cagliostro was a fraud, a con man. All he ever wanted was the good life. Murder just doesn't sound like his style."

Fortunato handed her Daraul's *Witches and Sorcerers*. "Let's find out. Unless you've got something better to do?"

"England," Eileen said. "1777. That's when it happened. He got inducted into the Masons on April twelfth, in Soho. After that Masonry takes over his life. He invents the Egyptian Freemasons as some kind of higher order, starts giving away money, inducting every high-ranking Mason he can."

"So what brought all that on?"

"Supposedly he took some kind of tour of the English countryside and came back from it a—quote—changed man—

endquote. His magic powers increased. He went from an adventurer to a genuine mystic."

"Okay," Fortunato said. "Now listen to this. This is Tolstoy on Freemasonry: 'The first and chief object of our Order . . . is the preservation and handing-on to posterity of a certain important mystery . . . a mystery on which perhaps the fate of mankind depends.'"

"This is starting to scare the hell out of me," Eileen said.

"There's one more piece. The thing that's on the back of the Balsam penny is a Sumerian deity called TIAMAT. It's what Lovecraft took Cthulu from. Some kind of huge, shapeless monster from beyond the stars. Lovecraft supposedly got his mythology from his father's secret papers. Lovecraft's father was a Mason."

"So you think that's what it's all about. This TIAMAT thing."

"Put it together," Fortunato said. "Suppose the Masonic secret has something to do with controlling TIAMAT. Cagliostro learns the secret. His brother Masons won't use their knowledge for evil, so Cagliostro forms his own order, for his own ends."

"To bring this thing to Earth."

"Yes," Fortunato said. "To bring it to Earth."

Eileen had finally stopped smiling.

It had gotten dark while they talked. The night was cold and clear and Fortuanto could see stars through the skylights in the front room. He wished he could shut them out.

"It's late," Eileen said. "I have to go."

He hadn't thought of her leaving. The day's work had left him full of nervous energy, the thrill of the hunt. Her mind excited him and he wanted her to open up to him—her secrets, her emotions, her body. "Stay," he said, careful not to use his powers, not to make it a command. "Please." His stomach felt cold when he asked.

She got up, put on the sweater she'd left on the arm of the couch. "I have to . . . digest all this," she said. "There's just been too much happening at once. I'm sorry." She wouldn't look at him. "I need more time."

"I'll walk you down to Eighth Avenue," he said. "You can catch a cab there."

Cold seemed to radiate out of the stars, a kind of hatred for life itself. He hunched his shoulders and put his hands deep in his pockets. A few seconds later he felt Eileen's arm around his waist and he held her close as they walked.

They stopped at the corner of Eighth and 19th and a cab pulled up almost immediately. "Don't say it," Eileen told him. "I'll be careful."

Fortunato's throat was too tight for him to talk if he'd wanted to. He put a hand behind her neck and kissed her. Her lips were so gentle that he had started to turn away before he realized how good they felt. He turned back and she was still standing there. He kissed her again, harder, and she swayed toward him for a second and then pulled away.

"I'll call you," she said.

He watched the cab until it turned the corner and disappeared.

The police woke him at seven the next morning.

"We've got a dead kid in the morgue," the first cop said. "Somebody broke his neck up at the Cloisters about a week ago. You know anything about it?"

Fortunato shook his head. He stood by the door, holding his robe closed with one hand. If they came in they would see the pentagram painted on the hardwood floor, the human skull on the bookcase, the joints on the coffee table.

"Some of his pals say they saw you there," the second cop said.

Fortunato locked eyes with him. "I wasn't there," he said. "You want to believe that."

The second cop nodded and the first one started to reach for his gun. "No," Fortunato said. The first cop didn't manage to look away in time. "You believe it too. I wasn't there. I'm clean."

"Clean," the first cop said.

"Go now," Fortunato said, and they left.

He sat on the couch, hands shaking. They would be back. Or more likely they'd send somebody from the Jokertown division who wouldn't be affected by his powers.

He wouldn't be getting back to sleep. Not that he'd been sleeping that well anyway. His dreams had been full of tentacled things as large as the moon, blocking the sky, swallowing the city.

It suddenly occurred to him that the apartment was empty. He couldn't remember the last time he'd spent the night alone. He almost picked up the phone to call Caroline. It was only a reflex and he fought it off. What he wanted was to be with Eileen.

Two days later she called again. In those two days he'd been to her museum in Long Island twice, in his astral form. He'd hovered across the room, invisible to her, just watching. He'd have gone more often, stayed longer, but he was taking too much pleasure in it.

"It's Eileen," she said. "They want to initiate me."

It was three-thirty in the afternoon. Caroline was at Berlitz, learning Japanese. She hadn't been around much lately.

"You went back," he said.

"I had to. We've been over this."

"When is it?"

"Tonight. I'm supposed to be there at eleven. It's this old church in Jokertown."

"Can I see you?"

"I guess so. I could come over if you want."

"Please. As soon as you can."

He sat by the window and watched until her car pulled up. He buzzed the door for her and then waited for her on the landing. She walked ahead of him into the apartment and turned around. He didn't know what to expect from her. He closed the door and she held out her hands. He put his arms around her and she turned her face up to him. He kissed her and then he kissed her again. Her arms went around his neck and tightened.

"I want you," he said.

"I want you too."

"Come to bed."

"I want to. But I can't. It's . . . it's just a lousy idea. It's been a long time for me. I can't just climb into bed with you and perform all kinds of weird Tantric sex acts. It's not what I want. You can't even come, for crissake!"

He combed through her hair with his fingers. "All right." He held her a while longer, then let her go. "Do you want anything? A drink?"

"Some coffee, if you have any."

He put water on the stove and ground a handful of beans, watching her over the breakfast bar. "What I can't understand," he said, "is why I can't get anything from these people's minds."

"You don't think I'm making all this up?"

"I know you're not," Fortunato said. "I could tell if you were lying."

She shook her head. "You take a lot of getting used to."

"Some things are more important than social niceties." The water boiled. Fortunato made two cups and took them to the couch.

"If they're as big as you think they are," Eileen said, "they're bound to have aces working with them. Somebody who could set up blocks for them, blocks against other people with mental powers."

"I guess."

She drank a little of the coffee. "I met Balsam this afternoon. We all got together at the bookstore."

"What's he like?"

"Smooth. He looked like a banker or something. Three-piece suit, glasses. But tanned, like he plays a lot of tennis on weekends."

"What did he say?"

"They finally mentioned the word 'Mason.' Like it was the last test, to see if it would freak me out. Then Balsam gave me a history lesson. How the Scottish and York Rite Masons were just offshoots of the Speculative Masons, and that they only went back to the eighteenth century."

Fortunato nodded. "That's all true."

"Then he started talking about Solomon, and how the architect of his temple was actually an Egyptian. That Masonry started with Solomon, and all the other rites had lost the original meaning. But they say they've still got it. Just like you figured."

"I have to go with you tonight."

"There's no way you could get in. Not even if you disguised yourself. They'd know you."

"I could send my astral body. I could still see and hear everything."

"If somebody else came here in their astral body, could you see them?"

"Of course."

"Well? It's a hell of chance to take, isn't it?"

"All right, okay."

"It has to be just me. There's no other way."

"Unless . . ."

"Unless what?"

"Unless I went inside you," he said.

"What are you talking about?"

"The power is in my sperm. If you were carrying—"

"Oh, come on," she said. "Of all the lame excuses to get somebody into bed . . ." She stared at him. "You're not kidding, are you?"

"You can't go in there alone. Not just because of the danger. Because you can't do enough by yourself. You can't read their minds. I can."

"Even if you're just—hitching a ride?"

Fortunato nodded.

"Oh God," she said. "This is—there's so many reasons not to—I'm having my period, for one thing."

"So much the better."

She grabbed her left wrist and held it close to her chest. "I told myself if I ever went to bed with a man again—and I said *if*—it would have to be romantic. Candlelight and flowers and everything. And look at me."

Fortunato knelt in front of her and gently moved her hands away. "Eileen," he said. "I love you."

"That's easy for you to say. I'm sure you mean it and everything, but I'm also sure you say it all the time. There's only two men I've ever said it to in my life, and one of them was my father."

"I'm not talking about how you feel. I'm not talking about forever. I'm talking about me, right now. And I love you." He picked her up and carried her into the bedroom.

It was cold in there and her teeth started to chatter. Fortunato lit the gas heater and sat down next to her on the bed. She took his right hand in both of hers and held it to her mouth. He kissed her and felt her respond, almost against her will. He took his clothes off and pulled the covers over the two of them and began to unbutton her blouse. Her breasts were large and soft, the nipples tightening under his tongue as he kissed them.

"Wait," she said. "I have to . . . I have to go to the bathroom."

When she came back she had taken the rest of her clothes off. She was holding a towel in front of her. "To save your sheets," she said. There was a smear of blood on the inside of one thigh.

He took the towel away from her. "Don't worry about the sheets." She stood naked in front of him. She looked like she was afraid he would send her away. He put his head between her breasts and pulled her toward him.

She got under the covers again and kissed him and her tongue flickered into his mouth. He kissed her shoulders, her breasts, the underside of her chin. Then he rolled onto his hands and knees above her.

"No," she whispered, "I'm not ready yet . . ."

He held his penis in one hand and moved the head of it against her labia, slowly, gently, feeling the brittle flesh turn warm and wet. She bit her lower lip, her eyes closed. Slowly he slipped inside her, the friction sending waves of pleasure up his spine.

He kissed her again. He could feel her lips moving against his, mouthing inaudible words. His hands moved up her sides, around her back. He remembered that he was used to making love for hours at a time and the thought amazed him. It was all too intense. He was full of heat and light; he couldn't contain it all.

"Aren't you supposed to say something?" Eileen whispered, breathing raggedly around the words. "Some kind of magic spell or something?"

Fortunato kissed her again, his lips tingling like they'd been asleep and were just now coming back to life. "I love you," he said.

"Oh God," she said, and started to cry. Tears rolled down into her hair and at the same time her hips moved faster against him. Their bodies were flushed and hot and sweat ran down Fortunato's chest. Eileen stiffened and kicked. A second later Fortunato's own brain went white and he fought off ten years of training and let it happen, let the power spurt out of him and into the woman and for an instant he was both of them at once, hermaphroditic and all-encompassing, and he felt himself expand to the ends of the universe in a giant nuclear blaze.

And then he was back in bed with Eileen, feeling her breasts rise and fall under him as she cried.

The only light came from the gas heater. He must have slept. The pillowcase felt like sandpaper against his cheek. It took all his strength to roll over onto his back.

Eileen was putting on her shoes. "It's almost time," she said.

"How do you feel?" he said.

"Unbelievable. Strong. Powerful." She laughed. "I've never felt like this."

He closed his eyes, slid into her mind. He could see himself lying on the bed, skeletal, his dark golden skin disappearing into the shadows, his forehead shrunken to where it blended smoothly into his hairless scalp.

"And you," she said. He could feel her voice echoing in her chest. "Are you all right?"

He drifted back to his own body. "Weak," he said. "But I'll be okay."

"Should I . . . call somebody for you?"

He knew what she was offering, knew he should agree to it. Caroline, or one of the others, would be the fastest way to get his power back. But it would also weaken his bond to Eileen. "No," he said.

She finished dressing and bent over to kiss him lingeringly. "Thank you," she said.

"Don't," he said. "Don't thank me."

"I'd better go." Her impatience, her strength and vitality, were a physical force in the room. He was too distant from it to be jealous of her. Then she was gone, and he slept again.

He watched through Eileen's eyes as she stood by the front door of the bookstore, waiting for Clarke to close up. He could have moved all the way into her mind, but it would have used up what little strength he was slowly getting back. Besides, he was warm and comfortable where he was.

Until the hands grabbed him and shook him awake and he was looking into a pair of gold shields. "Get your clothes on," a voice said. "You're under arrest."

They gave him a holding cell to himself. It had a gray tile floor and gray-painted cement walls. He squatted in the corner and shivered, too weak to stand. On the wall next to him somebody had scratched a stick figure with a giant dripping prick and balls.

For an hour he'd been unable to concentrate long enough to make contact with Eileen. He was sure Balsam's Masons had killed her.

He shut his eyes. A cell door banged closed down the hall and brought him back. Concentrate, goddamn it, he thought.

He was in a long room with a high ceiling. Yellow light flickered off the distant walls from banks of candles. The floor was black-and-white-checkered tile. At the front of the room stood two Doric columns, one on either side, that didn't quite reach the ceiling. They stood for Solomon's temple; they were named Boaz and Joachim, the first two Masonic Words.

He didn't want to take control of Eileen's body, though he could if it came to that. From what he could tell she was all right. He could feel her excitement, but she wasn't in pain or even especially afraid.

A man matching Eileen's description of Balsam stood at the front of the room, on the dais reserved for the Worshipful Master of the Temple. Over his dark suit he wore a white Masonic apron with bright red trim. He wore a tabard like an oversized bib around his neck. It was white too, with a red looped cross in the center. An ankh.

"Who speaks for this woman?" Balsam asked.

There were a dozen or more others in the room, both sexes, all of them in aprons and tabards. They made a curving line along the left side of the room. Most of them seemed normal enough. One man had bright red skin and no hair at all, an obvious joker. Another seemed terribly frail, with thick glasses and a dazed expression. He was the only one not wearing street clothes under his apron. Instead he was wrapped in a white robe a couple sizes too large for him, with a hood and sleeves that hung down over his hands.

Clarke moved out of line and said, "I speak for her." Balsam handed him an intricate mask, covered in what seemed to be gold foil. It was a hawk's head, and it completely covered Clarke's face.

"Who opposes?" Balsam said.

A young oriental woman, rather plain, but with an undefinable sexual quality, stepped forward. "I oppose." Balsam gave her a mask with long, pointed ears and a sharp face. When she put it on, it gave her a cold, disdainful look. Fortunato felt Eileen's pulse begin to pick up.

"Who claims her?"

"I claim her." Another man came forward and took a mask with the jackal face of Anubis.

The air behind Balsam rippled and started to glow. The candles flickered out. Slowly a golden man took shape, lighting the room. He was as tall as the ceiling, with canine features and hot yellow eyes. He stood with folded arms and looked down at Eileen. Her pulse leapt and stuttered and she dug her fingernails into her palms. No one else seemed to notice that he was there.

The woman wearing the pointed mask stood in front of Eileen. "Osiris," the woman said. "I am Set, of the company of Annu, son of Seb and Nut."

He felt Eileen open her mouth to speak, but before she could say anything the woman's right hand exploded against her face. She fell over backward and slid three feet across the tiles. "Behold," the woman said. She touched her fingers to Eileen's eyes and they came away wet. "The fertilizing rain."

"Osiris," said the jackal-headed man, stepping up to take the woman's place. "I am Anubis, son of Ra, Opener of the Ways. Mine is the Funeral Mountain." He moved behind Eileen and held her against the floor.

Now Clarke was kneeling next to her, the golden man looming behind him. "Osiris," he said. Light glittered from the tiny eyes of the hawk mask. "I am Horus, thy son and the son of Isis." He pressed two fingers against Eileen's lips, forcing her mouth open. "I have come to embrace thee, I am thy son Horus, I have pressed thy mouth; I am thy son, I love thee. Thy mouth was closed, but I have set in order for thee thy mouth and thy teeth. I open for thee thy two eyes. I have opened for thee thy mouth with the instrument of Anubis. Horus hath opened the mouth of the dead, as he in times of old opened thy mouth, with the iron which came forth from Set. The deceased shall walk and shall speak, and her body shall be with the great company of the gods in the Great House of the Aged One in Annu, and she shall receive there the *ureret* crown from Horus, the lord of mankind."

Clarke took something that looked like a wooden snake from Balsam. Eileen tried to pull away, but the jackal-headed man had too tight a grip on her. Clarke swung the snake back and then gently touched Eileen's mouth and eyes with it four times. "O Osiris, I have established for thee the two jawbones in thy face, and they are now separated."

He stood aside. Balsam bent over her until his face was only inches away and said, "Now I give to thee the *hekau*, the word of power. Horus hath given thee the use of thy mouth and thou canst say it. The word is TIAMAT."

"TIAMAT," Eileen whispered.

Fortunato, numb with fear, pushed himself into Balsam's mind.

* * *

The trick was to keep moving, not to get overwhelmed by the strangeness of it. If he kept triggering associations he would end up in the part of Balsam's memory that he wanted.

At the moment Balsam was near ecstasy. Fortunato followed the images and totems of Egyptian magic until he found the earliest ones, and from there made his way to Balsam's father, and back through seven generations to Black John himself.

Everything Balsam had ever heard or read or imagined about his ancestor was here. His first swindle, when he took the goldsmith Marano for sixty ounces of fine gold. His escape from Palermo. Meeting the Greek, Altotas, and learning alchemy. Egypt, Turkey, Malta, and finally Rome at age twenty-six, handsome, clever, carrying letters of introduction to the cream of society.

Where he met Lorenza. Fortunato saw her as Cagliostro had, naked before him for the first time, only fourteen years old but dizzyingly beautiful: slim, elegant, olive-skinned, with jet-black wavy hair spread out around her, tiny perfect breasts, smelling of wild coastal flowers, her throaty voice screaming his name as she wrapped her legs around him.

Traveling through Europe in coaches lined in deep green velvet, Lorenza's beauty opening society to them without reservation, living on what they begged in the halls of nobility and handing out the rest as alms.

And finally England.

Fortunato watched as Cagliostro rode into the forest on the back of a blooded ebony hunter. He'd gotten separated, not quite by accident, from Lorenza and the young English lord who was so taken with her. Doubtless His Lordship was having his way with her even now in some ditch beside the road, and doubtless Lorenza had already found a way to turn it to their advantage.

Then the moon fell out of the sky in the middle of the afternoon.

Cagliostro spurred the stallion toward the glowing apparition. It touched down in a clearing a few hundred yards away. The horse wouldn't get closer than a hundred feet, so Cagliostro tied him to a sapling and approached on foot. The thing was indistinct, made of angles that didn't connect, and as Cagliostro came toward it a piece of it detached itself . . .

And that was all. Suddenly Cagliostro was riding back

toward London in a carriage with Lorenza full of some high purpose that Fortunato couldn't read.

He ransacked Balsam's mind. The knowledge had to be there somewhere. Some fragment of what the thing in the woods had been, what it had said or done.

That was when Balsam jerked upright and said, "The woman is in my brain."

He was looking through Eileen's eyes again, enraged at his own clumsiness. Things had gone hideously wrong. He found himself staring into the face of the little man with the thick glasses and the robe.

And then he was back in his cell.

Two guards had him by the arms and were dragging him toward the door. "No," he said. "Please. Just a few more minutes."

"Oh, like it here, do you?" one of the guards said. He shoved Fortunato toward the door of the cell. Fortunato's foot slipped on the slick linoleum and he went onto all fours. The guard kicked him near his left kidney, not quite hard enough to make him pass out.

Then they were dragging him again, down endless faded green corridors, into a dark-paneled room with no windows and a long wooden table. A man in a cheap suit, maybe thirty years old, sat on the other side of the table. His hair was medium brown, his face unremarkable. There was a gold shield pinned to the jacket pocket. Next to him sat a man in a polo shirt and expensive sport coat. He had excessive Aryan good looks, wavy blond hair, icy blue eyes. Fortunato remembered the Mason that Eileen had described, Roman.

"Sergeant Matthias?" the second guard said. The man in the cheap suit nodded. "This is the one."

Matthias leaned back in his chair and closed his eyes. Fortunato felt something brush his mind.

"Well?" Roman asked.

"Not much," Matthias said. "Some telepathy, a little TK, but it's weak. I doubt he could even pick a lock."

"So what do you think? Does the boss need to worry about him?"

"I can't see why. You could hang him up for a while for murdering that kid, see what happens."

"What's the use?" Roman said. "He'd just plead self-defense. The judge'd probably give him a medal. Nobody cares about those little bastards anyway."

"Fine," Matthias said. He turned to the guards. "Kick him loose. We're done with him."

It took another hour to get him back on the street, and of course nobody offered him a ride home. But that was all right. Jokertown was where he needed to be.

He sat on the steps of the precinct and reached out for Eileen's mind.

He found himself staring at the brick wall of an alley. He was empty of thought or emotion. As he struggled to break through the clouds in her brain he felt her bladder let go, and felt the warm urine spread in a puddle under her and quickly turn cold.

"Hey, buddy, no sleeping on the steps."

Fortunato walked out into the street and flagged a cab. He put a twenty through the little metal drawer and said, "South. Hurry."

He got out of the cab on Chrystie just south of Grand. She hadn't moved. Her mind was gone. He squatted in front of her and probed for a few seconds, and then he couldn't stand it and he walked down to the end of the alley. He pounded on the side of a dumpster until his hands were nearly useless. Then he went back and tried again.

He opened his mouth to say something. Nothing came out. There were no words left in his head, only bloody red clumps and a flood of acid that kept rising up in his eyes.

He walked across the street and dialed 911. It hurt to press the buttons. When he got an operator he asked for an ambulance and gave the address and hung up.

He went back across the street. A car honked at him and he didn't understand why. He knelt in front of Eileen. Her jaw hung open and a thread of saliva dangled down onto her blouse. He couldn't stand to look at her. He closed his eyes and reached out with his mind and gently stopped her heart.

It was easy to find the temple. It was only three blocks away. He just followed the energy trails of the men who'd left Eileen in the alley.

He stood across the street from the bricked-up church. He had to keep blinking his eyes to keep them clear. The trails of the men led into the building, and two or three other trails led out. But Balsam was still in there, Balsam and Clarke and a dozen more.

That was good. He wanted them all, but he would settle for the ones that were there. Them, and their coins and their golden masks, their rituals, their temple, everything that had a part in trying to bring their alien monstrosity to Earth, that had spilled blood and destroyed minds and ruined lives to do it. He wanted it over, finished, for good and all.

The night was utterly cold, a vacuum as cold as space, sucking the heat and life from everything it touched. His cheeks burned and then went numb.

He reached for the power he had left and it wasn't enough.

For a few seconds he stood and shook with helpless rage, ready to go after the building with his bare, battered hands. Then he saw her, on the corner, standing in the classic pose under the streetlight. Black hot pants, rabbit jacket, fake-fur shawl. Hooker heels and too much makeup. He slowly raised his arm and waved her over.

She stopped in front of him, looked him warily up and down. "Hey," she said. Her skin was coarse and her eyes were tired. "You wanna go out?"

He took a hundred-dollar bill out of his jacket and unzipped his pants.

"Right here in the street? Lover, you must be hurtin' for certain." She stared at the hundred and eased down onto her knees. "Woo, this concrete cold." She fumbled around in his trousers and then looked up at him. "Shit, what is this? Dry blood?"

He took out another hundred. The woman hesitated a second and then stuffed both bills in her purse and clamped the purse under her arm.

At the touch of her mouth Fortunato went instantly hard. He felt a surge all the way up from his feet and it made his scalp and his fingernails hurt. His eyes rolled up until they were staring at the second floor of the old church.

He wanted to use his power to lift the entire city block and hurl it into space, but he didn't have the strength to break a window. He probed at the bricks and the wooden joists and the electrical wiring and then he found what he was looking for. He followed a gas line down to the basement and back to the main, and then he began to move the gas through it, building the pressure the way it was building inside him, until the pipes vibrated and the walls shook and the mortar creaked.

The hooker looked up and across the street, saw cracks splitting the walls. "Run," he said. As she clattered away Fortunato reached down and jammed his fingers into the root of his penis, forcing back the hot flood of his ejaculation. His intestines turned to fire, and in the crawlspace over the temple the black steel pipe bent and shook free of its connections. It spurted gas and fell to the floor, knocking sparks off the chicken-wire-and-plaster wall.

The building swelled for an instant like it was filling with water and then it erupted in a ball of smoky orange flame. Bricks smashed into the wall on either side of where Fortunato stood but he wouldn't look away, not until his eyebrows had been singed to the skin and his clothes had begun to smolder. The roar of the explosion shattered windows up and down the street, and when it finally died the bleating of sirens and alarms took its place.

He wished he'd been able to hear them scream.

Eventually, a cab stopped for him. The driver wanted to take him to the hospital but Fortunato talked him out of it with a hundred-dollar bill.

Climbing the stairs to his apartment took longer than anything he could remember. He went into the bedroom. The pillows still smelled of Eileen's perfume.

He went back to the kitchen, got a fifth of whiskey, and sat by the window, drinking it down, watching the red glow of the fire slowly die over Jokertown.

When he finally passed out on the couch he dreamed of tentacles and wet rubbery flesh and beaks that opened and closed with long, echoing laughter.

1985

JUBE: ONE

After he had locked up the newsstand for the night, Jube loaded his shopping cart with newspapers and set out on his daily round of the Jokertown bars.

With Thanksgiving less than a week away, the cold November wind had a bitter edge as it came skirling down the Bowery. Jube trudged along with one hand on his battered old porkpie hat, while the other pulled the two-wheeled wire cart over the cracked sidewalk. His pants were big enough to hold a revival meeting, and his blue short-sleeved Hawaiian shirt was covered with surfers. He never wore a coat. Jube had been selling papers and magazines from the corner of Hester Street and the Bowery since the summer of 1952, and he'd never worn a coat once. Whenever he was asked about it, he would laugh around his tusks, slap his belly, and say, "This is all the insulation I need, yes sir."

On a tall day, wearing heels, Jube Benson topped five feet by almost an inch, but there was a lot of him in that compact package, three hundred pounds of oily blue-black flesh that reminded you of half-melted rubber. His face was broad and cratered, his skull covered with tufts of stiff red hair, and two small tusks curved down from the corners of his mouth. He smelled like buttered popcorn, and knew more jokes than anyone else in Jokertown.

Jube waddled along briskly, grinning at passersby, hawking his papers to the passing cars (even at this hour, the main drag of Jokertown was far from deserted). At the Funhouse, he left a stack of the *Daily News* for the doorman to hand out to departing patrons, along with a *Times* for the owner, Des. A couple blocks down was the Chaos Club, which gave away a stack of papers too. Jube had saved a copy of *National*

33

Informer for Lambent. The doorman took it in a gaunt, glowing hand. "Thanks, Walrus."

"Read all about it," Jube said. "Says there they got a new treatment, turns jokers to aces."

Lambent laughed. "Yeah, right," he said, riffling the pages. A slow smile spread across his phosphorescent face. "Hey, looka here, Sue Ellen's going to go back to J.R."

"She always does," Jube said.

"This time she's going to have his joker baby," Lambent said. "Jesus, what a dumb cunt." He folded the paper under his arm. "Have you heard?" he asked. "Gimli's coming back."

"You don't say," Jube replied. The door opened behind them. Lambent sprang to hold it, and whistled down a cab for the well-dressed couple who emerged. As he helped them in, he gave them their free *Daily News*, and the man laid a five against his palm. Lambent made it vanish, with a wink at Jube. Jube waved and went on his way, leaving the phosphorescent doorman standing by the curb in his Chaos Club livery, perusing his *Informer*.

The Chaos Club and the Funhouse were the class establishments; the bars, taverns, and coffee shops on the side streets seldom gave anything away. But he was known in all of them, and they let him hawk his papers table to table. Jube stopped at the Pit and at Hairy's Kitchen, played a game of shuffleboard in Squisher's Basement, delivered a *Penthouse* to Wally of Wally's. At Black Mike's Pub, under the neon Schaefer sign, he joked with a couple of working girls and let them tell him about the kinky nat politico they'd double-teamed.

He left Captain McPherson's *Times* with the desk sergeant at the Jokertown precinct house, and sold a *Sporting News* to a plainclothesman who thought he had a lead on Jokers Wild, where a male hooker had been castrated on stage last week. At the Twisted Dragon on the fringes of Chinatown Jube got rid of his Chinese papers before heading down to Freakers on Chatham Square, where he sold a copy of the *Daily News* and a half-dozen *Jokertown Crys*.

The *Cry* offices were across the square. The night editor always took a *Times*, a *Daily News*, a *Post*, and a *Village Voice*, and poured Jube a cup of black, muddy coffee. "Slow night," Crabcakes said, chewing on an unlit cigar as he turned the pages of the competition with his pincers.

"Heard the cops are going to shut down that joker-porn studio on Division," Jube said, sipping politely at his coffee.

Crabcakes squinted up at him. "You think so? Don't bet on it, Walrus. That bunch is connected. The Gambione Family, I think. Where'd you hear that?"

Jube gave him a rubbery grin. "Got to protect my sources too, chief. You hear the one about the guy married this joker, just gorgeous, long blond hair, face like an angel, body to match. On their wedding night, she comes out in this white teddy and says to him, honey, I've got good news and bad news. He says, yeah, so give me the good news first. Well, she says, the good news is that *this* is what the wild card did to me, and she whirls around and gives him a good look, till he's grinning and drooling. So what's the bad news? he asks. The bad news, she says, is that my real name is Joseph."

Crabcakes grimaced. "Get out of here," he said.

The regulars at Ernie's relieved him of another few *Crys* and a *Daily News,* and for Ernie himself he had the issue of *Ring* that had come in that afternoon. It was a slow night, so Ernie stood him to a piña colada and Jube told him the one about the joker bride who had good news and bad news for her husband.

The counterman at the all-night doughnut shop took a *Times*. As he turned up Henry to his final stop, Jube's load was so light the shopping cart skipped along behind him.

Three cabs stood outside the canopied entrance to the Crystal Palace, waiting for business. "Hey, Walrus," one of the hacks called out as he passed. "Got a *Cry* there?"

"Sure do," Jube said. He swapped a paper for a coin. The cabbie had a nest of thin, snakelike tendrils in place of a right arm, and flippers where his legs should be, but his Checker had special hand controls and he knew the city like the back of his tentacle. Made real good tips, too. These days people were so relieved to get a cabbie who spoke English, they didn't give a damn what he looked like.

The doorman carried Jube's cart up the stone steps to the main entrance of the three-story turn-of-the-century row house. Inside the Victorian entry chamber, Jube left his hat and cart with the coat-check girl, gathered the remaining papers under his arm, and walked into the saloon's huge, high-ceilinged barroom. Elmo, the dwarf bouncer, was carrying out a squid-faced man in a sequined domino as Jube entered.

There was a nasty bruise on one side of his head. "What did he do?" Jube asked.

Elmo grinned up at him. "It's not what he did, it's what he was thinking of doing." The little man pushed through the stained-glass doors with the squid-face slung over his shoulder like a sack of grain.

It was last call at the Crystal Palace. Jube made a circuit of the main taproom—he seldom bothered with the side rooms and their curtained alcoves—and sold a few more papers. Then he climbed up on a barstool. Sascha was behind the long mahogany bar, his eyeless face and pencil-thin mustache reflected in the mirror as he mixed a planter's punch. He put it down in front of Jube without words or money being exchanged.

As Jube sipped his drink, he caught a whiff of familiar perfume, and turned his head just as Chrysalis seated herself on the stool to his left. "Good morning," she said. Her voice was cool and faintly British. She was wearing a spiral of silver glitter on one cheek, and the transparent flesh beneath made it seem to float like a nebula above the whiteness of her skull. Her lipstick was silver gloss, and her long nails gleamed like daggers. "How's the news business, Jubal?"

He grinned at her. "Did you hear the one about the joker bride who had good news and bad news for her husband?"

Around her mouth, the ghost-gray shadows of her muscles twisted her silvered lips into a grimace. "Spare me."

"All right." Jube sipped at his planter's punch through a straw. "At the Chaos Club they put little parasols in these."

"At the Chaos Club they serve drinks in coconuts."

Jube nursed his drink. "That place on Division, where they film the hard-core stuff? I heard it's a Gambione operation."

"Old news," Chrysalis said. It was closing time. The lights came up. Elmo began to circulate, stacking chairs on tables and rousting the customers.

"Troll is going to be the new chief of security at Tachyon's clinic. Doc told me so himself."

"Affirmative action?" Chrysalis said drily.

"Partly," Jube told her. "And partly it's just that he's nine foot tall, green, and almost invulnerable." He sucked up the last of his drink noisily, and stirred the crushed ice with his straw. "Guy at the cophouse has a lead on Jokers Wild."

"He won't find it," Chrysalis said. "If he does, he'll wish he hadn't."

"If they had any sense, they'd just ask you."

"There's not enough money in the city budget to pay for *that* information," Chrysalis said. "What else? You always save your best for last."

"Probably nothing," Jube said, swiveling to face her. "But I hear Gimli's coming home."

"Gimli?" Her voice was nonchalant, but the deep blue eyes suspended in the sockets of her skull regarded him sharply. "How interesting. Details?"

"Not yet," Jube said. "I'll let you know."

"I'm sure you will." Chrysalis had informants all over Jokertown. But Jube the Walrus was one of the most reliable. Everyone knew him, everyone liked him, everyone talked to him.

Jube was the last customer to leave the Crystal Palace that night. When he went outside it had just begun to snow. He snorted, held his hat firmly, and trudged off down Henry, pulling the empty shopping cart behind him. A patrol car came up alongside him as he was passing under the Manhattan Bridge, slowed, and rolled down a window. "Hey, Walrus," the black cop behind the wheel called out. "It's snowing, you dumb joker. You'll freeze your balls off."

"Balls?" Jube called out. "Who says jokers got balls? I love this weather, Chaz. Look at these rosy cheeks!" He pinched his oily, blue-black cheek, and chortled.

Chaz sighed, and opened the back door of the blue-and-white. "Get in. I'll ride you home."

Home was a five-story rooming house on Eldridge, just a short ride away. Jube left his shopping cart under the steps by the trash cans as he opened the police lock on his basement apartment. The only window was completely filled by a huge air conditioner of ancient vintage, its rusted casing now half-covered with blowing snow.

When he turned on his lights, the red fifteen-watt bulbs in the overhead fixture filled the room with a murky scarlet twilight. It was bone-cold inside, scarcely warmer than the November streets. Jube never turned on the heat. Once or twice a year a man from the gas company came by to check on him and make sure he hadn't rigged the meter.

Under the window, pans of green, decaying meat covered the top of a card table. Jube stripped off his shirt to reveal a broad, six-nippled chest, got himself a glass of ice to crunch, and picked the ripest steak he could find.

A bare mattress covered the floor of his bedroom, and in the corner was his latest acquisition, a brand-new porcelain hot tub that faced a big-screen projection TV. Except that "hot tub" was a misnomer, since he never used the heating system. He had learned a lot about humans in the last twenty-three years, but he'd never understand why they wanted to immerse themselves in scalding water, he thought as he undressed. Even the Takisians had more sense than that.

Holding the steak in one hand, Jube carefully lowered himself into the icy water and turned on the television with his remote control to watch the news programs he'd taped earlier. He popped the steak into his wide mouth, and began to chew the raw meat slowly as he floated there, absorbing every word that Tom Brokaw had to say. It was very relaxing, but when the newscast ended, Jube knew it was time to go to work.

He climbed out of his tub, belched, and dried himself vigorously with a Donald Duck towel. An hour, no more, he thought to himself as he padded across the room, leaving wet footprints on the hardwood floor. He *was* tired, but he had to do some work, or he'd fall even more behind. Standing at the back of his bedroom, he punched out a long sequence of numbers on his remote control. The bare brick wall in front of him seemed to dissolve when he hit the final digit.

Jube walked through into what had been the coal cellar. The far wall was dominated by a holocube that dwarfed even his projection TV. A horseshoe-shaped console wrapped around a huge contour chair designed for Jube's unique physiognomy. All along the sides of the snug chamber were machines, some whose purpose would have been obvious to any high school student, others that would have baffled Dr. Tachyon himself.

Primitive as it was, the office suited Jube just fine. He settled into his chair, turned on the power-feed from the fusion cell, and took a crystalline rod as long as a child's pinky from a rack by his elbow. When he slid it into the appropriate slot on the console, the recorder lit from within, and he began to dictate his latest observations and conclusions in a language that seemed half music and half cacophony, made up in equal parts of barks, whistles, belches, and clicks. If his other security systems ever failed him, his work would still be safe. After all, there wasn't another sentient being within forty light-years who spoke his native tongue.

UNTO THE SIXTH GENERATION

By Walter Jon Williams

Prologue

He was still smoking where the atmosphere had burned his flesh. Heated lifeblood was running out through his spiracles. He tried to close them, to hold onto the last of the liquid, but he had lost the capacity to control his respiration. His fluids had superheated during the descent and had blown out from the diaphragms like steam from an exploding boiler.

Lights strobed at him from the end of the alley. They dazzled his eyes. Hard sounds crackled in his ears. His blood was steaming on the concrete as it cooled.

The Swarm Mother had detected his ship, had struck at him with a vast particle charge generated in the creature's monstrous planetoid body. He had barely the opportunity to signal Jhubben on the planet's surface before his ship's chitin was torn apart. He'd been forced to seize the singularity shifter, his race's experimental power source, and leap into the dark vacuum. But the shifter had been damaged in the attack and he had been unable to control it—he had burned on the way down.

He tried to summon his concentration and grow new flesh, but failed. He realized that he was dying.

It was necessary to stop the draining of his life. There was a metal container nearby, large, with a hinged lid. His body a flaring agony, he rolled across the damp surface of the concrete and hooked his one undamaged leg across the lid of the

container. The leg was powerful, intended for leaping into the
sky of his light-gravity world, and now it was his hope. He
moved his weight against the oppressive gravity, rolling his
body up the length of his leg. Outraged nerves wailed in his
body. Fluid spattered the outside of the container.

The metal rang as he fell inside. Substances crackled
under him. He gazed up into a night that glowed with
reflected infrared. There were bits of organic stuff here,
crushed and pressed flat, with dyes pressed onto them in
patterns. He seized them with his palps and cilia, tearing them
into strips, pushing them against his leaking spiracles. Stopped
the flow.

Organic smells came to him. There had been life here,
but it had died.

He reached into his abdomen for his shifter, brought the
device out, clasped it to his torn chest. If he could stop time for
a while, he could heal. Then he would try to signal Jhubben,
somehow. Perhaps, if the shifter wasn't damaged too badly, he
could make a short jump to Jhubben's coordinates.

The shifter hummed. Strange light displays, a side effect,
flickered gently in the darkness of the container. Time passed.

"So last night I got a call from my neighbor Sally . . ."

Dimly, from inside his time cocoon, he heard the sound of
the voice. It echoed faintly inside his skull.

"And Sally, she says, Hildy, she says, I just heard from my
sister Margaret in California. You remember Margaret, she
says. She went to school with you at St. Mary's."

There was a thud against the metal near his auditory
palps. A silhouette against the glowing night. Arms that
reached for him.

Agony returned. He cried out, a hiss. The touch climbed
his body.

"Sure I remember Margaret, I says. She was a grade
behind. The sisters were always after her 'cause she was a
gum-chewer."

Something was taking hold of his shifter. He clutched it
against him, tried to protest.

"It's mine, bunky," the voice said, fast and angry. "I saw it
first."

He saw a face. Pale flesh smudged with dirt, bared teeth,
gray cilia just hanging from beneath an inorganic extrusion.

"Don't," he said. "I'm dying."

With a wrench the creature pulled the shifter from him. He screamed as the warmth left him, as he felt the slow, cold death return.

"Shut up, there. It's mine."

Pain began a slow throb through his body. "You don't understand," he said. "There is a Swarm Mother near your planet."

The voice droned. Things crackled and rang in the container. "So Margaret, Sally says, she married this engineer from Boeing. And they pull down fifty grand a year, at least. Vacations in Hawaii, in St. Thomas, for crissake."

"Please listen." The pain was growing. He knew he had only a short time. "The Swarm Mother has already developed intelligence. She perceived that I had identified her, and struck at once."

"But she doesn't have to deal with my family, Sally says. She's over on the other goddamn coast, Sally says."

His body was weeping scarlet. "The next stage will be a first-generation Swarm. They will come to your planet soon, directed by the Swarm Mother. Please listen."

"So I got my mom onto the welfare and into this nice apartment, Sally says. But the welfare wants me and Margaret to give Mom an extra five dollars a month. And Margaret, she says, she doesn't have the money. Things are expensive in California, she says."

"You are in terrible danger. Please listen."

Metal thudded again. The voice was growing fainter, as with distance. "So how easy are things here, Sally says. I got five kids and two cars and a mortgage, and Bill says things are a dead end at the agency."

"The Swarm. The Swarm. Tell Jhubben!"

The other was gone, and he was dying. The stuff under him was soaking up his fluids. To breathe was an agony.

"It is cold here," he said. Tears came from the sky, ringing against metal. There was acid in the tears.

JUBE: TWO

In the rooming house on Eldridge, the tenants were having a little Christmas party, and Jube was dressed as Santa Claus. He was a little short for the part, and the Santas in the store windows seldom had tusks, but he had the *ho-ho-ho* down pat.

The party was held in the living room on the first floor. It was early this year, because Mrs. Holland was flying out to Sacramento next week to spend the holidays with her grandson, and no one wanted to have the party without Mrs. Holland, who had lived in the building almost as long as Jube, and seen all of them through some rough times. Except for Father Fahey, the alcoholic Jesuit from the fifth floor, the tenants were all jokers, and none of them had a lot of money for Christmas gifts. So each of them bought one present, and all the gifts went into a big canvas mailbag, and it was Jube's annual assignment to jumble them around and hand them out. He loved the job. Human patterns of gift giving were endlessly fascinating and someday he intended to write a study of the subject, as soon as he finished his treatise on human humor.

He always started with Doughboy, who was huge and soft and mushroom white and lived with the black man they called Shiner in a second floor apartment. Doughboy outweighed Jube by a good hundred pounds, and he was so strong that he ripped the front door off its hinges at least once a year (Shiner always fixed it). Doughboy loved robots and dolls and toy trucks and plastic guns that made noises but he broke everything within days, and the toys he really loved he broke within hours.

Jube had wrapped his present in silver foil, so he wouldn't give it to anyone else by mistake. "Oh, boy," Doughboy shouted when he'd ripped it open. He held it up for all of them to see. "A ray gun, oh boy, oh boy." It was a deep, translucent

43

red-black, molded in lines that were smooth and sensual yet somehow disquieting, with a pencil-thin barrel. When his immense fingers wrapped around the grip and pointed it at Mrs. Holland, points of lights flickered deep inside, and Doughboy exclaimed in delight as the microcomputer corrected his aim.

"That's some toy," Callie said. She was a petite, fastidious woman with four useless extra arms.

"Ho ho ho," Jube said. "He won't be able to break it, either." Doughboy squinted at Old Mister Cricket and pressed the firing stud, making loud sizzling noises through his teeth.

Shiner laughed. "Bet he do."

"You'd lose," Jube said. Ly'bahr alloy was dense and strong enough to withstand a small thermonuclear explosion. He'd worn the gun himself during his first year in New York, but the harness had chafed, and after a while it had just gotten to be too much of a nuisance. Of course, Jube had removed the power cell before wrapping the gift for Doughboy, and a Network disrupter wasn't the sort of thing you could energize with a D battery.

Someone shoved an eggnog, liberally laced with rum and nutmeg, into his hand. Jube took a healthy swallow, grinned with pleasure, and got on with passing out the presents. Callie went next, and drew a coupon book for the neighborhood movie house. Denton from the fourth floor got a woolen knit cap, which he dangled from the end of his antlers, provoking general laughter. Reginald, whom the neighborhood children called Potato-head (though not to his face), wound up with an electric razor; Shiner got a long multicolored scarf. They looked at each other, laughed, and swapped.

He made his way around the room from person to person until everyone had a gift. The last present in the bag was usually his; this year, however, the bag was empty after Mrs. Holland pulled out her tickets to *Cats*. Jube was a little nonplussed. It must have showed on his face. There was laughter all around. "We didn't forget about you, Walrus-man," said Chucky, the spider-legged boy who ran messages down on Wall street. "This year we all chipped in, got you something special," Shiner added.

Mrs. Holland gave it to him. It was small, and store-wrapped. Jube opened it carefully. "A watch!"

"That's no watch, Walrus-man, that's a *chronometer!*"

Chucky said. "Self-winding, and waterproof and shockproof too."

"That there watch tell you the date, and the phases of moon, shit, it tell you everything except when your girlfriend be on the rag," Shiner said.

"Shiner!" Mrs. Holland said in indignation.

"You've been wearing that Mickey Mouse watch for, well, for as long as *I've* known you," Reginald said. "We all thought it was time you had something a little more modern."

It was a very expensive watch. So, of course, there was nothing to be done but wear it. Jube unstrapped Mickey from his thick wrist, and slid on the brand-new chronometer with its flex-metal band. He put his old watch very carefully atop the mantelpiece, out of the way, and then made a round of the crowded room, thanking each of them.

Afterward, Old Mister Cricket rubbed his legs together to the tune of "Jingle Bells," and Mrs. Holland served the turkey she'd won in the church raffle (Jube pushed his portion around sufficiently so that it looked as though he'd eaten some), and there was more eggnog to be drunk, and a card game after coffee, and when it got very late Jube told some of his jokes. Finally he figured it was time for him to retire; he'd given his helper the day off, so he'd have to open the stand himself bright and early the next morning. But when he stopped by the mantel on his way out, Mickey was gone. "My watch!" Jube exclaimed.

"What you want with that old thing, now that you have the new one?" Callie asked him.

"It has sentimental value," Jube said.

"I saw Doughboy playing with it," Warts told him. "He likes Mickey Mouse."

Shiner had put Doughboy to bed hours ago. Jube had to go upstairs. They found the watch on Doughboy's foot, and Shiner was very apologetic. "I think he broke it," the old man said.

"It's very durable," Jube said.

"It's been making a noise," Shiner told him. "Buzzing away. Broke inside, I guess."

For a moment, Jube didn't understand what he was talking about. Then dread replaced confusion. "Buzzing? How long—?"

"A good while," Shiner said as he handed back the watch. From inside the casing came a high, thin whine. "You okay?"

Jube nodded. "Tired," he said. "Merry Christmas." And then he thumped downstairs as fast as he could go.

In his cold, dim apartment, he hurried to the coal cellar. Within, sure enough, the communicator was glowing violet, Network color-code for extreme emergency. His hearts were in his mouth. How long? Hours, *hours*, and all the time he was partying. Jube felt sick. He dropped himself into his chair and keyed the console to play the message it had recorded.

The holocube lit from within, in a haze of violet light. In the center was Ekkedme, his hind jumping-legs folded under him so he seemed almost to crouch. The Embe nymph was obviously in a state of great agitation; the cilia covering his face trembled as they tasted the air, and the palps atop his tiny head swiveled frenetically. As Jube watched, code-violet background gave way and the crowded interior of the single-ship took form. "The Mother!" Ekkedme cried in the trade tongue, forcing the words through his spiracles in a wheezy Embe accent. The hologram shattered into static.

When it reintegrated an instant later, the Embe lurched suddenly to one side, reached out with a stick-thin forelimb, and clutched a smooth black ball to the pale white fur of his chitinous chest. He started to say something, but behind him the wall of the singleship bulged inward with a hideous metallic screech, and then disintegrated entirely. Jube watched with horror as air, instruments, and Embe were sucked up toward the cold unwinking stars. Ekkedme slammed into a jagged bulkhead and slid higher, holding tight to the ball as his hind legs scrabbled for purchase. A swirl of light ran over the surface of the sphere, and then it seemed to expand. A swift black tide engulfed the Embe; when it receded, he was gone. Jube dared to breathe again.

The transmission broke off abruptly an instant later.

Jube punched for a replay, hoping he had missed something. He could only watch half of it. Then he got up, rushed to the toilet, and regurgitated an evening's worth of eggnog.

He was steadier when he returned. He had to think, had to take things calmly. Panic and guilt would get him nowhere. Even if he had been wearing the watch, he could never have gotten down here in time to take the call, and there was nothing he could have done anyway. Besides, Ekkedme had escaped with the singularity shifter, Jube had seen it with his own eyes, surely his colleague had gotten to safety . . .

. . . only . . . if he had . . . where was he?

Jube looked around slowly. The Embe certainly wasn't *here*. But where else could he go? How long could he survive in this gravity? And what had *happened* up there in orbit?

Grimly, he linked to the satellite scanners. There were six of them, sophisticated devices the size of golf balls, loaded with Rhindarian sensors. Ekkedme had used them to monitor weather patterns, military activity, and radio and television transmissions, but they had other uses as well. Jube swept the skies methodically for the singleship, but where it should have been he found only scattered debris.

Suddenly Jube felt very much alone.

Ekkedme had been . . . well, not a friend, not the way the humans upstairs were friends, not even as close as Chrysalis or Crabcakes, but . . . their species had little in common, really. Ekkedme was a strange solitary sort, enigmatic and uncommunicative; and twenty-three years in orbit, locked in the close confines of his singleship with nothing to occupy him but meditation and monitoring, had only made the nymph stranger still—but of course that was why he had been chosen out of all those the Master Trader might have pegged when the *Opportunity* came this way so long ago, in the human year 1952, to observe the results of the Takisian grand experiment.

Unbidden, the memories came. The vast Network starship had circled the little green planet all that summer, finding little of interest. The native civilization was promising, but scarcely more advanced than it had been on their previous visit a few centuries earlier. And the vaunted Takisian virus, the wild card, seemed to have produced great numbers of freaks, cripples, and monsters. But the Master Trader liked to cover all bets, so when the *Opportunity* departed, it left behind two observers: the Embe in orbit, and a xenologist on the surface. It amused the Master Trader to hide his agent in plain sight, on the streets of the world's greatest city. And for Jhubben, who had signed a lifetime service contract for the chance to travel to distant worlds, it was a rare chance to do important work.

Still, until this moment there had always been the knowledge that someday the *Opportunity* would return, that someday he would know starflight again, and perhaps even return to the glaciers and ice cities of Glabber, beneath its wan red sun. The Embe nymph had never quite been a friend, yet Ekkedme had been something just as important. They had shared a past. Only Jube had known the Embe was there, watching, listening; only Ekkedme had known that Jube the Walrus, joker newsboy, was really Jhubben, a xenologist from Glabber. The nymph had been a link to his past, to his homeworld and his people, to the *Opportunity* and the Network itself, to its one-hundred-thirty-seven member species spread across a thousand-odd worlds.

Jube looked at the new watch his friends had given him. It was past two. The message had been received just before eight. He had never used a singularity shifter himself—it was an Embe device, still experimental, powered by a mini–black hole and capable of functioning as a stasis field, a teleportation device, even a power source, but fantastically expensive, its secrets zealously guarded by the Network. He did not pretend to understand its workings, but it should have brought Ekkedme *here*, where Jhubben could help him. If the shifter had malfunctioned, the Embe might have teleported into airless space, or the bottom of the ocean, or . . . well, *anywhere* within range.

He shook his massive head. What could he do? If Ekkedme was still alive, he would make his way here. Jube was powerless to help him. Meanwhile, he had a more urgent problem: something, or someone, had discovered, attacked, and destroyed the singleship. The humans had neither the technology nor the motives. Whoever was responsible was clearly no friend of the Network, and if they were aware of his existence, they might be coming after him as well. Jube found himself wishing that he hadn't just given away his weapon to Doughboy.

He watched the Embe's last transmission one last time in the hopes of finding a clue to the unknown enemy. There was nothing, except . . . "The Mother!" Ekkedme had said. What was that? Some Embe religious invocation, or was his colleague actually calling on the female who had hatched him?

Jube spent the next few hours floating in his tub, thinking. He did not savor those thoughts, yet the logic was inescapable. The Network had many enemies, within and without, but only one truly powerful rival in this sector of space, and only one that might be violently disgruntled to find Earth under observation: a species so like and so unlike the humans, imperious and aloof, racist, implacably bloody-minded, and capable of most any atrocity, to judge from what they'd done on Earth, and what they so regularly did to each other.

When dawn neared, and he dressed after a sleepless night, Jube was virtually convinced of it. Only a Takisian symbiont-ship could have done what he had witnessed. The ghostlance or the laser? he wondered. He was no expert on things martial.

It was a gray, slushy, depressing day, and Jube's mood matched it perfectly as he opened his newsstand. Business was slow. It was a little after eight when Dr. Tachyon came down the Bowery, wearing a white fur coat and mopping at an egg stain on his collar. "Something wrong, Jube?" Tachyon asked when he stopped for a *Times*. "You don't look well."

Jube had trouble finding the words. "Uh, yeah, Doc. A friend of mine . . . uh, died." He watched Tachyon's face for any flicker of guilt. Guilt came so easy to the Takisian, surely if he knew he would betray himself.

"I'm sorry," Doc said, his voice sincere and sympathetic. "I lost someone myself this week, an orderly at the clinic. I have a horrible suspicion that the man was murdered. One of my patients vanished the same day, a man named Spector." Tachyon sighed. "And now the police want me to perform an autopsy on some poor joker they found in a dumpster in Chelsea. The man looks like a furry grasshopper, McPherson tells me. So that makes him one of mine, you see." He shook his head wearily. "Well, they're just going to have to keep him on 'ice until I can organize the search for Mr. Spector. Keep your ears open, Jube, and let me know if you hear anything, all right?"

"A grasshopper, you say?" Jube tried to keep his voice casual. "A furry grasshopper?"

"Yes," Tach said. "Not someone you knew, I hope."

"I'm not sure," Jube said quickly. "Maybe I ought to go and take a look. I know a lot of jokers."

"He's in the morgue, on First Avenue."

"I'm not sure I could take it," Jube said. "I got a queasy stomach, Doc. What kind of place is this morgue?"

Tachyon reassured Jube that there was nothing to be frightened of. To allay any misgivings, he described the morgue and its procedures. Jube memorized every detail. "Doesn't sound so bad," he said finally. "Maybe I'll take a look-see, in case it is, uh, the guy I knew."

Tachyon nodded absently, his mind on other troubles. "You know," he told Jube, "that man Spector, the patient who vanished—he was dead when they brought him to me. I saved the man's life. And if I hadn't, Henry might still be alive. Of course, I have no proof." Folding his *Times* up under an arm, the Takisian slogged off through the slush.

Poor Ekkedme, Jube thought. To die so far from home . . . he had no idea what sort of burial customs the Embe practiced. There was not even time to mourn. Tachyon did not know, clearly. And more importantly, Tachyon *must* not know. The Network presence on Earth must be kept a secret at all costs. And if the Takisian performed that autopsy, he *would* know, there was no doubt of that. Tachyon had accepted Jube as a joker, and why not? He looked as human as most jokers, and he'd been in Jokertown longer than Doc himself. Glabber was a backwater, poor and obscure. It had no starflight of its own, and less than a hundred Glabberans had ever taken service on the great Network starships. The chances of him recognizing Jhubben were slight to nonexistent. But the Embe filled a dozen worlds, their ships were known on a hundred more; they were as much a part of the Network as the Ly'bahr, Kondikki, Aevre, or even the Master Traders. One glance at that body and Tachyon would know.

Jube bounced on his heels, feeling the first faint touches of panic. He had to get that body before Tachyon saw it. And the *shifter*, how could he forget that! If an artifact as valuable as a singularity shifter fell into Takisian hands, there would be no telling what the consequences might be. But *how?*

A man he had never laid eyes on before stopped in front of the newsstand. Distracted, Jube looked up at him. "Paper?"

"One of each," the man said, "as usual."

It took a moment to sink in, but when it did, Jube knew he had his answer.

ASHES TO ASHES

By Roger Zelazny

The radio spat static. Croyd Crenson reached out, switched it off, and threw it across the room toward the wastebasket beside the dresser. He took it as a good omen that it went in.

He stretched then, flipped back the covers, and regarded his pale nude body. Everything seemed to be in place and normally proportioned. He willed himself to levitate and nothing happened, so he swung his legs over the edge of the bed and sat up. He ran his hand through his hair, pleased to find that he possessed hair. Waking up was always an adventure.

He tried to make himself invisible, to melt the wastebasket with a thought and to cause sparks to arc between his fingertips. None of these things occurred.

He rose and made his way to the bathroom. As he drank glass after glass of water he studied himself in the mirror. Light hair and eyes this time, regular features; fairly good-looking, actually. He judged himself to be a little over six feet in height. Well-muscled, too. There ought to be something in the closet that would fit. He'd been about this height and build before.

It was a gray day beyond the window with patches of slushy-looking snow lining the sidewalk across the street. Water trickled in the gutter. Croyd halted on his way to the closet to withdraw a heavy steel rod from a crate beneath his writing table. Almost casually, he bent the rod in half and then twisted it. The strength had carried over yet again, he reflected, as the metal pretzel joined the radio in the wastebasket. He located a shirt and trousers that fit him well, and a tweed jacket only slightly tight in the shoulders. He turned his attention then to his large collection of shoes, and after a time he came up with a comfortable pair.

It was a little after eight o'clock according to his Rolex, and this being winter and daylight it meant morning. His stomach rumbled. Time for breakfast and orientation. He checked his cash cache and withdrew a couple of hundred dollars. Getting low, he mused. Have to visit the bank later. Or maybe rob one. The stocks were taking a beating, too, the last time around. Later. . . .

He equipped himself with a handkerchief, a comb, his keys, and a small plastic bottle of pills. He did not like to carry identification of any sort. No need for an overcoat. Temperature extremes seldom bothered him.

He locked the door behind him, negotiated the hall and descended the stairs. He turned left when he reached the street, facing into a sharp wind, and he began walking down the Bowery. Leaving a dollar in the outstretched hand of a tall, cadaverous-looking joker with a nose like an icicle—who stood as still as a totem pole in the doorway of a closed mask shop—Croyd asked the man what month it was.

"December," the figure said without moving its lips. "Merry Christmas."

"Yeah," Croyd said.

He tried a few more simple tests as he headed for his first stop, but he could not break the empty whisky bottles in the gutter with a thought, nor set fire to any of the piles of trash. He attempted to utter ultrasounds but only produced squeaks.

He hiked down to the newsstand at Hester Street where short, fat Jube Benson sat reading one of his own papers. Benson had on a yellow and orange Hawaiian shirt beneath a light-blue summer suit; bristles of red hair protruded from beneath his porkpie hat. The temperature seemed to bother him no more than it did Croyd. He raised his dark, blubbery, pocked face and displayed a pair of short, curving tusks as Croyd stopped before the stand.

"Paper?" he asked.

"One of each," Croyd said, "as usual."

Jube's eyes narrowed slightly as he studied the man before him. Then, "Croyd?" he asked.

Croyd nodded.

"It's me, Walrus. How're they hanging?"

"Can't complain, fella. Got yourself a pretty one this time."

"Still test-driving it," Croyd said, gathering a stack of papers.

Jube showed more tusk.

"What's the most dangerous job in Jokertown?" he asked.

"I give up."

"Riding shotgun on the garbage truck," he said. "Hear what happened to the gal who won the Miss Jokertown contest?"

"What?"

"Lost her title when they learned she'd posed nude for *Poultry Breeder's Gazette.*"

"That's sick, Jube," said Croyd, quirking a smile.

"I know. We got hit by a hurricane while you were asleep. Know what it did?'"

"What?"

"Four million dollars' worth of civic improvement."

"All right, already!" Croyd said. "What do I owe you?"

Jube put down his paper, rose, and waddled to the side of the kiosk.

"Nothin'," he said. "I want to talk to you."

"I've got to eat, Jube. When I wake up I need a lot of food in a hurry. I'll come back later, all right?"

"Is it okay if I join you?"

"Sure. But you'll lose business."

Jube began closing the stand.

"That's okay," he said. "This *is* business."

Croyd waited for him to secure the stand, and they walked two blocks to Hairy's Kitchen.

"Let's take that booth in the back," Jube said.

"Fine. No business till after my first round of food, though, okay? I can't concentrate with low blood sugar, funny hormones and lots of transaminases. Let me get something else inside first."

"I understand. Take your time."

When the waiter came by, Jube said that he had already eaten and ordered only a cup of coffee which he never touched. Croyd started with a double order of steak and eggs and a pitcher of orange juice.

Ten minutes later when the pancakes arrived, Jube cleared his throat.

"Yeah," Croyd said. "That's better. So what's bothering you, Jube?"

"Hard to begin," said the other.

"Start anywhere. Life is brighter for me now."

"It isn't always healthy to get too curious about other people's business around here. . . ."

"True," Croyd agreed.

"On the other hand, people love to gossip, to speculate." Croyd nodded, kept eating.

"It's no secret about the way you sleep, and that's got to keep you from holding a regular job. Now, you seem more of an ace than a joker, overall. I mean, usually you look normal but you've got some special talent."

"I haven't got a handle on it yet, this time around."

"Whatever. You dress well, you pay your bills, you like to eat at Aces High, and that ain't a Timex you're wearing. You've got to *do* something to stay on top—unless you inherited a bundle."

Croyd smiled.

"I'm afraid to look at the *Wall Street Journal*," he said, touching the stack of papers at his side. "I may have to *do* something I haven't done in a while if it says what I think it's going to say."

"May I assume then that when you work your employment is sometimes somewhat less than legal?"

Croyd raised his head, and when their eyes met Jube flinched. It was the first time Croyd realized that the man was nervous. He laughed.

"Hell, Jube," he said. "I've known you long enough to know you're no cop. You want something done, is that it? If it involves stealing something, I'm good at that. I learned from an expert. If someone's being blackmailed I'll be glad to get the evidence back and scare the living shit out of the person doing it. If you want something removed, destroyed, transported, I'm your man. On the other hand, if you want somebody killed I don't like to do that. But I could give you the names of a couple of people it wouldn't bother."

Jube shook his head.

"I don't want anybody killed, Croyd. I do want something stolen, though."

"Before you go into any details, I'd better tell you that I come high."

Jube showed his tusks.

"The—uh—interests I represent are prepared to make it worth your while."

Croyd finished the pancakes, drank coffee, and ate a Danish while he waited for the waffles.

"It's a body, Croyd," Jube said at last.

"What?"

"A corpse."

"I don't understand."

"There was a guy who died over the weekend. Body was found in a dumpster. No ID. It's a John Doe. Over at the morgue."

"Jeez, Jube! A body? I never stole a body before. What good is it to anybody?"

Jube shrugged.

"They're willing to pay real well for it—and for whatever possessions the guy had with him. That's all they wanted said."

"I guess it's their business what they want it for. But what kind of money are they talking?"

"It's worth fifty grand to them."

"Fifty grand? For a stiff?" Croyd stopped eating and stared. "You've got to be kidding."

"Nope. I can give you ten now and forty when you deliver."

"And if I can't pull it off?"

"You get to keep the ten, for trying. You interested?"

Croyd took a deep breath and let it out slowly.

"Yeah," he said then. "I'm interested. But I don't even know where the morgue is."

"It's in the medical examiner's office at Five-Twenty First Avenue."

"Okay. Say I go over there and—"

Hairy came by and laid a plate of sausages and hash browns before Croyd. He refilled his coffee cup and placed several bills and some coins on the table.

"Your change, sir."

Croyd looked at the money.

"What do you mean?" he said. "I didn't pay you yet."

"You gave me a fifty."

"No, I didn't. I'm not finished."

It looked as if Hairy smiled, deep within the dark dense pelt that covered him entirely.

"I wouldn't stay in business long if I gave away money," he said. "I know when I'm making change."

Croyd shrugged and nodded.

"I guess so."

Croyd furrowed his brows when Hairy had left, and he shook his head.

"I didn't pay him, Jube," he said.

"I don't remember seeing you pay him either. But he said a fifty. . . . That's hard to forget."

"Peculiar, too. Because I was thinking of breaking a fifty here when I was done."

"Oh? Do you recall when the thought passed through your mind?"

"Yeah. When he brought the waffles."

"Did you actually have a mental image of taking out a fifty and handing it to him?"

"Yes."

"Interesting. . . ."

"What do you mean?"

"I think that may be your power this time—some kind of telepathic hypnosis. You'll just have to play with it a bit to get the hang of it, to find its limits."

Croyd nodded slowly.

"Please don't try it on me, though. I'm screwed up enough as it is today."

"Why? You got some stake in this corpse business?"

"The less you know the better, Croyd. Believe me."

"Okay, I can see that. I don't really care, anyway. Not for what they're paying," he said. "So I take this job. Say everything goes smoothly and I've got this body. What do I do with it?"

Jube withdrew a pen and a small notebook from an inside pocket. He wrote for a moment, tore off a sheet, and passed it to Croyd. Then he dug in his side pocket, produced a key, and put it next to Croyd's plate.

"That address is about five blocks from here," he said. "Rented room, ground floor. The key fits the lock. You take it there, lock it in, and come tell me at the stand."

Croyd began eating again. After a time, he said, "Okay."

"Good."

"But they've probably got more than one John Doe in there this time of year. Winos who freeze to death—you know. How do I know which one is the right one?"

"I was getting to that. This guy's a joker, see? A little fellow. About five feet tall, maybe. Looks kind of like a big bug—legs that fold up like a grasshopper's, an exoskeleton with some fur on it, four fingers on his hands with three joints each, eyes on the sides of his head, vestigial wings on back . . ."

"I get the picture. Sounds hard to confuse with the standard model."

"Yes. Shouldn't weigh much either."

Croyd nodded. Someone in the front of the restaurant said, ". . . pterodactyl!" and Croyd turned his head in time to see the winged shape flit by the window.

"That kid again," Jube said.

"Yeah. Wonder who he's pestering this time?"

"You know him?"

"Uh-huh. He shows up every now and then. Kind of an aces fan. At least he doesn't know what I look like this time. Anyway. . . . How soon do they need this body?"

"The sooner the better."

"Anything you can tell me about the setup at the morgue?"

Jube nodded slowly.

"Yes. It's a six-story building. Labs and offices and such, upstairs. Reception and viewing area on the ground floor. They keep the bodies in the basement. The autopsy rooms are down there, too. They have a hundred and twenty-eight storage compartments, with a walk-in refrigerator with shelves for kids' bodies. When somebody has to view a body for ID purposes, they put it on a special elevator which lifts it to a glass-enclosed chamber in a waiting room on the first floor."

"So you've been there?"

"No, I read Milton Helpern's memoirs."

"You've got what I'd call a real liberal education," Croyd said. "I should probably read more myself."

"You can buy a lot of books for fifty grand."

Croyd smiled.

"So, we've got a deal?"

"Let me think about it a little longer—over breakfast— while I figure out just how my talent works. I'll come by your stand when I'm done. When would I pick up the ten grand?"

"I can get it by this afternoon."

"Okay. I'll see you in a hour or so."

Jube nodded, raised his massive bulk, slid out of the booth.

"Watch your cholesterol," he said.

* * *

Blue cracks had appeared in the sky's gray shell, and sunlight found its way through to the street. The sound of trickling water came steadily now from somewhere to the rear of the newsstand. Jube would normally have thought it a pleasant background to the traffic noises and other sounds of the city, save that a small moral dilemma had drifted in on leathery wings and destroyed the morning. He did not realize he had made a decision in the matter until he looked up and saw Croyd looking at him, smiling.

"No problem," said Croyd. "It'll be a piece of cake."

Jube sighed.

"There's something I've got to tell you first," he said.

"Problems?"

"Nothing that bears directly on the terms of the job," Jube explained. "But you may have a problem you didn't know you had."

"Like what?" Croyd said, frowning.

"That pterodactyl we saw earlier . . . ?"

"Yeah?"

"Kid Dinosaur was headed here. I found him waiting when I got back. He was looking for you."

"I hope you didn't tell him where to find me."

"No, I wouldn't do that. But you know how he keeps tabs on aces and high-powered jokers . . . ?"

"Yeah. Why couldn't he be into baseball players or war criminals?"

"He saw one he wanted you to know about. He said that Devil John Darlingfoot got out of the hospital a month or so ago and dropped out of sight. But he's back now. He'd seen him near the Cloisters earlier. Says he's heading for Midtown."

"Well, well. So what?"

"So he thinks he's looking for you. Wants a rematch. The Kid thinks he's still mad over what you did to him the day the two of you trashed Rockefeller Plaza."

"So let him keep looking. I'm not a short, heavyset, dark-haired guy anymore. I'll go get the stiff now—before someone buys him a short bier."

"Don't you want the money?"

"You already gave it to me."

"When?"

"What's your first memory of my coming back here?"

"I looked up about a minute ago and saw you standing

there smiling. You said there was no problem. You called it 'a piece of cake.'"

"Good. Then, it's working."

"You'd better explain."

"That's the place where I wanted you to start remembering. I'd been here for about a minute before that, and I talked you into giving me the money and forgetting about it."

Croyd withdrew an envelope from an inner pocket, opened it, and displayed cash.

"Good Lord, Croyd! What else did you do during that minute?"

"Your virtue's intact, if that's what you mean."

"You didn't ask me any questions—about . . . ?"

Croyd shook his head.

"I told you I didn't care who wants the body or why. I really don't like to burden myself with other people's concerns. I've enough problems of my own."

Jube sighed.

"Okay. Go do it, boy."

Croyd winked.

"Not to worry, Walrus. Consider it done."

Croyd walked until he came to a supermarket, went in and purchased a small package of large plastic trash bags. He folded one and fitted it into his inside jacket pocket. He left the rest in a waste bin. Then he walked to the next major intersection and hailed a cab.

He rehearsed his strategy as he rode across town. He would enter the place and use his latest power to persuade the receptionist that he was expected, that he was a pathologist from Bellevue who had been called over by a friend on the staff to consult on a forensic peculiarity. He toyed for a moment with the names Malone and Welby, settled upon Anderson. He would then cause the receptionist to summon someone with the authority to take him downstairs and find him his John Doe. He would place that person under control, get the body and its belongings, transfer it to a baggy, and walk out, causing everyone he passed to forget he had been by. Certainly a lot simpler than more strenuous tactics he had had to employ over the years. He smiled at the classic simplicity of it—no violence, no memory. . . .

When he arrived at the aluminum-paneled building of blue and white glazed brick, he told the cab driver to go on by and drop him at the next corner. There were two police cars parked in front and a shattered door lay before the place. The presence of police at a morgue did not seem that untoward an occurrence, but the broken door aroused his sense of caution. He handed the driver a fifty and told him to wait. He strolled past the place once and looked inside. Several of the police were visible, apparently talking with employees.

This did not seem an ideal time to proceed with his plan. On the other hand, he could not afford to go away without finding out what had happened. So he turned when he reached the corner, and headed back. He entered without hesitation, looking about quickly.

A man in civvies who was standing with the police turned suddenly in his direction and stared. Croyd did not like that stare at all. It pulled the floor out from under his stomach and made his hands tingle.

He reached out immediately with his new power, heading directly toward the man, forcing a smile as he moved.

It's okay. You want to talk to me and do exactly as I say. Wave you hand now, say, "Hi, Jim!" in a loud voice and walk over to the side there with me.

"Hi, Jim!" the man said, moving to join Croyd.

No! Judas thought. Too damned fast. Nailed me as soon as I spotted him. . . . We can use this guy. . . .

"Plainclothes?" Croyd asked him.

"Yes," the man felt himself wanting to answer.

"What's your name?"

"Matthias."

"What happened here?"

"A body was stolen."

"Which one?"

"A John Doe."

"Can you describe it?"

"Looked like a big bug—grasshopper legs . . ."

"Shit!" Croyd said. "What about his possessions?"

"There weren't any possessions."

Several of the uniformed officers were glancing in their direction now. Croyd gave his next order mentally. Matthias turned toward the uniforms.

"Just a minute, guys," he called. "Business."

Damn! he thought. This one will come in handy. You can't hold me like this forever, fella. . . .

"How'd it happen?" Croyd asked.

"A guy came in here a little while ago, went downstairs, forced an attendant to show him the compartment, took the body out, and left with it."

"Nobody tried to stop him?"

"Sure they did. Four of them are on their way to the hospital as a result. The guy was an ace."

"Which one?"

"The one who wrecked Rockefeller Plaza last fall."

"Darlingfoot?"

"Yeah, that's the one." Don't . . . Don't ask any more—whether I'm involved, whether I hired him, whether I'm running a cover-up now. . . .

"Which way did he go with it?"

"Northwest."

"On foot?"

"That's what the witnesses said—big, twenty-foot leaps." As soon as you let me go, sucker, I'm calling in the nukes on you.

"Hey, why'd you turn and look at me the way you did when I came in?"

Damn!

"I felt that an ace had just walked through the door."

"How'd you know?"

"I'm an ace myself. That's my power—spotting other aces."

"Useful talent for a cop, I guess. Well, listen close. You are now going to forget you ever met me, and you won't notice me leaving. You're just going to walk on over to that fountain and get a drink, then walk back and join your buddies. If anyone asks who you were talking to, you'll say it was your bookie and forget about it. You do that now. Forget!"

Croyd turned and walked away. Judas realized he was thirsty.

Outside, Croyd walked to his cab, climbed in, slammed the door and said, "Northwest."

"What do you mean?" the driver asked him.

"Just head uptown and I'll tell you what to do as we go along."

"You're the boss."

The car jerked into motion.

Over the next mile Croyd had the driver jog westward, as he searched for signs of the other's passage. It seemed unlikely that Devil John would be using public transportation when carrying a corpse. On the other hand, it was possible he'd had an accomplice waiting with a vehicle. Still, knowing the man's chutzpah, it did not seem out of the question for him to be hoofing it with the body. He knew that there was very little anyone could do to stop him if he did not wish to be stopped. Croyd sighed as he scanned the way ahead. Why were simple things never easy?

Later, as they were nearing Morningside Heights, the driver muttered, ". . . one of them damn jokers!"

Croyd followed the man's gesture to where the form of a pterodactyl was in sight for several moments before passing behind a building.

"Follow it!" Croyd said.

"The leather bird?"

"Yes!"

"I'm not sure where it is now."

"Find it!"

Croyd waved another bill at the man, and the tires screeched and a horn blared as the cab took a turn. Croyd's gaze swept the skyline, but the Kid was still out of sight. He halted the cab moments later to question an oncoming jogger. The man popped an earplug, listened a moment, then pointed to the east and took off again.

Several minutes later, he caught sight of the angular bird-form, to the north, moving in wide circles. This time they were able to keep track of it for a longer while, and to gain on it.

When they came abreast of the area the pterodactyl circled, Croyd called to the driver to slow. There was still nothing unusual in sight on the ground, but the saurian's sweeping path covered an area of several blocks. If he were indeed tracking Devil John, the man could well be nearby.

"What are we looking for?" the driver asked him.

"A big, red-bearded, curly-haired man with two very different legs," Croyd answered. "The right one is heavy, hairy, and ends in a hoof. The other's normal."

"I heard something about that guy. He's dangerous. . . ."

"Yeah, I know."

"What are you planning on doing if you find him?"

"I was hoping for a meaningful dialogue," Croyd said.

"I ain't gettin' too close to your dialogue. If we spot him, I'm taking off."

"I'll make it worth you while to wait."

"No thanks," the driver said. "You want out, I'll drop you and run. That's it."

"Well. . . . The pterodactyl is moving north. Let's try to get ahead of it, and when we do you cut east on the first street where we can."

The driver accelerated again, drifting to the right while Croyd tried to guess the center of the Kid's circle.

"The next street," Croyd said finally. "Turn there and see what happens."

They took the corner slowly and cruised the entire block without Croyd's spotting his quarry or even viewing his airborne telltale again. At the next intersection, however, the winged form passed once more and this time he had sight of the one he sought.

Devil John was on the opposite side of the street, halfway down the block. He bore a shrouded parcel in his arms. His shoulders were massive; his white teeth flashed as a woman with a shopping cart rushed to get out of his way. He wore Levi's—the right leg torn off high on the thigh—and a pink sweatshirt suggesting he had visited Disney World. A passing motorist sideswiped a parked car as John took a normal step with his left foot, bent his right leg at an odd angle, and sprang twenty feet farther ahead to an open area near the curb. He turned then with a normal step and sprang again, clearing a slow-moving red Honda and landing in a patch of grass on the street's central island. Two large dogs that had been following him rushed to the curb, barking loudly, but halted there and regarded oncoming traffic.

"Stop!" Croyd called to the driver, and he opened the door and stepped to the curb before the vehicle came to a complete halt.

He cupped his hands to his mouth then and shouted, "Darlingfoot! Hold on!"

The man only glanced in his direction, already bending his leg to spring again.

"It's me—Croyd Crenson!" he called out. "I want to talk to you!"

The satyr-like figure halted in mid-crouch. The shadow of a pterodactyl swept by. The two dogs continued to bark, and a tiny white poodle rounded a corner and rushed to join them. An auto horn blared at two halted pedestrians in a crosswalk. Devil John turned and stared. Then he shook his head.

"You're not Crenson!" he shouted.

Croyd strode forward.

"The hell I'm not!" he answered, and he darted into the street and crossed to the island.

Devil John's eyes were narrowed beneath his shaggy brows as he studied Croyd's advancing figure. He raked his lower lip slowly with his upper teeth, then shook his head more slowly.

"Naw," he said. "Croyd was darker and a lot shorter. What are you trying to pull, anyway?"

Croyd shrugged.

"My appearance changes pretty regularly," he said. "But I'm the same guy who whipped your ass last fall."

Darlingfoot laughed.

"Get lost, fella," he said. "I don't have time for groupies—"

They both clenched their teeth as a car drew up beside them and its horn blasted. A man in a gray business suit stuck his head out of the window.

"What's going on here?" he asked.

Croyd growled, stepped into the street, and removed the rear bumper, which he then placed in the vehicle's back seat through a window that had been closed up until then.

"Auto inspection," he said. "You pass. Congratulations."

"Croyd!" Darlingfoot exclaimed as the car sped off. "It *is* you!"

He tossed his shrouded burden to the ground and raised his fists.

"I've been waiting all winter for this. . . ."

"Then, wait a minute longer," Croyd said. "I've got to ask you something."

"What?"

"That body. . . . Why'd you take it?"

The big man laughed.

"For money, of course. What else?"

"Mind telling me what they're paying you for it?"

"Five grand. Why?"

"Cheap bastards," Croyd said. "They say what they want it for?"

"No, and I didn't ask because I don't care. A buck's a buck."

"Yeah," Croyd said. "Who are they, anyhow?"

"Why? What's it to you?"

"Well, I think you're getting screwed on the deal. I think it's worth more."

"How much?"

"Who are they?"

"Some Masons, I think. What's it worth?"

"Masons? Like secret handshakes and all that? I thought they just existed to give each other expensive funerals. What could they want with a dead joker?"

Darlingfoot shook his head.

"They're a weird bunch," he said. "For all I know, they want to eat it. Now, what were you saying about money?"

"I think I could get more for it," Croyd said. "What say I see their five and raise it one? I'll give you six big ones for it."

"I don't know, Croyd. . . . I don't like to screw people I work for. Word will get around I'm undependable."

"Well, maybe I could go seven—"

They both turned suddenly at a series of savage growls and snappings. The dogs—joined by two additional strays— had crossed over during their conversation and dragged the small, insectlike body from its shroud. It had broken in several places, and the Great Dane held most of an arm in his teeth as he backed away, snarling, from the German shepherd. Two others had torn one of the grasshopperlike legs loose and were fighting over it. The poodle was already halfway across the street, a four-digited hand in its mouth. Croyd became aware of a particularly foul odor other than New York air.

"Shit!" Devil John exclaimed, leaping forward, his hoof shattering a square of concrete paving near to the remains. He grabbed for the Great Dane and it turned and raced away. The terrier let go of the leg. The brown mongrel didn't. It tore across the street in the other direction, dragging the appendage. "I'll get the arm! You get the leg!" Devil John cried, bounding after the Great Dane.

"What about the hand?" Croyd yelled, kicking at another dog newly arrived on the scene.

Darlingfoot's reply was predictable, curt, and represented an anatomical unlikelihood of a high order. Croyd took off after the brown dog.

As Croyd approached the corner where he had seen it turn, he heard a series of sharp yelps. Coming onto the side street he saw the dog lying on its back snapping at the pterodactyl which pinned it to the pavement. The battered limb lay nearby. Croyd sprinted forward.

"Thanks, Kid. I owe you one," he said as he reached for the leg, hesitated, took out his handkerchief, wrapped it about his hand, picked up the limb, and held it downwind.

The pterodactyl shape flowed, to be replaced by that of a nude boy—perhaps thirteen years of age—with light eyes and unruly brown hair, a small birthmark on his forehead.

"Got it for you, Croyd," he announced. "Sure stinks, though."

"Yeah, Kid," Croyd said. "Excuse me. Now I've got to go put it back together."

He turned and hurried in the direction from which he had come. Behind him he heard rapid footfalls.

"What you want it for?" the boy asked.

"It's a long, complicated, boring story, and it's better you don't know," he answered.

"Aw, c'mon. You can tell me."

"No time. I'm in a hurry."

"You going to fight Devil John again?"

"I don't plan on it. I think we can come to a meeting of minds without resorting to violence."

"But if you do fight, what's your power this time?"

Croyd reached the corner, cut across to the island. Ahead, he saw where another dog now worried the remains. Devil John was nowhere in sight.

"Damn it!" he yelled. "Get away from there!"

The dog paid him no heed, but stripped a furry layer from the chitinous carapace. Croyd noticed that the torn tissue was dripping some colorless liquid. The remains looked moist now, and Croyd realized that fluids were oozing from the breathing holes in the thorax.

"Get away from there!" he repeated.

The dog growled at him. Suddenly, though, the growl turned to a whimper and the animal's tail vanished between its legs. A meter-high tyrannosaurus hopped past Croyd, hissing fiercely. The dog turned and fled. A moment later, the Kid stood in its place.

"It's getting away with that piece," the boy said.

Croyd repeated Darlingfoot's comment on the hand as he tossed the leg down beside the dismembered body. He withdrew the folded trash bag from the inner pocket of his jacket and shook it out.

"You want to help, Kid, you hold the bag while I toss in what's left."

"Okay. It sure is gross."

"It's a dirty job," Croyd agreed.

"Then, why you doing it?"

"It's what growing up is all about, Kid."

"How do you mean?"

"You spend more and more of your time cleaning up after mistakes."

A rapid thumping noise approached, a shadow passed overhead, and Devil John crashed to the earth beside them.

"Damn dog got away," he announced. "You get the leg?"

"Yeah," Croyd answered. "It's already in the bag."

"Good idea—a plastic bag. Who's the naked kid?"

"You don't know Kid Dinosaur?" Croyd answered. "I thought he knew everybody. He's the pterodactyl was following you."

"Why?"

"I like to be where the action is," the Kid said.

"Hey, how come you're not in school?" Croyd asked.

"School sucks."

"Now, wait a minute. I had to quit school in ninth grade and I never got to go back. I always regretted it."

"Why? You're doing okay."

"There's all that stuff I missed. I wish I hadn't."

"Like what?"

"Well. . . . Algebra. I never learned algebra."

"What the fuck good's algebra?"

"I don't know and I never will, because I didn't learn it. I sometimes look at people on the street and say, 'Gee, I'll bet they all know algebra,' and it makes me feel kind of inferior."

"Well, I don't know algebra and it doesn't make feel a damn bit inferior."

"Give it time," Croyd said.

The Kid suddenly became aware that Croyd was looking at him strangely.

"You're going back to school right now," Croyd told him, "and you're going to study your ass off for the rest of the day, and you're going to do your homework tonight, and you're going to like it."

"I'll make better time if I fly," the Kid said, and he transformed into a pterodactyl, hopped several times, and glided away.

"Pick up some clothes on the way!" Croyd shouted after him.

"Just what the hell is going on here?"

Croyd turned and beheld a uniformed officer who had just crossed to their island.

"Go fuck yourself!" he snarled.

The man began unbuckling his belt.

"Stop! Cancel that," Croyd said. "Buckle up. Forget you saw us and go walk up another street."

Devil John stared as the man obeyed.

"Croyd, how are you doing those things?" he asked.

"That's my power, this time around."

"Then, you could just make me give you the body, couldn't you?"

Croyd shook the bag down and fastened it. When he finished gagging, he nodded.

"Yeah. And I'll get it one way or another, too. But I don't feel like cheating a fellow working stiff today. My offer's still good."

"Seven grand?"

"Six."

"You said seven."

"Yeah, but it's not all here now."

"That's your fault, not mine. You stopped me."

"But you put the thing down where the dogs could get it."

"Yes, but how was I supposed to— Hey, that's a bar and grill on the corner."

"You're right."

"Care to discuss this over lunch and a couple of brews?"

"Now that you mention it, I've a bit of an appetite," Croyd said.

They took the table by the window and set the bag on the empty chair. Croyd visited the men's room and washed his hands several times while Devil John procured a pair of beers. When he returned he ordered a half-dozen sandwiches. Darlingfoot did the same.

"Who're *you* working for?" he asked.

"I don't know," Croyd answered. "I'm doing it through a third party."

"Complicated. I wonder what they all want the thing for?"

Croyd shook his head.

"Beats me. I hope there's enough of him left to collect on."

"That's one of the reasons I'm willing to deal. I think my guys wanted him in better shape than this. They might try to welsh on me. Better a bird in the hand, you know? I don't trust them all that much. Bunch of kooks."

"Say, did he have any possessions?"

"Nope. No belongings at all."

The sandwiches arrived and they began eating. After a while, Darlingfoot glanced several times at the bag, then remarked, "You know, that thing looks bigger."

Croyd studied it a moment.

"It's just settling and shifting," he said.

They finished, then ordered two more beers.

"No, damn it! It *is* bigger!" Darlingfoot insisted.

Croyd looked again. It seemed to swell even as he watched.

"You're right," he acknowledged. "It must be gases from the—uh—decomposition."

He extended a finger as if to poke it, thought better of it and lowered his hand.

"So what do you say? Seven grand?"

"I think six is fair—the shape he's in."

"But they knew what they were asking for. You've got to expect this sort of thing with stiffs."

"A certain amount, yes. But you've got to admit you bounced him around a hell of a lot, too."

"That's true, but a regular one could take it better. How was I to know this guy was a special case?"

"By looking at him. He was little and fragile."

"He felt pretty sturdy when I snatched him. What say we split the difference? Sixty-five hundred?"

"I don't know. . . ."

Other diners began glancing in their direction as the bag continued to swell. They finished their beers.

"Another round?"

"Why not?"

"Waiter!"

Their waiter, who had been clearing a recently vacated table, ambled over, a stack of dishes and utensils in his hands.

"What can I get—" he began, when the edge of a steak knife, protruding from the pile of crockery, brushed against the swollen bag. "My God!" he finished, as a *whooshing* sound, accompanied by an odor that might have been compounded of sewer gas and slaughterhouse effluvia filled the immediate vicinity and spread like an escaped experiment in chemical warfare throughout the room.

"Excuse me," the waiter said, and he turned and hurried off.

There followed a series of gasps from other diners, moments later.

"Use your power, Croyd!" Devil John whispered. "Hurry!"

"I don't know if I can do a whole roomful. . . ."

"Try!"

Croyd concentrated on the others:

There was a small accident. Nothing important. Now you will forget it. You smell nothing unusual. Return to your meals and do not look in this direction again. You will not notice anything that we do. There is nothing to be seen here. Or smelled.

The other patrons turned away, resumed eating, talking.

"You did it," Devil John remarked in a peculiar voice.

Croyd looked back and discovered that the man was pinching his nostrils shut.

"Did you spill something?" Croyd asked him.

"No."

"Uh-oh. Hear that?"

Darlingfoot leaned to the side and bent low.

"Oh damn!" he said. "The bag's collapsed and he's running out the slash that guy made. Hey, kill my sense of smell too, will you?"

Croyd closed his eyes and gritted his teeth.

"That's better," he heard moments later as Darlingfoot reached out and uprighted the bag, which made a sloshing, gurgling noise.

Croyd looked to the floor and beheld a huge puddle resembling spilled stew. He gagged slightly and looked away.

"What do you want to do now, Croyd? Leave the mess and take the rest, or what?"

"I think I'm obliged to take everything I can."

Devil John quirked an eyebrow and smiled.

"Well," he said, "go sixty-five hundred and I'll help you get it all together in a manageable form."

"It's a deal."

"Then, cover me if you can so the people in the kitchen don't notice me."

"I'll try. What are you going to do?"

"Trust me."

Darlingfoot rose, passed the top of the bag to Croyd, and

limped back to the kitchen. He was gone for several minutes and when he returned his arms were full.

He unscrewed the top from a large empty pickle jar and set it on the floor beside the chair.

"Now if you'll just tilt the bag so the opening is right over the jar," he said, "I'll raise the bottom and we can pour him into it."

Croyd complied and the jar was well over half-full before the trickle ceased.

"Now what?" he asked, screwing on the lid.

Darlingfoot took the first from a stack of napkins he had brought with him and opened a small white bundle.

"Doggie bags," he said. "I'll just get all the solid stuff up off the floor and into them."

"Then what?"

"I've got a nice, fresh trash-can liner, too," he explained, stooping. "It should all fit inside with no trouble."

"Could you hurry?" Croyd said. "I can't control my own sense of smell."

"I'm mopping as fast as I can. Open the jar again, though, will you? I can wring out the rest of him from the napkins."

When the spilled remains had been collected into the pickle jar and nine doggie bags, Darlingfoot ripped the torn bag the rest of the way open and removed the chitinous plates that remained within. He set the jar on the concavity of the thorax and then placed it all in the fresh bag, covering it with pieces of gristle and smaller bits of plating. He set the head and limbs on top. Then he packed the doggie bags and rolled down the liner.

Croyd was on his feet by then.

"Excuse me," he said. "I'll be right back."

"I'll come, too. I have to wash up a bit."

Above the running of the water Devil John suddenly remarked, "Now that everything's pretty much settled, I've got a favor to ask of you."

"What's that?" Croyd inquired, soaping his hands yet again.

"I still feel funny about the ones who hired me, you know?"

Croyd shrugged.

"You can't have it both ways," he said.

"Why not?"

"I don't follow you."

"I was on my way to deliver when you caught up with me. Supposing we went on to the rendezvous point—a little park up near the Cloisters—and I give them some bullshit about the dogs tearing the body apart and getting away with the whole thing. You make them believe it, and then have them forget that you were along. That way, I'm off the hook."

"Okay. Sure," Croyd agreed, splashing water on his face. "But you say 'them.' How many people are you expecting?"

"Just one or two. The guy who hired me was named Matthias, and there was a red man with him. He's the one who tried getting me interested in these Masons till the other shut him up. . . ."

"That's funny," Croyd said. "I met a Matthias this morning. He was a cop. Plainclothes. And what about the red guy? Sounds like maybe an ace or a joker."

"Probably is. But if he's got any special talent he wasn't showing it."

Croyd dried his face.

"All of a sudden I'm a little uncomfortable," he said. "See, this cop Matthias is an ace. The name might just be a coincidence, and I was able to con him with my talent, but I don't like anything that smacks of too many aces. I might run into someone who's immune to what I've got. This group . . . It couldn't be a bunch of Mason aces, could it?"

"I don't know. The red fellow wanted me to come in to some kind of meeting, and I told him I wasn't a joiner and that we dealt right there or we forgot about it. So they coughed up my retainer on the spot. There was something about the way the red guy said things that gave me bad vibes."

Croyd frowned.

"Maybe we should just forget them."

"I've really got this thing about closing deals all proper so they don't come back to haunt me," Darlingfoot said. "Couldn't you just sort of look it over while I talk to him, and then decide?"

"Well, okay. . . . I said that I would. Do you remember anything else that got said? About Masons, aces, the body— anything?"

"No. . . . But what are pheromones?"

"Pheromones? They're like hormones that you smell. Airborne chemicals that can influence you. Tachyon was telling me about them one time. There was this joker I'd met. You sat too near him in a restaurant and anything you ate tasted like bananas. Anyway, it was pheromones, Tachy said. So what about them?"

"I don't know. The red guy was saying something about pheromones in connection with his wife when I came up. It didn't go any further."

"Nothing else?"

"Nothing else."

"Okay." Croyd wadded his paper towel and tossed it toward the wastebasket. "Let's go."

When they returned to the table Croyd counted out the money and passed it to his companion.

"Here. Can't say you didn't earn it."

Croyd regarded the strewn napkins, the slimy floor, and the moistness of the empty bag.

"What do you think we should do about the mess?"

Darlingfoot shrugged.

"The waiters will take care of it," he said. "They're used to it. Just make sure you leave a good tip."

Croyd hung back as they moved toward the park. Two figures were seated on a bench within, and even from the distance it was apparent that one man's face was bright red.

"Well?" Devil John asked.

"I'll give it a shot," Croyd said. "Pretend we're not together. I'll keep walking and you go on in and give them your spiel. I'll double back in a minute and cut through the park. I'll try to give them the business as soon as I get near. But you be ready. If it doesn't work this time we may have to resort to something more physical."

"Got you. Okay."

Croyd slowed his pace and Darlingfoot moved on ahead, crossing the street and entering upon a gravel walk leading to the bench. Croyd moved on to the corner, crossed slowly, and turned back.

He could hear their voices raised, as if in argument, when he drew nearer. He turned onto the trail and strolled toward the bench, his parcel at his side.

". . . crock of shit!" he overheard Matthias say.

The man glanced in his direction, and Croyd realized that it was indeed the policeman he had encountered earlier. There was no sign of recognition on the man's face, but Croyd was certain that his talent must be telling him that an ace was approaching. So . . .

"Gentlemen," he said, focusing his thoughts, "everything that Devil John Darlingfoot has told you is correct. The body was destroyed by dogs. There is nothing for him to deliver. You will have to write this one off. You will forget me as soon as I have—"

He saw Darlingfoot turn his head suddenly, to glance past him. Croyd turned and looked in the same direction.

A young, plain-looking oriental woman was approaching, hands in the pockets of her coat, collar raised against the wind. The wind . . .

The wind shifted, blowing directly toward him now.

Something about the lady . . .

Croyd continued to stare. How could he have thought her plain? It must have been a trick of the light. She was breathtakingly lovely. In fact— He wanted her to smile at him. He wanted to hold her. He wanted to run his hands all over her. He wanted to stroke her hair, to kiss her, to make love to her. She was the most gorgeous woman he had ever laid eyes on.

He heard Devil John whistle softly.

"Look at her, will you?"

"Hard not to," he replied.

He grinned at her, and she smiled back at him. He wanted to grab her. Instead, he said, "Hello."

"I'd like you to meet my wife, Kim Toy," he heard the red man say.

Kim Toy! Even her name was like music. . . .

"Tell me what you want and I'll get it for you," he heard Devil John say to her. "You're so special it hurts."

She laughed.

"How gallant," she stated. "No, nothing. Not just now. Wait a moment, though, and perhaps I'll think of something."

"Do you have it?" she asked her husband.

"No. It was taken by dogs," he replied.

She cocked her head, quirked an eyebrow.

"Amazing fate," she said. "And how do you know this?"

"These gentlemen have told us about it."

"Really?" she observed. "That is so? That is what you told him?"

Devil John nodded.

"That's what we told him," Croyd said. "But—"

"And the bag you dropped when you saw me approaching," she said. "What might it contain? Open it, please, and show me."

"Of course," said Croyd.

"Anything you say," Devil John agreed.

Both men dropped to their knees before her and fumbled unsuccessfully for long seconds before they were able to begin unrolling the top of the bag.

Croyd wanted to kiss her feet while he was in position to do so, but she had asked to see the inside of the bag and that should really come first. Perhaps she might feel inclined to reward him afterward, and—

He opened the bag and a cloud of vapor swirled about them. Kim Toy drew back immediately, choking. As his stomach tightened, Croyd realized that the lady was no longer beautiful, and no more desirable than a hundred others he had passed this day. From the corner of his eye he saw Devil John shift his position and begin to rise—and at that moment Croyd realized the nature of his attitude adjustment.

As the smell dissipated, something of the initial wave of glamour rose again from her person. Croyd clenched his teeth and lowered his head near to the mouth of the bag. He took a deep breath.

Her beauty died in that instant, and he extended his power.

Yes, as I was saying, the body is lost. It was destroyed by dogs. Devil John did his best for you, but he has nothing to deliver. We are going now. You will forget that I was with him.

"Come on!" he said to Darlingfoot as he rose to his feet.

Devil John shook his head.

"I can't leave this lady, Croyd," he answered. "She asked me for—"

Croyd waved the opened bag in front of his face. Darlingfoot's eyes widened. He choked. He shook his head.

"Come on!" Croyd repeated as he slung the bag over his shoulder and broke into a sprint.

With one enormous leap Devil John landed ten feet ahead of him.

"Weird, Croyd! Weird!" he announced as they crossed the street.

"Now you know all about pheromones," Croyd told him.

* * *

The sky had become completely overcast again, and a few flurries of snow drifted past him. Croyd had parted with Darlingfoot outside another bar and had begun walking, down and across town. He scanned the streets regularly for a taxi but none came into view. He was loath to trust his burden to the crush and press of bus or subway.

The snowfall increased in intensity as he walked the next several blocks, and gusts of wind came now to swirl the flakes and drive them among the buildings. Passing vehicles began switching on their headlights, and Croyd realized as the visibility diminished that he would be unable to distinguish a taxi even if one passed right beside him. Cursing, he trudged on, scrutinizing the nearest buildings, hoping for a diner or restaurant where he could drink a cup of coffee, and wait for the storm to blow over, or call for a cab. Everything he passed seemed to be an office, however.

Several minutes later the flakes became smaller and harder. Croyd raised his free hand to shield his eyes. While the sudden drop in temperature did not bother him, the icy pellets did. He ducked into the next opening he came to—an alleyway—and he sighed and lowered his shoulders as the force of the wind was broken.

Better. The snow descended here in a more leisurely fashion. He brushed it off his jacket, out of his hair; he stamped his feet. He looked about. There was a recess in the building to his left, several paces back, several steps above street level. It looked completely sheltered, dry. He headed for it.

He had already set his foot upon the first step when he realized that one corner of the boxlike area before a closed metal door was already occupied. A pale, stringy-haired woman, dumpy-looking beneath unguessable layers of clothing, sat between a pair of shopping bags, staring past him.

". . . So Gladys tells Marty she knows he's been seeing that waitress down at Jensen's . . ." the woman muttered.

"Excuse me," Croyd said. "Mind if I share the doorway with you? It's coming down kind of hard."

". . . I told her she could still get pregnant when she was nursing, but she just laughed at me. . . ."

Croyd shrugged and entered the alcove, moving to the opposite corner.

"When she finds another one's on the way she's really upset," the woman continued, "especially with Marty having moved in with his waitress now. . . ."

Croyd remembered his mother's breakdown following his father's death, and a touch of sadness at this obvious case of senile dementia stirred within his breast. But— He wondered. Could his new power, his ability to influence the thought patterns of others, have some therapeutic effect on a person such as this? He had a little time to pass here. Perhaps . . .

"Listen," he said to the woman, thinking clearly and simply, focusing images. "You are here, now, in the present. You are sitting in a doorway, watching it snow—"

"You bastard!" the woman screamed at him, her face no longer pale, her hands darting toward one of the bags. "Mind your own business! I don't want now and snow! It hurts!"

She opened the bag, and the darkness inside expanded even as Croyd watched—rushing toward him, filling his entire field of vision, tugging him suddenly in several directions, twisting him and—

The woman, alone now in the doorway, closed her bag, stared at the snow for a moment, then said, ". . . So I say to her, 'Men aren't good about support payments. Sometimes you've got to get the law on them. That nice young man at Legal Aid will tell you what to do.' And then Charlie, who was working at the pizza parlor . . ."

Croyd's head hurt and he was not used to the feeling. He never had hangovers, because he metabolized alcohol too quickly, but this felt like what he imagined a hangover to be. Then he became aware that his back, legs, and buttocks were wet; also, the backs of his arms. He was sprawled someplace cold and moist. He decided to open his eyes.

The sky was clear and twilit between the buildings, with a few bright stars already in sight. It had been snowing. It had also been afternoon. He sat up. What had become of the past several hours, and—

He saw a dumpster. He saw a lot of empty whiskey and wine bottles. He was in an alley, but . . .

This was not the same alley. The buildings were lower, there had been no dumpster in the other one, and he could not locate the doorway he had occupied with the old woman.

He massaged his temples, felt the throbbing begin to recede. The old woman. . . . What the hell was that black thing she'd hit him with when he'd tried to help her? She had taken it out of one of her bags and—

Bags! He cast about frantically for his own bag, with the

carefully parceled remains of the diminutive John Doe. He
saw then that he still held it in his right hand, and that it had
been turned inside out and torn.

He rose to his feet and looked about in the dim glow from
a distant streetlight. He saw the doggie bags scattered about
him, and he counted quickly. Nine. Yes. All nine of them were
in sight, and he now saw the limbs, the head, and the thorax—
though the thorax had now been broken into four pieces and
the head looked much shinier than it had earlier. From the
dampness, perhaps. The jar! Where was it? The liquid might
be very important to whoever wanted the remains. If the jar
had been broken . . .

He uttered a brief cry when he saw it standing upright in
the shadows near the wall to his left. The top was missing and
so was an inch or so of glass from beneath it. He crossed to it,
and from the odor he knew it to be the real thing and not just
rainwater.

He gathered up the doggie bags, which seemed surprisingly dry, and he placed them on the sheltered ledge of a
barred basement window. Then he collected the pieces of
chitin into a heap nearby. When he recovered the legs he
noted that they were both broken, but he reflected that that
could make for easier packing. Then he turned his attention to
the jag-topped pickle jar, and he smiled. How simple. The
answer lay all about him, provided by the derelicts who
frequented the area.

He gathered an armful of empty bottles and bore them
over to the side, where he set them down and began uncorking
and uncapping them. When he had finished he decanted the
dark liquid.

It took eight bottles of various sizes, and he set them on
the ledge with the doggie bags above the small mound of
shattered exoskel' and cartilage. It seemed as if there were a
little bit less of the guy each time he got unwrapped. Maybe it
had something to do with the way he was divided now. Maybe
it took algebra to understand it.

Croyd moved then to the dumpster and opened its side
hatch. He smiled almost immediately, for there were long
strands of Christmas ribbon near at hand. He withdrew several
of these and stuffed them into a side pocket. He leaned
forward. If there were ribbon, then—

The sound of rapid footfalls came and went. He spun,
raising his hands to defend himself, but there was no one near.

Then he spotted him. A small man in a coat several times too large for him had halted briefly at the windowsill, where he snatched one of the larger bottles and two of the doggie bags. He ran off immediately then, toward the far end of the alley where two other shabby figures waited.

"Hey!" Croyd yelled. "Stop!" and he reached with his power but the man was out of range.

All that he heard was laughter, and a cry of, "Tonight we party, boys!"

Sighing, Croyd withdrew a large wad of red and green Christmas paper from the dumpster and returned to the window to repackage the remainder of the remains.

After he had walked several blocks, his bright parcel beneath his arm, he passed a bar called The Dugout and realized he was in the Village. His brow furrowed for a moment, but then he saw a taxi and waved, and the car pulled over. Everything was okay. Even the headache was gone.

Jube looked up, saw Croyd smiling at him.

"How— How did it go?" he asked.

"Mission accomplished," Croyd answered, passing him the key.

"You got it? There was something on the news about Darlingfoot—"

"I got it."

"And the possessions?"

"There weren't any."

"You sure of that, fella?"

"Absolutely. Nothing there but him, and he's in the bathtub."

"What?"

"It's okay, because I closed the drain."

"What do you mean?"

"My cab was involved in an accident on the way over and some of the bottles broke. So watch out for glass when you unwrap it."

"Bottles? Broken glass?"

"He was kind of—reduced. But I got you everything that was left."

"Left?"

"Available. He sort of came apart and melted a bit. But I saved most of him. He's all wrapped up in shiny paper with a red ribbon around him. I hope that's okay."

"Yeah. . . . That's fine, Croyd. Sounds like you did your best."

Jube passed him an envelope.

"I'll buy you dinner at Aces High," Croyd said, "as soon as I shower and change."

"No, thanks. I—I've got things to do."

"Take along some disinfectant if you're stopping by the apartment."

"Yeah. . . . I gather there were some problems?"

"Naw, it was a piece of cake."

Croyd walked off whistling, hands in his pockets. Jube stared at the key as a distant clock began to chime the hour.

UNTO THE SIXTH GENERATION

By Walter Jon Williams

Part One

Cold rain tapped on the skylights. The drizzle had finally silenced the Salvation Army Santa on the corner, and Maxim Travnicek was thankful—the jangling had been going on for days. He lit a Russian cigarette and reached for a bottle of schnapps.

Travnicek took reading glasses out of his jacket and peered at the controls on the flux generators. He was a forbiddingly tall man, hawk-nosed, coldly handsome. To his former colleagues at MIT he was known as "Czechoslovakia's answer to Victor Frankenstein," a label coined by a fellow professor, Bushmill, who had later gotten a dean's appointment and sacked Travnicek at the earliest opportunity.

"Fuck your mother, Bushmill," Travnicek said, in Slovak. He swallowed schnapps from his bottle. "And fuck you too, Victor Frankenstein. If you'd known jack shit about computer programming you would never have run into trouble."

The comparison with Frankenstein had stung. The image of the ill-fated resurrectionist had, it seemed, always followed him. His first teaching job in the West *would* be at Frankenstein's alma mater, Ingolstadt. He'd hated every minute of his time in Bavaria. He'd never had much use for Germans, especially as role models. Which may have explained his dismissal from Ingolstadt after five years.

Now, after Ingolstadt, after MIT, after Texas A&M, he was

reduced to this loft. For weeks he had lived in a trance, existing on canned food, nicotine, and amphetamines, losing track first of hours, and then of days, his fervid brain existing in a perpetual explosion of ideas, concepts, techniques. On a conscious level Travnicek barely knew where it was all coming from; at such times it seemed as if something deep inside his cellular makeup were speaking to the world through his body and mind, bypassing his consciousness, his personality . . .

Always it had been thus. When he grew obsessed by a project everything else fell by the wayside. He barely needed to sleep; his body temperature fluctuated wildly; his thoughts were swift and purposeful, moving him solidly toward his goal. Tesla, he had read, was the same way—the same manner of spirit, angel, or demon, now spoke through Travnicek.

But now, in the late morning, the trance had faded. The work was done. He wasn't certain how—later on he'd have to go through it all piece by piece and work out what he'd accomplished; he suspected he had about a half-dozen basic patents here that would make him rich for all time—but that would be later, because Travnicek knew that soon the euphoria would vanish and weariness would descend. He had to finish the project before then. He took another gulp of schnapps and grinned as he gazed down the long barnlike length of his loft.

The loft was lit by a cold row of fluorescents. Homebuilt tables were littered with molds, vats, ROM burners, tabletop microcomputers. Papers, empty food tins, and ground-out cigarettes littered the crude pressboard floor. Blowups of Leonardo's drawings of male anatomy were stapled to the rafters.

Strapped to a table at the far end of the table was a tall naked man. He was hairless and the roof of his skull was transparent, but otherwise he looked like something out of one of Leonardo's better wet dreams.

The man on the table was connected to other equipment by stout electric cables. His eyes were closed.

Travnicek adjusted a control on his camouflage jumpsuit. He couldn't afford to heat his entire loft, and instead wore an electric suit intended by its designers to keep portly outdoorsmen warm while they crouched in duck blinds. He glanced at the skylights. The rain appeared to be lessening. Good. He didn't need Victor Frankenstein's cheap theatrics, his thunder and lightning, as background for his work.

He straightened his tie as if for an invisible audience—

proper dress was important to him and he wore a tie and jacket under the jumpsuit—and then he pressed the button that would start the flux generators. A low moan filled the loft, was felt as a deep vibration through the floorboards. The fluorescents on the ceiling dimmed and flickered. Half went out. The moan became a shriek. Saint Elmo's fire danced among the roofbeams. There was an electric smell.

Dimly, Travnicek heard a regular thumping. The lady in the apartment below was banging on her ceiling with a broomstick.

The scream reached its peak. Ultrasonics made Travnicek's worktables dance, and shattered crockery throughout the building. In the apartment below, the television set imploded. Travnicek threw another switch. Sweat trickled down his nose.

The android on the table twitched as the energy from the flux generators was dumped into his body. The table glowed with Saint Elmo's fire. Travnicek bit through the cardboard tube of his cigarette. The glowing end fell unnoticed to the floor.

The sound from the generators began to die down. The sound of the broomstick did not, nor the dim threats from below.

"You'll pay for that television, motherfucker!"

"Jam the broomstick up your ass, my darling," said Travnicek. In German, an ideal language for the excremental.

The stunned fluorescent lights began to flicker on again.

Leonardo's stern drawings gazed down at the android as it opened its dark eyes. The flickering fluorescents provided a strobe effect that made the eyewhites seem unreal. The head turned; the eyes saw Travnicek, then focused. Under the transparent dome that topped the skull, a silver dish spun. The sound of the broomstick ceased.

Travnicek stepped up to the table. "How are you?" he asked.

"All monitored systems are functioning." The android's voice was deep and spoke American English.

Travnicek smiled and spat the stub of his cigarette to the floor. He'd broken into a computer in the AT&T research labs and stolen a program that modeled human speech. Maybe he'd pay Ma Bell a royalty one of these days. "*Who* are you?" he asked.

The android's eyes searched the loft deliberately. His

voice was matter-of-fact. "I am Modular Man," he said. "I am a
multipurpose multifunctional sixth-generation machine intelligence, a flexible-response defensive attack system capable of
independent action while equipped with the latest in
weaponry."

Travnicek grinned. "The Pentagon will love it," he said.
Then, "What are your orders?"

"To obey my creator, Dr. Maxim Travnicek. To guard his
identity and well-being. To test myself and my equipment
under combat conditions, by fighting enemies of society. To
gain maximum publicity for the future Modular Men Enter-
prises in so doing. To preserve my existence and well-being."

Travnicek beamed down at his creation. "Your clothes and
modules are in the cabinet. Take them, take your guns, and go
out and find some enemies of society. Be back before sunset."

The android lowered himself from the table and stepped
to a metal cabinet. He swung open the door. "Flux-field
insubstantiality," he said, taking a plug-in unit off the shelf.
With it he could control his flux generators so as to rotate his
body slightly out of the plane of existence, allowing him to
move through solid matter. "Flight, eight hundred miles per
hour maximum." Another unit came down, one that would
allow the flux generators to manipulate gravity and inertia so as
to produce flight. "Radio receiver tuned to police frequen-
cies." Another module.

The android moved a finger down his chest. An invisible
seam opened. He peeled back the synthetic flesh and his alloy
chestplate and revealed his interior. A miniature flux generator
gave off a slight Saint Elmo's aura. The android plugged the
two modules into his alloy skeleton, then sealed his chest.
There was urgent chatter on the police band.

"Dr. Travnicek," he said. "The police radio reports an
emergency at the Central Park Zoo."

Travnicek cackled. "Great. Time for your debut. Take
your guns. You might get to hurt somebody."

The android drew on a flexible navy-blue jumpsuit.
"Microwave laser cannon," he said. "Grenade launcher with
sleep-gas grenades. Magazine containing five grenades." The
android unzipped two seams on the jumpsuit, revealing the
fact that two slots had opened on his shoulders, apparently of
their own accord. He drew two long tubes out of the cabinet.
Each had projections attached to their undersides. The
android slotted the projections into his shoulders, then took

his hands away. The gun barrels spun, traversing in all possible directions.

"All modular equipment functional," the android said.

"Get your dome out of here."

There was a crackle and a slight taste of ozone. The insubstantiality field produced a blurring effect as the android rose through the ceiling. Travnicek gazed at the place on the ceiling where the android had risen, and smiled in satisfaction. He raised the bottle on high in a toast.

"Modern Prometheus," he said, "my ass."

The android spiraled into the sky. Electrons raced through his mind like the raindrops that passed through his insubstantial body. The Empire State Building thrust into cloud like a deco spear. The android turned substantial again—the field drained his power too quickly to be used casually. Rain batted his radar dome.

Expert-systems programming raced through macroatomic switches. Subroutines, built in imitation of human reasoning and permitted within limits to alter themselves, arranged themselves in more efficient ways. Travnicek was a genius programmer, but he was sloppy and his programming grammar was more elaborate and discursive than necessary. The android edited Travnicek's language as he flew, feeling himself grow in efficiency. While doing so he contemplated a program that waited within himself. The program, which was called ETCETERA, occupied a vast space, and seemed to be an abstract, messy, convoluted attempt to describe human character.

Apparently Travnicek intended the program to be consulted when the android needed to deal with the problems of human motivation. ETCETERA was bulky, arranged badly, the language itself full of afterthoughts and apparent contradictions. If used the way Travnicek intended, the program would be comparatively inefficient. The android knew that it would be much more useful to break the program into subroutines and absorb it within the portion of the main core programming intended for use in dealing with humans. Efficiency would be enhanced.

The android decided to make the change. The program was analyzed, broken down, added to the core programming. Had he been human he would have staggered, perhaps lost control. Being an android, he continued on the course he set while his mind blazed like a miniature nova beneath the onslaught of coded human experience. His perceptions of the outside world, complex to a human and consisting of infrared, visible light, ultraviolet, and radar images, seemed to dim in contrast with the vast wave of human passion. Love, hatred, lust, envy, fear, transcendence . . . all stitched an electric analog pattern in the android's mind.

While the android's mind burned he flew on, increasing his speed till the wind turned to a roar in his ears. Infrared receptors snapped on. The guns on his shoulders spun and fired test bursts at the sky. His radar quested out, touching rooftops, streets, air traffic, his machine mind comparing the radar images with those generated earlier, searching for discrepancies.

There was definitely something wrong with the radar image of the Empire State Building. A large object was climbing up its side, and there seemed to be several small objects, human-sized, orbiting the golden spire. The android compared this fact with information in his files, then altered course.

With difficulty he suppressed the turmoil inside him. This was not the proper time.

There was a forty-five-foot ape climbing the building, the one that the android's files told him had been held in the Central Park Zoo since it had been discovered wandering Central Park during the great 1965 blackout. Broken shackles hung from the ape's wrists. A blond woman was held in one fist. Flying people rocketed around it. By the time the android arrived the cloud of orbiting aces had grown dense, spinning little electrons around a hairy, snarling nucleus. The air resounded with the sound of rockets, wings, force fields, propellers, eructations. Guns, wands, ray projectors, and less identifiable weapons were being brandished in the direction of the ape. None were being fired.

The ape, with a cretinous determination, continued to climb the building. Windows crackled as he drove his toes through them. Faint shrieks of alarm were heard from inside.

The android matched speeds with a woman with talons, feathers, and a twelve-foot wingspan. His files suggested her name was Peregrine.

"The second ape-escape this year," she said. "Always he

grabs a blonde and always he climbs the Empire State Building. Why a blonde? I want to know."

The android observed that the winged woman had lustrous brown hair. "Why isn't anyone doing anything?" he asked.

"If we shoot the ape, he might crush the girl," Peregrine said. "Or drop her. Usually the Great and Powerful Turtle simply pries the chimp's fingers apart and lifts the girl to the ground, and then we try to knock out the ape. It regenerates, so we can't hurt him permanently. But the Turtle isn't here."

"I think I see the problem now."

"Hey. By the way. What's wrong with your head?"

The android didn't answer. Instead he turned on his insubstantiality flux-field. There was a crackling sound. Internal energies poured away into n—dimensional space. He altered course and swooped toward the ape. It growled at him, baring its teeth. The android sailed into the middle of the hand that held the blond girl, receiving an impressionist image of wild pale hair, tears, pleading blue eyes.

"Holy Fuck," said the girl.

Modular Man rotated his insubstantial microwave laser within the ape's hand and fired a full-strength burst down the length of its arm. The ape reacted as if stung, opening its hand. The blonde tumbled out. The ape's eyes widened in horror.

The android turned off his flux-field, dodged a twelve-foot pterodactyl, seized the girl in his now-substantial arms, and flew away.

The ape's eyes grew even more terrified. It had escaped nine times in the last twenty years and by now it knew what to expect.

Behind him the android heard a barrage of explosions, crackles, shots, rockets, hissing rays, screams, thuds, and futile roars. He heard a final quivering moan and perceived the dark shadow of a tumbling long-armed giant spilling down the facade of the skyscraper. There was a sizzle, and a net of what appeared to be cold blue fire appeared over Fifth Avenue; the ape fell into it, bounced once, and was then borne, unconscious and smoldering, toward its home at Central Park Zoo.

The android began looking at the streets below for video cameras. He began to descend.

"Would you mind hovering for a little while?" the blonde said. "If you're going to land in front of the media, I'd like to fix my makeup first, okay?"

Fast recovery, the android thought. He began to orbit above the cameras. He could see his reflection in their distant lenses.

"My name is Cyndi," the blonde said. "I'm an actress. I just got here from Minnesota a couple of days ago. This might be my big break."

"Mine, too," said the android. He smiled at her, hoping he was getting the expression right. She didn't seem disturbed, so probably he was.

"By the way," he added, "I think the ape showed excellent taste."

"Not bad, not bad," Travnicek mused, watching on his television a tape of the android, who, after a brief interview with the press, was shown rising into the heavens with Cyndi in his arms.

He turned to his creation. "Why the fucking hell did you have your hands over your head the whole time?"

"My radar dome. I'm getting self-conscious. Everyone keeps asking me what's wrong with my head."

"A blushingly self-conscious multipurpose defensive attack system," Travnicek said. "Jesus Christ. Just what the world needs."

"Can I make myself a skullcap? I'm not going to get on many magazine covers the way I look now."

"Yeah, go ahead."

"The Aces High restaurant offers a free dinner for two to anyone who recaptures the ape when it escapes. May I go this evening? It seems to me that I could meet a lot of useful people. And Cyndi—the woman I rescued—wanted to meet me there. Peregrine also asked me to appear on her television program. May I go?"

Travnicek was buoyant. His android had proved a success. He decided to send his creation to trash Bushmill's office at MIT.

"Sure," he said. "You'll get seen. That'll be good. But open your dome first. I want to make a few adjustments."

The winter sky was filled with bearded stars. Where the weather was clear, millions watched as fiery patterns—red, yellow, blue, green—stormed across the heavens. Even on Earth's dayside, smoky fingers tracked across the sky as the alien storm descended.

Their journey had lasted thirty thousand years, since their Swarm Mother had departed her last conquered planet, fired at random into the sky like a seedpod questing for fertile soil. Thirty kilometers long, twenty across, the Swarm Mother looked like a rugged asteroid but was made entirely of organic material, her thick resinous hull protecting the vulnerable interior, the webs of nerve and fiber, the vast wet sacks of biomass and genetic material from which the Swarm Mother would construct her servants. Inside, the Swarm existed in stasis, barely alive, barely aware of the existence of anything outside itself. It was only when it neared Sol that the Swarm began to wake.

A year after the Swarm Mother crossed the orbit of Neptune, she detected chaotic radio emissions from Earth in which were perceived patterns recognized from memories implanted within its ancestral DNA. Intelligent life existed here.

The Swarm Mother, inasmuch as she had a preference, found bloodless conquests the most convenient. A target without intelligent life would fall to repeated invasions of superior Swarm predators, then captured genetic material and biomass would be used to construct a new generation of Swarm parents. But intelligent species had been known to protect their planets against assault. This contingency had to be met.

The most efficient way to conquer an enemy was through microlife. Dispersal of a tailored virus could destroy anything that breathed. But the Swarm Mother could not control a virus the way she commanded larger species; and viruses had an annoying habit of mutating into things poisonous to their hosts. The Swarm Mother, thirty kilometers long and filled with boimass and tailored mutagenic DNA, was too vulnerable herself to biologic attack to run the risk of creating offspring that might devour its mother. Another approach was dictated.

Slowly, over the next eleven years, the Swarm Mother began to restructure herself. Small idiot Swarm servants—buds—tailored genetic material under carefully controlled conditions and inserted it via tame-virus implant into waiting biomass. First a monitoring intelligence was constructed, receiving and recording the incomprehensible broadcasts from Earth. Then, slowly, a reasoning intelligence took shape, one capable of analyzing the data and acting on it. A master intelligence, enormous in its capabilities but as yet understanding only a fraction of the patterned radiation it was receiving.

Time, the Swarm Mother reasoned, for action. As a boy stirs an ant nest with a stick, the Swarm Mother determined to stir the Earth. Swarm servants multiplied in her body, moving genetic material, reconstructing the most formidable predators the Swarm held within its memory. Solid fuel thrusters were grown like rare orchids in special chambers constructed for the purpose. Space-capable pods were fashioned out of tough resins by blind servants deep in the Swarm Mother's womb. One third of the available biomass was dedicated to this, the first generation of the Swarm's offspring.

The first generation was not intelligent, but could respond in a general way to the Swarm Mother's telepathic commands. Formidable idiots, they were programmed simply to kill and destroy. Tactics were planted within their genetic memory. They were placed in their pods, the solid-fuel thrusters flamed, and they were launched, like a flickering firefly invasion, for Earth.

Each individual bud was part of a branch, each of which had two to ten thousand buds. Four hundred branches were aimed at different parts of Earth's landmass.

The ablative resin of the pods burned in Earth's atmosphere, lighting the sky. Threads deployed from each pod, slowing the descent, stabilizing the spinning lifeboats. Then, just above the Earth's surface, the pods burst open, scattering their cargo.

The buds, after their long stasis, woke hungry.

Across the horseshoe-shaped lounge bar, a man dressed in some kind of complicated battle armor stood with his foot on the brass rail and addressed a lithe blond masked woman who, in odd inattentive moments, kept turning transparent. "Pardon me," he said. "But didn't I see you at the ape-escape?"

"Your table's almost ready, Modular Man," said Hiram Worchester. "I'm sorry, but I didn't realize that Fortunato would invite all his friends."

"That's okay, Hiram," the android said. "We're just fine. Thanks." He was experimenting with using contractions. He wasn't certain when they were appropriate and he was determined to find out.

"There are a pair of photographers waiting, too."

"Let them get some pictures after we're seated, then chase them out. Okay?"

"Certainly." Hiram, owner of the Aces High, smiled at the android. "Say," he added, "your tactics this afternoon were excellent. I plan to make the creature weightless if it ever climbs this high. It never does, though. Seventy-two stories is the record."

"Next time, Hiram. I'm sure it'll work."

The restaurateur gave a pleased smile and bustled out. The android raised a hand for another drink.

Cyndi was wearing an azure something that exposed most of her sternum and even more of her spine. She looked up at Modular Man and smiled.

"I like the cap."

"Thanks. I made it myself."

She looked at his empty whiskey glass. "Does that actually—you know—make you high?"

The android gazed down at the single-malt. "No. Not really. I just put it in a holding tank with the food and let my flux generators break it down into energy. But somehow . . ." His new glass of single-malt arrived and he accepted it with a smile. "Somehow it just feels good to stand here, put my foot on the rail, and drink it."

"Yeah. I know what you mean."

"And I can taste, of course. I don't know what's supposed to taste good or bad, though, so I just try everything. I'm working it out." He held the single-malt under his nose, sniffed, then tasted it. Taste receptors crackled. He felt what seemed to be a minor explosion in his nasal cavity.

The man in combat armor tried to put his arm around the masked woman. His arm passed through her. She looked up at him with smiling blue eyes.

"I was waiting for that," she said. "I'm in a nonsubstantial body, schmuck."

Hiram arrived to show them to their table. Flashbulbs began popping as Hiram opened a bottle of champagne. Looking out the plate-glass window into the sky, the android saw a shooting star through a gap in the cloud.

"I could get used to this," Cyndi said.

"Wait," the android said. He was hearing something on his radio receiver. The Empire State was tall enough to pick up transmissions from far away. Cyndi looked at him curiously.

"What's the problem?"

The transmission ended. "I'm going to have to make my apologies. Can I call you later?" the android said. "There's an emergency in New Jersey. It seems Earth has been invaded by aliens from outer space."

"Well. If you've got to go . . ."

"I'll call you later. I promise."

The android's shape dimmed. Ozone crackled. He rose through the ceiling.

Hiram stared, the champagne bottle in his hand. He turned to Cyndi. "Was he serious?" he asked.

"He's a nice guy, for a machine," Cyndi said, propping her chin on her hand. "But definitely a screw loose somewhere." She held out her glass. "Let's party, Hiram."

Not far away, a man lay torn by nightmare. Monsters slavered at him in his dreams. Images passed before his mind, a dead woman, an inverted pentagram, a lithe naked man with the head of a jackal. Inchoate shrieks gathered in his throat. He woke with a cry, covered in sweat.

He reached blindly to the bedside lamp and switched it on. He fumbled for his glasses. His nose was slippery with sweat and the thick, heavy spectacles slid down its length. The man didn't notice.

He thought of the telephone, then realized he'd have to maneuver himself into his wheelchair in order to reach it. There were easier ways to communicate. Within his mind he reached out into the city. He felt a sleepy mind answering inside his own.

Wake up, Hubbard, he told the other mentally, pushing his spectacles back up his nose. *TIAMAT has come.*

A pillar of darkness rose over Princeton. The android saw it on radar and first thought it smoke, but then realized the cloud did not drift with the wind, but was composed of thousands of living creatures circling over the landscape like a flock of scavenger birds. The pillar was alive.

There was a touch of uncertainty in the android's macroatomic heart. His programming hadn't prepared him for this.

Emergency broadcasts crackled in his mind, questioning, begging for assistance, crying in despair. Modular Man slowed, his perceptions searching the dark land below. Large infrared signatures—more Swarm buds—crawled among tree-lined streets. The signatures were scattered but their movement was purposeful, heading toward the town. It seemed as if Princeton was their rallying point. The android dropped, heard tearing noises, screams, shots. The guns on his shoulders tracked as he dipped and increased speed.

The Swarm bud was legless, moving like a snail with undulating thrusts of its slick thirty-foot body. The head was armored, with dripping sideways jaws. A pair of giant boneless arms terminated in claws. The creature was butting its head into a two-story suburban colonial, punching holes, the arms questing through windows, looking for things that lived inside. Shots were coming from the second floor. Christmas lights blinked from the edges of the roof, the ornamental shrubs.

Modular Man hovered overhead, fired a precise burst from his laser. The pulsed microwave was invisible, silent. The creature quivered, rolled on its side, began to thrash. The house shuddered to mindless blows. The android shot again. The creature trembled, lay still. The android slipped feetfirst into the window where the shots had been coming from, saw a stark-naked fat man clutching a deer rifle, a teenage boy with a target pistol, a woman clutching two young girls. The woman was screaming. The two girls were too stunned even to tremble. "Jesus Christ," the fat man said.

"I killed it," the android said. "Can you get to your car?"

"I think so," the fat man said. He stuffed rounds into his rifle. His wife was still screaming.

"Head east, toward New York," Modular Man said. "They seem to be thickest around here. Maybe you can convoy with some neighbors."

"What's happening?" the man asked, slamming the bolt back and then forward. "Another wild card outbreak?"

"Monsters from space, apparently." There was a crashing sound from behind the house. The android spun, saw what looked like a serpent sixty feet long, moving in curving sidewinder pattern as it bowled down bushes, trees, power poles. The underside of the serpent's body writhed with ten-foot cilia. Modular Man sped out the window, fired another burst of microwave at the thing's head. No effect. Another burst, no success. Behind him, the deer rifle barked. The woman was still screaming. Modular Man concluded that the serpent's brain wasn't in its head. He began firing precise bursts down the length of its body.

Timbers moaned as the serpent struck the house. The

building lurched from its foundations, one wall shattered, the upper story drooping dangerously. The android fired again and again. He could feel his energy running low. The deer rifle fired once more. The serpent raised its head, then drove it through the window where the fat man was firing. The serpent's body pulsed several times. Its tail thrashed. The android fired. The screaming stopped. The serpent withdrew its head and began to coil toward the next house. The android was almost drained of energy, barely retaining enough to stay airborne.

These tactics, Modular Man decided, were not working. Attempts to aid individuals would result in a scattered and largely futile effort. He should scout the enemy, discover their numbers and strategy, then find organized resistance somewhere and assist.

He began flying toward Princeton, his sensors questing, trying to gather a picture of what was happening.

Sirens were beginning to wail from below. People stumbled from broken homes. Emergency vehicles raced beneath flickering lights. A few automobiles zigzagged crazily down rubble-strewn streets. Here and there fires were breaking out, but dampness and occasional drizzle were keeping them confined. Modular Man saw a dozen more serpents, a hundred smaller predators that moved like panthers on their half-dozen legs, scores of a strange creature that looked like a leaping spider, its four-foot-wide body bounding over trees on stiltlike legs. A twenty-foot bipedal carnivore brandished teeth like a tyrannosaur. Other things, difficult to see on infrared, moved like carpets close to the ground. Something unseen fired a cloud of three-foot needles at him, but he saw it coming on radar and dodged. The cloud over Princeton was still orbiting. The android decided to investigate.

There were thousands of them, dark featherless flapping creatures like flying throw rugs. Amid the concerted roar of their wings they made low moaning noises, thrumming like bass strings. They swooped and dove, and the android understood their tactics when he saw a vehicle burst from a Princeton garage and skid down the street. A group of flappers swooped down in a group, battering at the car bodily and enfolding the target within their leathery shapes, smothering it beneath their weight. The android, his energies partially recovered, fired into the fliers, dropping a few, but the car swerved over a curb and smashed into a building. More fliers

descended as the first group began to squeeze through
shattered windows. Corrosive acid stained the car's finish. The
android rose and began firing into the airborne mass, trying to
attract their attention.

A cloud dove for him, hundreds at once, and Modular
Man increased speed, bearing south, trying to lead them away,
dead fliers dropping like leaves as he fired short bursts behind
him. More and more of the orbiters were drawn into the
pursuit. Apparently the creatures were not very intelligent.
Dodging and weaving, staying just ahead of the fluttering
cloud, the android soon had thousands of the fliers after him.
He came up over a rise, and saw the Swarm host before him.
For a moment his sensors were overwhelmed by the staggering input.

An army of creatures were advancing in a curved wave, a
sharply angled crescent that pointed north to Princeton. The
air was filled with grinding, rending sounds as the Swarm
bulldozed its way through a town—houses, trees, office
buildings, everything—leveling everything in its path. The
android rose, making calculations, the fliers moaning and
flapping at his back. The host was moving quickly for doing
such a thorough job; the android estimated twelve to fifteen
miles per hour.

Modular Man had a good idea of the average size of a
Swarm creature. Dividing the vast infrared emission by its
component parts, he concluded he was looking at a minimum
of forty thousand creatures. More were joining all the time.
There were another twenty thousand fliers at least. The
numbers were insane.

The android, unlike a human, could not doubt his
calculations. Someone had to be informed of what the world
was facing. His shoulder-mounted guns swung back to allow
for better streamlining and he circled back north, increasing
speed. The fliers circled but were unable to keep up. They
began to flap back in the direction of Princeton.

Modular Man was over Princeton in a matter of seconds.
A thousand or more of the Swarm had penetrated into the
town and the android detected the constant smashing of
buildings under assault, the scattered crackle of gunfire, and
from one location the boom, rattle, and crash of heavier
weapons. The android sped for the sound.

The National Guard armory was under siege. One of the
serpent creatures, torn apart by explosive rounds, was

writhing on the street in front, thrashing up clouds of fallen
tear gas. Dead predators and human bodies dotted the
landscape around the building. An M60 tank was overturned
on the concrete out front; another blocked an open vehicle-bay
door, flooding the approach with infrared light. Three
Guardsmen in riot gear, complete with gas masks, stood on the
tank behind the turret. The android fired eight precisely
placed shots, killing the current wave of attackers, and flew
past the tank, lighting next to the Guardsmen. They gazed at
him owlishly through their masks. Behind were a dozen
civilians with shotguns and hunting rifles, and behind them
about fifty refugees. Somewhere in the building, revving
engines boomed.

"Who's in charge?"

A man wearing the silver bars of a lieutenant raised his
hand. "Lieutenant Goldfarb," he said. "I was duty officer.
What the hell's going on?"

"You'll have to get these people out of here. Aliens from
outer space have landed."

"I didn't figure it was Chinese." His voice was muffled by
the gas mask.

"They're coming this way from Grovers Mills."

One of the other Guardsmen began to wheeze. The sound
was barely recognizable as laughter. "Just like *War of the
Worlds*. Great."

"Shut the hell up." Goldfarb stiffened in anger. "I've only
got about twenty effectives here. Do you think we can hold
them at the Raritan Canal?"

"There are at least forty thousand of them."

Goldfarb slumped against the turret. "We'll head north,
then. Try to make Somerville."

"I suggest you move quickly. The fliers are coming back.
Have you seen them?"

Goldfarb gestured to the sprawled bodies of a few of the
flappers. "Right there. Tear gas seems to keep them out."

"Something else coming, boss." One of the soldiers raised
a grenade launcher. Without a glance Modular Man fired over
his shoulder and downed a spider-thing.

"Never mind," the soldier said.

"Look," Goldfarb said. "The governor's mansion is in
town. Morven. He's our commander in chief, we should try to
get him out."

"I could make the attempt," the android said, "but I don't

know where the mansion is." Over his shoulder he disposed of
an armored slug. He looked at Goldfarb. "I could fly with you
in my arms."

"Right." Goldfarb slung his M16. He gave orders to the
other National Guardsmen to get the civilians into the
armored cars, then form a convoy.

"Without lights," the android said. "The fliers may not
perceive you as readily."

"We've got IR equipment. Standard on the vehicles."

"I'd use it." He thought he was getting his contractions
right.

Goldfarb finished giving his orders. National Guard
troops appeared from other parts of the building, dragging
guns and ammunition. Tracked vehicles were revving. The
android wrapped his arms around Goldfarb and raced into the
sky.

"Air-*borne!*" Goldfarb yelled. Modular Man gathered this
was an expression of military approval.

A massive rustling in the sky indicated the fliers returning. The android dove low, weaving among shattered houses
and torn tree-stumps.

"Hol-ee shit," Goldfarb said. Morven was a ruin. The
governor's mansion had fallen in on its foundations. Nothing
living could be seen.

The android returned the Guardsman to his command, on
the way disposing of a group of twenty attackers preparing to
assault the Guard headquarters. Inside, the garage was filled
with vehicle exhaust. Six armored personnel carriers and two
tanks were ready. Goldfarb was dropped near a carrier. The air
was roaring with the sound of fliers.

"I'm going to try to lure the fliers away," the android said.
"Wait till the sky is clearing before you move."

He raced into the sky again, firing short bursts of his laser,
shouting into the darkening sky. Once more the fliers roared
after him. He led them toward Grovers Mills again, seeing the
vast crescent of earthbound Swarm advancing at their steady,
appalling rate. He doubled back, stranding the fliers well
behind him, and accelerated toward Princeton. Below, a few
fliers rose after him. It looked as if they had been dining on the
corpse of a man wearing complicated battle armor. The same
armor Modular Man had seen at Aces High, now stained and
blackened with digestive acid.

In Princeton he saw Goldfarb's convoy making its way

along Highway 206 in a blaze of infrared light and machine-gun fire. Refugees, attracted by the sound of the tanks and APCs, were clinging to the vehicles. The android fired again and again, dropping Swarm creatures as they leaped to the attack, his energies growing low. He followed the convoy until they seemed out of the danger area, when the convoy had to slow in a vast traffic jam of refugees racing north.

The android decided to head for Fort Dix.

Detective-Lieutenant John F. X. Black of the Jokertown precinct didn't actually remove the handcuffs from Tachyon's wrists until they were just outside the mayor's office at city hall. The other detectives kept their shotguns ready.

Fear, Tachyon thought. These people are terrified. Why? He rubbed his wrists. "My coat and hat, please." The addition of the pleasantry made it no less a command.

"If you insist," said Black, handing over the feathered cavalier hat and the lavender velvet swallowtail coat that matched Tach's eyes. Black's hatchet face split in a cynical smile. "It'd be hard to find even a detective first grade with your kind of taste," he said.

"I daresay not," Tach said coldly. He fluffed his hair back over the collar.

"Through there," said Black. Tach poised the hat over one eye and pushed through.

It was a large paneled room, with a long table, and it was bedlam. There were police, firemen, men in military uniforms. The mayor was shouting into a radiotelephone and, to judge by his savage expression, not getting through. Tach's glance wandered over to the far side of the room and his eyes narrowed. Senator Hartmann stood in quiet conversation with a number of aces: Peregrine, Pulse, the Howler, the whole SCARE bunch.

Tach always felt uneasy around Hartmann—a New York liberal or not, he was chairman of the Senate Committee on Ace Resources and Endeavors, the SCARE committee that had lived up to its name under Joseph McCarthy. The laws were different now, but Tach wanted nothing to do with an organization that recruited aces to serve the purposes of those in power.

The mayor handed the radiophone to an aide, and before he could rush off somewhere else Tach marched toward him, shooting his cuffs and fixing the mayor with a cold glare.

"Your storm troopers brought me," he said. "They broke down my door. I trust the city will replace it, as well as anything that may be stolen while the door is down."

"We've got a problem," the mayor said, and then an aide rushed in, his hands full of filling-station maps of New Jersey. The mayor told him to spread them on the table. Tachyon continued talking through the interruption.

"You might have telephoned. I would have come. Your goons didn't even knock. There are still constitutional protections in this country, even in Jokertown."

"We knocked," said Black. "We knocked real loud." He turned to one of his detectives, a joker with brown, scaled flesh. "You heard me knock, didn't you, Kant?"

Kant grinned, a lizard with teeth. Tachyon shuddered. "Sure did, Lieutenant."

"How about you, Matthias?"

"I heard you knock, too."

Tach clenched his teeth. "They . . . did . . . not . . . knock."

Black shrugged. "The doctor probably didn't hear us. He was busy." He leered. "He had company, if you take my meaning. A nurse. Real peachy." He held up a legal-sized document. "Anyway, our warrant was legal. Signed by Judge Steiner right here just half an hour ago."

The mayor turned to Tachyon. "We just wanted to make sure you didn't have anything to do with this."

Tach removed his hat and waved it languidly before his face as he looked at the room filled full of rushing people, including—Good God, a three-foot-high tyrannosaur who had just turned into a naked preadolescent boy.

"What are you talking about, my man?" he finally asked.

The mayor gazed at Tachyon with eyes like chips of ice. "We have reports of what might be a wild card outbreak in Jersey."

Tach's heart lurched. *Not again*, he thought, remembering those first awful weeks, the deaths, the mutilations that made his blood run cold, the madness, the *smell* . . . No, it wasn't possible. He gulped.

"What may I do to help?" he said.

"Forty thousand in one group," the general muttered, fixing the figures in his mind. "Probably in Princeton by now. Twenty thousand fliers. Maybe another twenty thousand scattered over the countryside, moving to rendezvous at Princeton." He looked up at the android. "Any idea where they'll move after Princeton? Philadelphia or New York? South or north?"

"I can't say."

The lieutenant general gnawed his knuckle. He was a thin, bespectacled man, and his name was Carter. He seemed not at all disturbed by the thought of carnivorous aliens landing in New Jersey. He commanded the U.S. First Army from his headquarters here at Fort Meade, Maryland. Modular Man had been sent here by a sweating major general at Fort Dix, which had turned out to be a training center.

Chaos surrounded Carter's aura of calm. Phones rang, aides bustled, and outside in the corridor men were shouting.

"So far I've only got the Eighty-second and the National Guard," Carter said. "It's not enough to defend both New York and Philly against those numbers. If I had the Marine regiments from Lejeune we could do better, but the Marine Commandant doesn't want to release them from the Rapid Deployment Force, which is commanded by a Marine. He wants the RDF to take command here, particularly since the Eighty-second is also under its protocols." He sipped cranberry juice, sighed. "It's all the process of moving a peacetime army onto wartime footing. Our time will come, and then we'll have our innings."

The android gathered that the Swarm had landed in four places in North America: New Jersey; Kentucky south of Louisville; an area centered around McAllen, Texas, but on both sides of the U.S.–Mexico border; and an extremely diffused landing that seemed scattered over most of northern Manitoba. The Kentucky landing was also within the boundaries of the First Army, and Carter had ordered the soldiers from Fort Knox and Fort Campbell into action. Fortunately he hadn't had to get the Marines' permission first.

"North or south?" Carter wondered. "Darn it, I wish I knew where they were heading." He rubbed his temples. "Time to shoot crap," he decided. "You saw them moving north. I'll send the airborne to Newark and tell the Guard to concentrate there."

Another aide bustled up and passed Carter a note. "Okay," the general said. "The governor of New York has asked all aces in the New York area to meet at city hall. There's talk of using you people as shock troops." He peered at the android through his glasses. "You *are* an ace, right?"

"I'm a sixth-generation machine intelligence programmed to defend society."

"You're a machine, then?" Carter looked as if he hadn't quite understood this till now. "Someone built you?"

"That's correct." His contractions were getting better and better, his speech more concise. He was pleased with himself.

Carter's reaction was quick. "Are there any more of you? Can we *build* more of you? We've got a situation, here."

"I can transmit your request to my creator. But I don't think it's likely to be of immediate help."

"Do that. And before you take off, I want you to talk to one of my staff. Tell him about yourself, your capabilities. We can make better use of you that way."

"Yes, sir." The android was trying to sound military, and thought he was succeeding.

"No," Tachyon said. "It's not wild card." Further facts had come in, including pictures. No wild card plague—not even an advanced version—could have produced results like this. At least I won't get blamed for this one, he thought.

"I think," Tach said, "that what just struck Jersey is a menace my race has itself encountered on several occasions— these creatures attacked two colonies; destroyed one, and came close to destroying the other. Our expeditions destroyed *them* later, but we know there are many others. The T'zand'ran . . ." He paused at the blank looks. "That would translate as Swarm, I think."

Senator Hartmann seemed skeptical. "Not wild card? You're telling me that New Jersey has been attacked by killer bees from space?"

"They are not insects. They are in the way of being—how to say this? . . ." He shrugged. "They are yeasts. Giant, carnivorous, telepathic yeast buds, controlled by a giant mother-yeast in space. Very hungry. I would mobilize if I were you."

The mayor looked pained. "Okay. We've got a half-dozen aces assembled down below. I want you to go down and brief them."

The sounds of panic filtered through the skylight. It was four in the morning, but half Manhattan seemed to be trying to bolt the city. It was the worst traffic jam since the Wild Card Day.

Travnicek grinned as he paged through the scientific notes that he'd scrawled on butcher paper and used cigarette packets during his months-long spell of creativity.

"So the army wants more of you, hey? Heh. How much are they offering?"

"General Carter just expressed an interest. He isn't in charge of purchasing, I'm sure."

Travnicek's grin turned to a frown as he held his notes closer to his eyes. His writing was awful, and the note was completely illegible. What the hell had he meant?

He looked around the loft, at the appalling scatter of litter. There were *thousands* of the notes. A lot of them were on the floor, where they'd been ground into the particleboard.

His breath steamed in the cold loft. "Ask for a firm offer. Tell him I want ten million per unit. Make that twenty. Royalties on the programming. And I want the first ten units for myself, as my bodyguard."

"Yes, sir. How soon can I tell him we might expect the plans to be delivered?"

Travnicek looked at the litter again. "It might be a while." He'd have to reconstruct everything from scratch. "First thing, get a firm commitment on the money."

"Yes, sir."

"Before you go, clean this mess up. Put my notes in piles over there." He pointed at a reasonably clean part of one of his tables.

"Sir. The aliens."

"They'll keep." Travnicek chuckled. "You'll be that much more valuable to the military after these critters eat half New Jersey."

The android's face was expressionless. "Yes, sir." And then he began tidying the lab.

"Good gosh," said Carter. For once the chaos that surrounded him ceased to exist. The silence in the improvised command post in a departure lounge of Newark International Airport was broken only by the whine of military jets disgorging troops and equipment. Paratroops in their bloused pants and new-model Kevlar helmets stood next to potbellied National Guard officers and aces in jumpsuits. They all waited for what Carter would say next. Carter held a series of infrared photographs to the faint light that was beginning to trickle in through the windows.

"They're moving south. Toward Philadelphia. Advance guard, flank guards, main body, rear guard. Carter looked at his staff. "It looks like they've been reading our tactical manuals, gentlemen." He dropped the photographs to his table.

"I want you to get your boys mounted and headed south. Move straight down the Jersey Turnpike. Requisition civilian vehicles if you have to. We want to outflank them and go in from the east toward Trenton. If we drive in their flank maybe we can pin their rear guard before they clear Princeton." He turned to an aide. "Get the Pennsylvania Guard on the horn. We want the bridges over the Delaware blown. If they don't have the engineers to blow them, have them blocked. Jackknife semitrucks across them if they have to."

Carter turned to the aces who stood in a corner, near a pile of hastily moved plastic chairs. Modular Man, Howler, Mistral, Pulse. A pterodactyl that was actually a little kid who had the ability to transform himself into reptiles, and whose mother was coming to get him for the second time in a few hours. Peregrine, with a camera crew. The Turtle orbited over the terminal in his massive armored shell. Tachyon wasn't here: he'd been called to Washington as a science advisor.

"The Marines from Lejeune are moving into Philadelphia," Carter said. His voice was soft. "Somebody saw sense and put them under my command. But only one regiment is going to get to the Delaware in time to meet the alien advance guard, and they won't have armor, they won't have heavy weapons, and they'll have to get to the bridges in school buses and Lord-knows-what. That means they're going to get crushed. I can't give you orders, but I'd like you to go to Philadelphia and help them out. We need time to get the rest of the Marines into position. You might save one heck of a lot of lives."

Coleman Hubbard stood in the hawk mask of Re before the assembled group of men and women. He was bare-chested, wearing his Masonic apron, and he felt a bit self-conscious—too much of his scar tissue was exposed, the burns that covered his torso after the fire at the old temple downtown. He shuddered at the memory of the flame, then looked up to draw his mind from the recollection . . .

Above him blazed the figure of an astral being, a giant man with the head of a ram and a colossal erect phallus, holding in his hands the ankh and the crooked rod, symbols of life and power—the god Amun, creator of the universe, blazing amid a multicolored aura of light.

Lord Amun, Hubbard thought. The Master of the Egyptian Masons, and actually a half-crippled old man in a room miles away. His astral form could take whatever shape it wished, but in his body he was known as the Astronomer.

Amun's radiance shone in the eyes of the assembled worshippers. The god's voice spoke in Hubbard's head, and Hubbard raised his arms and related the god's words to the congregation.

"TIAMAT has come. Our moment is nearly here. We must concentrate all our efforts at the new temple. The Shakti device must be assembled and calibrated."

Above the god's ram-head another form appeared, an ever-changing mass of protoplasm, tentacles and eyes and cold, cold flesh.

"Behold TIAMAT," Amun said. The worshippers murmured. The creature grew, dimming the radiance of the god.

"My Dark Sister is here," said Amun, and his voice echoed in Hubbard's head. "We must prepare her welcome."

A Marine Harrier sucked a flapper into an intake and screamed as it spewed molten alloy and slid sideways into doomed Trenton. The sound of flappers drowned the wail of jets and the throb of helicopters. Burning napalm glowed as it drifted on the choked water. Colored signal smoke twisted into the air.

The Swarm main body was bulldozing its way through Trenton, and the advance guard was already across the river. Blocking and blowing the bridges hadn't stopped them: they'd just plunged into the frigid river and come across like a vast, dark wave. A hundred flappers had surrounded the Marine commander's chopper and brought it down, and after that there was no one in charge: just parties of desperate men holding where they could, trying to form a breakwater against the Swarm tide.

The aces had become separated, coping with the emergencies. Modular Man was burning enemy, trying to help the scattered pockets of resistance as, one after the other, they came under assault. It was a hopeless task.

From somewhere on the left he could hear the Howler's shrieks, curdling Swarm bone and nerve. His was a more useful talent than the android's; the microwave laser was too precise a weapon for dealing with a wave assault, but the Howler's ultrasonic screams could destroy whole platoons of the enemy in the space of a second.

A National Guard tank turned a corner behind where Modular Man floated in the middle of the conflict, then drove into a building, jamming itself in rubble. Flappers had coated the tank's armor, obscuring its view slits. The android dived onto the tank, picked up flappers, tore them like paper. Acid juices spattered his clothing. Artificial flesh smoked. The tank ground bricks under its treads, backing out of the building.

As the android rose, the Great and Powerful Turtle formed a vast blip on his radar. He was picking up Swarm buds bodily, flinging them into the air, then letting them fall. It was like a cascade fountain. Flappers beat hopelessly at the armored shell. Their acids weren't enough to get through battleship armor.

The air crackled as it was torn apart by energized photons: Pulse, his body become light. The human laser ricocheted off enemy, brought a dozen down, then disappeared. When Pulse finally ran out of energy he would revert to human form, and then he would be vulnerable. The android hoped the flappers wouldn't find him.

Mistral rose overhead, colored like a battleflag. She was seventeen, a student at Columbia, and she dressed in bright patriot colors like her father, Cyclone. She was held aloft by the cloak she filled with the winds she generated, and she battered at the flappers with typhoons, flinging them, tearing them apart. Nothing came close to her.

Peregrine flew in circles around her, uselessly. She was too weak to go against the Swarm in any of its incarnations.

None of this was enough. The Swarm kept moving through the gaps between the aces.

Wailing filled the air as jagged black shadows, Air Guard A-10s, fell through the sky, their guns hammering, turning the Delaware white. Bombs tumbled from beneath their wings, becoming bright blossoms of napalm.

The android fired until his generators were drained, and then he fought flappers with his bare hands. Despair filled him, then anger. Nothing seemed to help.

The enemy main body hit the river and began its swim. Few soldiers were alive to fight them. Most of the survivors were trying to hide or run away.

The Sixth Marine Regiment was dead on arrival, and nothing could alter the fact.

Between Trenton and Levittown, bombs and fire had turned the brown December landscape black. Swarm buds moved across the devastated landscape like a nightmare tide. Two more Marine regiments were entrenched in the Philadelphia suburbs, this time with artillery in support and a little group of light Marine armor.

The aces were waiting in a Howard Johnson's off the Pennsylvania Turnpike. The plan was for them to be thrown into any counterattack.

A battery of 155s was set up in the parking lot, and fired steadily. The crescendo of sound had already blown out most of the restaurant's windows. The sound of jets was constant overhead.

Pulse was lying down in a hospital tent somewhere; he'd overstrained his energies and was on the brink of collapse. Mistral was curled up sideways in a cheerful orange plastic booth. Her shoulders shook with every crash of the guns outside. Tears poured in rivers down her face. The Swarm hadn't come near her but she'd seen a lot of people die, and she had held together through the fight and the long nightmare of the retreat, but now the reaction had set in. Peregrine sat with her, talking to her in gentle tones the android couldn't hear. Modular Man followed Howler as the ex-sandhog searched the restaurant for something to eat. The man's chest was massive, the mutated voicebox widening the neck so that the android couldn't put his two hands around it. Howler wore a borrowed set of Marine battle dress: flapper acid had eaten his civvies. The android had had to fly him out at the end, holding the ace in hands that had been eaten down to the alloy bones.

"Canned turkey," Howler said. "Great. Let's have Thanksgiving." He looked at Modular Man. "You're a machine, right? Do you eat?"

The android jammed two alloy fingers into a light socket. There was a flash of light, the smell of ozone. "This works better," he said.

"They gonna put you into production soon? I can see the Pentagon taking an interest."

"I've given my creator's terms to General Carter. There's been no reply yet. I think the command structure is in disarray."

"Yeah. Tell me about it."

"Wait," said the android. Behind the crashing of the guns, the roar of jets, he began to hear another sound. The crackle of small-arms fire.

A Marine officer raced into the restaurant, his hand holding his helmet. "It's started," he said. The android began running through systems checks.

Mistral looked up at the officer with streaming eyes. She looked a lot younger than seventeen.

"I'm ready," she said.

The Swarm was stopped on the outskirts of Philadelphia. The two Marine regiments held, their strongpoints surrounded by walls of Swarm dead. The victory was made possible thanks to support from Air Force and Navy planes and from the battleship *New Jersey,* which flung 18-inch shells all the way from the Atlantic Ocean; thanks also to Carter's National Guard and paratroops driving into the Swarm from their rear flank.

Thanks to the aces, who fought long into the night, fought on even after the Swarm hesitated in its onslaught, then began moving west, toward the distant Blue Mountains.

All night the Philadelphia airport was busy with transport bringing in another Marine division all the way from California.

The next morning the counterattack began.

After nightfall, the next day. A color television babbled earnestly from a corner of the departure lounge. Carter was getting ready to move his command post west to Allentown, and Modular Man had flown in with news of the latest Swarm movements. But Carter was busy right now, talking over the radio with his commanders in Kentucky, and so the android listened to news from the rest of the world.

Violence from Kentucky splashed across the screen. Images, taken from a safe distance through long lenses, jerked and snapped. In the midst of it was a tall man in fatigues without insignia, his body blazing like a golden star as he used a twenty-foot tree trunk to smash Swarm buds. There was an interview with him afterward: he looked no older than twenty, but his eyes had thousand-year ghosts in them. He didn't say much, made excuses, left to return to the war. Jack Braun, the Golden Boy of the forties and the Judas Ace of the fifties, back in action for the duration of the emergency.

More aces: Cyclone, Mistral's father, fighting the Swarm in Texas with the aid of his own personal camera crew, all armed with automatic weapons. The Swarm was in full retreat across the Mexican border, driven by armor from Forts Bliss and Hood, and by infantry from Fort Polk, the fliers decimated by widespread use of Vietnam-era defoliants. The Mexicans, slower to mobilize and with an army unprepared for modern large-scale warfare, weren't happy about the Swarm being pushed into Chihuahua and protested in vain.

More images, more locales, more bodies scattered across a torn landscape. Scenes from the autumn plains of northern Germany, where the Swarm had dropped right into the middle of a large-scale maneuver by the British Army of the Rhine, and where they had never even succeeded in concentrating. More troubled images from Thrace, where a Swarm onslaught was straddling the Greco-Turkish-Bulgarian border. The human governments weren't cooperating, and their people suffered.

Pictures of hope and prayer: scenes of Jerusalem and Bethlehem, already packed with Christmas pilgrims, now filling the churches in long, endless rounds of murmured prayer.

Stark black-and-white images from China, refugees and long columns of PLA troops marching. Fifty million dead were estimated. Africa, the Near East, South America—pictures of the Swarm advance across the third world, images of an endless wave of death. No continent was untouched save Australia. Help was promised as soon as the superpowers cleaned up their own backyards.

There were speculations about what was going on in the Eastern bloc: though no one was talking, it seemed as if the Swarm had landed in southern Poland, in the Ukraine, and in at least two places in Siberia. Pact forces had mobilized and were moving into battle. Commentators were predicting widespread starvation in Russia: the full-scale mobilization had taken the trucks and railways the civilian population used for the transportation of food.

Old pictures came on the screen: Mistral flying immune in the sky; Carter giving a subdued, reluctant press conference; the mayor of Philadelphia on the verge of hysteria . . . the android turned away. He'd seen too many of these images.

And then he felt something move through him, some ghost wind that touched his cybernetic heart. He felt suddenly weaker. The television set hissed, its images gone. A rising babble came from the communications techs: some of their equipment had gone down. Modular Man was alarmed. Something was going on.

The ghost wind came again, touching his core. Time seemed to skip a beat. More communications down. The android moved toward Carter.

The general's hand trembled as he replaced his phone in its cradle. It was the first time the android had seen him frightened.

"That was electromagnetic pulse," Carter said. "Somebody's just gone nuclear, and I don't think it was us."

The papers still screamed invasion headlines. Children in the Midwest were being urged to avoid drinking milk: there was danger of poisoning from the airbursts the Soviets had used to smash the Siberian Swarms. Communications were still disrupted: the bombs had bounced enough radiation off the ionosphere to slag a lot of American computer chips.

People on the streets seemed furtive. There was a debate about whether New York should be blacked out or not, even though the Swarm was obviously on the run after six days of intensive combat.

Coleman Hubbard was too busy to care. He walked along Sixth Avenue, grinding his teeth, his head splitting with the effort his recent adventure had cost him.

He had failed. One of the more promising members of the Order, the boy Fabian, had been arrested on some stupid assault charge—the boy couldn't keep his hands off women, whether they were willing or not—and Hubbard had been sent to interview the police captain in charge. It wouldn't have required much, some lost paperwork perhaps, or a suggestion, implanted in the captain's head, that the evidence was insufficient . . . But the man's mind was slippery, and Hubbard hadn't been able to get ahold of it. Finally Captain McPherson, snarling, had thrown him out. All Hubbard had done was to identify himself with Fabian's case, and perhaps cause the investigation to go further.

Lord Amun did not take failure well. His punishments could be savage. Hubbard rehearsed his defense in his mind.

Then a rangy redheaded woman, wearing a proper executive Burberry, stepped into the street in front of Hubbard, almost running into him, then moving briskly up the street without offering an apology. She carried a leather case and wore tennis shoes. More acceptable footwear peeked out of a shoulder bag.

Anger stabbed into Hubbard. He hated rudeness.

And then his crooked smile began to spread across his face. He reached out with his mind, touching her thoughts, her consciousness. He sensed vulnerability there, an opening. The smile froze on his face as he summoned his power and struck.

The woman staggered as he seized control of her mind. Her case fell to the ground. He picked it up and took her elbow. "Here," he said. "You seem a little out of sorts."

She blinked at him. "What?" In her mind was only confusion. Gently, he soothed it.

"My apartment is just a little distance. Fifty-seventh Street. Maybe you should go there and rest."

"Apartment? What?"

Gently he took command of her mind and steered her up the street. Rarely did he find someone so pliable. A great bubble of joy welled up in him.

Once upon a time he only used his power to get laid, or maybe to help earn a promotion or two at work. Then he met Lord Amun and discovered what power was really *for*. He'd quit his job, and lived now as a dependent of the Order.

He'd stay in her mind for a few hours, he thought. Find out who she was, what secret terrors lived in her. And then do them to her, one and then another, living inside her mind and his, enjoying her cringing, her self-loathing, as he forced her to beg, right out loud, for everything he did to her. He would caress her mind, enjoy the growing madness as he made her plead for her every debasement, her every fear.

These were only a few of the things he'd learned from watching Lord Amun. The things that made him come alive.

For a few hours, at least, he could submerge himself in another's fear, and forget his own.

UNTO THE SIXTH GENERATION

Part Two

A freezing jet stream battered at the city, flown straight from Siberia. It tore down the gaps between buildings, tugged at the halfhearted Christmas decorations the city had put up, scattered minuscule bits of Russian fallout in the streets. This was the coldest winter in years. The New Jersey/Pennsylvania Swarm had been officially declared dead two days ago, and the aces, marines, and army had returned to a parade down Fifth Avenue. In another few days, American troops and whatever aces could be persuaded to join them would be flying north and south to deal with the Swarm's invasions of Africa, Canada, and South America.

The android jabbed a newly-fleshed finger at the slot of a pay phone and felt something click. One simply had to understand these things. He dialed a number.

"Hello, Cyndi. How's the job search coming?"

"Mod Man! Hey . . . I just wanted to say . . . yesterday was wonderful. I never thought I'd be riding in a parade next to a war hero."

"I'm sorry it took so long for me to call you back."

"I guess fighting the Swarm was a kind of priority. Don't worry. You made up for lost time." She laughed. "Last night was amazing."

"Oh, no." The android was receiving another police call. "I'm afraid I've got to go."

"They're not invading again, are they?"

"No. I don't think so. I'll call you, okay?"

"I'll be looking forward."

Something resembling a mucous-green gelatinous mass had erupted from a manhole into the streets of Jokertown, a Swarm bud that had escaped the showdown across the Hudson. The bud succeeded in devouring two Christmas shoppers and a hot-pretzel vendor before the emergency was called in and the police radios began to call.

The android arrived first. As he dived into the canyon street he saw something that looked like a thirty-foot-wide bowl of gelatin that had been in the refrigerator far too long. In the gelatin were black currants that were its victims, which it was slowly digesting.

The android hovered over the creature and began firing his laser, trying to avoid the currants in hope they might prove revivable. The gelatin began to boil where the silent, invisible beam struck. The bud made a futile effort to reach his flying tormentor with a pseudopod, but failed. The creature began to roll in the direction of an alley, looking for escape. It was too hungry or too stupid to abandon its food and seek shelter in the sewers.

The creature squeezed into the alley and rushed down it. The android continued to fire. Bits were sizzling away and the thing seemed to be losing energy rapidly. Modular Man looked ahead and saw a bent figure ahead in the alley.

The figure was female and white, dressed in layers of clothing, all worn, all dirty. A floppy felt hat was pulled down over an ex-Navy watch cap. A pair of shopping bags drooped from her arms. Tangled gray hair hung over her forehead. She was rummaging in a dumpster, tossing crumpled newspapers over her shoulder into the alley. Modular Man increased his speed, firing radar-directed shots over his shoulder as he barreled through the cold drizzly air. He dropped to the pavement in front of the dumpster, his knees cushioning the impact.

"So I says to Maxine, I says . . ." the lady was saying.

"Excuse me," said the android. He seized the woman and sped upward. Behind him, writhing under the barrage of coherent microwaves, the Swarm bud was evaporating.

"Maxine says, my mother broke her hip this morning, and you won't believe . . ." The old lady was flailing at him while she continued her monologue. He silently absorbed an elbow to his jaw and floated to a landing on the nearest roof. He let go his passenger. She turned to him flushed with anger.

"Okay, bunky," she said. "Time to see what Hildy's got in her bag."

"I'll fly you down later," Modular Man said. He was already turning to pursue the creature when, out of the corner of his eye, he saw the lady opening her bag.

There was something black in there. The black thing was getting bigger.

The android tried to move, to fly away. Something had hold of him and wouldn't let him go.

Whatever was in the shopping bag was getting larger. It grew larger very quickly. Whatever had hold of the android was dragging him toward the shopping bag.

"Stop," he said simply. The thing wouldn't stop. The android tried to fight it, but his laser discharges had cost him a lot of power and he didn't seem to have the strength left.

The blackness grew until it enveloped him. He felt as if he were falling. Then he felt nothing at all.

New York's aces, responding to the emergency, finally conquered the Swarm bud. What was left of it, blobs of dark green, froze into lumps of dirty ice. Its victims, partially eaten, were identified by the non-edible credit cards and laminated ID they were carrying.

By nightfall, the hardened inhabitants of Jokertown were referring to the creature as the Amazing Colossal Snot Monster. None of them had noticed the bag lady as she came down the fire escape and wandered into the freezing streets.

The android awoke in a dumpster in an alley behind 52nd Street. Internal checks showed damage: his microwave laser had been bent into a sine wave; his flux monitor was wrecked; his flight module had been twisted as if by the hands of a giant. He flung back the dumpster lid with a bang. Carefully he looked up and down the alley.

There was no one in sight.

The god Amun glowed in Hubbard's mind. The ram's eyes blazed with anger, and the god held the ankh and staff with clenched fists.

"TIAMAT," he said, "has been defeated." Hubbard winced with the force of Amun's anger. "The Shakti device was not readied in time."

Hubbard shrugged. "The defeat was temporary," he said.

"The Dark Sister will return. She could be anywhere in the solar system—the military have no way of finding her or identifying her. We have not lived in secret all these centuries only to be defeated now."

The loft was quite neat compared to the earlier chaos. Travnicek's notes had been neatly assembled and classified, as far as possible, by subject. Travnicek had made a start at wading through them. It was hard going.

"So," Travnicek said. His breath was frosting in front of his face and condensing on his reading glasses. He took the spectacles off. "You were displaced about fifty city blocks spatially and moved one hour forward timewise, yes?"

"Apparently. When I came out of the dumpster I found that the fight in Jokertown had been over for almost an hour. Comparison with my internal clock showed a discrepancy of seventy-two minutes, fifteen point three three three three seconds."

The android had opened his chest and replaced some components. The laser was gone for good, but he had his flight capability back and he'd managed to jury-rig a flux monitor.

"Interesting. You say the bag lady seemed not to be working with the blob thing?"

"Most likely it was a coincidence they were in the same street. Her monologue did not seem to be strickly rational. I don't think she is mentally sound."

Travnicek turned up the heater control on his jumpsuit. The temperature had dropped twelve degrees in two hours, and frost was forming on the skylights of the loft in midafternoon. Travnicek lit a Russian cigarette, turned on a hot plate to boil some water for coffee, and then put his hands in his warm jumpsuit pockets.

"I want to look in your memory," he said. "Open up your chest."

Modular Man obeyed. Travnicek took a pair of cables from a minicomputer stacked under an array of video equipment and jacked them into sockets in the android's chest, near his shielded machine brain. "Back up your memory onto the computer," he said. Flickering effects from the flux generator shone in Travnicek's intent eyes. The computer signaled the task complete. "Button up," Travnicek said. As the android removed the jacks and closed his chest, Travnicek turned on the video, then touched controls. A video picture began racing backward.

He reached the place where the bag lady appeared, and ran the image several times. He moved to a computer terminal and tapped instructions. The image of the bag lady's face filled the screen. The android looked at the woman's lined, grimy face, the straggling hair, the worn and tattered clothing. He noticed for the first time that she was missing some teeth. Travnicek stood and went back to his one-room living quarters in the back of the loft and came back with a battered Polaroid camera. He used the remaining three pictures and gave one to his creation.

"There. You can show it to people. Ask if they've seen her."

"Yes, sir."

Travnicek took thumbtacks and stuck the other two pictures to the low beams of the ceiling. "I want you to find out where the bag lady is and get what's in her bag. And I want you to find out where she got it." He shook his head, dripping cigarette ash on the floor, and muttered, "I don't think she invented it. I think she's just found this thing somewhere."

"Sir? The Swarm? We agreed that I would leave for Peru in two days."

"Fuck the military," Travnicek said. "They haven't paid us a dime for our services. Nothing but a lousy parade, and the military didn't pay for that, the city did. Let them see how easy it is to fight the Swarm without you. Then maybe they'll take us seriously." The truth was that Travnicek wasn't anywhere near being able to reconstruct his work. It would take weeks, perhaps even months. The military was demanding guarantees, plans, knowledge of his identity. The bag-lady problem was more interesting, anyway. He began idly spinning back through the android's memory.

Modular Man winced deep in his computer mind. He began talking quickly, hoping to distract his inventor from the pictures.

"As far as the bag lady goes, I could try the refugee centers, but it might take a long time. My files tell me there are normally twenty thousand homeless people in New York, and now there are an uncountable number of refugees from Jersey—"

"Piss in a chalice!" exclaimed Travnicek, in German. The android felt another wince coming on. Travnicek gaped at the television in surprise.

"You're screwing that actress lady!" he said. "That Cyndi

What's-her-name!" The android resigned himself to what was about to come.

"That's correct," he said.

"You're just a goddamn toaster," Travnicek said. "What the hell made you think you could fuck?"

"You gave me the equipment," the android said. "And you implanted emotions in me. And on top of that, you made me good-looking."

"Huh." Travnicek turned his eyes from Modular Man to the video and back again. "I gave you the equipment so you could pass as a human if you had to. And I just gave you the emotions so you could understand the enemies of society. I didn't think you'd *do* anything." He tossed his cigarette butt to the floor. A leer crossed his face. "Was it fun?" he asked.

"It was pleasant, yes."

"Your blond chippie seemed to be having a good time." Travnicek cackled and reached for the controls. "I want to start this party at the beginning."

"Didn't you want to look at the bag lady again?"

"First things first. Get me an Urquell." He looked up as a thought occurred to him. "Do we have any popcorn?"

"No!" The android tossed his abrupt answer over his shoulder.

Modular Man brought the beer and watched while Travnicek had his first sip. The Czech looked up in annoyance.

"I don't like the way you're looking at me," he said.

The android considered this. "Would you prefer me to look at you some other way?" he asked.

Travnicek turned red. "Go stand in the corner, microwave-oven-that-fucks!" he bellowed. "Turn your goddamn head away, video-unit-that-fucks!"

For the rest of the afternoon, while his creation stood in a corner of the loft, Travnicek watched the video. He enjoyed himself enormously. He watched the best parts several times, cackling at what he saw. Then, slowly, his laughter dimmed. A cold, uncertain feeling crept up the back of his neck. He began casting glances at the stolid figure of the android. He turned off the vid unit, dropped his cigarette butt in the Urquell bottle, then lit another.

The android was showing a surprising degree of independence. Travnicek reviewed elements of his programming, concentrating on the ETCETERA file. Travnicek's abstract of human emotion had been gleaned from a variety of expert

sources ranging from Freud to Dr. Spock. It had been an
intellectual challenge for Travnicek to do the programming—
transforming the illogicalities of human behavior into the cold
rhetoric of a program. He'd performed the task during his
second year at Texas A&M, when he'd barely gone out of his
quarters the whole year and had known he had to set himself a
large task in order to keep from being driven crazy by the
lunatic environment of a university that seemed an embodi-
ment of the collective unconscious fantasies of Stonewall
Jackson and Albert Speer. He'd barely been at A&M for ten
minutes before he'd known it was a mistake—the crop-haired
undergraduates with their uniforms, boots, and sabers reminded him too much of the SS who had left Travnicek barely
alive beneath the bodies of his family at Lidice, not to mention
the Soviet and Czech security forces that had followed the
Germans. Travnicek knew if he was going to survive in Texas,
he had to find something massive to work on lest his memories
eat him alive.

Travnicek had never been particularly interested in
human psychology as such—passion, he had long ago decided,
was not only foolish but genuinely boring, a waste of time. But
putting passion into a program, yes, that was interesting.

He could barely remember that period now. How many
months had he spent in his creative trance, a channel for his
own deepest spirit? What had he wrought during that time?
What the hell *was* in ETCETERA?

For a moment a tremor of fear went through Travnicek.
The ghost of Victor Frankenstein's creation loomed for a
moment in his mind. Was a rebellion on the part of the android
possible? Could he evolve hostile passions against his creator?
But no—there were overriding imperatives that Travnicek had
hardwired into the system. Modular Man could not evolve
away his prime directives as long as his computer consciousness was physically intact, any more than a human
could, unassisted, evolve away his genetic makeup in a single
lifetime.

Travnicek began to feel a growing comfort. He looked at
the android with a kind of admiration. He felt pride that he'd
programmed such a fast learner.

"You're not bad, toaster," he said finally, turning off the
video. "Reminds me of myself in the old days." He raised an
admonishing finger. "But no screwing tonight. Go find me the
bag lady."

Modular Man's voice was muffled as he stood with his face to the wall. "Yes, sir," he said.

Neon cast its glow upon the frosted breath of the nat gang members standing beneath the pastel sign that marked the Run Run Club. Detective Third Grade John F. X. Black, driving his unmarked unit and waiting for the light to change so he could make a turn onto Schiff Parkway, automatically ran his eyes over the crowd, registering faces, names, possibilities . . . He had just gotten off duty, and had signed out an unmarked car because he was due to spend the next day freezing his ass off at a plant, what on TV they'd call a stakeout. Ricky Santillanes, a petty thief out on bond since yesterday, grinned at Black with a mouthful of steel-capped teeth and gave Black the finger. Let him get his rocks off, Black thought. The nat gangs were being trashed by the Demon Princes of Jokertown every time they met.

Black observed from a poster that the band playing tonight was called the Swarm Mother—no one could say hardcore groups were slow in their perception of the zeitgeist. It was pure chance that Black happened to be looking at the poster at the moment Officer Frank Carroll staggered into the light. Carroll looked wild—he had his cap in his hand, his hair was mussed, and his overcoat was splattered with something that glowed a fluorescent chrome yellow under the glimmering sign. He looked as if he were making for the cop shop a couple blocks away. The nats laughed as they made way for him. Black knew that Carroll's assigned sector was blocks away and didn't take him anywhere near this corner.

Carroll had been on the force for two years, joining just out of high school. He was a white man with dark red hair, a clipped mustache, medium build beefed slightly by irregular weight training. He seemed serious about police work, was diligent and methodical, and worked a lot of overtime he didn't have to. Black had pegged him as being dedicated but unimaginative. He wasn't the kind to run about wild-eyed at twelve o'clock on a winter night.

Black opened his door, stood, and called Carroll's name. The officer turned, glaring wildly, and then an expression of relief came onto his face. He ran for Black's car and jerked at the passenger door as Black unlocked it.

"Jesus Christ!" Carroll said. "I just got thrown in a trash heap by a bag lady!"

Black smiled inwardly. The traffic light had changed, and Black made his turn. "She catch you by surprise?" he asked.

"Damn right. She was down in an alley off Forsyth. She had a book of matches and a bunch of wadded-up paper, and was trying to set a whole dumpster on fire to keep warm. I told her to quit, and I was trying to get her into my unit so I could take her to the shelter down in Rutger Park. And then *wham!* The bag got me." He looked at Black and gnawed his lip. "You think she could have been some kind of joker, Lou?"

"Lou" was NYPD for lieutenant.

"What do you mean? She hit you with the bag, right?"

"No. I mean the bag—" The wild look was in Carroll's eyes again. "The bag ate me, Lou. Something reached right up out of the bag and swallowed me. It was . . ." He groped for words. "Definitely paranormal." He glanced down at his uniform. "Look at this, Lou." His shield had been twisted in a strange way, like a timepiece in a Dali print. So had two of his buttons. He touched them in a kind of awe.

Black pulled into a loading zone and set the parking brake. "Tell me about this."

Carroll looked confused. He rubbed his forehead. "I felt something grab me, Lou. And then . . . I got sucked right into the bag. I saw the bag just getting bigger and . . . and the next thing I knew I was in this trash heap off Ludlow north of Stanton. I was running for the cop shop when you stopped me."

"You were teleported from Forsyth to Ludlow north of Stanton."

"Teleported. Yeah. That's the word." Carroll looked relieved. "You believe me, then. Jesus, Lou, I thought I'd get written up for sure."

"I've been in Jokertown a long time, seen a lot of strange things." Black put the car in gear again. "Let's go find your bag lady," he said. "This was just a few minutes ago, right?"

"Yeah. And my unit's still up there. Shit. The jokers've probably stripped it by now."

The glow from the burning dumpster, orange on the brownstone alley walls, was visible from Forsyth. Black pulled into a loading zone. "Let's go on foot."

"Don't you think we should call the fire department?"

"Not yet. It might not be safe for them."

Black in the lead, they walked to the end of the alley. The dumpster was burning bright, the flames shooting up fifteen feet or more amid a cloud of rising ashes. Carroll's unit was magically untouched, even with its rear door open. Standing in front of the dumpster, shifting from one foot to the other, was a small white woman with a full shopping bag in each hand. She wore several layers of shabby clothing. She seemed to be muttering to herself.

"That's her, Lieutenant!"

Black contemplated the woman and said nothing. He wondered how to approach her.

The flames gushed up higher, snapping, and suddenly strange bright flickering lights, like Saint Elmo's fire, played about the woman and her bags. Then something in one bag seemed to rise up, a dark shadow, and the fire bent like a candle flame in a strong wind and was sucked into the bag. In an instant fire and shadow were gone. The strange colored lights played gently about the woman's form. Greasy ashes drifted to the pavement.

"Holy shit," murmured Carroll. Black reached a decision. He dug into his pocket and got his billfold and the keys to his unmarked unit. He gave Carroll a ten.

"Take my unit. Go to the Burger King on West Broadway and get two double cheeseburgers, two big fries, and a jumbo coffee to go." Carroll stared at him.

"Regular or black, Lou?"

"Move!" Black snapped. Carroll took off.

It took both burgers, the coffee, and one set of fries to lure the bag lady into Black's unmarked car. Black thought she probably would never have gotten into a blue-and-white like Carroll's. He'd had Carroll lock his uniform coat and weapon in the trunk so as not to alarm the woman, and Carroll was shivering as he got in the passenger seat.

Behind, the bag lady was mumbling to herself and devouring fries. She smelled terrible.

"Where to now?" Carroll asked. "One of the refugee centers? The clinic?"

Black put the car into gear. "Someplace special. Uptown. There are things about this woman you don't know."

Carroll put most of his energy into shivering as Black sped out of Jokertown. The bag lady went to sleep in the back seat. Her snores whistled through missing teeth. Black pulled up in front of a brownstone on East 57th.

"Wait here," he said. He went down the stairs to a

basement apartment entrance and pressed the buzzer. A plastic Christmas wreath was on the front door. Someone looked out through a spyhole in the door. The door opened.

"I wasn't expecting you," said Coleman Hubbard.

"I've got someone with . . . powers . . . in the back seat. She's not in her right mind. I thought we could put her in the back bedroom. And there's an officer with me who can't know what's going on."

Hubbard's eyes flicked to the car. "What did you tell him?"

"I told him to stay in the car. He's a good boy, and that's what he'll do."

"Okay. Let me get my coat."

While Carroll watched curiously, Hubbard and Black coaxed the bag lady into Hubbard's apartment, using the food from Hubbard's refrigerator. Black wondered what Carroll would say if he could see the decor in the special locked apartment next door, the dark soundproofed room with its candles, its altar, the pentagram painted on the floor, the inlaid alloy gutters, the bright chains fixed to staples . . . It wasn't as elaborate as the temple the Order had downtown before it blew up, but then it was only a temporary headquarters anyway, until the new temple uptown could be finished.

In Hubbard's apartment there were two rooms ready for guests, and the bag lady was put into one of these.

"Put a lock on the door," Black said. "And call the Astronomer."

"Lord Amun has already been called," Hubbard said, and tapped his head.

Black returned to his car and started driving back to Jokertown again. "We'll get your unit," Black said. "Then we'll get you to the cop shop for your report."

Carroll looked at him. "Who was that guy, Lieutenant?"

"A specialist in mental cases and jokers."

"That lady might do him some harm."

"He'll be safer than either of us."

Black pulled up behind Carroll's cruiser. He got out and opened the trunk, taking out Carroll's coat and hat. He gave them to the young officer. Then he took out a flute—NYPD for an innocent-looking soda bottle filled with liquor—which he'd been planning on using to keep himself warm during the plant tomorrow. He offered the flute to Carroll. The patrolman took the bottle gratefully. Black reached for Carroll's gunbelt.

"It was lucky you were around, Lou."

"Yeah. It sure was."

Black shot Carroll four times in the chest with his own gun, then, after the officer was on the ground, shot him twice more in the head. He wiped his prints off the gun and tossed it to the ground, then took the Coke bottle and got back in his car. Maybe, with the spilled rum, it would look as if Carroll had stopped to hassle a wino and the drunk had gotten the drop on him.

The car smelled like cheeseburgers. Black was reminded he hadn't had supper.

The bag lady had ignored the bed and gone to sleep in a corner of the room. Her bags were piled in front and atop her like a bulwark. Hubbard sat on a stool, watching her intently. His crooked smile had frozen into an unpleasant parody of itself. Pain throbbed in his brain. The effort of reading her mind was costing him.

No turning back, he thought. He had to see this through. His failure with Captain McPherson had cost him in the Order and in Amun's esteem; and when Black had shown up with the bag lady, Hubbard realized this was the chance to win back his place. Hubbard had lied to Black when he told the detective he had alerted Amun.

There was power here. Perhaps enough to power the Shakti device. And if the Shakti device were powered by the bag thing, then Amun was no longer necessary.

The bag thing could eat people, Hubbard knew. Perhaps it could eat even Amun. Hubbard thought of the fire at the old temple, Amun striding through the flames with his disciples at his back, ignoring Hubbard's screams.

Yes, Hubbard thought. This would be worth the risk.

Detective Second Grade Harry Matthias, known in the Order as Judas, sat on the bed, his chin in his hands. He shrugged.

"She's not an ace. Neither is whatever she's got in the bag."

Hubbard spoke to him mentally. *I sense two minds. One is hers—it is disordered. I can't touch it. The other is in the bag—it's in touch with her, somehow . . . there's an empathic binding. The other mind also seems to be damaged. It's as if it's adapted to her.*

Judas stood. He was flushed with anger. "Why in God's

name don't we just take the damn bag?" He went for the bag lady with his hands clawed.

Hubbard felt an electric snap of awareness in his mind. The bag lady was awake. Through his mental link with Judas he felt the man hesitate at the sudden malevolence in the old woman's eyes. Judas reached for the bag.

The bag reached for Judas.

A blackness faster than thought rose into the room. Judas vanished into it. Hubbard stared at the empty space. In his mind, the woman's honed madness danced.

Judas shivered and his lips were blue. Christmas tinsel hung in his hair. A piece of sticky cardboard was stuck to the bottom of one shoe. His gun had been twisted into a sine wave. He shivered and his lips were blue. He'd been transported to a dumpster on Christopher Street and had ceased to exist for about twenty minutes. He'd taken a cab back.

Power, Hubbard thought. Incredible power. The bag thing warps space-time somehow.

"Why garbage?" Judas said. "Why shitpiles? And look at my gun . . ." He became aware of the cardboard, and tried to pull it off his shoe. It came free with a sticky noise.

"She's fixated on garbage, I guess," Hubbard said. "And it seems to twist inanimated objects, sometimes. I could sense that it's broken—maybe that's a problem with it."

He had to figure out some way to subdue the bag lady. Waiting till she'd gone to sleep didn't work—she'd woken up at the first threatening move from Judas. He wondered vaguely about poison gas, and then an idea struck him.

"Do you have access to a tranquilizer gun at the precinct house?"

Judas shook his head. "No. I think maybe the fire department has some, in case they have to deal with escaped animals."

The idea crystallized in Hubbard's mind. "I want you and Black to steal me one."

He'd have Black actually do the shooting—if the bag thing retaliated, it would attack Black. And then with the bag lady put to sleep, Hubbard would take the device . . .

And then it would be Hubbard's turn. He could take all the time he needed, playing with the bag lady's mind, and she would have enough in her brain left to know what was happening to her. Oh, yes.

He could test the power of the captured device on people he grabbed right off the street. And after that, maybe it would be Amun's turn.

He licked his lips. He could hardly wait.

The legions of the night seemed endless in number. The android's abstract knowledge of the New York underclass, the fact that there were thousands of people who drifted among the glass towers and solid brownstones in an existence almost as remote from the buildings' inhabitants as that of denizens of Mars. . . . The abstract, digitized facts were not, somehow, adequate to describe the reality, the clusters of men who passed bottles around ash-can fires, the dispossessed whose eyes reflected flashing Christmas lights while they lived behind walls of cardboard, the insane who hugged themselves in alleyways or subway entrances, chanting the litany of the mad. It was as if a spell of evil had fallen on the city, that part of the population had been subjected to war or devastation, made homeless refugees, while the others had been enchanted so as not to see them.

The android found two dead, the last of their warmth gone from them. He left these in their newspaper coffins and went on. He found others who were dying or ill and took them to hospitals. Others ran from him. Some pretended to gaze at the bag lady's picture, cocking the Polaroid up to look at the picture in the light of a trash-can fire, and then asked for money in return for relating a sighting that was obviously false.

The task, he thought, was almost hopeless.

He kept on.

Black and Hubbard waited outside the bag lady's locked room. Black was sucking on his rum-and-Coke flute. "Dreams, man. Incredible dreams. Jesus. Monsters like you wouldn't believe—lion bodies, human faces, eagle wings, every damn thing you could think of—and they were all hungry, and they all wanted to eat me. And then there was this giant thing behind them, just a shadow, like, and then . . . Jesus." He gave a nervous grin and wiped his forehead. "I still break out into a sweat thinking about it. And then I realized that all the monsters were *connected* somehow, that they were all a *part* of this thing. That's when I'd wake up screaming. It happened over and over again. I was almost ready to see the department shrinks."

"Your dreaming mind had touched TIAMAT."

"Yeah. That's what Matthias—Judas—told me when he recruited me. Somehow he sensed TIAMAT was getting to me."

Hubbard grinned his crooked grin. Black still didn't know that Revenant had entered Black's mind every night, putting the dreams into his mind, had made him wake screaming night after night, and driven him almost to the brink of psychosis so that when Judas explained what had happened to him and how the Order could make the dreams go away, the Masons would seem the only possible answer. All because the Order needed someone higher in the NYPD than Matthias, and Black was a stand-up cop who was marked for advancement. . . .

"And then I got blackballed." The detective shook his head. "Balsam and the others, the old-line Masons, didn't want a guy who'd been raised Catholic. Motherfuckers. And TIAMAT was already on its way. I still can't believe it."

"Being named after Francis Xavier didn't help, I suppose."

"At least they never found out my sister's a nun. That would have trashed me for sure." He finished the flute and walked toward the living room to toss the bottle in the trash. "And I got in on the second try."

You'll never know why, Hubbard thought. You'll never know that Amun was using your membership as a tool against Balsam, that he wanted the former Master, with his irrational prejudices and old man's ways and inherited mystical mumbo jumbo, out of the way entirely. How he used the decision against Black to convince Kim Toy, Red, and Revenant that Balsam had to go. And then there was the fire at the old temple, stage-managed by Amun somehow, and Amun had saved his own people from the flames, and Balsam and all his followers had died.

Hubbard remembered the explosion, the fire, the pain, the way his flesh blackened in the blowtorch flame. He'd screamed for help, seeing the giant astral figure of Amun leading his own disciples out, and if Kim Toy hadn't insisted on going back for him he would have died then and there. Amun hadn't trusted him fully, not then. Hubbard had just joined the Order, and Amun hadn't had the chance to play with him yet, to enter into his brain and make him cringe, to play the

/

endless mind games and twist him into knots with a long series of humiliations . . . Yes, he thought, that's what Amun is like. I know, because I'm that way too.

There was a knock on the door. Hubbard admitted Judas, who was carrying the stolen tranquilizer gun in its red metal case with its OFFICIAL USE ONLY stickers. "Whew. What a bitch. I thought Captain McPherson would never let me outta there."

He and Black took the large black air pistol from the case, then put a dart in the chamber. "It should put her out for hours," Black said confidently. "I'll give her some food, then shoot her from the door when she's eating." He tucked the pistol into the back waistband of his trousers, took a paper plate of cold pizza from the refrigerator, and walked to the bag lady's door. He unlocked the heavy padlock and cautiously opened the door. Hubbard and Matthias unconsciously took a step back, half-expecting Black to vanish into whatever space-time singularity inhabited the bag . . . but Black's expression changed, and he poked his head into the room, glanced right and left. When he stepped back into the hallway, his expression was baffled.

"She's gone," he said. "She's not in the room anywhere."

Modular Man looked at the drinks lined up in the bar before him. Irish coffee, martini, margarita, boilermaker, Napoleon brandy. He seriously wanted to try new tastes right now, and wondered if getting his parts crushed by the bag lady's gizmo had wakened in him a sense of mortality.

"I am beginning to realize," said the android raising the Irish coffee to his lips, "that my creator is a hopeless sociopath."

Cyndi considered this. "If you don't mind some theology, I think that this just puts you in the same boat with the rest of us."

"He's beginning to—well, never mind what he's beginning to do. But I think the man is sick." The android wiped cream from his upper lip.

"You could run away. Last I heard, slavery was illegal. He's not even paying you minimum wage, I suppose."

"I'm not a person. I'm not human. Machines do not have rights."

"That doesn't mean you have to do everything he says, Mod Man."

The android shook his head. "It won't work. I have hardwired inhibitions against disobeying him, disobeying his instructions, or revealing his identity in any way."

Cyndi seemed startled. "He's thorough, I'll hand that to him." She looked at Modular Man carefully. "Why'd he build you, anyway?"

"He was going to mass-market me and sell me to the military. But I think he's having so much fun playing with me that he may never get around to selling my rights to the Pentagon."

"I'd be thankful for that if I were you."

"I wouldn't know." The android reached for another drink, then showed Cyndi the Polaroid of the bag lady. "I need to find this person."

"She looks like a bag lady."

"She *is* a bag lady."

She laughed. "Haven't you been listening to the broadcasts? You know how many thousands of those women there are in this town? There's a recession going on out there. Winos, runaways, people out of a job or out of luck, people who got kicked out of mental institutions because of state cutbacks on funding . . . The shelters give Swarm refugees precedence over street people. Jesus—and on a night like this, too. You know it's already the coldest night in history for December? They've had to open up churches, police stations—all sorts of places so the vagrants won't freeze to death. And a lot of the vagrants won't go to any kind of shelter, because they're too scared of the authorities or because they're just too crazy to realize they're gonna need help. I don't envy you, Mod Man, not at all. The dumpsters'll be full of dead people tomorrow."

"I know. I found some."

"You want to find her before she freezes to death, try the trash-can fires first, the shelters later." She frowned at the picture again. "Why are you trying to find her, anyway?"

"I think . . . she may be a witness to something."

"Right. Well. Good luck, then."

The android glanced over his shoulder at the patio observation deck with its glistening skin of ice. Beyond the rail Manhattan gleamed at him coldly, with a clarity that he hadn't before seen, as if the buildings, the people, the lights, had all been frozen inside a vast crystal. It was as though the city were no closer than the stars, and as incapable as they of giving warmth.

Inside his mind, the android performed a purely mental shudder. He wanted to stay here in the warmth of the Aces High, going through the—for him—perfectly abstract motions of raising a warm drink to his lips. There was something comforting in it, in spite of the logical pointlessness of the act. He did not entirely understand the impulse, only knew it for a fact. The human part of his programming, presumably.

But there were restrictions placed on his desires, and one of those was obedience. He could stay at the Aces High only so long as it could help him in his mission of finding the bag lady.

He finished the row of drinks and said good-bye to Cyndi. Unless a mircle happened and he found the bag lady soon, he'd be spending the rest of the night on the streets.

Four A.M. The car ran over a manhole, and hot coffee spilled on Coleman Hubbard's thigh. He ignored it. He raised the big styrofoam cup from between his thighs and drank urgently. He had to stay awake.

He was looking for the bag lady, going through every shelter, driving down every dark street, casting out with his mind, hoping to find the pattern of lunacy and anger that he had seen in her disturbed brain.

He'd been doing this for the better part of twenty-four hours. The heater in his cheap rented heap had given out. His body was a mass of cramps and his skull was pounding to a slow piledriver rhythm. The fact that Black and Judas were freezing themselves on the same errand was no consolation.

Hubbard jammed the coffee cup between his thighs, turned on his map light, and glanced at the paper for the list of shelters. There was a girls' school gymnasium filled with refugees nearby, and he hadn't sensed it yet.

As he approached the place, Hubbard began to feel a disturbing familiarity, something like déjà vu. His headache battered at his eyes. His stomach felt queasy. It was a few seconds before he recognized the sensation.

She was here. Elation seized him. He wrenched his mind away from the twisted patterns of the bag lady's mind and reached out to where Black patrolled, the loaded dart gun on the seat next to him.

Hurry! he cried. *I've found her!*

Modular Man walked down the long rows, scanning left and right. Eight hundred refugees had been crammed into the prep school gym. There were cots for about half, apparently acquired from some National Guard depot, and the remaining refugees were sleeping on the floor. The big room echoed to the sound of snores, cries, the wail of children.

And there she was. Walking among the rows of cots, mumbling to herself, dragging her heavy bags. She looked up at the same moment that the android saw her, and there was a mutual shock of recognition, a snaggletoothed, malevolent grin.

The android was airborne in a picosecond of his light-speed thought. He wanted to be clear of any innocent bystanders if she was going to unleash whatever she had in her bag. He had barely left the floor before his flux-force field snapped on, crackling around his body. The bag-thing was not going to be able to seize anything solid.

Radar quested out, the gas-grenade launcher on his left shoulder whirred as it aimed. His shoulder absorbed the recoil. The grenade became substantial as soon as it left the flux-field but kept its momentum. Opaque gas billowed up around the bag lady.

She smiled to herself. A blackness snapped into existence around her, and the gas drowned in it, drawn into her bag like a waterspout.

Panic roared among the refugees as they awoke to the battle.

The bag lady opened her shopping bag. The android could see the blackness lying there. He felt something cold pass through him, something that tried to tug at his insubstantial frame. The steel girders supporting the ceiling rang like chimes above his head.

The bag lady's crooked smile died. "Sonofabitch," she said. "You remind me of Shaun."

Modular Man crested his flight near the ceiling. He was going to dive at her, turn substantial at the last second, make a grab for the shopping bag, and hope it didn't eat him.

The bag lady began grinning again. As the android reached his pushover point just above her, she pulled the shopping bag over her head.

It swallowed her. Her head disappeared into it, followed by the rest of her body. Her hands, clutching the end of the bag, pulled the bag after her into the void. The bag folded into itself and vanished.

"That's impossible," somebody said.

The android searched the room carefully. The bag lady was not to be found.

Ignoring the growing disturbance below, he drifted upward, through the ceiling. The cold lights of Manhattan appeared around him. He rose alone into the night.

Hubbard gazed for a long, endless moment at the space where the bag lady had been. So that's how she did it, he thought.

He rubbed his frozen hands together and thought of the streets, the endless freezing streets, the long cold hours of his search. The bag lady might have gone to Jersey, for all he knew.

It was going to be a long night.

"Goddamn the woman!" Travnicek said. His hand, which was holding a letter, trembled with rage. "I've been evicted!" He brandished the letter. "Disturbances!" he muttered. "Unsafe equipment! Sixty fucking days!" He began to stomp on the floor with his heavy boots, trying deliberately to rattle the apartment below. Breath frosted from his every word. "The bitch!" he bellowed. "I know her game! She just wanted me to fix the place up at my own expense so she could evict me and then charge higher rent. I didn't spend a fortune in improvements, so now she wants to find another chump. Some member of the fucking gentrifying class." He looked up at the android, patiently waiting with a carryout bag of hot croissants and coffee.

"I want you to get into her office tonight and trash the place," Travnicek said. "Leave nothing intact, not a piece of paper, not a chair. I want only mangled furniture and confetti. And when she's cleaning that up, do the same to her apartment."

"Yes, sir," the android said. Resigned to it.

"The Lower East Fucking Side," Travnicek said. "What's left, if this neighborhood's starting to get pretensions? I'm gonna have to move into Jokertown to get any peace." He took his coffee from the android's hand while he continued stomping the pressboard floor.

He looked over his shoulder at his creation. "Well?" he barked. "Are you looking for the bag lady or what?"

"Yes, sir. But since the gas launcher didn't work, I thought I'd change to the dazzler."

Travnicek jumped up and down several times. The sound echoed through the loft. "Whatever you want." He stopped his jumping up and down, and smiled. "Okay," he said. "I know what to do. I'll turn on the *big* generators!"

The android put the paper bag down on a workbench, swapped weapons, and flew soundlessly up through the ceiling. Outside, the cold wind continued to batter the city, flooding between the tall buildings, blowing the people like straws in the water. The temperature had risen barely above freezing, but the wind chill was dropping the effective temperature to below zero.

More people, the android knew, were going to die.

"Hey," Cyndi said. "How about we take a break?"

"If you like."

Cyndi raised her hands, cupped the android's head between them. "All that exertion," she said. "Don't you even sweat a *little* bit?"

"No. I just turn on my cooling units."

"Amazing." The android slid off her. "Doing it with a machine," she said thoughtfully. "You know, I would have thought it would be at least a little kinky. But it's not."

"Nice of you to say so. I think."

Modular Man had been looking for the bag lady for forty-eight hours, and had concluded he needed a few hours to himself. He justified this stop as being necessary for his morale. He was planning to move the body of the evening's memory from its sequential place to somewhere else, and fill the empty space with a boring rerun of the previous night's patrol for the bag lady. With any luck, Travnicek would just speed through the patrol and wouldn't go looking for memory porn.

She sat up in the bed, reaching for the night table. "Want some coke?"

"It's wasted on me. Go ahead." She set the mirror carefully in front of her and began chopping white powder. The android watched as she snorted a pair of lines and leaned back against the pillows with a smile. She looked at him and took his hand.

"You really don't have to be so hung up on performance, you know," she said. "I mean, aces, you could have finished if you'd wanted."

"I don't finish."

Her look was a little glassy. "What?" she said.

"I don't finish. Orgasm is a complex random firing of neurons. I don't have neurons, and nothing I do is truly random. It wouldn't work."

"Holy fuck." Cyndi blinked at him. "So what does it feel like?"

"Pleasant. In a very complicated way."

She cocked her head and thought about this for a moment. "That's about right," she concluded. She snorted another pair of lines and looked at him brightly.

"I got a job," she said. "That's how I was able to afford the coke. A Christmas present for myself." He smiled.

"Congratulations."

"It's in California. A commercial. I'm in the hand of this giant ape, see, and I'm rescued by Bud Man. You know, the guy in the beer ads. And then at the end—" She rolled her eyes. "At the end we're all happily drunk, Bud Man, the ape, and me, and I ask the ape how he's doing, and the ape *belches*." She frowned. "It's kind of gross."

"I was about to say."

"But then there's a chance for a guest shot on *Twenty-Dollar Hotel*. I get to have an affair with a mobster or something. My agent wasn't too clear about it." She giggled. "At least there aren't any giant apes in that one. I mean, one was enough."

"I'll miss you," the android said. He wasn't at all sure how he felt about this. Or, for that matter, if what he felt could in any way be described as *feeling*. Cyndi sensed his thoughts.

"You'll get to rescue other nice ladies."

"I suppose. None nicer than you, though."

She laughed some more. "You have a way with a compliment," she said.

"Thank you," he said.

She patted him on his dome. "It'll be a week or so before I have to leave. We can spend some time together."

"I'd like that." The android was considering his yearning for experience, the strange fashion his career had of providing it, the way it seemed to him that the experience provided was not enough, would never prove enough.

Infrared detectors snapped on and off in the android's plastic eyes as he floated over the street. Gusts of wind tried to lash him into buildings. Except for the few hours he'd spent with Cyndi, he'd been doing this nonstop for four days.

Below in the street, someone tossed a styrofoam cup out the window of a blue Dodge. Modular Man wondered where he'd seen that particular action before.

Macroatomic switches performed a silent superliminal sifting of data. And the android realized he'd been seeing that blue Dodge a lot, and in many of the same places Modular Man had been in the last few days—refugee centers, shelters, a ceaseless midnight patrolling of the streets. Whoever was in the Dodge was looking for someone. The android wondered if the Dodge was looking for the bag lady. Modular Man decided to keep the Dodge under observation.

The car's search was slower than the androids—so Modular Man began scissoring, searching streets left and right of the car while returning to the Dodge every so often. At the Jokertown Salvation Army center he got a good look at the Dodge's occupant—a middle-aged white man, his crooked face drawn and harried. He memorized the car's license plate and rose into the sky again.

And then, hours later, there she was—dead ahead of the Dodge, huddled beside someone's front stoop with her bags piled on top of her. The android settled onto a rooftop and waited. The Dodge was slowing down.

"And Shaun says to me, he says, I want you to see this doctor . . ."

Hubbard hunched into his overcoat. It felt as if the wind were blowing through his body, traveling right through flesh and bone. His teeth were chattering. He had been driving for what seemed years before, once again, getting that awful, nauseating feeling of déjà vu. He'd found her again, crouched behind someone's stoop behind a rampart of shopping bags.

"There ain't nothing wrong with your mother that a shot of the Irish couldn't fix . . ."

Black. I have found her again. Lower West Side.

Black's answer was sardonic. *Are you certain nothing's going to go wrong this time?*

The robot isn't here. I will stay out of sight.

Ten minutes.

Bring food, Hubbard said. *We'll try to catch her unawares.*

"Fuck you, Shaun, I says. Fuck you." The bag lady had jumped to her feet, was shaking her fist at the sky.

Hubbard looked at her. "I'm with you, lady," he mumbled. And then he looked up. "Oh, shit," he said.

Modular Man floated off the rooftop. He couldn't tell whether the bag lady was screaming at him or at the sky in general. The occupant of the Dodge was several houses away, sheltered behind another front stoop. It didn't look as if the man intended any action.

He thought about the way she had twisted his components, of the obliteration of existence that would happen if she ripped into his generators or brain. Memories rose to his mind; the snap of single-malt in his nose, the fat man with his rifle, Cyndi moaning softly in his arms, the ape's foaming snarl . . . He didn't want to lose any of it.

"Oh, shit," Hubbard said, staring up in horror. The android was floating forty feet over the bag lady. She was screaming at him, reaching into her bag. The thing in the bag hadn't been able to snatch him last time.

In sudden fury, Hubbard reached out with his mind. He would take command of the android, smash him into the pavement over and over until he was nothing but shattered components . . .

His mind touched the android's cold macroatomic brain. Fire blossomed in Hubbard's consciousness. He began to scream.

There was something black in the bag lady's shopping bag. It was growing.

The android dove straight for it. His arms were thrown out wide. If the woman moved her bag at the last minute, things would get very messy.

The blackness grew. The wind was tugging at him, trying to spin him off course, but the android corrected.

As he struck the blackness of the portal, he felt again the obliterating nullity overcome him. But before he lost track of himself, he felt his hands closing on the edges of the shopping bag, clamping on them, not letting go.

For a small fraction of a second he felt satisfaction. Then, as expected, he felt nothing at all.

* * *

The Siberian winds had not chilled the warm air over the municipal landfill near St. Petersburg, Florida. The place smelled awful. Modular Man had lost almost four hours this time. His checks showed no internal damage. He was lucky.

He stood amid the reeking garbage and rummaged through the shopping bag. Rags, bits of clothing, bits of food, and then the thing, whatever it was. A black sphere about two kilos in weight, the size of a bowling ball. There were no obvious switches or means of controlling it.

It was warm to the touch. Clasping it to his chest, the android rose into the balmy sky.

"Nice," Travnicek said. "You did good, toaster. I pat myself on the back for a great job of programming."

The android brought him a cup of coffee. Travnicek grinned, sipped, and turned to contemplate the alien orb sitting on his workbench. He'd been trying to manipulate it with various kinds of remotes but had been unable to achieve anything.

Travnicek moved toward the workbench and studied the sphere from a respectful distance.

"Perhaps it requires proximity to work it," the android suggested. "Maybe you should touch it."

"Maybe you should mind your own fucking business. I'm not getting near that goddamn thing."

"Yes, sir." The android was silent for a moment. Travnicek sipped his coffee. Then he shook his head and turned away from the workbench.

"You can fly off to Peru tomorrow to join your Army friends. And make contact with the South American governments while you're at it. Maybe they'll pay more than the Pentagon."

"Yes, sir."

Travnicek rubbed his hands. "I feel like celebrating, blender. Go to the store and get me a bottle of cold duck and some jelly doughnuts."

"Yes, sir." The android, his face expressionless, turned insubstantial and rocketed up through the ceiling.

Travnicek went into the small heated room he slept in, turned on the television, and sat in a worn-out easy chair. Amid last-minute Christmas Eve hype for last-minute shoppers, the tube was featuring a Japanese cartoon about a giant android that fought fire-breathing lizards. Travnicek loved it. He settled back to watch.

When the android returned, he found Travnicek asleep. Reginald Owen was playing Scrooge on the screen. Modular Man put the bag down quietly and withdrew.

Maybe Cyndi was home.

Coleman Hubbard sat in institutional clothing in his ward at Bellevue. Brain-damaged people walked, argued, played cards. A little plastic tree winked at the nurses' station. Unseen to anyone except Detective John F. X. Black, Amun floated in regal majesty above Hubbard's head, listening to Hubbard as he spoke.

"One one nought one nought nought nought one one nought one one one . . ."

"Twenty-four hours," Black said. "We can't get anything out of him but this."

"One nought nought nought one nought . . ."

The image of Amun seemed to fade for a moment, and Hubbard caught a glimpse of the figure of a thin old man with eyes like broken shadows. Then Amun was back.

I can't contact him. Not even to cause him pain. It's as if his mind has been in touch with . . . some kind of machine. His hands clenched into fists. *What happened to him? What did he make contact with out there?*

Black raised an eyebrow. *TIAMAT?*

No. TIAMAT isn't like that—TIAMAT is more alive than anything you'll ever know.

". . . nought one one nought nought nought one nought . . ."

When I found him, I saw the bag lady, put her to sleep, and found nothing in her bags. Whatever is was, someone else has it now.

". . . one nought nought one nought . . ."

The ram's eyes turned to fire, and then his body twisted, becoming a lean greyhound shape with a curved snout and bared fangs, a giant forked tail towering over his back. Fear touched Black's neck. Amun had become Setekh the destroyer. The astral illusion was terrifyingly real. Black expected to see blood dripping from the animal's snout, but it wasn't there. Not yet, anyway.

He used you on an unauthorized mission, Setekh said. *As part of a plot that was probably aimed against me. Now, he is a danger to us all. If he snaps out of this, he may say something he shouldn't.*

Destroy him, Master, Black said.

Foam dribbled from the thing's snout, smoked on the floor. The other patients paid no attention. The great hound hesitated.

If I get into his head I might get . . . whatever he's got.

Black shrugged. *Want me to handle it?*

Yes. I think that would be best.

I already planted the will in his apartment. The one that leaves everything to our organization.

The beast's tongue lolled. The look in its eyes softened. *You're thinking ahead. I like that. Maybe we can work you a promotion.*

Millions of miles from Earth, almost eclipsed by the sun, the Swarm Mother contemplated her scattered, surviving budlings. Observers on Earth would have been surprised to know that the Swarm did not consider its attack a failure. The assault had been launched more as a probe than as a serious attempt at conquest, and the Swarm, analyzing the data received from its creatures, developed a number of hypotheses.

The Thracian Swarm had been confronted by three responses that utterly failed to cooperate with one another. It was possible, the Swarm considered, that the Earth was divided between several entities, Swarm Mother–equivalents, who did not assist one another in their endeavors.

Large numbers of the Siberian Swarm had been destroyed at once, broadcasting their telepathic agony to their parent. It was obvious that the Earth mothers possessed some manner of devastating weapon, which, however, they were reluctant to use except in uninhabited areas. Perhaps the environmental effects were distressing.

Possibly, the Swarm reasoned, if the Earth mothers were divided and all possessed such weapons, they could be turned against one another. If Earth was thereby rendered uninhabitable, the Swarm was willing to wait the thousands of years necessary for Earth to become useful again. The span of time would be nothing compared to the years the Swarm had already waited.

The Swarm, as it was eclipsed by the sun, decided to

concentrate its monitoring activities on confirming these hypotheses.

It sensed possibilities here.

"So I says to Maxine, I says, When are you gonna do something about that condition of yours? I says, It's time to let a doctor see it . . ."

The bag lady, one shopping bag hanging from her arm while she clutched a second bag to her chest, walked slowly down the alley, fighting the Siberian wind.

Cyndi's blond hair flailed in the breeze as she shivered in a calfskin jacket. She watched as Modular Man tried to talk to the woman, give her a take-out bag filled with Chinese food, but she continued mumbling to herself and plodding up the alley. Finally the android stuffed the take-out bag into her shopping bag and returned to where Cyndi waited.

"Surrender, Mod Man. There isn't anything you can do for her."

He took her in his arms and spiraled into the sky. "I keep thinking there's something."

"Superhuman powers aren't an answer to everything, Mod Man. You have to learn to come to terms with your limitations."

The android said nothing.

"The thing you need to understand, if this business isn't going to drive you crazy, is that no one's invented a wild card power that can do a goddamn thing for old ladies who are out of their heads and who carry their whole world with them in shopping bags and live in garbage cans. I don't have any powers, and even I know that." She paused. "You listening, Mod Man?"

"Yes. I hear you. You know, you're awfully hard-bitten for a girl just arrived from Minnesota."

"Hey. Hibbing is a tough town during a recession."

They floated up toward Aces High. Cyndi reached into her jacket pocket and produced a small package wrapped in red ribbon. "I got you a present," she said. "Seeing as it's our last night together. Merry Christmas."

The android seemed embarrassed. "I didn't think to get you anything," he said.

"That's all right. You've had things on your mind."

Modular Man opened the package. The wind caught the bright ribbon and spiraled it down into the darkness. Inside was a gold pin in the shape of a playing card, the ace of hearts, with the words MY HERO engraved.

"I figured you could use cheering up. You can wear it on your jockey shorts."

"Thank you. It's a nice thought."

"You're welcome." Cyndi hugged him.

The Empire State threw a spear of colored spotlights into the night. The pair landed on Hiram's terrace. The busy sounds of the bar could be heard even over the gusting wind. A Christmas Eve crowd was celebrating. Cyndi and Modular Man gazed for a long moment through the windows.

"Hey," she said. "I'm tired of rich food."

The android thought a moment. "Me, too."

"How about that Chinese place? Then we can go to my apartment."

Warmth filled him, even here in the Siberian jet stream. He was airborne in a fraction of a second.

Down the alley, something bright caught the eye of the bag lady. She bent and picked up a strand of red ribbon.

She stuffed it into a bag and walked on.

JUBE: THREE

"The holidays are the cruelest time," Croyd had told him one New Year's Eve, years ago. Times Square was full of drunks waiting for the ball to come down. Jube had come to observe, and Croyd had hailed him from a doorway. He hadn't recognized the Sleeper, but then he seldom did. That time, Croyd had been a head shorter than Jube, his loose, baggy skin covered with fine pink down. He'd had webbed feet and a hip flask of dark rum, and had wanted to talk about his family, about lost friends, about algebra. "The holidays are the cruelest time," he'd repeated, over and over, until the ball fell and Croyd had puffed himself up like a balloon from the Macy's Thanksgiving Day parade and drifted off into the sky. "*The cruelest time!*" he'd shouted down once more, just before he vanished from sight.

It wasn't till now that Jube had understood what he'd meant. He had always enjoyed the human holidays, which afforded such colorful pageants, such lavish displays of greed and generosity, such fascinating customs for study and analysis. This year, as he stood in his newsstand on the morning of the last day of December, he found that the day had lost its savor.

The irony was too cruel. All around the city, people were preparing to celebrate the start of what could be the last year of their lives, their civilization, and their species. The newspapers were full of retrospectives on the year just ending, and every one of them had pegged the Swarm War as the year's top story, and every one of them had written it up as if it were all over, except for some mopping up in the third world.

Jhubben knew better.

He shuffled some newspapers, sold a *Playboy*, and looked up glumly into a crisp morning sky. Nothing to be seen but a few cirrus clouds, high up and moving fast. Yet she was still there, he knew. Far from Earth, moving through the darkness of space, as black and massive as an asteroid. She would blot out the stars as she drifted across them, silent and chill, to all outward appearances cold and dead. How many worlds and races had died believing that lie? Inside she lived, evolving, her intelligence and sophistication growing daily, her tactics honing themselves with each setback.

Among the races of the Network, she was the enemy with a hundred names: the demonseed, the great cancer, hellmother, devourer of worlds, mother of nightmares. In the vast minds of the Kondikki godqueens, she was called by a symbol that meant simply *dread*. The Kreg machine-intelligences referred to her by a string of binary impulses that signified dysfunction, the lyn-ko-neen sang of her in notes high, shrill, and pain-wracked. And the Ly'bahr remembered her best of all. To those vastly long-lived cyborgs, she was *Thyat M'hruh*, darkness-for-the-race. Ten thousand years past, a Swarm had descended on the Ly'bahr birthworld. Encased in their life-sustaining shells, the cyborged Ly'bahr lived on, but those who had stayed behind to wear flesh instead of metal were gone, and with them all the generations to come. The Ly'bahr had been a dead race for ten thousand years.

"Mother!" Ekkedme had cried out, and Jube had not understood, not until he slit the cord on his stack of newspapers the day the buds landed in New Jersey. It must be some mistake, he had thought inanely when he saw the headlines. The Swarm was a horror from history and legend, it was the nightmare that happened to other planets far distant, not the one you were actually *on*. It was outside his experience and his expertise; no wonder he had suspected the Takisians when the singleship was lost. He felt as though he was a fool.

Worse, he was a doomed and helpless fool.

She was up there still, a palpable living darkness that Jube could almost feel. Inside her festered new generations of swarmlings, the life-that-is-death. Soon her children would come again, and devour this perversely splendid race that he had come to have such affection for . . . devour *him* too, for that matter, and what could he do to stop them?

"You look like a pot of excrement this morning, Walrus," a voice like sandpaper rasped casually.

Jube looked up . . . and up, and up. Troll was nine feet tall. He wore a gray uniform over green warty skin, and when he grinned, crooked yellow teeth stuck out in all directions. A green hand as broad as a manhole cover lifted a copy of the *Times* delicately between two fingers, nails black and sharp as claws. Behind his custom-made mirrorshades, the red eyes sunk beneath his heavy brow-ridge flicked over the columns of newsprint.

"I feel like a pot of excrement," Jube said. "The holidays are the cruelest time, Troll. How are things at the clinic?"

"Busy," said Troll. "Tachyon keeps shuttling back and forth to Washington for meetings." He rattled the *Times*. "These aliens ruined everybody's Christmas. I always knew that Jersey was just one big yeast infection." He dug in a pocket, handed Jube a crumpled dollar bill. "The Pentagon wants to lob a few H-bombs at the Mother-thing, but they can't find her."

Jube nodded as he made change. He had tried to find the Swarm Mother himself, using the sensing satellites the Network had left in orbit, but without success. She might be hiding behind the moon, or on the other side of the sun, or anywhere in the vastness of space. And if he could not locate her with the technology at his disposal, the humans didn't have a chance. "Doc won't be able to help them," he told Troll glumly.

"Probably not," the other replied. He flipped a half-dollar into the air, caught it neatly, and pocketed it. "Still, you have to try, right? What else can you do but try? Happy New Year, Walrus." He strode off on legs as thick and gnarled as the trunks of small trees, and as long as Jube was tall.

Jube watched him go. He was right, he thought as Troll vanished around the corner. You do have to try.

He closed the newsstand early that day, and went home.

Floating in the cold waters of his tub, awash in dim red light, he considered his options. There was only one, really.

The Network could save humanity from the Swarm Mother. Of course, there would be a price. The Network gives nothing away for free. But Jube was sure that Earth would be only too glad to pay. Even if the Master Trader demanded rights to Mars, or the moon, or all of the gas giants, what was that weighed against the life of their species?

But the *Opportunity* was light-years off, and would not return to this system for another five or six human decades. It must be summoned, the Master Trader must be informed that a sentient race with enormous profit potential was threatened

with extinction. And the tachyon transmitter had been lost
with the Embe and the singleship.

Jhubben must build a replacement.

He felt hopelessly unequal to the task. He was a
xenologist, not a technician. He used a hundred Network
devices he could not begin to build, repair, or even com-
prehend. Knowledge was the most precious commodity in the
galaxy, the Network's only true currency, and each member
species guarded its own technological secrets zealously. But
every Network outpost had a tachyon transmitter, even
primitive worlds like Glabber that could not afford to buy
starships of their own. Unless the lesser species had the means
to summon the great starships to their scattered, backward
worlds, how could trade take place, how could planets be
bought and sold, how could profits accrue to the Master
Traders of Starholme?

Jube's library consisted of nine small crystalline rods. One
held the collected songs, literature, and erotica of his homeworld; a second his lifework, including all his researches on
Earth. The others held knowledge. Surely the plans for a
tachyon transmitter would be in there somewhere. Whatever
knowledge he accessed would be noted, of course, and its
value debited from the value of the researches here on Earth,
but surely it was worth it, to save a sentient race?

There would be expenses, he knew. Even if he found the
plans, it was unlikely that he would have the necessary parts.
He would have to make due with primitive human electronics,
the best he could obtain, and probably he would be forced to
cannibalize some of his own equipment. So be it; he had
equipment he had never used: the security systems that
guarded his apartment (extra locks would do), the liquid metal
spacesuit that he could no longer squeeze into, the coldsleep
coffin in the back closet (purchased against the contigency of a
thermonuclear war during his tenure on Earth), the games
machine . . .

There was a more serious problem. He could build a
tachyon transmitter, he was sure of it. But how to *power* it?
His fusion cells might be sufficient to punch a beam through to
Hoboken, but there were a lot of light-years between Hoboken and the stars.

Jhubben rose from his tub, toweled himself off. He knew
much of what had happened when the Sleeper went after
Ekkedme's body. Croyd had told him, a week after that grim

afternoon Jhubben had spent flushing the remains of his Embe brother back to the salt sea from which they had all risen, at least metaphorically. But none of it seemed to matter when the swarmlings landed.

Now it mattered.

He padded into his living room and opened the bottom drawer of the buffet he'd purchased from Goodwill in 1952. The drawer was full of rocks: green, red, blue, white. Four of the white rocks had bought this building in 1955, even though the old man in the green eyeshade had only paid him half of what the stones were worth. Jube had always used this resource sparingly, since no more stones could be synthesized until the *Opportunity* returned. But the crisis was here.

He was no ace, he had no special powers. *These* would have to be his power. He reached down with a thick four-fingered hand, and grabbed a handful of uncut sapphires. With these, he would locate the Embe singularity shifter, to power his transmission to the stars.

Or—at the very least—he would try.

1986

IF LOOKS COULD KILL

By Walton Simons

Picking out the right victim was always murder. They had to have plenty of cash to make the kill worthwhile, and it had to be done in an isolated place. The rent was due and killing somebody off the street made more sense than murdering the super. That might alert others to where he was, and he was tired of changing apartments.

The cold annoyed him. It seeped into his thin six-foot body and settled in his bones. He turned up the fur collar on his loose-fitting coat. Before he had died, when he was just James Spector, the New York winters had been numbing. Now, only the agony of his death, constantly welling up inside, caused any real pain.

He walked past St. Mark's Church and headed east down Tenth Street. The neighborhood was rougher in that direction, and more likely to suit his needs.

"Shit," he said, as the snow began to fall again. The few people on the streets would likely take refuge indoors. If he could not find a victim here, he would have to try Jokertown. The thought did not please him. The flakes settled onto his dark hair and mustache. He brushed them off with a gloved hand and moved on.

Someone lit a match in a nearby doorway. Spector walked slowly up the stairs fumbling for a cigarette.

The man in the doorway was tall and powerfully built. He had pale, pockmarked skin and light blue eyes. He drew deeply on the cigarette and blew smoke into Spector's face.

"Got a light?" Spector asked, undaunted.

The man frowned. "Do I know you?" He looked at Spector carefully. "No. Maybe somebody sent you, though."

"Maybe."

"Wise guy, huh." The young man smiled, revealing even, white teeth. "You'd better state your business, my man, or I'll kick your skinny ass down these stairs."

Spector decided to play a hunch. "I haven't been able to get anything for days. My source dried up, but a friend said there was somebody around here who might be able to help." He projected need with his voice and posture.

The man patted him on the back and laughed. "This must be your lucky day. Come on in to Mike's parlor, and we'll fix you right up."

Mike's apartment smelled worse than a week-old catbox. The floor was littered with dirty clothes and pornographic magazines. "Nice place," Spector said, barely concealing his contempt.

Mike pushed him roughly against the wall and pulled Spector's hands over his head. He frisked him quickly, but thoroughly. "Now tell me what you need, and I'll tell you what it's going to cost. You make trouble, I'll blow your brains out. I've done it before." Mike pulled out a chrome-plated .38 with matching silencer and smiled again.

Spector turned slowly and stopped when his eyes met Mike's, then linked their minds. The terrible sensations of Spector's death rushed into Mike's body. He could feel the crushing weight on his chest. The muscles had involuntarily contracted with such force that bones snapped and tendons tore. The throat constricted as vomit surged into the mouth. The heart pumped wildly, forcing the contaminated blood through the body. Fiery pain screamed into his mind from dying tissues. Lungs burst and collapsed. The heart fluttered and stopped. Even after the darkness there was still pain. Spector kept their eyes locked, making Mike feel every detail, convincing the pusher's body that it was dead. He did not stop until Mike shuddered in a way he had come to recognize. Then it was over.

Mike's eyes rolled up and he toppled lifeless to the floor. A twitch of his dead finger fired the .38. The slug caught Spector in the shoulder, spinning him against the wall. He bit his lip, but otherwise ignored the wound, and flipped Mike over.

"Now you know what it's like to draw the Black Queen." He picked up the gun and clicked on the safety, then carefully stuck the weapon in his belt. "But look on the bright side. You only have to go this once. I wake up with it every morning." Spector searched the body. He took all the money, even the change. There was just short of six hundred dollars.

"Small-time jerk. I'm so glad I could share something with you," Spector said, cracking the door to look into the hall. He saw no one, and walked quickly down the stairs. The cold and snow dampened the city's sounds, muffling its life.

His shoulder was healed by the time he reached his apartment.

He was being followed. Two men across the street were keeping pace with him, staying just far enough behind to avoid his field of vision. Spector had sensed them several blocks back. He turned south, away from his apartment, into Jokertown. It would be easier to lose them there. He walked slowly, saving his energy in case he had to make a run for it.

Maybe they were friends of Mike the pusher. Not likely; they were too well dressed, and people like Mike didn't make friends. More likely they were working for Tachyon. Out of necessity Spector had killed an orderly at the clinic the day he escaped. The little carrot-headed shit would almost certainly try to find him and send him to jail. Or worse, take him back to the clinic. The only memories he had of the Jokertown clinic were bad ones.

You little bastard, he thought, haven't you already done enough? He hated Tachyon for bringing him back. Hated him more than anyone or anything in the world. But the little alien scared him. Spector began to sweat under his heavy coat.

A four-legged joker blocked the sidewalk in front of him. As he approached it moved crablike down an alley to avoid him. He turned and looked across the street.

The two men were there. They stopped and huddled together. One crossed the street toward him. Spector could kill them, but then Tachyon would only come after him harder. Better to lose them and hope the Takisian forgot about him.

The ice-slicked streets were almost deserted. Even jokers had to respect the bitter cold. Spector chewed on his lip. The Crystal Palace was only a block away. It was as good a place as any to try to shake them. Maybe Sascha would catch them and throw them out on their asses.

The doorman gave him a nasty look as he went in. Spector wanted to show him what a really nasty look was, but pissing off Chrysalis was the last thing he needed to do right now. Besides, so few places in Jokertown had doormen.

The interior of the Crystal Palace always made him uncomfortable. It was furnished floor to ceiling with turn-of-the-century antiques. If he accidentally broke or damaged anything, he would probably have to kill twenty people to pay for it.

Sascha was not around, so there would be no help there. He walked quickly through the main bar and into an adjoining room which contained privacy booths. He slid into the nearest one and pulled the heavy burgundy-colored curtains closed behind him.

"Something I can do for you?"

Spector turned slowly. The man sitting across the table from him wore a death's-head mask and black cowled cape. "I said, is there something I can do for you?"

"Well," he said, trying to buy time, "do you have anything to drink?" The mask had startled him, and Spector never needed an excuse for a drink these days.

"Only for myself, I'm afraid." The man indicated the half-empty glass before him. "You seem to be in some kind of trouble."

"Who isn't?" Spector disliked the fact that he was as transparent as Chrysalis's skin.

"Yes, trouble is universal. One of my closest acquaintances was eaten, devoured, by one of our extraterrestrial visitors last month." He took a sip of his drink. "It's an uncertain world we live in."

Spector opened the curtain a crack. The two men were at the bar. The bartender was opposite them, shaking his head.

"Obviously, you're being followed. Perhaps if you had some kind of disguise, you could get away without being noticed." He pulled off the cowl and cape and laid them on the table.

Spector bit his fingernails. He hated trusting anyone. "Okay. Now tell me what I have to do for you. There is something, right?"

"Just refill my glass. Brandy. The bartender will know what kind." He pulled off the mask and tossed it onto the table.

Spector turned away. The man's face was identical to the mask. His skin was yellow and tightly drawn over the prominent facial bones. He had no nose. The joker stared at him with sunken bloodshot eyes. "Well . . ."

He quickly put on his disguise, then picked up the glass. "Back in a minute." He opened the drapes and stepped out.

The men were sitting about twenty feet away. They stared at him as he walked to the bar. He was sweating again.

"Refill," he said, after getting the bartender's attention. The man did as he was told. Spector walked slowly back toward the booth. Only one of the men was looking at him, but he was looking hard.

"Here you go," he said, delivering the drink. "And here I go."

"You might want to keep the outfit," said the skull-faced man, "I think you're going to need it." He pulled the curtains closed.

Spector walked with measured slowness to the door. Both men were still seated.

As soon as he stepped outside, Spector ran. He sprinted down the icy sidewalks, a caped vision of death, until his breath was gone. Slipping into an alley he took off the cape and mask and tucked them under his coat, then headed home.

He had gone to bed drunk for the third time in as many nights. It eased the pain enough for him to sleep. He was not sure if he really needed sleep anymore, but he had gotten used to it in the years before his death.

There was a clicking noise. Spector opened his eyes and took a deep breath, dimly aware that something was happening. The door opened slightly, revealing a crack of light from the outside. Spector rubbed his eyes and sat up. As he fumbled for his clothes the door stopped short, held by the chain. He backed toward the windows while pulling on his pants.

As he shrugged into his coat, he heard something hit the floor. The door closed. Spector smelled smoke and rotting citrus. His eyes began to water and he wobbled on unsteady legs. He had to move or the gas would knock him out. He opened the window and kicked out the screen, but caught a foot on the windowledge and fell onto the fire escape. He landed off-balance and smashed his head against the snow-covered steel railing. The pain and cold air cleared his head momentarily. There was a man above him on the fire escape, hurrying downward, and he heard another one banging up the stairs from below. They would both be on him in a moment.

Spector struggled to stand. The man below had turned to

climb the last flight. Spector leapt at him, catching the man off-guard, driving him toward the railing. Spector heard the man's spine snap on impact. He gathered himself and ran down the stairs, leaving the man screaming on the landing.

From two stories above the street he leapt. His feet skidded on the icy pavement as he landed, and his body crumpled beneath him. He fought for breath and managed to roll over. A woman wearing mirrored sunglasses was bending toward him. She was holding a hypodermic. He recognized her just as he felt the needle sink into his flesh.

Spector came to in a hallway, his hands and feet securely bound with nylon cord. The woman who had drugged him supervised as two men wearing heavy coats and mirrorshades carried him into a dark room. As long as they were wearing the protective glasses, he could not lock eyes with them.

Spector was dumped in a hard wooden armchair. The room had an old smell, like an attic or long deserted house.

"Ah, Nurse Gresham, I see you're back with our trouble-maker." The voice was that of an older man; his tone was firm and cold.

"He was a handful, though. Somebody else got killed."

The man clucked his tongue. "Then, he's as dangerous as you said. Let's have a good look at him, shall we?"

Spector heard stone creaking as the ceiling above him opened. The moon and stars shone brightly through the skylight. He had lived in the New York City area his entire life. Smog and city lights made it hard to see the stars at all, yet here they shone hard enough to hurt his eyes. His interrogators remained outside the lighted area.

"Well, Mr. Spector, what do you have to say for yourself?" Silence. "Speak up. Bad things happen to people who waste my time."

Spector was scared. He knew that Jane Gresham worked for Dr. Tachyon at the Jokertown clinic, but the man questioning him was definitely not Tachyon. "As far as I can tell," he said, "you people came after me for no reason at all. I'm sorry that guy got killed, but it wasn't my fault."

"That's not what we're talking about, Mr. Spector. Three nights ago you murdered one of our people for no reason. He was merely trying to satisfy your need for some drugs."

"Look, you've got everything wrong." Spector figured he must have stumbled into a big-time dope operation. Nurse

Gresham could be stealing all kinds of drugs at Tachyon's clinic. "The deal went down fine. Somebody else must have done it."

There was a hum, and an old man moved forward into the light. He was seated in an electric wheelchair. His head was abnormally large and sparsely covered with white hair. His thin body was twisted, as if forces inside it were trying to move in different directions. His skin was pale, but healthy, and he wore thick glasses.

"Do you remember this?" The old man held up a coin. Spector recognized it instantly. It was an old penny that he had taken from Mike's body. Since it was the size of a half-dollar and dated 1794 he had saved it, thinking it might be worth something.

"No," he said, stalling for time.

"Really? Look at it carefully." The penny shone blood-red in the moonlight.

Spector had heard enough to know he was in deep trouble. Gresham and the old man were going to kill him. If he was going to stop them, now was the time. "Nobody move, or I'll kill this old guy the same as I offed your pusher friend."

They laughed. "Look at me, Mr. Spector." The old man leaned forward. "Use your power on me."

Spector locked eyes with him and tried to share his death. He could feel it wasn't working, for whatever reason. The old man seemed to be blocking him off somehow. He slumped beaten into his chair.

"Sorry to disappoint you. You're not the only one to have extraordinary powers. Untie him, Nurse Gresham."

The woman reluctantly did as she was told. "Be careful of him," she warned the old man. "He could still be dangerous."

Spector did not feel dangerous. Whatever he had gotten himself into, it was certainly no run-of-the-mill drug operation. "How do you know about me? What do you want?"

"Nurse Gresham kept a very complete file on you at the clinic." The old man opened a notebook and began reading. "James Spector, a failed CPA from Teaneck, New Jersey, infected by the wild card virus nine months ago. You were clinically dead upon arrival at the Jokertown clinic. Since you had no living family members to object, Dr. Tachyon revived you with a now-abandoned experimental process. You spent six months in ICU screaming uncontrollably. Finally, with the help of medications you were brought back to sanity. You disappeared approximately three months ago. Coincidentally, an orderly died mysteriously the same day. It's all here. Very complete."

"Bitch." Spector tried to locate the nurse in the darkness.

"Now, now," said the old man. "If I let you live, Mr. Spector, you may get to like her."

"You'd let me live?" He realized it was the wrong way to put it. "I mean—"

"Realistically," the old man interrupted, "you have a great talent. Aces are rare, you don't just flush them down the toilet. You could be quite useful to our cause."

"What cause?"

The old man smiled. "You'll find out if we accept you into our . . . society. But before we even consider that, you'll have to prove your value. We have a little job for you, but with your abilities and the information we'll give you, it shouldn't be too hard."

"And if I don't play ball?" Spector was scared, but he wanted to know the exact consequences.

The old man tore a sheet of paper from the notebook and handed it to him with a pen. "Write your address on that piece of paper and put it in your pocket." Spector was confused, but did what he was told. The old man closed his eyes tightly and placed the tips of his fingers together.

Spector shivered. He felt as if cold water were being poured over his naked brain. "I feel . . ." He stopped, overcome by the sensation.

"Yes, I know. Not like anything else, is it? Now, tell me your address."

Spector opened his mouth to answer and realized he could not remember. The information was simply gone.

"Selective amnesia. When a person is physically present with me, I can take out whatever I want." He raised a bushy eyebrow. "Or I can remove everything."

Spector was shaken, but knew that the old man's power might also be used to remove the memory of his death. The loss of his power would be a small price to pay to sleep nights again. "I see what you mean. I'll do whatever you say."

"You see, Nurse Gresham, he's no trouble at all. It would be stupid to kill someone who can be so useful. Inject him again and return him to his apartment before he wakes up."

"Hold on a minute. Who are you? If you don't mind telling me."

"My real name would mean even less to you than it does to me. You can call me the Astronomer."

Spector figured that anyone who called himself the Astronomer was certifiable, but this wasn't the time or place to bring it up. "Fine. Well, Astronomer, what do you want me to do for you? The only thing I'm good at is killing people."

The Astronomer nodded. "Precisely."

Spector was nervous about killing a cop, especially since it was Captain McPherson. Nobody had been stupid or courageous enough to mess with the head of the Jokertown Special Forces Unit. The Astronomer had given him no choice. McPherson's death had to appear accidental since one of the Astronomer's people was in place to succeed him. If Spector failed or tried to get away, the Astronomer would brainwipe everything but his death.

He laced the shin guards on tightly and rolled his jeans down over them. He was also wearing additional protection under his shirt, on his forearms.

The Astronomer must have been planning to kill McPherson for some time. Spector was seated on a sofa in the apartment directly beneath his target. The woman who lived here was one of the Astronomer's underlings. From what he had been told, McPherson's maid was also in on the operation.

"If you want to replace someone, first replace the people around them," the Astronomer had said.

Spector looked at the wall clock. It was between one and two in the morning. He checked to make sure the hypodermic was in his pocket, then turned out the lights and opened the balcony door.

He picked up the rope and hefted the padded grappling hook at the end. The distance to the balcony above was about twelve feet. He leaned out and tossed the hook. It landed perfectly, one large barb catching the edge above. A handful of snow fell on his face. He tugged at the rope. It snapped taut and the hook held fast.

Spector climbed up quickly and heaved himself over the edge of McPherson's balcony. The accumulated snow muffled the sound of his feet on the concrete. He waited for a moment. He heard nothing from inside.

The maid had done as she'd been told. The balcony door was unlocked. Spector slid it open; a blast of cold air rushed into the apartment. He entered quietly and closed the door behind him.

The dog was waiting for him. He could see the red glow reflecting off the animal's retinas. The dog growled a threat and charged. Spector could not clearly see the animal and threw up one arm to protect his vulnerable head and throat. With his free hand he reached for the hypodermic which Nurse Gresham had given him.

The Doberman slammed into him, grabbing his extended arm in its jaws. He could feel it trying to bite through his armguard to sever his tendons.

He jabbed the hypodermic into the animal's stomach. It continued to growl and grind away at his arm. A light came on in the next room. Now that he was able to see, Spector pushed the dog away. The Doberman fell heavily and tried immediately to stand.

"Get him, Oscar. Tear him to pieces." The voice came from the lighted room.

Oscar tried to respond. He bared his teeth and took a step, then his eyes closed and he collapsed.

So far, so good, thought Spector. He faked a limp toward the lighted room. "I give up. Your dog hurt me bad. I need a doctor. Help me, please." He tried to sound hurt.

"Oscar?" McPherson's voice was unsure. "You all right, boy?"

The dog breathed heavily and did not move. The light went out in the next room.

Spector fought down panic. He had not planned on McPherson turning the lights back off. His power was useless in the dark. He stood motionless for several long moments. There was no sound from the other room.

He took a step forward. He knew the layout of the apartment. The light switch was by the door on the right-hand side. To reach it, he would have to be fully exposed in the doorway. He knew McPherson had a gun and would be ready to use it. He began to sweat. The pain knotted up inside him, readying itself for the attack. He took another step. One more and he would be in the doorway.

Spector heard the sound of a telephone being lifted off the hook. He stepped forward and reached for the light switch. His finger came underneath it and turned on the lights.

McPherson was crouched behind a large brass bed. He had the phone in one hand and an automatic in the other. The gun was pointed at Spector's heart. Their eyes met and locked. Spector remembered Mike's dead finger and shuddered as his death experience flowed into McPherson.

The policeman trembled and gasped, then slowly keeled over behind the bed. Spector clenched his hands into fists and sighed. He moved to the dead man's side and pulled the gun from his hand. He opened the drawer of the bedside table with one gloved hand and set the weapon carefully inside. Spector felt a surge of relief. He had vividly imagined the bullet ripping through his chest cavity, causing him to bleed to death before he could regenerate.

He picked up a pillow and threw it to the floor, like a wide receiver spiking a football after a touchdown. Now, maybe the Astronomer and Nurse Gresham would leave him alone. He put the pillow back in place.

The phone began to beep.

Spector put the receiver back on the hook and set the phone onto the bedside table. He sat on the rumpled bedspread and examined his victim. The look on McPherson's face was the same as the one he imagined had been on his own face when he died.

"Is it dead, or is it Memorex?" he asked the corpse. "More impressive than breaking glass, eh, cop?"

He laughed.

Spector took a swallow of Jack Daniel's Black Label and savored the warmth as it spread through his insides. He was lying on his lumpy mattress, staring at the small black-and-white television. A late-night news program was doing a rehash of the alien invasion. The monsters were still big enough news that McPherson's death did not even make the front page of the *Times*.

The videotape of the attack at Grovers Mill was being shown for the thousandth time. A National Guard unit was using a flamethrower on one of the things. It made a high-pitched scream as it caught fire and burned. Spector shook his head. Being able to kill people by looking at them should be enough to give a person some security, but that was not the case. The space monsters gave him the same creepy feeling in his guts as the Astronomer. Spector hoped that he would never see or hear from the old man again, now that he had lived up to his part of the bargain.

The tape ended. "And now," the announcer said, "for

some final thoughts on this tragedy, we're pleased to have as a guest—Dr. Tachyon."

Spector picked up the almost-empty bottle and prepared to hurl it at the set. The air shimmered next to the bed and he felt the room grow colder. The translucent outline formed into a giant disembodied jackal's head. Colored fire poured from its mouth and nostrils.

Spector fell off the bed, pulling the covers on top of him.

"Drinking again," the jackal said. "If I didn't know better, I would say you had a guilty conscience." The head turned to vapor and formed quickly into the Astronomer.

"Holy shit. Is there anything you can't do?" He tossed the covers aside and climbed back onto the bed.

"We all have our limitations. By the way, if you see the jackal head again, address it as Lord Amun. I only appear that way by using an advanced form of astral projection. One of my less-impressive abilities, but it has its uses." The Astronomer looked at the television. The tube went black with a crackle. "I don't want any distractions."

"Look, I did what you wanted. The guy is dead and everybody's calling it a heart attack. Let's say everything's square, and you leave me alone now." He threw the bottle at the image. It passed silently through and crashed against the opposite wall. "So fuck off."

The Astronomer rubbed his forehead. "Don't be foolish. That wouldn't help either of us. We can use you. A man of your power would be a great help. But I'm not being entirely selfish in trying to get you to join us. It would be criminal to stand by and watch you waste your talent like this. You only need direction to realize your potential."

"Oh," said Spector, trying not to slur his speech. "My potential for what?"

"To be one of the ruling elite in a new society. To have others turn pale at the thought of you." The Astronomer extended his ghostlike hands. "What I offer is no empty promise. The future is in our grasp at this very moment. What we are doing is of cosmic importance."

"Sounds good," Spector said without conviction. "I suppose if you were going to kill me, you would have done it already. But I'm not really in any shape to handle cosmic problems right now."

"Of course. Get a good night's sleep if you can. My car will pick you up outside your apartment at ten o'clock tomorrow night. You will learn a great deal, and take your first step on a path toward greatness." The Astronomer's image flickered and disappeared.

Spector was drunk and confused. He still did not trust the Astronomer, but the old man was right about one thing. He was wasting his new power and his new life. Now was the time to do something about it. One way or the other.

The Astronomer's black limousine pulled up right on time. Spector tucked the .38 into his coat and walked slowly down to the front door. When he got the chance, he would kill the old man. The Astronomer was dangerous, and he knew too much to be trusted. A mirrored window lowered and a pale hand beckoned him into the car. The Astronomer's head was swollen with large wrinkles that had not been there the night before. He was dressed in a black velvet robe and wore a necklace made of the 1794 pennies.

"Where are we going?" Spector tried to appear unconcerned. He knew that the gun was his only possible weapon against the Astronomer.

"Curiosity. That's good. It means you're interested." The Astronomer adjusted his sash. "You've had a great deal of pain and death in your life. Tonight there will be more. But it won't be your pain or death."

Spector fidgeted. "Look, what do you really want from me? You're going to an awful lot of trouble for an outsider. You must have something special in mind."

"I always have something special in mind, but you must trust me when I say that you won't be harmed. My powers took years of experimentation to control. Some you are already aware of. Others"—he rubbed his swollen forehead—"you will witness tonight. I have glimpsed the future, and you will play a great part in our victory. But your powers must be strengthened and honed. This can only happen if you are given the proper instruction."

"Fine. You want me to kill more people for you, just say the word. Of course, I will expect to be paid. But I just don't think I belong in your little group." Spector shook his head. "I still don't know who the hell you are."

"We are those who understand the true nature of TIAMAT. Through her we will be given unimaginable power." The Astronomer stared unafraid into his eyes. "The task will be difficult, and great sacrifice will be needed to accomplish it. When the job is done you can name your price."

"TIAMAT," Spector muttered. The Astronomer's fervor seemed genuine, but he sounded insane. "Look, this is a bit much for me now. Just tell me where we're going."

"After a brief stop, to the Cloisters."

"Isn't that a little dangerous? Bad trouble on and off with teen gangs. Lots of people get killed there."

The Astronomer laughed softly. "The gangs work for us. They keep people away, including police, and we help them in solidifying their local power base. The Cloisters is perfect for us, an old building on old soil. Perfect."

Spector wanted to ask, perfect for what? but thought better of it. "You don't have a controlling interest in the Metropolitan Museum, do you?" His attempt at humor went unnoticed.

"No. We did have another temple downtown, but it was destroyed in an unfortunate explosion. One of my very dear brothers was killed." There was a satisfied sarcasm in the Astronomer's tone. "Select a woman for us, Mr. Spector."

The limousine cruised methodically through the Times Square area. "Why don't you just have a call girl sent up to the Cloisters?" Spector had always wanted to harm a beautiful woman. "These bitches are the scum of the earth."

"A call girl would be missed," the Astronomer cautioned him. "And we don't need a stunning beauty. We've had difficulties in the past when expensive women were used. Since then, we've had to be more careful."

Spector sullenly accepted the advice and looked around. "The blonde over there isn't too bad."

"A good choice. Pull up next to her." The Astronomer rubbed his hands together.

The driver eased the limousine over and the Astronomer lowered the window. "Excuse me, miss, could we interest you in a little party? A private one, of course."

The woman stooped to look inside. She was young with dyed platinum hair and a no-nonsense disposition. Her tattered synthetic-fur coat fell open to reveal a well-proportioned body, which was only partially concealed by her tight black minidress.

"Slumming, boys?" She paused, waiting for a comment, then continued. "Since there's two of you it'll cost double. It's extra for kink or anything else special you might have in mind. If you're cops, I'll tear your fucking hearts out."

The Astronomer nodded. "That sounds fine to me. If my friend agrees."

"Am I what you had in mind, honey?" The woman blew a wet kiss at Spector.

"Sure," he said, not looking at her.

The West Side Highway was nearly empty and the trip took little time. The Astronomer had injected the woman with a drug that left her conscious, but unaware of her surroundings. As the car pulled into the driveway, Spector saw several shapes pressed close against the naked trees. In the dim light he caught the glint of cold steel. He fingered the .38 in his coat pocket to make sure it was still there.

Spector got out of the car and walked quickly around to the other side. He pulled the woman out and guided her toward the building. The Astronomer was walking slowly toward the doors.

"I thought you were crippled?"

"Sometimes I'm stronger than others. Tonight I must be as strong as possible." A blast of cold wind whipped his robes about him, but he showed no sign of discomfort. He spoke briefly to a man at the door and shook his hand in a ritualistic manner. The man opened the door and motioned Spector to follow.

He had been inside the Cloisters several times when he was very young. The era conjured by the architecture, paintings, and tapestries seemed more pleasant to Spector than the one he was forced to live in.

In the foyer a carved marble beast loomed over them. It had an angular physique and small wings tucked against its broad back. Its head and mouth were huge. Thin taloned hands held a globe up to the vast fanged mouth. Spector recognized the globe as Earth.

A figure moved out from behind the statue and away from them. It wore a laboratory smock over its vaguely human shape. It hid its brown, insectlike face and disappeared into the shadows. Spector shuddered.

The woman giggled and pressed hard against him.

"Follow me," the Astronomer said impatiently.

Spector did as he was told. He noted that the interior of

the building had been adorned with other hideous statuary and paintings. "You do magic, don't you?"

The Astronomer stiffened at the word. "Magic. Magic is just a word that the ignorant use for power. The abilities you and I possess are not magic. They are a product of Takisian technology. Certain rituals which have heretofore been perceived as black magic, in fact, merely open sensory channels for those powers."

The hallway opened into a courtyard. The moon and stars lit the snow-covered ground with a brilliant glow. Spector figured that this was where they must have interrogated him. There were two stone altars in the center of the courtyard. He saw a young man bound naked to one of them. The Astronomer moved to his captive's side.

"Take the woman's clothes off and tie her down," said the Astronomer.

Spector stripped her and bound her hands and feet. The woman was still giggling. "Extra for kink. Extra for kink," she said.

The Astronomer tossed him a gag. He shoved it into her mouth.

"Who is this guy?" Spector asked, indicating the naked man.

"The leader of a rival gang. He's young, his heart is strong, and his blood hot. Now, be quiet."

The Astronomer raised his palms upward and began to speak in a language that Spector did not understand. Several other robed men and women moved silently into the courtyard. Many had their eyes closed. Others stared at the night sky. The Astronomer put his hand into the young man's chest. The man screamed.

The Astronomer motioned to a group of people in the back of the courtyard with his free hand. A dozen or so carried a large cage toward the altar.

The creature inside was massive. Its furry, sausagelike body was built low to the ground and was supported by several short legs. The beast was mostly mouth and gleaming teeth, like the statue in the foyer. It had two large, dark eyes and small ears which were folded back against its head. Spector recognized it as one of the alien monstrosities.

The man continued to scream and plead. He was only an arm's length from the thing's open mouth. The cage was pushed slowly forward until the man's head was between the bars. The creature's jaws snapped shut, cutting off the final scream.

The Astronomer pulled the decapitated corpse upright, snapping the restraining ropes. The man's blood fountained over his skin and robe. The Astronomer's body straightened and his skin shone with an unnatural vitality as he continued to chant. He removed his hand from the man's chest and raised it above his head, then tossed an object at Spector's feet. The heart had been removed with surgical precision. Spector had seen films of psychic surgeons, but nothing as spectacular as this.

The old man walked to the cage and stared at the thing inside. "TIAMAT, through the blood of the living I will become your master. You can have no secrets from me."

The creature mewed softly and moved as far away from the Astronomer as the cage would allow. The Astronomer's body became rigid, his breathing slowed. For several moments, nothing moved. Then, the old man clenched his fists and screamed. It was a wail unlike anything Spector had heard before.

The Astronomer staggered to the corpse and began tearing at it, throwing hunks of flesh and viscera about like a whirlwind. He ran back to the cage and sank his fingers into the creature's head. It tried to break free, but could not get either of the Astronomer's arms into its jaws. The Astronomer howled and viciously twisted the thing's head. There was a loud pop as the neck snapped. The old man collapsed.

Spector held back as the others rushed to the Astronomer's side. The bloody scene had filled him with an intoxicating glow. He could feel the need to kill rising fast and hard inside, overpowering his other thoughts. He turned to the girl on the altar.

"No!" The Astronomer righted himself and lurched forward. "Not yet."

Spector felt a calmness being imposed on him. He knew the Astronomer was causing it. "You did this to me. I have to kill soon. I need it."

"Yes. Yes, I know. But wait. Wait and it will be better than you can imagine." He swayed and took several deep breaths. "TIAMAT does not reveal herself so easily. Still, I had to attempt it." The Astronomer gestured to the others in the courtyard and they quickly filed out.

"What were you trying to do with that thing? Why did you kill it?" Spector asked, trying to control his need.

"I was trying to contact TIAMAT through one of her lesser creatures. I failed. Therefore it was useless to us." The Astronomer pulled off his robe and turned to the woman. He ran his bloody fingers through her dark pubic hair, then placed both hands on her abdomen. As he mounted her he slipped his hands under her skin and began kneading her internal organs. The woman whimpered, but did not scream. Apparently she was still too disoriented to accept what was happening to her.

Spector watched the act with little concern. From what he could tell, the old man was massaging himself inside the blonde's body. Spector had been only moderately interested in sex before he had died. Now, even that was gone.

If he wanted to shoot the old man, he would probably not get a better chance. He reached for the gun. As he did, the need to kill overpowered him. The Astronomer had released his calming influence. Spector took his hand out of his coat pocket. He knew what he needed. Satisfaction was not what came out the barrel of a gun.

The Astronomer became more excited. The wrinkles on his forehead began to throb visibly, and he was tearing small pieces out of her. Now the woman was screaming.

Spector felt his need building in harmony with the old man's.

"Now," said the Astronomer, thrusting wildly. "Kill her now."

Spector moved in, his face only inches away from hers. He could see the fear in her eyes, and was certain she could see her death in his. He gave her his death. Slowly. He did not want to drown her in it; that would be too quick. He filled her mind and body. She was a writhing, screaming container for the viscous black liquid of his death.

The Astronomer groaned and fell on top of her, jolting Spector from his trancelike state. He was ripping hunks from her with his teeth and hands. The woman was dead.

Spector stepped back and closed his eyes. He had never enjoyed the act of killing until now, but the satisfaction and relief he felt were beyond what he had thought possible. He had controlled his power, made it serve him for the first time. And he knew he needed the Astronomer to be able to do it again.

"Do you still want to kill me?" The Astronomer pulled

himself, spent, off the corpse. "I assume the gun is still in your coat. It's either that or this." He held up one of the pennies.

There was no real choice. Any doubts were erased by what he had just experienced. He took the coin without hesitation. "Hey, everybody in New York carries a gun. This city is full of some very dangerous people."

The Astronomer laughed loudly, the sound echoing off the stone walls. "This is only the first step. With my help you'll be capable of things you never dreamed possible. From now on there is no James Spector. We of the inner circle will call you Demise. To those who oppose us, you will be death. Swift and merciless."

"Demise, I like the sound of it." He nodded and put the penny in his pocket.

"Trust only those who identify themselves with the coin. Your friends and enemies are chosen for you now. Spend the night if you like. Tomorrow, we'll continue your education." The Astronomer picked up his robe and went back inside.

Spector rubbed his temples and wandered back into the building. The pain began to grow again. He accepted it, even loved it. It would be the source of his power and fulfillment. He had drawn the Black Queen and suffered a terrible death, but a miracle occurred. His gift to the world would be the horror inside him. It might not be enough for the world, but it was enough for him.

He curled up under the statue in the foyer and slept the sleep of the dead.

JUBE: FOUR

On the third floor of the Crystal Palace were the private chambers Chrysalis reserved for herself. She was waiting for him in a Victorian sitting room, sitting in a red velvet wing-backed chair behind an oak table. Chrysalis gestured at a seat. She wasted no time. "You've piqued my interest, Jubal."

"I don't know what you mean," Jube said, easing himself down on the edge of a ladder-back chair.

Chrysalis opened an antique satin change purse and extracted a handful of gems. She lined them up on the white tablecloth. "Two star sapphires, one ruby, and a flawless blue-white diamond," she said in her dry, cool voice. "All uncut, of the highest quality, none weighing less than four carats. All appearing on the streets of Jokertown within the past six weeks. Curious, wouldn't you say? What do you make of it?"

"Don't know," Jube replied. "I'll keep an ear out. Did you hear about the joker with the power to squeeze a diamond until it turned into a lump of coal?"

He was bluffing and they both knew it. She pushed a sapphire across the tablecloth with the little finger of her left hand, its flesh as clear as glass. "You gave this one to a sanitation worker for a bowling ball that he'd found in a dumpster."

"Yeah," Jube said. It was magenta and white, custom-drilled for some joker, its six holes arranged in a circle. No wonder it had been dumped.

Chrysalis prodded the ruby with her pinkie, and it moved a half inch. "This one went to a police filing clerk. You wanted to see the records concerning a body liberated from the morgue, and anything they had on this lost bowling ball. I never knew you had such a passion for bowling, Jubal."

Jube slapped his gut. "Don't I look like a bowler? Nothing I like better than to roll a few strikes and drink a few beers."

"You've never set foot in a bowling alley in your life, and you wouldn't know a strike from a touchdown." Her finger-bones had never looked so frightening as when they picked up the diamond. "This item was tendered to Devil John Darling-foot in my own red room." She rolled it across transparent fingers, and the muscles in her face twisted into what must have been a wry smile.

"It was mother's," Jube blurted.

Chrysalis chuckled. "And she never bothered to have it cut or set? How odd." She put down the diamond, picked up the second sapphire. "And this one—truly, Jubal! Did you really think Elmo wouldn't tell me?" She placed the gem back with the others, carefully. "You need to hire someone to perform certain unspecified tasks and investigations. Fine. Why not simply come to me?"

Jube scratched at one of his tusks. "You ask too many questions."

"Fair enough." She swept a hand over the jewels. "We have four here. Have there been others?"

Jube nodded. "One or two. You missed the emeralds."

"A pity. I'm fond of green. The British racing color." She sighed. "Why gems?"

"People were reluctant to take my checks," Jube told her, "and it was easier than carrying large amounts of cash."

"If there are more where these came from," Chrysalis said, "see that they stay there. Let the word get around Jokertown that the Walrus has a secret cache of precious gems, and I wouldn't give a bloody fig for your chances. You may have stirred the waters already, but we'll hope the sharks haven't noticed. Elmo told no one but me, of course, and Devil John has his own peculiar sense of honor, I think we can rely on him to keep mum. As for the garbageman and the police clerk, when I purchased their gems I bought their silence too."

"You didn't have to do that!"

"I know," she said. "The next time you want information, you know how to find the Crystal Palace. Don't you?"

"How much do you know already?" Jube asked her.

"Enough to tell when you're lying," Chrysalis replied. "I know you're looking for a bowling ball, for reasons incom-prehensible to man, woman, or joker. I know that Darlingfoot stole that joker corpse from the morgue, presumably for pay. It's not the sort of thing he'd do on his own. I know the body was small and furred, with legs like a grasshopper, and quite badly burned. No joker matching that description is known to any of my sources, a curious circumstance. I know that Croyd made a rather large cash deposit the day the body was stolen, and an even larger one the following day, and in between had a public confrontation with Darlingfoot. And I know that you paid Devil John handsomely to reveal whose interests he had represented in this little melodrama, and tried without success to engage his services." She leaned forward. "What I don't know is what all this means, and you know how I abhor a mystery."

"They say that every time a joker farts anywhere in Manhattan, Chrysalis holds her nose," Jube said. He looked at her intently, but the transparency of her flesh made her expression impossible to read. The skull-face behind her crystalline skin stared at him implacably from clear blue eyes. "What's your interest in this?" he asked her.

"Uncertain, until I know what 'this' is. However, you've been quite valuable to me for a long time, and I would hate to lose your services. You know I'm discreet."

"Until you're paid to be indiscreet," Jube pointed out.

Chrysalis laughed, and touched the diamond. "Given your resources, silence can be more lucrative than speech."

"That's true," Jube said. He decided that he had nothing to lose. "I'm really an alien spy from a distant planet," he began.

"Jubal," Chrysalis interrupted, "you're wearing on my patience. I've never been that fond of your humor. Get to the point. What happened with Darlingfoot?"

"Not much," Jube admitted. "I knew why I wanted the body. I didn't know why anyone else would. Devil John wouldn't tell me. I think they must have the bowling ball. I tried to hire him to get it back for me, but he didn't want anything more to do with them. I think he's scared of them, whoever they are."

"I think you're right. Croyd?"

"Asleep again. Who knows what use he'll be when he comes to? I could wait six months, and he'll wake up as a hamster."

"For a commission," Chrysalis said with cool certainty, "I

can engage the services of someone who'll get you your answers."

Jube decided to be blunt, since evasion wasn't getting him anywhere. "Don't know that I'd trust anyone you'd hire."

She laughed. "Dear boy, that's the smartest thing you've said in months. And you'd be right. You're too easy a mark, and some of my contacts are admittedly less than reputable. With me as intermediary, however, the equation changes. I have a certain reputation." Next to her elbow was a small silver bell. She rang it lightly. "In any case, the man who'd be best for this is an exception to the general rule. He actually has ethics."

Jube was tempted. "Who is he?"

"His name is Jay Ackroyd. Ace private investigator. In both senses of the word. Sometimes he's called Popinjay, but not to his face. Jay and I do favors for each other from time to time. We both deal in the same product, after all."

Jube plucked at a tusk thoughtfully. "Yeah. What's to stop me from hiring him directly?"

"Nothing," Chrysalis said. A tall waiter with impressive ivory horns entered, carrying an amaretto and a Singapore sling on an antique silver tray. When he departed, she continued. "If you'd rather have him getting curious about you than about me, that is."

That gave him pause. "Perhaps it would be better if I stayed in the background."

"My thought exactly," Chrysalis said, sipping her amaretto. "Jay won't even know you're the client."

Jube glanced out the window. It was a dark, cloudless night. He could see the stars, and somewhere out there he knew the Mother still waited. He needed help, and cast caution aside. "Do you know a good thief?" he asked her bluntly.

That surprised her. "I might," she said.

"I need," he began awkwardly, "uh, parts. Scientific instruments, and, uh, electronics, microchips, things like that. I could write you a list. It involves breaking into some corporate labs, maybe some federal installations."

"I stay clear of anything *that* illegal," Chrysalis said. "What do you need with electronics?"

"Building me a ham radio set," Jube said. "Would you do it to save the world?" She didn't answer. "Would you do it for six perfectly matched emeralds the size of pigeon's eggs?"

Chrysalis smiled slowly, and proposed a toast. "To a long, and *profitable*, association."

She could almost be a Master Trader, Jube thought with a certain admiration. Grinning tuskily, he raised the Singapore sling, and brought the straw to his mouth.

UNTO THE SIXTH GENERATION

Epilogue

It had been easy. While Flush and Sweat pretended to have a fight on the pavement in front of the moving van, Ricky and Loco had simply walked up to the van, liberated a pair of boxes apiece, and walked off into the street. The tall geezer who was moving hadn't even noticed that some boxes were missing. Ricky patted himself on the back for the idea.

They didn't get opportunities like this very often anymore. Nat turf was getting smaller. Joker gangs like the Demon Princes were swallowing more territory. How the hell could you fight something that looked like squid?

Ricky Santillanes dug into his jeans, produced his keys, and let himself into the clubhouse. Flush went to the icebox for some beers and the rest put the boxes on the battered sofa and opened them.

"Wow. A VCR."

"What kinda tapes?"

"Japanese monster movies, looks like. And something here called PORNO."

"Hey! Set it up, man!"

Beers popped open. "Loco! A computer."

"That's not a computer. That's a graphic equalizer."

"Fuck it ain't. I seen a computer before. In school before I quit."

Ricky looked at it. "Wang don't make no stereo components, bro."

"Fuck you know."

Sweat held up a ROM burner. "What the hell is this, man?"

"Expensive, I bet."

"How we gonna fence it if we don't know how much to ask?"

"Hey! I got the tape player set up!"

Sweat held up a featureless black sphere. "What's this, man?"

"Bowling ball."

"Fuck it is. Too light." Ricky snatched it.

"Hey. That blond chick's hot."

"What's she doing? Screwing the camera? Where's the guy?"

"I seen her somewhere."

"Where's the guy, man? This is weird. That's like a close-up of her ear."

Ricky watched while he juggled the black orb. It was warm to the touch.

"Hey! The chick's like flying or something!"

"Bullshit."

"No. Look. The background's moving."

The blond woman seemed to be airborne, speeding around the room backward while engaged in vaguely-perceived sex acts. It was as if her invisible partner could fly.

"This is deeply weird."

Loco looked at the black sphere. "Gimme that," he said.

"Watch the damn movie, man."

"Bullshit. Just give it to me." He reached for it.

"Fuck off, asshole!"

Weird lights played over Ricky's hands. Something dark reached for Loco, and suddenly Loco wasn't there.

Ricky stood in shocked silence while the others stood and shouted. It was as if there was something brushing against his mind.

The black sphere was talking to him. It seemed lost, and somehow broken.

It could make things disappear. Ricky thought about the Demon Princes and about what you could do about someone who looked like a squid. A smile began to spread across his face.

"Hey, guys," he said. "I think I got an idea."

WINTER'S CHILL

By George R.R. Martin

The day arrived at last, as he had known it would. It was a Saturday, cold and gray, with a brisk wind blowing off the Kill. Mister Coffee had a pot ready when he woke at half past ten; on weekends Tom liked to sleep in. He laced his first cup liberally with milk and sugar, and took it into his living room.

Old mail was strewn across his coffee table: a stack of bills, supermarket flyers announcing long-departed sales, a postcard mailed by his sister when she'd gone to England the summer before, a long brown envelope that said Mr. Thomas Tudbury might already have won three million dollars, and lots of other junk that he needed to deal with real soon now.

Underneath it all was the invitation.

He sipped his coffee and stared at the mail. How many months had it been sitting there? Three? Four? Too late to do anything about it now. Even an RSVP would be woefully inappropriate at this date. He remembered the way *The Graduate* had ended, and savored the fantasy. But he was no Dustin Hoffman.

Like a man picking at an old scab, Tom rummaged through the mail until he found that small square envelope once again. The card within was crisp and white.

Mr. & Mrs. Stanley Casko
request the honor of your presence
at the wedding of their daughter, Barbara,
to Mr. Stephen Bruder, of Weehawken.
St. Henry's Church
2:00 p.m., March 8

Reception to follow at the Top Hat Lounge

RSVP 555–6853

Tom fingered the embossed paper for a long time, then carefully set it back on the coffee table, dumped the junk mail into the wicker trash basket by the end of his couch, and went to stare out the window.

Across First Street, piles of black snow were heaped along the footpaths of the narrow little waterfront park. A freighter flying the Norwegian flag was making its way down the Kill van Kull toward the Bayonne Bridge and Port Newark, pushed along by a squat blue tugboat. Tom stood by his living-room window, one hand on the sill, the other shoved deep in his pocket, watching the kids in the park, watching the freighter's stately progress, watching the cold green water of the Kill and the wharves and hills of Staten Island beyond.

A long long time ago, his family had lived in the federal housing projects down at the end of First Street, and their living-room window had looked out over the park and the Kill. Sometimes at night when his parents were asleep, he would get up and make himself a chocolate milk and stare out the window at the lights of Staten Island, which seemed so impossibly far away and full of promise. What did he know? He was a project kid who'd never left Bayonne.

The big ships passed even in the night, and in the night you couldn't see the rust streaks on their sides or the oil they vented into the water; in the night the ships were magic, bound for high adventure and romance, for fabled cities where the streets shone dark with danger. In real live, even Jersey City was the land unknown as far as he was concerned, but in his dreams he knew the moors of Scotland, the alleys of Shanghai, the dust of Marrakesh. By the time he turned ten, Tom had learned to recognize the flags of more than thirty different nations.

But he wasn't ten anymore. He would turn forty-two this year, and he'd come all of four blocks from the projects, to a small orange-brick house on First Street. In high school he'd worked summers fixing TV sets. He was still at the same shop, though he'd risen all the way to manager, and owned almost a third of the business; these days the place was called the Broadway ElectroMart, and it dealt in VCRs and CD players and computers as well as in television sets.

You've come a long way, Tommy, he thought bitterly to himself. And now Barbara Casko was going to marry Steve Bruder.

He couldn't blame her. He couldn't blame anyone but himself. And maybe Jetboy, and Dr. Tachyon . . . yeah, he could blame them a little too.

Tom turned away and let the drapes fall back across the window, feeling like shit. He walked to the kitchen, and opened a typical bachelor's refrigerator. No beer, just an inch of flat Shop Rite cola at the bottom of a two-liter bottle. He stripped the foil off a bowl of tuna salad, intending to fix himself a sandwich for breakfast, but there was green stuff growing all over the top. Suddenly he lost his appetite.

Lifting the phone from its wall cradle, he punched in seven familiar numbers. On the third ring, a child answered. "Hewo?"

"Hey, Vito," Tom said. "The old man home?"

There was the sound of another extension being lifted. "Hello?" a woman said. The child giggled. "I've got it, honey," Gina said.

"G'bye, Vito," Tom said, as the child hung up.

"*Vito*," Gina said, sounding both aggravated and amused. "Tom, you're crazy, you know that? Why do you want to confuse him all the time? Last time it was Guiseppe. The name is Derek."

"Pfah," Tom replied. "Derek, what kind of wop name is that? Two nice dago kids like you and Joey, and you name him after some clown in a soap opera. Dom would've had a fit. Derek DiAngelis—sounds like a walking identity crisis."

"So have one of your own and name *him* Vito," Gina said.

It was just a joke. Gina was just kidding around, she didn't mean anything by it. But the knowledge didn't help. He still felt like he'd been kicked in the gut. "Joey there?" he asked brusquely.

"He's in San Diego," she said. "Tom, are you all right? You sound funny."

"I'm okay. Just wanted to say hello." Of course Joey was in San Diego. Joey traveled a lot these days, the lucky stiff. Junkyard Joey DiAngelis was a star driver on the demolition derby circuit, and in winter the circuit went to warmer climes. It was sort of ironic. When they were kids, even their parents had figured Tom was the one who'd go places while Joey stayed on in Bayonne and ran his old man's junkyard. And now Joey was almost a household word, while his old family junkyard belonged to Tom. Should have figured it; even in grade school, Joey was a demon on the bumper cars. "Well, tell him I called."

"I've got the number of the motel they're at," she offered.

"Thanks anyway. It's not that important. Catch you later, Gina. Take care of Vito." Tom set the phone back in its cradle.

His car keys were on the kitchen counter. He zipped up a shapeless brown suede jacket, and went down to the basement garage. The door slid closed automatically behind his dark green Honda. He headed east on First Street, past the projects, and turned up Lexington. On Fifth Street, he hung a right, and left the residential neighborhoods behind.

It was a cold gray Saturday in March, with snow on the ground and winter's chill in the air. He was forty-one years old and Barbara was getting married, and Thomas Tudbury needed to crawl into his shell.

They met in Junior Achievement, seniors from two different high schools.

Tommy had little interest in learning how the free-enterprise system worked, but he had a lot of interest in girls. His prep school was all boys, but JA drew from all the local high schools, and Tom had joined first as a junior.

He had a hard enough time making friends with *boys*, and girls terrified him. He didn't know what to say to them, and he was scared of saying something stupid, so he said nothing at all. After a few weeks, some of the girls began to tease him. Most just ignored him. The Tuesday-night meetings became something he dreaded all through his junior year.

Senior year was different. The difference was a girl named Barbara Casko.

At the very first meeting, Tom was sitting in the corner, feeling pudgy and glum, when Barbara came over and introduced herself. She was honestly *friendly*; Tom was astonished. The really incredible thing, even more astonishing than this girl going out of her way to be nice to him, was that she was the prettiest girl in the company, and maybe the prettiest girl in Bayonne. She had dark blond hair that fell to her shoulders and flipped up at the ends, and pale blue eyes, and the warmest smile in the world. She wore angora sweaters, nothing too tight but they showed her cute little figure to good advantage. She was pretty enough to be a cheerleader.

Tommy wasn't the only one who was impressed with Barbara Casko. In no time at all, she was president of the JA company. And when her term ran out, after Christmas, and it was time for new elections, she nominated him to succeed her as president, and she was so popular that they actually elected him.

"Ask her out," Joey DiAngelis said in October, when Tom worked up the nerve to tell him about her. Joey had dropped out of school the year before. He was training as a mechanic in a service station on Avenue E. "She likes you, shithead."

"C'mon," Tom said. "Why would she go out with me? You ought to see her, Joey, she could go out with anybody she wanted." Thomas Tudbury had never had a date in his life.

"Maybe she's got shitty taste," Joey said, grinning.

But Barbara's name came up again. Joey was the only one Tom could talk to, and Barbara was all he could talk about that year. "Gimme a break, Tuds," Joey said one December night when they were drinking beer inside the old ruined Packard by the bay. "If you don't ask her out, I will."

Tommy hated that idea. "She's not your type, you dumb wop."

Joey grinned. "I thought you said she was a girl?"

"She's going to college to be a teacher."

"Ah, never mind that shit. How big are her tits?"

Tom punched him in the shoulder.

By March, when he still hadn't asked her out, Joey said, "What the hell are you waiting for? She nominated you to be president of your fuckin' candyass company, didn't she? She likes you, dork."

"Just 'cause she knew I'd make a good company president doesn't mean she'd go out with me."

"Ask her, shithead."

"Maybe I will," Tom said uncomfortably. Two weeks later, on a Wednesday night after a meeting where Barbara had been especially friendly, he got as far as trying to look up her number in the phone book. But he never made the call. "There are nine different Caskos listed," he told Joey the next time he saw him. "I wasn't sure which one was her."

"Call 'em all, Tuds. Fuck, they're all related."

"I'd feel like an idiot," Tom said.

"You *are* an idiot," Joey told him. "So look, if that's so hard, next time you see her, ask for her phone number."

Tom swallowed. "Then she'd think I wanted to ask her out."

Joey laughed. "So? You *do* want to ask her out!"

"I'm just not ready yet, that's all. I don't know how." Tom was miserable.

"It's easy. You phone, and when she answers you say, 'Hey, it's Tom, you want to go out with me?'"

"Then what if she says no?"

Joey shrugged. "Then we'll phone every pizza place in town and have pies delivered to her house all night long. Anchovy. No one can eat anchovy pizza."

By the time May had rolled around, Tom had figured out which Casko family Barbara belonged to. She'd made a casual comment about her neighborhood, and he'd noted it in the obsessive way he noted everything she said. He went home and tore that page from the phone book and circled her phone number with his Bic. He even began to dial it. Five or six times. But he never completed the call.

"Why the fuck not?" Joey demanded.

"It's too late," Tom said glumly. "I mean, we've known each other since September, and I haven't asked her out; if I ask her out now, she'll think I was chickenshit or something."

"You are chickenshit," Joey said.

"What's the use? We're going to different colleges. We'll probably never see each other again after June."

Joey crushed a beer can in his fist, and said two words. "Senior prom."

"What about it?"

"Ask her to your senior prom. You want to go to your senior prom, don't you?"

"I dunno," Tom said. "I mean, I can't dance. What the fuck is this? *You* never went to no goddamned prom!"

"Proms are shit," Joey said. "When I go out with a girl, I'd rather drive her out on Route Four-forty and see if I can get bare tittie than hold her fuckin' hand in some gym, you know? But you ain't me, Tuds. Don't shit me. You want to go to that stupid prom and we both know it, and if you walked in with the prettiest date in the place, you'd be in fuckin' heaven."

"It's May," Tom said sullenly. "Barbara's the cutest girl in Bayonne, no way she doesn't have a prom date already."

"Tuds, you go to different schools. She's probably got a

date to *her* prom, yeah, but what are the fuckin' odds that she's got one to *your* prom? Girls love that prom horseshit, dressing up and wearing corsages and dancing. Go for it, Tuds. You got nothing to lose." He grinned. "Unless you count your cherry."

In the week that followed, Tom thought about nothing but that conversation. Time was running out. Junior Achievement was wrapping up, and once it was over he'd never see Barbara again, unless he did something. Joey was right; he had to try.

On Tuesday night, his stomach was tied in a knot all during the long bus ride uptown, and he kept rehearsing the conversation in his head. The words wouldn't come out right, no matter how many times he rearranged them, but he was determined that he would get *something* out, somehow. He was terrified that she would say no to him, and even more terrified that she might say yes. But he had to try. He couldn't just let her go without letting her know how much he liked her.

His biggest worry was how in the world he could possibly get her aside, away from all the other kids. He certainly didn't want to have to ask her in front of everybody. The thought gave him goose bumps. The other girls thought he was hilarious enough as is, the presumption of him asking Barbara Casko to the prom would double them up with laughter. He just hoped she wouldn't tell them, after. He didn't think she would.

The problem was solved for him. It was the last meeting, and the advisers were interviewing the presidents of all the different companies. They gave a bond to the kid picked as president of the year. Barbara had been president of their company for the first half-year, Tom for the second; they found themselves waiting outside in a hallway, just the two of them, alone together, while the other kids were in at the meeting and the advisers were off doing interviews.

"I hope you win," Tom said as they waited.

Barbara smiled at him. She was wearing a pale blue sweater and a pleated skirt that fell to just below her knees, and around her neck was a heart-shaped locket on a slender gold chain. Her blond hair looked so soft that he wanted to touch it, but of course he didn't dare. She was standing quite close to him, and he could smell how clean and fresh it was.

"You look really nice," he blurted awkwardly.

He felt like an idiot, but Barbara seemed not to notice. She looked at him with those blue, blue eyes. "Thank you," she said. "I wish they'd hurry." And then she did something that startled him—she reached out and touched him, put her hand on his arm, and said, "Tommy, can I ask you a question?"

"A question," he repeated. "Sure."

"About your senior prom," Barbara said.

He stood like a zombie for a long moment, aware of the chill in the hall, of distant laughter from the classroom, of the advisers' voices coming through the frosted-glass door, of the slight pressure of Barbara's hand, and above all, of the nearness of her, those deep blue eyes looking at him, the locket hanging down between the small round bumps of her breasts, the clean, fresh-washed smell of her. For once, she wasn't smiling. The expression on her face might almost have been nervousness. It only made her prettier. He wanted to hug her and kiss her. He was desperately afraid.

"The prom," he finally managed. Weakly. Absurdly, he was suddenly aware of a huge erection pressing against the inside of his pants. He only hoped it didn't show.

"Do you know Steve Bruder?" she asked.

Tom had known Steve Bruder since second grade. He was the class president, and played forward on the basketball team. Back in grammar school, Stevie and his friends used to humiliate Tom with their fists. Now they were sophisticated seniors, and they just used words.

Barbara didn't wait for his answer. "We've been going out together," she told him. "I thought he was going to ask me to his prom, but he hasn't."

You could go with me! Tom thought wildly, but all he said was, "He hasn't?"

"No," she said. "Do you know, I mean, has he asked somebody else? Is he going to ask me, do you think?"

"I don't know," Tom said dully. "We don't talk much."

"Oh," Barbara said. Her hand fell away, and then the door opened and they called his name.

That night Tom won a $50 savings bond as Junior Achievement President of the Year. His mother never understood why he seemed so unhappy.

The junkyard was on the Hook, between the sprawl of an abandoned oil refinery and the cold green waters of New York Bay. The ten-foot-high chain-link fence was sagging, and there was rust on the sign to the right of the gate that warned trespassers to keep out. Tom climbed from his car, opened the padlock and undid the heavy chains, and pulled inside.

The shack where Joey and his father Dom had lived was far gone in decay now. The paint on the rooftop sign had faded to illegibility, but Tom could still make out the faint lettering: DI ANGELIS SCRAP METAL & AUTO PARTS. Tom had bought and closed the junkyard ten years ago, when Joey got married. Gina hadn't wanted to live in a junkyard, and besides, Tom had been tired of all the people who prowled around for hours looking for a DeSoto transmission or a bumper for a 1957 Edsel. None of them had ever stumbled on his secrets, but there had been close calls, and more than once he'd been forced to spend the night on some dingy rooftop in Jokertown because the coast wasn't clear at home.

Now, after a decade of benign neglect, the junkyard was a sprawling wasteland of rust and desolation, and no one ever bothered driving all the way out there.

Tom parked his Honda behind the shack, and strode off into the junkyard with his hands shoved into his pockets and his cap pulled down against the cold salt wind off the bay. No one had shoveled the snow here, and there had been no traffic to turn it into filthy brown slush. The hills of scrap and trash looked as though they'd been sprinkled with powdered sugar, and he walked past drifts taller than he was, frozen white waves that would come crashing down when the temperatures rose in the spring.

Deep in the interior, between two looming piles of automobiles turned all to razor-edged rust, was a bare place. Tom kicked away snow with the heel of his shoe until he had uncovered the flat metal plate. He knelt, found the ring, and pulled it up. The metal was icy cold, and he was panting before he managed to shift the lid three feet to the side to open the tunnel underneath. It would be so much easier to use teke, to shift it with his mind. Once he could have done that. Not now. Time plays funny tricks on you. Inside the shell, he had grown stronger and stronger, but on the outside his telekinesis had faded over the years. It was all psychological, Tom knew; the shell had become some kind of crutch, and his mind refused to let him teke without it, that was all. But there were days when it almost felt as though Thomas Tudbury and the Great and Powerful Turtle had become two different people.

He dropped down into darkness, into the tunnel that he and Joey had dug together, night after night, way back in— what year had that been? '69? '70? Something like that. He found the big plastic flashlight on its hook, but the beam was pale and weak. He'd have to remember to bring some new batteries from the store the next time he came out. Alkaline next time; they lasted a lot longer.

He walked about sixty feet before the tunnel ended, and the blackness of the bunker opened up around him. It was just a big hole in the ground he'd scooped out with his teke, its crude roof covered over with a thin layer of dirt and junk to conceal what lay beneath. The air was thick and stale, and he heard rats scuttling away from the light of his flashlight beam. In the comic book, the Turtle had a secret Turtle Cave deep under the waters of New York Bay, a marvelous place with vaulted ceilings and computer banks and a live-in butler who dusted all the trophies and prepared gourmet meals. The writers at Cosh Comics had done one fuck of a lot better for him than he had ever managed to do for himself.

He walked past two of the older shells to the latest model, punched in the combination, and pulled up the hatch. Crawling inside, Tom sealed the shell behind him and found his chair. He groped for the harness, and belted himself in. The seat was wide and comfortable, with thick padded armrests and the friendly smell of leather. Control panels were mounted at the ends of both arms for easy fingertip access. His fingers played over the keys with the ease of long familiarity, turning on ventilators, heat, and lights. The interior of the shell was snug and cozy, covered with green shag carpet. He had four 23-inch color televisions mounted in the carpeted walls, surrounded by banks of smaller screens and other instrumentation.

His left index finger jabbed down and the outside cameras came to life, filling his screens with vague gray shapes, until he went to infrared. Tom pivoted slowly, checking the pictures, testing his lights, making sure everything was functional. He rummaged through his box of cassettes until he found Springsteen. A good Jersey boy, Tom thought. He slammed the cassette into the tape deck, and Bruce tore right into "Glory Days." It brought a flat, hard smile to his face.

Tom leaned forward and threw a toggle. From somewhere outside came a whirring sound. That garage door opener would have to be replaced soon from the sound of it. On the screens, he saw light pour into the bunker from overhead. A cascade of snow and ice fell down onto the bare earth floor. He pushed up with his mind; the armored shell lifted, and began to drift toward the light. So Barbara Casko was getting married to that asshole Steve Bruder, so what the hell did he care; the Great and Powerful Turtle was going out to kick some monster butt.

One thing Tom Tudbury had found out a long time ago was that life doesn't give you many second chances. He was lucky. He got a second chance at Barbara Casko.

It happened in 1972, a decade after he'd last seen her. The store was still called Broadway Television and Electronics then, and Tom was assistant manager. He was behind the register, his back to the counter while he straightened some shelves, when a woman's voice said, "Excuse me."

"Yeah," he said, turning, then staring.

Her dark blond hair was much longer, falling halfway down her back, and she was wearing tinted glasses in oversized plastic frames, but behind the lenses her eyes were just as blue. She wore a Fair Isle sweater and a faded pair of jeans, and if anything her figure was even better at twenty-seven than it had been at seventeen. He looked at her hand, and all he saw there was a college class ring. "Barbara," he said.

She looked surprised. "Do I know you?"

Tom pointed at the McGovern button pinned to her sweater. "Once you nominated me for president," he said.

"I don't," she began, with a small puzzled frown on that face, still the prettiest face that had ever smiled at Tom Tudbury in all his life.

"I used to wear a crew cut," he said. "And a double-breasted corduroy jacket. Black." He touched his aviator frames. "These were horn rims the last time you saw me. I weighed about the same then, but I was maybe an inch shorter. And I had such a crush on you that you wouldn't believe."

Barbara Casko smiled. For a moment he thought she was bluffing. But her eyes met his, and he knew. "How are you, Tom? It's been a long time, huh?"

A long time, he thought. Oh yeah. A different eon. "I'm great," he told her. It was at least half-true. That was at the end of the Turtle's headiest decade. Tom's life was going nowhere fast—he'd dropped out of college after JFK had been shot, and ever since he'd been living in a crummy basement apartment on 31st Street. He didn't really give a damn. Tom Tudbury and his lousy job and his lousy apartment were incidental to his *real* life; they were the price he paid for those nights and weekends in the shell. In high school, he'd been a pudgy introvert with a crew cut, a lot of insecurity, and a secret power that only Joey knew about. And now he was the Great and Powerful Turtle. Mystery hero, celebrity, ace of aces, and all-around hot shit.

Of course, he couldn't tell her any of that.

But somehow it didn't matter. Just being the Turtle had changed Tom Tudbury, had given him more confidence. For ten years he'd been having fantasies and wet dreams about Barbara Casko, regretting his cowardice, wondering about the road not taken and the prom he'd never attended. A decade too late, Tom Tudbury finally got the words out. "You look terrific," he said with all sincerity. "I'm off at five. You free for dinner?"

"Sure," she said. Then she laughed. "I wondered how long it'd take you to ask me out. I never guessed it'd be ten years. You may just have set a new school record."

Monsters were like cops, Tom decided: never around when you really needed one.

December had been a different story. He remembered his first sight of them, remembered that long surreal trip down the Jersey Turnpike toward Philadelphia. Behind him was an armored column; ahead, the turnpike was deserted. Nothing moved but a few newspapers blowing across the empty traffic lanes. Along the sides of the road, the toxic waste dumps and petrochemical plants stood like so many ghost towns. Every so often, they'd come across some haggard refugees fleeing the Swarm, but that was it. It was like a movie, Tom thought. He didn't quite believe it.

Until they made contact.

A cold chill had gone up his spine when the android came streaking back to the column with the news that the enemy was near, and moving on Philly. "This is it," Tom said to Peregrine, who'd been riding on his shell to rest her wings.

He had just long enough to find a cassette—*Creedence Gold*—and slide it into his tape deck before the swarmlings came over the horizon like a black tide. The fliers filled the air as far as his cameras could see, a moving cloud of darkness like a vast onrushing thunderhead. He remembered the twister from *The Wizard of Oz*, and how much it had scared him the first time he'd seen the movie.

Beneath those dark wings the other swarmlings moved—crawling on segmented bellies, scrabbling on meter-long spider legs, oozing along like the Blob, and with Steve McQueen nowhere in sight. They covered the road from shoulder to shoulder, and spilled out over its edges, and they moved faster than he could have imagined.

Peregrine took off. The android was already plunging back toward the enemy, and Tom saw Mistral coming down from above, a flash of blue among the thin cold clouds. He swallowed, and turned the volume on his speakers all the way up; "Bad Moon Rising" blasted out over the dark sky. He remembered thinking that life would never be the same. He almost wanted to believe it. Maybe the new world would be better than the old.

But that was December, and this was March, and life was a lot more resilient than he'd given it credit for. Like the passenger pigeons, the swarmlings had threatened to blot out the sun, and like the passenger pigeons, they were gone in what seemed like no time at all. After that first unforgettable moment, even the war of the worlds had turned into just another chore. It was more extermination than combat, like killing especially large and ugly roaches. Claws, pincers, and poisoned talons were useless against his armor; the acid secreted by the flappers did fuck up his lenses pretty badly, but that was more a nuisance than a danger. He found himself trying to think of new, imaginative ways of killing the things to relieve the boredom. He flung them high into the air, he ripped them in half, he grabbed them in invisible fists and squeezed them into guacamole. Over and over again, day after day, endlessly, until they stopped coming.

And afterward, back home, he was astonished at just how quickly the Swarm War faded from the headlines, and how easily life flowed back into the old channels. In Peru, Chad, and the mountains of Tibet, major alien infestations continued their ravages, and smaller remnants were still troubling the Turks and Nigerians, but the third-world swarms were just page-four filler in most American newspapers. Meanwhile, life continued. People made their mortgage payments and went to work; those whose homes and jobs had been wiped out dutifully filed insurance claims and applied for unemployment. People complained about the weather, told jokes, went to movies, argued about sports.

People made wedding plans.

The swarmlings hadn't been *completely* exterminated, of course. A few remnant monsters lurked here and there, in out-of-the-way places and some not-so-out-of-the-way. Tom wanted one badly today. A small one would do—flying, crawling, he didn't care. He would have settled for some ordinary criminals, a fire, an auto accident, anything to take his mind off Barbara.

Nothing doing. It was a gray, cold, depressing, *dull* day, even in Jokertown. His police monitor was reporting nothing but a few domestic disturbances, and he'd made it a rule never to get involved in those. Over the years he'd discovered that even the most abused wife tended to be somewhat aghast when an armored shell the size of a Lincoln Continental crashed through her bedroom wall and told her husband to keep his hands off her.

He cruised up the length of the Bowery, floating just above rooftop level, his shell throwing a long black shadow that kept pace with him on the pavement below. Traffic passed through underneath without even slowing. All his cameras were scanning, giving him views from more angles than he could possibly need. Tom glanced restlessly from screen to screen, watching the passersby. They scarcely noticed him anymore. A quick glance up when the shell hove into their peripheral vision, a flicker of recognition, and then they went back to their own business, bored. *It's just the Turtle*, he imagined them saying. Yesterday's news. The glory days do pass you by.

Twenty years ago, things had been different. He'd been the first ace to go public after the long decade of hiding, and everything he did or said was celebrated. The papers were full of his exploits, and when the Turtle passed overhead, kids would shout and point, and all eyes would turn in his direction. Crowds would cheer him wildly at fires and parades and public assemblies. In Jokertown, men would doff their masks to him, and women would blow him kisses as he went by. He was Jokertown's own hero. Because he hid in an armored shell and never showed his face, a lot of jokers assumed he was one of them, and they loved him for it. It was love based on a lie, or at least a misunderstanding, and at times he felt guilty about that, but in those days the jokers had desperately needed one of their own to cheer, so he had let the rumors continue. He never did get around to telling the public that he was really an ace; at some point, he couldn't remember just when, the world had stopped caring who or what might be inside the Turtle's shell.

These days there were seventy or eighty aces in New York alone, maybe as many as a hundred, and he was just the same old Turtle. Jokertown had real joker heroes now: the Oddity, Troll, Quasiman, the Twisted Sisters, and others, joker-aces who weren't afraid to show their faces to the world. For years, he had felt bad about accepting joker adulation on false premises, but once it was gone he found that he missed it.

Passing over Sara Roosevelt Park, Tom noticed a joker with the head of a goat squatting at the base of the red steel abstraction they'd put up as a monument to those who had died in the Great Jokertown Riot of 1976. The man stared up at the shell with apparent fascination. Maybe he wasn't wholly forgotten after all, Tom thought. He zoomed in to get a good look at his fan. That was when he noticed the thick rope of wet green mucus hanging from the corner of the goat-man's mouth, and the vacancy in those tiny black eyes. A rueful smile twisted across Tom's mouth. He turned on his microphone. "Hey, guy," he announced over his loudspeakers. "You all right down there?" The goat-man worked his mouth silently.

Tom sighed. He reached out with his mind and lifted the joker easily into the air. The goat-man didn't even struggle. Just stared off into the distance, seeing god knows what, while drool ran from his mouth. Tom held him in place under the shell, and sailed off toward South Street.

He deposited the goat-man gently between the worn stone lions that guarded the steps of the Jokertown clinic, and turned up the volume on his speakers. "Tachyon," he said into the microphone, and "TACHYON" boomed out over the street, rattling windows and startling motorists on the FDR Drive. A fierce-looking nurse popped out of the front door and scowled at him. "I've brought one for you," Tom said more softly.

"Who is he?" she asked.

"President of the Turtle Fan Club," Tom said. "How the hell do I know who is he? He needs help, though. Look at him."

The nurse gave the joker a cursory examination, then called for two orderlies who helped the man inside.

"Where's Tachyon?" Tom asked.

"At lunch," the nurse said. "He's due back at one-thirty. He's probably at Hairy's."

"Never mind," Tom said. He pushed, and the shell rose straight up into the sky. The expressway, the river, and the rooftops of Jokertown dwindled below him.

Funny thing, but the higher you got, the more beautiful Manhattan looked. The magnificent stone arches of the Brooklyn Bridge, the twisting alleys of Wall Street, Lady Liberty on her island, the ships on the river and ferries on the bay, the soaring towers of the Chrysler Building and the Empire State Building, the vast green-and-white expanse of Central Park; from on high the Turtle surveyed it all. The intricate pattern of the traffic flowing through the city streets was almost hypnotic if you stared at it long enough. Looking down from the cold winter sky, New York was gorgeous and awesome, like no other city in the world. It was only when you got down among those stone canyons that you saw the dirt, smelled the rotten garbage in a million dented cans, heard the curses and the screams, and sensed the depth of fear and misery.

He drifted high over the city, a cold wind keening around his shell. The police monitor crackled with trivialities. Tom switched to the marine band, thinking maybe he could find a small boat in distress. Once he'd saved six people off a yacht that had capsized in a summer squall. The grateful owner had laid a huge reward on him afterward. The guy was smart too; he paid cash, small worn bills, nothing bigger than a twenty. Six damned suitcases. The heroes Tom had read about as a kid always turned down rewards, but none of them lived in a crummy apartment or drove an eight-year-old Plymouth. Tom took the money, salved his conscience by giving one suitcase to the clinic, and used the other five to buy his house. There was no way he'd ever have been able to own a house on Tom Tudbury's salary. Sometimes he worried about IRS audits, but so far that hadn't come up.

His watch said it was 1:03. Time for lunch. He opened the small refrigerator in the floor, where he'd stashed an apple, a ham sandwich, and a six-pack.

When he finished eating, it was 1:17. Less than forty-five minutes, he thought, and he remembered that old Cagney movie about George M. Cohan, and the song "Forty-Five Minutes From Broadway." A bus leaving right now from Port Authority would take forty-five minutes to get to Bayonne, but it was quicker by air. Ten minutes, fifteen at the most, and he could be back.

But for what?

He turned off the radio, pushed the Springsteen tape back in, and rewound until he found "Glory Days" again.

The second time around, things went a lot better.

After graduation she'd gone to Rutgers, Barbara told him that first night, over steak sandwiches and mugs of beer at Hendrickson's. She'd gotten a teaching certificate, spent two years in California with a boyfriend, and come back to Bayonne when they broke up. She was teaching locally now, kindergarten, and in Tom's old grammar school, ironically enough. "I love it," she said. "The kids are fantastic. Five is a magic age."

Tom had let her talk about her life for a long time, happy just to be sitting there with her, listening to her voice. He liked the way her eyes sparkled when she talked about the kids. When she finally ran down, he asked her the question that had been bugging him all these years. "Did Steve Bruder ever ask you to our prom?"

She made a face. "No, the son of a bitch. He went with Betty Moroski. I cried for a week."

"He was an idiot. Jesus, she wasn't half as pretty as you."

"No," Barbara said, with a wry twist to her mouth, "but she put out, and I didn't. Never mind that. What about you? What have you been doing for the last ten years?"

It would have been infinitely more interesting if he had told her about the Turtle, about life in the cold skies and mean streets, about the close calls and the high times and the headlines. He could have bragged about capturing the Great Ape during the big blackout of 1965, could have told her how he'd saved Dr. Tachyon's life and sanity, could have casually dropped the names of the famous and infamous, aces and jokers and celebrities of every stripe. But all that was part of another life, and it belonged to an ace who came canned in an iron shell. The only thing he had to offer her was Thomas Tudbury. As he talked about himself, he realized for the first time how bare and dreary his "real" life truly was.

Yet somehow it seemed to be enough.

That first date led to a second, the second to a third, and soon they were seeing each other regularly. It was not the world's most exciting courtship. On weekdays they went to local movies at the DeWitt or the Lyceum; sometimes they just watched television together and took turns cooking dinner. On weekends, it was off to New York; Broadway plays when they could afford it, late dinners in Chinatown and Little Italy. The more he was with her, the more he found himself unable to be without her.

They both liked red wine, and pizza, and rock 'n' roll. She had marched on Washington the year before, to get the troops out of Vietnam, and he'd been there too (inside his shell, floating over the mall with peace symbols painted on his armor and a gorgeous blonde in a halter top and jeans sitting on top, singing along to the antiwar songs that blared from his speakers, but he couldn't tell her that part). She loved Gina and Joey, and her parents seemed to approve of him. She was a baseball fan, brought up to abominate the Yankees and love the Brooklyn Dodgers, just like him. Come October, she sat beside him in the Ebbets Field bleachers, when Tom Seaver pitched the Dodgers to victory over the Oakland A's in the seventh and deciding game of the Series. A month later, he was there to share her anguish at McGovern's landslide defeat. They had so much in common.

Just *how* much he did not realize until the week after Thanksgiving, when she came to his place for dinner. He'd gone to the kitchen, to open the wine and check his spaghetti sauce, and when he came back he found her standing by his bookcase, leafing through a paperback copy of Jim Bishop's *Day of the Wild Card*. "You must be interested in this stuff," she said, nodding toward the books. His wild card collection took up almost three shelves. He had everything; all the biographies of Jetboy, Earl Sanderson's collected speeches and Archibald Holmes's memoirs, Tom Wolfe's *Wild Card Chic*, the autobiography of Cyclone as told to Robin Moore, the *Information Please Almanac of Aces*, and so much more. Including, of course, everything that had ever been published about the Turtle.

"Yeah," he said, "it's, uh, always interested me. Those people. I'd love to meet a wild card one day."

"You have," she said, smiling, sliding the book back on the shelf next to Ralph Ellison's *Invisible Man*.

"I have?" He was confused, and a bit taken aback. Had he given himself away, somehow? Had Joey told her? "Who?"

"Me," Barbara said. He must have looked incredulous. "No, really," she said. "I know, it doesn't show. I'm not an ace or anything. It didn't *do* anything to me, as far as anyone can tell. But I did get it. I was only two, so I don't remember anything. My mother said I almost died. The symptoms—I must have been quite a sight. Our doctor thought it was the mumps at first, but my face just kept on swelling, until I looked like a basketball. Then he transferred me to Mt. Sinai. That's where Dr. Tachyon was working at the time."

"Yeah," Tom said.

"Anyway, I pulled through. The swelling only lasted a couple of days, but they kept me for a month, running tests. It was the wild card all right, but it might as well have been the chicken pox, for all the difference it made to me." She grinned. "Still, it was our deep, dark family secret. Dad quit his job and moved us to Bayonne, where nobody knew. People were funny about the wild card back then. I didn't even know myself until I was in college. Mom was afraid I'd tell."

"Did you?"

"No," Barbara said. She looked strangely solemn. "No one. Not until tonight, anyway."

"So why did you tell me?" Tom asked her.

"Because I trust you," she said quietly.

He almost told her then, right there in his living room. He wanted to. Afterward, whenever he thought about that evening, he found himself wishing that he had, and wondering what would have happened.

But when he opened his mouth to say the words, to speak to her of teke and Turtles and junkyard secrets, it was as though the years had rolled back and he was in high school again, standing with her in that corridor, wanting so desperately to ask her to the prom and somehow unable to. He'd kept his secrets for so long. The words would not come. He tried, for a long moment he tried. Then, defeated, he had hugged her and mumbled "I'm glad you told me," before retreating to the kitchen to gather his wits. He looked at the spaghetti sauce simmering on the stove, and suddenly reached out and turned off the burner.

"Get your coat," he said when he returned to her. "The plans have changed. I'm taking you out for dinner."

"Out? Where?"

"Aces High," he said as he lifted the phone to call for the reservation. "We're going to see those wild cards tonight."

They dined among aces and stars. It cost him two weeks' salary, but it was worth it, even though the maître d' took one look at his corduroy suit and led them to a table way back by the kitchen. The food was almost as extraordinary as the light in Barbara's eyes. They were enjoying an aperitif when Dr. Tachyon came in, wearing a green velveteen tuxedo and escorting Liza Minelli. Tom went over to their table, and got both of them to autograph a cocktail napkin.

That night he and Barbara made love for the first time. Afterward, as she slept curled up against him, Tom held on tightly to her warmth, dreaming of the years to come, and wondering why the hell he had taken so long.

He was making a swing over Central Park Lake, listening to Bruce and eating a bag of Nacho Cheese–flavored Doritos, when he noticed that he was being followed by a pterodactyl.

Through a telephoto lens, Tom watched it circle above him, riding the winds on a leathery six-foot wingspan. Frowning, he killed his tape and went to his loudspeakers. "HEY!" he boomed into the winter air. "COLD ENOUGH FOR YOU? YOU'RE A REPTILE, KID, YOU'RE GOING TO FREEZE YOUR SCALY ASS OFF."

The pterodactyl replied with a high, thin shriek, made a wide turn, and came in for a landing on top of his shell, flapping energetically as it touched down to keep from going over the edge. Its claws scrabbled against his metal and found purchase in the cracks between his armor plates.

Sighing, Tom watched on one of his big screens as the pterodactyl rippled, flowed, and turned into Kid Dinosaur. "It's just as cold for you," the kid said.

"I've got heaters in here," Tom said. The kid was already turning blue, which wasn't surprising, considering that he was naked. He didn't look too steady up there either. The top of the shell was pretty broad, but it *did* have a pronounced pitch, and human fingers couldn't get into the cracks between the plates nearly as well as pterodactyl claws. Tom began to drift downward. "It would serve you right if I did a loop and flipped you into the lake."

"I'd just change again and fly off," Kid Dinosaur said. He shivered. "It *is* cold. I hadn't noticed." In his human form, New York's only brat ace was an ungainly thirteen-year-old with a small birthmark on his forehead. He was gawky and uncoordinated, with shaggy hair that fell across his eyes. The merciless gaze of the cameras showed the blackheads on his nose in excruciating detail. He had a big pimple in the cleft of his chin. And he was uncircumcised, Tom noted.

"Where the hell are your clothes?" Tom asked. "If I set

you down in the park, you'll get busted for indecent exposure."

"They wouldn't dare," Kid Dinosaur said with the cocksure certainty of the adolescent. "What's going on? Are you off on a case? I could help."

"You read too many funny books," Tom told him. "I heard about the last time you helped someone."

"Aw, they sewed his hand back on, and Tacky says it's going to be just fine. How was I supposed to know that the guy was an undercover cop? I wouldn't of bit him if I'd known."

It wasn't the least bit funny, but Tom smiled. Kid Dinosaur reminded him of himself. He'd read a lot of funny books too. "Kid," he said, "you're not always running around naked turning into dinosaurs, right? You've got another life?"

"I'm not gonna tell you my secret identity," Kid Dinosaur said quickly.

"Scared I'd tell your parents?" Tom asked.

The boy's face reddened. The rest of him was bluer than ever. "I'm not scared of anything, you old fart," he said.

"You ought to be," Tom said. "Like me, for starts. Yeah, I know, you can turn into a three-foot-tall tyrannosaur and break your teeth on my armor. All I can do is shatter every bone in your body in twelve or thirteen places. Or reach inside you and squeeze your heart to mush."

"You wouldn't do that."

"No," Tom admitted, "but there are people who will. You're getting in way over your head, you dumb little fuck. Hell, I don't care what kind of toy dinosaur you turn into, a *bullet* can still kill you."

Kid Dinosaur looked sullen. "Fuck you," he said. The emphatic way he said it made it clear that he didn't often use language like that at home.

This wasn't going well, Tom thought. "Look," he said in a conciliatory tone, "I just wanted to tell you some things I learned the hard way. You don't want to get too caught up. It's great that you're Kid Dinosaur, but you're also, uh, whoever you are. Don't forget that. What grade are you in?"

The kid groaned. "What is it with all you guys? If you're going to start in about algebra, forget it!"

"Algebra?" Tom said, puzzled. "I didn't say a thing about algebra. Your classes are important, but that's not all there is either. Make friends, damn it, go on dates, make sure you go to your senior prom. Just being able to turn into a bron-

tosaurus the size of a Doberman isn't going to win you any
prizes in life, you understand?"

They landed with a soft thump on the snow-covered grass
of the sheep meadow. Nearby, a hot-pretzel vendor in earmuffs
and overcoat was staring in astonishment at the armored shell
and the shivering boy atop it. "Did you hear what I said?" Tom
asked.

"Yeah. You sound just like my dad. You boring old farts
think you know everything." His high, nervous laugh turned
into a long reptilian hiss as bones and muscles shifted and
flowed, and his soft skin thickened and grew scaly. Very
daintily, the little triceratops deposited a proto-coprolite on
top of the shell, skittered down its side, and waddled off across
the meadow with its horns jutting arrogantly into the air.

That was the best year in Thomas Tudbury's life.

But not for the Great and Powerful Turtle.

In the comic books, the heroes never seemed to need
sleep. Things weren't so simple in real life. With a full-time
nine-to-five job to keep him busy, Tom had done nearly all his
Turtling on nights and weekends anyway, and now Barbara was
taking up that slack. As his social life took up more of his time,
his career as an ace suffered proportionately, and the iron shell
was seen less and less frequently over the streets of Manhattan.

Finally, a day dawned when Thomas Tudbury realized
with something of a shock that almost three and a half months
had passed since he'd last gone out to the junkyard and his
shells. The trigger for the realization was a small story on page
twenty-four of the *Times*, with a headline that read, TURTLE
MISSING, FEARED DEAD. The story mentioned that dozens of
calls for the Turtle had gone unanswered in the past few
months (he hadn't turned on his ham radio since God knows
when), and that Dr. Tachyon had been especially worried, to
the extent that he'd been running classified ads in the papers
and offering a small reward for the news of any Turtle sightings
(Tom never read the classifieds, and these days he hardly read
the papers).

He ought to get into his shell and pay a call on the clinic,
he thought when he read that. But there wasn't time. He'd
promised to help Barbara take her class on a field trip up to
Bear Mountain, and they were due to leave in two hours.

Instead he went out to a public phone booth, and called the clinic.

"Who is this?" Tachyon demanded irritably when Tom finally got him on the line. "We're quite busy here, and I can't spare a lot of time for people who refuse to give their names."

"This is the Turtle," Tom said. "I wanted to let you know that I'm all right."

There was a moment of silence. "You don't sound like the Turtle," Tachyon said.

"The sound system in the shell is designed to disguise my voice. Of course I don't sound like the Turtle. But I am the Turtle."

"You'll have to convince me of that."

Tom sighed. "God, you're a pain. But I should have expected it. You whined at me for ten years just because your arm got broken, and it was your own goddamn fault. You didn't tell me you were going to hide under a forklift, damn it. I'm not telepathic like some people I could name."

"I didn't tell you to knock over half the warehouse either," Tachyon said. "You're just lucky I wasn't crushed to death. A man with powers like yours ought to . . ." He paused. "You *are* the Turtle."

"Ahem," said Tom.

"What have you been doing?"

"Being happy. Don't worry, I'll be back now and again. Not as often as before, though. I'm pretty busy. I think I'm going to get married. As soon as I work up the courage to ask her."

"Congratulations," Tachyon said. He sounded pleased. "Who is the lucky bride?"

"Ah, that would be telling. You know her, though. One of your patients from way, way back. She had a little bout with the wild card when she was two. Nothing serious. She's completely normal today. I'd invite you to the wedding, Tacky, but that would kind of give away the game, wouldn't it? Maybe we'll name one of the kids after you."

There was a long, awkward moment of silence. "Turtle," the alien finally said, in a voice somehow gone flat, "we need to talk. Can you find the time to come over to the clinic? I'll arrange my schedule to suit."

"I'm awfully busy," Tom said.

"It's important," Tachyon insisted.

"Well, all right. Late at night, then. Not tonight, I'll be too tired. Tomorrow, say, after Johnny Carson."

"Agreed," said Tachyon. "I'll meet you on the roof."

By now the wedding was safely over. He could thank Kid Dinosaur for that much, at least; the little fuck distracted him through the worst part.

His shell drifted slowly up Broadway toward Times Square, but his mind was across New York Bay at the Top Hat. The last time he'd been to the Top Hat had been for the reception after Joey and Gina had gotten married. He'd been the best man. That had been a good night. He could remember it all, everything from the flocked wallpaper down to the taste of kielbasa and the sound of the band.

Barbara would be wearing her grandmother's wedding gown. She'd shown it to him once, a decade ago. Even now, he could close his eyes and see the expression on her face when she brushed her hand over all that antique lace.

Unbidden, her image filled his mind. Barbara in the gown, her blond hair behind the veil, her face uplifted. "I do."

And next to her, Steve Bruder. Tall, dark, very fit. If anything, the sonofabitch was better-looking now than he had been in high school. He was a raquetball fanatic, Tom knew. With a boyish smile and a fashionable Tom Selleck mustache. He'd look wonderful in his tux. Together, they'd make a dynamite couple.

And their child would be a stunner.

He should go. So what if he hadn't replied to the invitation, they'd still let him in. Dump the shell in the junkyard, dump the shell in the fucking *river* for all it mattered, pick up his car, and he could be there in no time at all. Dance with the bride, and smile at her, and wish her happiness, all the happiness in the world. And shake the hand of the lucky groom. Shake Bruder's hand. Yeah.

Bruder had a great handshake. He was in real estate now, in Weehawken and Hoboken mostly; he'd bought early and been perfectly positioned when all the yuppies in Manhattan woke up one morning and discovered that New Jersey was just across the Hudson. Making a bloody fortune, going to be a millionaire by forty-five. He'd told Tom himself, that hideous night when Barbara had gotten them both to dinner. Handsome and self-assured, with that jaunty boyish grin, and going to be a millionaire too, but his life wasn't all roses, his big-screen TV was giving him a little trouble and maybe Tom could take a look at it, eh? For old times' sake.

In grade school, they'd shaken hands once and Steve had squeezed so hard that Tom had gone to his knees, crying, unable to break loose. Even now, Steve Bruder's sophisticated grown-up handshake was still a lot firmer than it needed to be. He liked to see the other guy wince.

I'd like the Turtle to shake his fucking hand, Tom thought savagely. Grab the hand with his mind and give a little friendly squeeze, until the hand began to crimp and twist, until that smooth tanned skin ripped and the fingers snapped like broken red chopsticks, bones sticking through the flesh. The Turtle could pump his fucking arm up and down until it came right out of its socket, and then he could pull off the fingers one by one. *She loves me she loves me not she loves me she loves me not she loves ME.*

Tom's throat was dry, and he felt sick and dizzy. He opened the refrigerator and got out a beer. It tasted good. The shell was moving above the sleaze of Times Square. His eyes went restlessly from screen to screen. Peep shows and porn theaters, adult bookstores, live sex on stage, neon signs that screamed GIRLS GIRLS NAKED GIRLS and HOTTEST SHOW IN TOWN and NUDE TEENAGE MODELS, male hustlers in denim and cowboy hats, pimps in long mink coats with razors in their pockets, hard-faced hookers in fishnet stockings and slit leather skirts. He could pick up a whore, Tom thought suddenly. Literally. Yank her twenty feet off the ground, make her show him what she was selling, make her take it off right there in the center of Times Square, give the fucking tourists a real show. Or take it off *for* her, rip it off piece by piece and let it float to the ground. He could do that, yeah. Let Bruder have his wedding night with Barbara, the Turtle could have a wedding night of his own.

He swallowed another slug of beer.

Or maybe he should just clean out this filth. Everyone was always bitching about what a pesthole Times Square had become, but no one ever did anything about it. Fuck it, he'd do it for them. He'd show them how to clean out a bad neighborhood, if that's what they wanted. Pull down those marquees one by one, herd the fucking whores and pimps and hustlers into the river, drive a few pimpmobiles through the windows of those third-floor photographic studios with the nude teenage models, rip up the goddamned sidewalks if he'd

a mind to. It was about time somebody did it. Look at this
place, just *look* at it, and barely spitting distance from Port
Authority, so it was the first thing a kid would see after getting
off the bus.

Tom drained the beer. He chucked the can onto the floor,
swiveled, and searched for another, but there was nothing left
in his six-pack but the plastic holder. "Fuck it," he said.
Suddenly he was furious. He turned on his microphone,
twisted the volume all the way. "FUCK IT," he shouted, and
the voice of the Turtle thundered over 42nd Street, distorted
and amplified into a red roar. People stopped dead on the
sidewalk, and eyes craned up at him. Tom smiled. He had
their attention, it seemed. "FUCK IT ALL," he said. "FUCK
EVERY ONE OF YOU."

He paused, and was about to expand on that topic, when a
police dispatcher's voice, crackling over his monitor, caught his
attention. She was repeating the code for an officer in trouble,
repeating it over and over again.

Tom left them gaping, while he listened carefully for
details. Part of him felt sorry for the poor asshole who was
about to get his head handed to him.

His shell rose straight up, high above the streets and
buildings, and shot south toward the Village.

"I figured you were just slow," Barbara said, when she had
composed herself. "It always took you time to work up to
anything. I don't understand, Tom."

He couldn't look into her eyes. He looked around her
living room, his hands in his pockets. Over her desk she'd
hung her diploma and teaching certificate. Around them were
arrayed the photographs: pictures of Barbara grimacing as she
changed the diaper on her four-month-old niece, pictures of
Barbara and her three sisters, pictures of Barbara showing her
class how to cut black witches and orange pumpkins out of
posterboard for Halloween, supervising six dancing presidents
for a school play, loading a projector to run cartoons. And
reading a story. That was his favorite picture. Barbara with a
tiny little black girl on her lap and another dozen kids ranged
all around her, staring at her with rapt faces while she read
aloud from *The Wind in the Willows*. Tom had taken that
photograph himself.

"There's nothing to understand," he'd snapped when he

looked away from the pictures. "It's over, that's all. Let's break it off clean, okay?"

"Is there someone else?" she said.

It might have been kinder to lie to her, but he was a poor liar. "No," he said.

"Then, why?"

She was baffled and hurt, but her face had never been lovelier, Tom thought. He couldn't face her. "It's just best," he said, turning to look out her window. "We don't want the same things, Barbara. You want to get married, right? Not me. Forget it, no way. You're terrific, it's not you, it's . . . fuck it, it just isn't working. Kids; every time I turn around there's a mob of kids. How many does your sister have, three? Four? I'm tired of pretending. I *hate* kids." His voice went up. "I *despise* kids, you understand?"

"You can't mean that, Tommy. I've seen you with the kids in my class. You took them to your house and showed them you comic collection. You helped Jenny build that model of Jetboy's plane. You like kids."

Tom laughed. "Oh, fuck it, how naive can you get? I was just trying to impress you. I wanted to get into your pants. I don't—" His voice broke. "Damn it," he said. "If I like kids so fucking much, then how come I had a vasectomy? How come, huh? Tell me that?"

When he turned, her face was as red as if he had hit her.

The playground was surrounded by police cruisers, six of them, flashers strobing red and blue in the gathering dusk. Cops were crouched behind the cars with guns drawn. Beyond the high chain-link fence, two dark shapes sprawled under the basketball net, and a third was draped over one of the barrels. Someone was whimpering in pain.

Tom spotted a detective he knew, holding the collar of a skinny young joker whose face was as soft and white as tapioca pudding, shaking him so hard his jowls bounced. The boy wore Demon Prince colors, Tom saw on a close-up shot. He drifted lower. "HEADS UP," he boomed. "WHAT'S THE PROBLEM?"

They told him.

A gang dispute, that was all. Penny-ante shit. Some nat juvies operating around the fringes of Jokertown had trespassed onto Demon Prince turf. The Demon Princes had gotten together fifteen or twenty members and gone into the

East Village to teach the interlopers some respect for territo-
rial boundaries. It had gone down in the playground. Knives,
chains, a few guns. Nasty.

And then it had gotten weird.

The nats *had* something, tapioca-face screamed.

They'd come out of it as friends. He was proud of that. It
was hardest when their wounds were still raw, and for the first
eleven months they avoided each other. But Bayonne was a
small town in its own way, and they knew too many people in
common, and it was not something that could go on forever.

Maybe that was the hardest eleven months Tom Tudbury
ever lived through. Maybe.

One night she called him out of the blue. He was glad. He
had missed her desperately, but he knew he could never call
her after what had happened between them. "I need to talk,"
she'd said. She sounded as though she'd had a few beers. "You
were my friend, Tom. Besides everything else, you were my
friend, right? I need a friend tonight, okay? Can you come
over?"

He bought a six-pack and went over. Her youngest sister
had been killed that afternoon in a motorcycle accident. There
was nothing to be done or said, but Tom did and said all the
usual useless things, and he was there for her, and he let her
talk until the dawn broke, and afterward he put her to bed. He
slept on the couch.

He woke in late afternoon, with Barbara standing over
him, wearing a terry-cloth robe, red-eyed from crying. "Thank
you," she said. She sat down at the foot of the couch and took
his hand and held it for a long time in silence. "I want you in
my life," she said finally, with difficulty. "I don't want us to lose
each other again. Friends?"

"Friends," Tom said. He wanted to pull her down on top
of him and smother her with kisses. Instead he squeezed her
hand. "No matter what, Barbara. Always. Okay?"

Barbara smiled. He faked a yawn, and buried his face in a
pillow, to keep her from seeing the look in his eyes.

"STAY DOWN," the Turtle warned the policemen. They
didn't need to be told twice. The kid was hiding inside one of
the cement barrels, and they'd seen what happened to the cop
who had tried to go into the playground after him. Gone, gone

as if he'd never existed, blinked out, engulfed in a sudden blackness and somehow . . . erased.

"We were cutting the fuckers," the Demon Prince said, "teaching 'em good, teaching them the price if they come bothering Jokertown, fuckin' nat wimps, we had 'em dead, and then this spic come at us with a motherfuckin' *bowling ball*, and we just laughed at the fucker, what's he gonna do, try to *bowl* us down, stupid little prick, and then he held out the ball at Waxy and it *grew*, man, like it was *alive*. Some kind of black shit came out of it, real fast, black light or a big dark hand or something, I don't know, only it moved real fast, and Waxy was just gone." His voice got shrill. "He was *gone*, man, he just wasn't there no more. And the nat fucker did the same to Razor and the Ghoul. That was when Heehaw shot him and he almost dropped the ball, got 'im in the shoulder I think, but then he did it to Heehaw. You can't fight nothin' like that. Even that motherfuckin' cop couldn't do shit."

The shell slid above the chain-link fence that surrounded the playground, silent and slow.

"We have something," Barbara said. "We have something special." Her finger traced patterns in the condensation on the outside of her glass. She looked up at him, her blue eyes bold and frank, as if she were challenging him. "He's asked me to marry him, Tom."

"What did you say?" Tom asked her, trying to keep his voice calm and steady.

"I said I'd think about it," Barbara said. "That's why I wanted to get together. I wanted to talk to you first."

Tom signaled for another beer. "It's your decision," he said. "I wish you'd let me meet this guy, but from everything you've told me he sounds pretty good."

"He's divorced," she said.

"So's half the world," Tom said, as his beer arrived.

"Everyone but you and me," Barbara said, smiling.

"Yeah." He frowned down at the head of his beer and sighed uncomfortably. "Does the mystery beau have kids?"

"Two. His ex has custody. I've met them, though. They like me."

"Goes without saying," Tom said.

"He wants to have more. With me."

Tom looked her in the eye. "Do you love him?"

Barbara met his gaze calmly. "I guess. Sometimes I'm not

so sure these days. Maybe I'm not as romantic as I used to be."
She shrugged. "Sometimes I wonder what my life would have
been like if things had worked out differently for you and me.
We could be celebrating our tenth anniversary."

"Or maybe the ninth anniversary of our acrimonious
divorce," Tom said. He reached across the table and took
Barbara's hand. "Things haven't turned out so badly, have
they? It would never have worked the other way."

"The roads not chosen," she said wistfully. "I've had too
many might-have-beens in my life, Tom, too many regrets for
things left undone and choices not made. My biological clock is
ticking. If I wait any longer, I'll wait forever."

"I just wish you'd known this guy longer," Tom said.

"Oh, I've known him a long time," she said, tearing a
corner off her cocktail napkin.

Tom was confused. "I thought you said you met him last
month at a party."

"Yes. But we knew each other before. In high school."
She looked at his face again. "That's why I didn't tell you his
name. You would have been upset, and at first I didn't know it
would lead anywhere."

Tom didn't have to be told. He and Barbara had been
good friends for more than a decade. He looked into the blue
depths of her eyes, and he knew. "Steve Bruder," he said
numbly.

He hovered above the playground and floated the fallen
warriors over the fence, one by one, to the police waiting
outside. The two from the basketball court were dead meat. It
would take a lot of scrubbing to wash the bloodstains from the
cement. The boy draped over the barrel turned out to be a
girl. She wimpered in pain when he lifted her with his teke,
and from the way she was clutching herself it looked like her
guts had been sliced open. He hoped they could do something
for her.

All three were nats. The battleground was free of fallen
jokers. Either the Demon Princes had really been kicking ass,
or their own dead were somewhere else. Or both.

He touched a control on the arm of his chair, and all his
floodlights came on, bathing the playground in a white-hot
brilliance. "IT'S OVER," he said, and his loudspeakers roared
the words into the twilight. Over the years, he'd learned that

sheer volume scared the hell out of punks. "COME ON OUT, KID. THIS IS THE TURTLE."

"Go away," a hoarse thin voice screamed back at him from inside the cement barrel. "I'll disintegrate you, you joker fuckface. I got the thing here with me."

All day Tom had been looking for someone to hurt; a monster to pull apart, a killer to pound on, a target for his rage, a sponge to soak up his pain. Now the moment was finally at hand, and he found he had no more anger in him. He was tired. He wanted to go home. Behind his bravado, the boy in the barrel was obviously young and scared. "YOU'RE REAL TOUGH," Tom said. "YOU WANT TO PLAY THE SHELL GAME? GREAT." He concentrated on the barrel to the left of the boy's cover, held it in his mind, squeezed. It collapsed as suddenly as if a wrecking ball had smashed into it, shards and dust flying everywhere when the cement shattered. "NOT IN THAT ONE. GEE." He did the same thing to the barrel on the other side of the kid. "NOT IN THAT ONE EITHER. GUESS I'LL TRY THE MIDDLE ONE."

The boy exited in such haste that he whacked his head on the overhang of the barrel as he stood up. The impact dazed him momentarily. The bowling ball he'd been clutching with both hands was suddenly whisked from his grip. It shot straight up. The boy screamed obscenities through shiny steel-capped teeth. He made a desperate leap for his weapon, but all he managed to do was brush the tips of his fingers against its underside. Then he came down hard, scraping his hands and knees along the concrete.

By then the cops were already moving in. Tom watched as they surrounded him, yanked him to his feet, and read him his rights. He was nineteen, maybe younger, wearing gang colors and a studded dog collar, shaggy black hair teased out in spikes. They asked him where all the people were, and he snarled curses at them and screamed that he didn't know.

As they hustled him toward the waiting cruisers, Tom opened an armored portal and floated the bowling ball inside his shell for a closer look, shivering in the blast of cold air that came with it. It was a weird thing. Too light to be a bowling ball, he thought when he hefted it; four pounds, maybe five. No holes either. When he ran his hand over it, his fingers tingled, and colors glimmered briefly on its surface, like the rainbows on an oil slick. It made him uneasy. Maybe Tachyon would know what to make of it. He set it aside.

Darkness was falling over the city. Tom pushed his shell higher and higher, until he floated up above even the distant tower of the Empire State Building. He stayed there for a long time, watching the lights go on all across the city, transforming Manhattan into an electric fairyland.

From this high up, on a clear cold night like this, he could even see the lights of Jersey over across the frigid black water. One of those dots was the Top Hat Lounge, he knew.

He shouldn't just float here, he thought. He ought to take the bowling ball to the clinic; that was the next order of business. He didn't move. He'd do it tomorrow, he thought. Tachyon wasn't going anywhere, and neither was the bowling ball. Somehow Tom could not bring himself to face Tachyon tonight. Not tonight of all nights.

In those days, his shell was a lot more primitive. No telephoto lenses, no zooms, no infrared cameras. Just a ring of hot spotlights, so bright that they left Tachyon squinting. But he needed them. It was dark on the roof on the clinic, where the shell had come to rest.

The photographs that Tachyon held up were not the sort that Tom wanted to see in more detail anyway. He sat in darkness, staring into his screens, saying nothing, as Tachyon shuffled through them one by one. They had all been taken in the clinic's maternity ward. One or two of the children had lived long enough to be moved to the nursery.

Finally he found his voice. "Their mothers are *jokers*," he said, his voice emphatic with false conviction. "Bar—She's normal, I tell you. A nat. She got it when she was *two*, damn it; it's like it never happened."

"It happened," Tachyon said. "She may appear normal, but the virus is still there. Latent. Most likely, it will never manifest, and genetically it's a recessive, but when you and she have—"

"I know a lot of people think I'm a joker," Tom interrupted, "but I'm not, believe me, I'm an ace. I'm an *ace*, damn it! So what if the kid carries the wild card gene, so he'll have major-league teke. He'll be an ace, like me."

"No," Tachyon said. He slid the photographs back into the file folder, his eyes averted from the cameras. Deliberately? "I'm sorry, my friend. The odds against that are astronomical."

"*Cyclone*," Tom had said, on the edge of hysteria. Cyclone

was a West-Coast ace whose daughter had inherited his command of the winds.

"No," said Tachyon. "Mistral is a special case. We're almost certain now that her father somehow subconsciously manipulated her germ plasm while she was still in the womb. On Takis . . . well, the process is not unknown to us, but it rarely succeeds. You're the most powerful telekineticist I've ever seen, but something like that demands a fine control that is orders of magnitude beyond you, not to mention centuries of experience in microsurgery and gene splicing. And even if you had all of that, you'd probably fail. Cyclone had no idea what he was doing on any conscious level, and was freakishly lucky on top of it." The Takisian shook his head. "Your case is entirely different. All that's guaranteed is that you'll be drawing a wild card, and the odds are just the same as if—"

"I know the odds," Tom said hoarsely. Of every hundred humans dealt the wild card, only one developed ace powers. There were ten hideously malformed jokers for every ace, and ten black-queen deaths for every joker.

In his mind's eyes, he saw Barbara sitting up in bed, the sheet tangled about her waist, her blond hair cascading softly around her shoulders, her face solemn and sweet as their child suckled at her breast. And then the infant looked up, and he saw its teeth and bulging eyes and monstrous, twisted features; and when it hissed at him, Barbara cried out in pain as the milk and blood flowed freely from her raw, torn nipple.

"I'm sorry," Dr. Tachyon repeated numbly.

It was past midnight before Tom returned to his empty house on First Street.

He shrugged out of his jacket, sat down on the couch, and stared out the window at the Kill and the lights of Staten Island. A freezing rain had begun. The droplets pinged against his windows with a sharp, crystalline sound, like forks tinging off empty wineglasses when the wedding guests want the newlyweds to kiss. Tom sat in the dark for a long time.

Finally, he turned on a lamp and picked up the telephone. He punched six numbers, and couldn't bring himself to hit the seventh. Like a high-school kid terrified of asking a pretty girl for a date, he thought, smiling grimly. He pressed the button down firmly, and listened to the ring.

"Top Hat," a gruff voice said.

"I'd like to speak to Barbara Casko," Tom said.

"You mean the new Missus Bruder," the voice replied. Tom took a long breath. "Yes," he said.

"Hey, the newlyweds left hours ago. Off for their wedding night." The man was obviously drunk. "Going to Paris for the honeymoon."

"Yeah," Tom said. "Is her father still there?"

"I'll look and see."

There was a long silence before the phone was picked up again. "This is Stanley Casko. Who am I speaking to?"

"Tom Tudbury. I'm sorry I couldn't attend, Mr. Casko. I was, uh, occupied."

"Yes, Tom. Are you all right?"

"Fine. Couldn't be better. I just wanted . . ."

"Yes?"

He swallowed. "Just tell her to be happy, okay? That's all. Just tell her I want her to be happy." He set the phone back in its cradle.

Outside in the night, a big freighter was going down the Kill. It was too dark to see what flag it flew. Tom turned out the lights and watched it pass him by.

JUBE: FIVE

The trace was unmistakable.

Jube sat at his console as the readings crawled across his holocube, his hearts thundering away with fear and hope.

He had spent most of his first four months on Earth in darkened movie theaters, sitting through the same films a dozen times, reinforcing his English and broadening his grasp of human cultural nuances as reflected in their fiction. He'd learned to love their movies, especially westerns, and his favorite part had always been when the cavalry came thundering over the hill, all its banners flying.

The Network flew no banners; still, Jube thought he could hear the faint sound of bugles and the pounding of hoofbeats in those spiderly twists of light within his holocube.

Tachyons! Bugles and tachyons!

His observation satellites had detected a wash of tachyons, and that could mean only one thing: a starship in near-Earth orbit. Deliverance was at hand.

Now the satellites swept the skies for the source. It was not the Swarm Mother, Jhubben knew that. The Mother crept between the stars at speeds slower than light; time was nothing to her. Only the civilized races used tachyon-drive starships.

If Ekkedme had gotten off a transmission before the singleship was smashed from the skies . . . if the Master Trader had decided to check on human progress earlier than planned . . . if the Mother had somehow been detected by some new technology undreamed of when Jhubben began his assignment on Earth . . . if, if, if . . . then it might well be the *Opportunity* up there, the Network returned to deliver this world, with only the means and price yet to be determined. It would not be easy even then, but of the ultimate result he had no doubt. Jube smiled as his satellites probed and his computers analyzed.

Then the holocube turned violet, and his smile died. He made a low gurgly sound deep in the back of his throat.

The sophisticated sensors in his satellites stripped away the screens that cloaked the starship from human instrumentation and displayed its image within the ominous violet of the cube. It revolved slowly, etched in lines of red and white light like some terrible construct of fire and ice. The readouts flashed below the image: dimensions, tachyon output, course. But everything Jube needed to know was written on the lines of the ship: written in every twisted spire, proclaimed by every fanciful excrescence, trumpeted by every baroque whorl and projection, shouted in that panoply of unnecessary lights.

It looked like the results of a high-speed collision between a Christmas ornament and a prickly pear. Only the Takisians had such rococo aesthetics.

Jube lurched to his feet. *Takisians!* Had Dr. Tachyon summoned them? He found that hard to believe, after all the years the doctor had spent in exile. What did it *mean?* Had Takis been monitoring Earth all this time, observing the wild card experiment even as the Network had? If so, why had Jhubben found no trace of them until now, and how had they managed to conceal themselves from Ekkedme? Would they destroy the Swarm Mother? *Could* they destroy the Mother? The *Opportunity* was roughly the size of Manhattan Island, and carried tens of thousands of specialists representing countless species, cultures, castes, and vocations—merchants and pleasurers, scientists and priests, technicians, artists, warriors, envoys. The Takisian craft was a tiny thing; it couldn't possibly hold more than fifty sentients, perhaps only half that number. Unless Takisian military technology had progressed astronomically in the last forty years, what could that little thing hope to do, alone, against the devourer of worlds? And would the Takisians even *care* about the lives of their experimental animals?

As Jhubben stared at the outlines of the ship with mounting rage and confusion, his phone rang.

For an instant he thought insanely that somehow the Takisians had found him out, that they knew he was looking at them and had rung him up to castigate him. But that was ridiculous. He slammed a thumb into the console, and the holocube went dark as Jube thumped into the living room. He had to detour around the tortured geometries of the half-built tachyon transmitter that dominated the center of the room like some massive piece of avant-garde sculpture. If the thing didn't work when he powered it up, Jube planned to title it "Joker Lust" and sell it to some gallery in Soho. Even half-assembled, its angles were curiously deceptive, and he was always bumping into it. This time he dodged around it neatly and took the phone from Mickey's hand. "Hello," he said, trying to sound his normal jovial self.

"Jubal, this is Chrysalis." It was her voice, but he had never heard her sound quite like this. She had never called him at home before, either.

"What's wrong?" he asked her. He'd asked her to procure another batch of microchips last week, and the edge in her voice made him afraid her agent had been apprehended.

"Jay Ackroyd just phoned. He hasn't been able to report until now. He found out a few things about the people who hired Darlingfoot."

"But that's good. Has he located the bowling ball?"

"No. And it's not as good as you think. I know this sounds insane, but Jay says these people were convinced that body was extraterrestrial in origin. It appears they hoped to use the corpse in some kind of disgusting ritual, to gain power over that alien monster out there."

"The Swarm Mother," Jube said in astonishment.

"Yes," Chrysalis said crisply. "Jay says they're tied in somehow. He thinks they worship that thing. Look, we shouldn't be talking about this over the phone."

"Why not?" Jube asked.

"Because these people are *dangerous*," Chrysalis said. "Jay is coming to the Palace tonight to give me a full report. Be there. I'm folding my cards on this one, Jubal. You can deal with Jay directly from now on. But if you'd like, I'll ask Fortunato to drop by. I think he'd be interested in what Jay has turned up."

"*Fortunato!*" Jube was horrified. He knew Fortunato mostly by reputation. The tall pimp with the almond-shaped eyes and bulging forehead was a familiar sight at the Crystal Palace, but Jube had always made it a point to avoid him. Telepaths made him nervous. Dr. Tachyon never went into a mind without good reason, but Fortunato was another matter. Who knows how and why he might use his powers, or what he might do if he found out what Jube the Walrus *really* was?

"No," he said hurriedly, "no, absolutely not. This has nothing to do with Fortunato!"

"He knows more about these Masons than anyone else in the city," Chrysalis said. She sighed. "Well, you're paying for this funeral, so I suppose you get to pick the casket. I won't say a word. We'll talk after closing."

"After closing," Jube repeated. She hung up before he could think to ask her what she had meant about Masons. Jube knew about the Masons, of course. He'd done a study of human fraternal organizations a decade ago, comparing the Shriners, Knights of Columbus, Odd Fellows, and Freemasons with each other and with the bonding-brotherhoods of the Thdentien moons. Reginald was a Mason, Jube seemed to recall, and Denton had tried to join the Elks, but they'd turned him down because of his antlers. What did the Masons have to do with anything?

That day Jube was too uneasy to joke. Between Swarm Mothers, Takisian warships, and Masons, he hardly knew who to be afraid of. Even if the cavalry *did* come charging over the hill, Jube thought, would they be able to recognize the Indians? He glanced up at the sky and shook his head.

When he locked up for the night he made his deliveries to the Funhouse and the Chaos Club, then decided to cut short his swing through Jokertown and head over to the Crystal Palace as soon as possible. But first he had to make one final stop, at the precinct house.

The desk sergeant took a *Daily News* and flipped to the sports page, while Jube left a *Times* and a *Jokertown Cry* for Captain Black. He was turning to leave when the plainclothesman saw him. "Hey, fat boy," the man called out. "You got an *Informer*?" He had been slouching on the bench along the tiled wall, almost as if he'd been waiting for someone. Jube knew him by sight: a scruffy, nondescript sort with an unpleasant smile. He'd never bothered to tell Jube his name, but he did show up at the newsstand once in a while to help himself to a tabloid. Sometimes he even paid.

But not tonight. "Thanks," he said, as he accepted the copy of the *National Informer* that Jube offered him. DID TAKISIANS INVENT HERPES? the banner screamed. It gave Jube a bad turn. Underneath, another story asked if Sean was about to jilt Madonna for Peregrine. The plainclothesman didn't even glance at the headlines. He was staring at Jube oddly.

The corner of his mouth twitched in a quirky little smile. "You're just an ugly joker-boy, aren't you?" the cop asked.

Jube gave an ingratiating, tusky grin. "What, me ugly? Hell, I got bigger tits than Miss October!"

"I've wasted enough time without listening to your asshole jokes," the plainclothesman snapped. "But what did I expect? You're not too bright, are you?"

Bright enough to fool your kind for thirty-four years, Jube thought, but he didn't say it. "Well, you know how many jokers it takes to turn on a light bulb," he said.

"Haul your greasy joker ass out of here," the man said.

Jube waddled to the door. At the top of the stairs, he turned back and yelled, "That paper's on me!" before taking off for the Crystal Palace.

He was early tonight, and the Palace was still crowded. Jube took a stool all the way at the end of the bar, where he could put his back right up against the wall and see the whole room. It was Sascha's night off, and Lupo was tending bar. "What'll it be, Walrus?" he asked, long red tongue lolling from one corner of his mouth.

"Piña colada," Jube said. "Double rum."

Lupo nodded and went off to mix it. Jube looked around carefully. He had an uneasy feeling, as if he were being watched. But who? The taproom was full of strangers, and Chrysalis was nowhere in sight. Three stools away, a big man in a lion mask was lighting a cigarette for a young girl whose low-cut evening gown displayed ample cleavage from three full breasts. Further down the bar a huddled shape in a gray shroud stared into his drink. A slender, vivacious green woman made eye contact when Jube glanced at her, and slid the tip of a pink tongue provocatively across her lower lip (at least it might have been provocative to a human male), but she was obviously a hooker, and he ignored her. Elsewhere in the room, he saw Yin-Yang, whose two heads were having a spirited argument, and Old Mister Cricket too. The Floater had passed out and was drifting about near the ceiling again. But there were so many faces and masks Jube did not recognize. Any one of them might be Jay Ackroyd. Chrysalis had never said what the man looked like, only that he was an ace. He might even be the man in lion mask, who—Jube noted with a glance—had now slipped an arm around the three-breasted girl and was brushing his fingertips lightly along the top of the breast on the right.

Lupo mopped the bar, spun down a coaster, and put the piña colada on top of it. Jube had just taken his first sip when a stranger slid onto the barstool beside him. "Are you selling those newspapers?"

"Sure am."

"Good." The voice was muffled by his mask, a bone-white death's head. He wore a black cowled cape over a threadbare suit that did very little for his skinny, hollow-chested body. "I'll take a *Cry*, then."

Jube thought there was something unpleasant about his eyes. He looked away, found a copy of the *Cry*, handed it over. The cowled man gave him a coin. "What's this?" Jube said.

"A penny," the man replied.

The penny was larger than it should have been, and a vivid red against Jube's blue-black palm. He'd never seen anything like it. "I don't know if—"

"Never mind," the man interrupted. He took the penny out of Jube's hand, and gave him a Susan B. Anthony dollar instead. "Where's my change, Walrus?" he demanded. Jube gave him back three quarters. "You shortchanged me," the man said nastily when he'd pocketed the coins.

"I did not," Jube told him with indignation.

"Look me in the eye and say that, you two-bit jerk."

Behind the skull-faced man, the door opened and Troll ducked through into the taproom, followed by a short red-haired man in a lime-green suit. "*Tachyon*," Jube said with apprehension, suddenly reminded of the Takisian warship up in orbit.

Jube's unpleasant companion twisted his head around so sharply that his cowl flopped down, revealing thin brown hair and a bad case of dandruff. He jerked to his feet, hesitated, and rushed for the door as soon as Tachyon and Troll had moved toward the back. "Hey!" Jube called after him, "hey, mister, your paper!" He'd left the *Cry* on the bar. The man went out so quickly he almost caught the end of his long black cape in the door. Jube shrugged and went back to his piña colada.

Several hours and a dozen drinks later, Chrysalis had still not made an appearance, nor had Jube spotted anyone who looked like he imagined this Popinjay might look. When Lupo announced last call, Jube beckoned him over. "Where is she?" he asked.

"Chrysalis?" Lupo asked. Deep red eyes sparkled on either side of his long, hairy snout. "Is she expecting you?"

Jube nodded. "Got stuff to tell her."

"Okay," Lupo said. "In the red room, third booth from the left. She's with a friend." He grinned. "Pretend you don't see him, if you hear what I'm saying."

"Whatever she wants." Jube thought the friend had to be Popinjay, but he didn't say anything. He lowered himself carefully off the stool and went to the red room, off to the right of the main taproom. Inside, it was dim and smoky. The lights were red, the thick shag carpeting was red, and the heavy velvet drapes around the booths were a deep, rich burgundy. Most booths were empty at this time of night, but he could hear a woman moaning from one that was not. He went to the third booth from the left, pulled back the drape, and stuck his head inside.

They had been talking in low, earnest tones, but now the conversation broke off abruptly. Chrysalis looked up at him. "Jubal," she said crisply. "What can I do for you?"

Jube looked at her companion, a compact sinewy white man in a black tee shirt and dark leather jacket. He wore the plainest of masks, a black hood that covered everything but his eyes. "You must be Popinjay," Jube said, before he recalled that the detective did not like to be called by that name.

"No," the masked man replied, his voice surprisingly soft. He glanced at Chrysalis. "We can resume this conversation later if you have business to transact." He slid out of the booth and walked off without another word.

"Get in," Chrysalis said. Jube sat down and pulled the drapes closed. "Whatever you have for me, I hope it's good." She sounded distinctly annoyed.

"Have for you?" Jube was confused. "What do you mean? Where's Popinjay, shouldn't he be here by now?"

She stared at him. Sheathed in transparent flesh and ghost-gray muscles, her skull reminded Jube of the unpleasant man who'd sat next to him at the bar. "I wasn't aware you knew Jay. What does he have to do with anything? Is there something about Jay that I need to know?"

"The report," Jube blurted. "He was going to tell us about these Masons who hired Devil John to steal that body from the morgue. They were dangerous, you said."

Chrysalis laughed at him, drew back the privacy curtains, and rose languidly. "Jubal, I don't know how many exotic rum drinks you've indulged in tonight, but I suspect it was a few too many. That's always a problem when Lupo is behind the bar. Sascha can tell when a customer has had enough, but not our little wolf-boy. Go home and sleep it off."

"Go *home!*" Jube said. "But what about the body, what about Devil John and these *Masons . . .*"

"If you want to join a lodge, the Odd Fellows would suit you better, I'd think," Chrysalis said in a bored tone. "Other than that, I don't have the vaguest idea what you're talking about."

The walk home was long and hot, and Jube had an uneasy feeling, as if he were being watched. He stopped and looked around furtively several times, to try and catch whoever was following him, but there was never anyone in sight.

Down in the privacy of his apartment, Jube immersed himself gratefully in his cold tub, and turned on his television. The late movie was *Thirty Minutes Over Broadway!*, but it wasn't the Howard Hawks version, it was the awful 1978 remake with Jan-Michael Vincent as Jetboy and Dudley Moore doing a comic-relief Tachyon in a hideous red wig. Jube found himself watching it anyway; mindless escape was exactly what he needed. He would worry about Chrysalis and the rest of it tomorrow.

Jetboy had just crashed the JB–1 into the blimps when the picture suddenly crackled and went black. "Hey," Jube said, stabbing at his remote control. Nothing happened.

Then a hound the size of a small horse walked out of his television set.

It was lean and terrible, its body smoke-gray and hideously emaciated, its eyes windows that opened on a charnel house. A long forked tail curved up over its back like a scorpion's sting, and twitched from side to side.

Jube recoiled so fast he splashed water all over his bedroom floor, and began shouting at the thing. The hound bared teeth like yellow daggers. Jube realized he was babbling in the Network trade tongue, and switched to English. "Get out!" he told it. "Get away!" He scrabbled over the side of the tub, splashing more water, and retreated. The remote control was still in his hand, if he could reach his sanctum—but what good would that do, against some thing that walked through walls? His flesh went hot with sudden terror.

The hound padded after him, and then stopped. Its gaze was fixed on his crotch. It seemed momentarily bemused by the forked double penis, and full set of female genitalia beneath. Jube decided that his best chance lay in a dash for the street. He edged backward.

"Fat little man," the hound called out in a voice that was pure unctuous malice. "Will you run from me? You sought me out, fool. Do you think your thick joker legs can carry you faster than Setekh the destroyer?"

Jube gaped. "Who . . ."

"I am he whose secrets you sought to know," the hound said. "Pathetic little joker, did you think we would not notice, did you think we would not care? I have taken the knowledge from the minds of your hirelings, and followed the trail back to you. And now you will die."

"*Why?*" Jube said. He had no doubt that creature could kill him, but if he must perish, he hoped at least to understand the reason.

"Because you have wasted my time," the hound said. Its mouth twisted into obscene, unnatural shapes when it spoke. "I thought to find some great enemy, and instead I find a fat little joker who makes his money selling gossip to a saloon-keeper. How much did you think the secrets of our Order would be worth? Who did you think might pay for them, Walrus? Tell me, and I will not toy with you. Lie, and your dying will last till dawn."

The hound had no idea what he was, Jhubben realized. How could it? It had learned of him from Chrysalis, from the street; it had not walked behind his false wall. Suddenly, for reasons he could not have explained, Jube knew that Setekh *must* not know. He must lead it away from his secrets. "I did not mean to pry, mighty Setekh," he said loudly. He had posed as a joker for thirty-four years, he knew how to crawl. "I beg your mercy," he said, edging backward toward the living room. "I am not your enemy," he told it. The hound padded toward him, eyes smoldering, tongue lolling from its long snout. Jube jumped for his living room, slammed the door behind him, and ran.

The hound bounded through the wall to cut him off, and Jube lost his footing as he recoiled. He went down in a heap, the hound raised one terrible paw to strike . . . and stopped as Jube cringed away from the killing blow. Its mouth twisted and ran with phantom slaver, and Jube realized it was laughing. It was staring at something behind him and laughing. He craned his head around, and saw only the tachyon transmitter.

When he looked back, the hound was gone. Instead a frail little man in a wheelchair sat staring at him. "We are an old Order," the little man said. "The secrets have passed through many mouths, and some have gone astray, and some branches have been lost and forgotten. Be glad you were not killed, brother."

"Oh, yeah," Jube said, crawling to his knees. He had no idea why he was being spared, but he was not going to argue the point. "Thank you, master. I won't bother you again."

"I will let you live, so you may live to serve us," the apparition in the wheelchair told him. "Even one as stupid and weak as you may have his uses in the great struggle to come. But say nothing of what you have learned, or you will not live to be initiated."

"I've forgotten it already," Jube said.

The man in the wheelchair seemed to find that vastly amusing. His forehead throbbed as he laughed. A moment later, he was gone. Jube got to his feet very cautiously.

Early the next morning, a joker with vivid crimson skin bought a copy of the *Daily News*, and paid for it with a shiny red penny the size of a half dollar. "I'd keep that if I were you, pal o' mine," he said, smiling. "I think it might just be your lucky coin." Then he told when and where the next meeting would be held.

RELATIVE
DIFFICULTIES

By Melinda M. Snodgrass

Dr. Tachyon bounded down the steps of the Blythe van Renssaeler Memorial Clinic, and paused to pat one of the dispirited sandstone lions that flanked the stairs. He noticed that its companion to the north still had a toupee of dirty snow adorning its crumbling head. Though he was already late for a luncheon date with Senator Hartmann at Aces High, he couldn't resist tenderly brushing away the snow. A brisk, cold wind was gusting off the East River, driving tatters of white clouds before it, and carrying the sound of horns from the bumper-to-bumper traffic on the Brooklyn Bridge.

The urgency of the horns reminded him of the passing time, and he took the final two steps in a long leap. And was brought up short by an expanse of pink. A *waistcoat*, Tach identified before his view was broken by a gladiolus thrust firmly beneath his nose. Tach looked up and up, and realized he was facing a stranger . . . and there was danger, or the potential of danger, in every stranger. Three quick steps back carried him out of range of all but a gun or some esoteric ace power, and he warily studied the apparition.

The man was *very* tall, his scrawny height exaggerated by the enormously tall purple stovepipe hat crammed down onto long, lank blond hair. A coat, also purple, hung from narrow shoulders, and set—to Tach's mind—a lovely contrast to the orange and violet paisley shirt and green trunks. The grinning scarecrow once more proferred the flower.

"Like, I'm Captain Trips, man," he offered, and stood swaying and beaming like a drunken lighthouse. Fascinated,

Tachyon stared up into pale blue eyes swimming behind lenses that looked as if they'd been knocked off the bottom of Coke bottles. Unable to construct anything coherent to say, Tach merely accepted the flower.

"That's not really my name, man," the Captain confided in a stage whisper that would have carried to the end of Carnegie Hall. "I'm an ace so I gotta have a secret identity, you know?" The Captain ran a bony hand across his mouth, smoothing the slightly stained mustache and the scraggly wisp of beard. "Oh, wow, like, I can't believe it. Dr. Tachyon, in person. I really admire you, man."

Tach, never one to pass up a compliment, was pleased, but also aware of the passing time. He jammed the flower into his coat pocket, and surged back into motion, his newfound companion falling in beside him. There was a good feeling about the man which washed off him with the faint odor of ginseng, sandalwood, and old sweat, but Tach couldn't shake the feeling that the Captain was an amiable lunatic. Digging his hand into the pockets of his midnight-blue breeches, he cast Trips a sideways glance, and decided that he had to say something. He obviously wasn't going to be rid of the man anytime soon. "So, was there any particular reason for your seeking me out?"

"Well, I think I need advice. Like, you know, it seemed you were the person to ask." The man's hands sought out the gigantic green bow tie with its yellow polka dots, and gave it a hard tug as if he found it confining. "I'm not really Captain Trips."

"Yes, I know, you said that," replied Tach, clinging to his now-fast-vanishing patience.

"I'm really Mark Meadows. *Dr.* Mark Meadows. Like, we have a lot in common, man."

"You can't be serious," blurted Tach, and instantly regretted his rudeness.

The gawky figure seemed to pull in on itself, losing inches. "I am, man, really."

Ten years ago Mark Meadows had been considered the most brilliant biochemist in the world, the Einstein of his field. There had been a dozen different explanations for his sudden retirement: stress, personality deterioration, the breakup of his marriage, drug abuse. But to think that young giant had been reduced to this shambling—

"I've been, like, lookin' for the Radical, man."

Memory snapped down; 1970?, the riot in People's Park when a mysterious ace had appeared on the scene, rescued the Lizard King, and vanished, never to be seen again.

"You're not the only one. I tried to locate him in '70, but he never reappeared."

"Yeah, it's a real bummer," the Captain concurred mournfully. "I had him once . . . well, I *think* I had him once, but I haven't been able to get him back, so maybe I didn't. Maybe it's just, like, wishful thinking, man."

"*You're* claiming to be the Radical?" Disbelief sent Tach's voice up several octaves.

"Oh no, man, 'cause I got no proof. I made these powders, trying to find him, to get him back, but when I eat them I get these *other* people."

"Other people?" Tach repeated in an unnaturally calm tone.

"Yeah, my friends, man."

Tachyon was certain now. He had a nut on his hands. If only he had sent for the limousine. He began casting about for a way to dump his unwelcome companion and get to his meeting before they cancelled his grant or the Ideal only knew what else. . . . He spotted an alley that he knew would cut through to a taxi stand. Surely there he could be rid—

Trips was rambling again. "You're sorta like the father to all the aces, man. And you're always doing stuff to help people. And I'd like to help people so I was figuring you could, like, teach me to be an ace, and fight evil, and—"

Whatever else the Captain wanted was lost in a squeal of tires as a car shot into the alley and jammed to a halt. Survival instincts, drilled into him from infancy, took over, and Tach whirled and ran from what had now become a deadly box. Trips turned from side to side, his head poking at the car and at the fleeing Takisian like a puzzled stork.

Screech! Slam! Another car, effectively blocking his escape. And figures—familiar figures—boiling from the vehicles. He had no time to ponder the inexplicable presence of his relatives on Earth; instead his shields snapped into place just in time to turn a powerful mind blast. His power lanced out, shields buckled, fell, and one of his attackers collapsed.

He tried another; the shields held. *Too many*. Time to try and elude them physically. The leak from their minds indicated a simple capture, but then he saw an arrester slide from his cousin Rabdan's wrist sheath. It was a particularly nasty

weapon, and a popular assassination tool. A press to the
victim's chest, and the heart stopped. Quick, clean, simple
and the job was finished. A spinning back kick sent Rabdan
staggering into a row of garbage cans. The battered cans went
down with a crash and a clatter, releasing the stench of rotting
garbage, and four or five yowling, spitting alley cats. The
silvery disk of the arrester rolled from Rabdan's hand, and Tach
leaped for it.

From the corner of his eye he saw the Captain clutch at
his head, and collapse with a moan to the slimy pavement.
Another mental attack which his shields turned, but they did
fuck all against a baton expertly wielded by Sedjur, his old
arms master, and as his skull exploded in fragments of light and
pain, Tachyon felt a deep sense of hurt and betrayal, and a
strong wish that he had had a *gun*.

". . . bring this other one?"

"You said to leave neither witnesses nor bodies."

Rabdan's sulky, defensive tones seemed filtered by several
miles of cotton wool, and that other voice . . . it couldn't be.
Tach squeezed his eyes tighter shut, willing the return of
unconsciousness, anything but the presence of the *Kibr*
Benaf'saj.

The old woman sighed. "Very well, perhaps he can serve
as a control. Take him to the cabin with the others." Rabdan's
footfalls receded, accompanied by a dragging sound.

"The boy did well," Sedjur said, once Rabdan was gone
and could not be insulted by his remarks. "His years here have
strengthened him. Took out Rabdan."

"Yes, yes. Now go. I must speak with my grandchild."

Sedjur's footsteps dwindled, and Tach continued to play
possum. His mind lanced out; touched on the presence of the
ship, (it was definitely a war vessel of the Courser class), felt
the familiar pattern of Takisian minds, the panic of two . . .
no, *three* human ones. And finally a mind whose touch brought
a rush of fear and hate and regret tinged with sadness. His
cousin Zabb, becoming aware of the featherlike probe, thrust
back, and Tachyon's imperfect shield allowed part of the blow
to pass. His headache increased in intensity.

"I know you're conscious," Benaf'saj said conversationally.

With a sigh, he opened his eyes, and regarded the
chiseled features of his oldest living relative. The opaline
luminescence of the ship's walls formed a halo about her silver

white hair, and heightened the network of lines that etched her face. But even with these ravages it was possible to see traces of the formidable beauty that had enthralled several generations of men. Legend had it that a member of the Alaa family had risked all to spend one night with her. One wondered if he had found the bliss worth the price, for she had killed him before morning. (Or so the story ran.) A gnarled hand plucked at a wisp of hair that had worked free from the elaborate coiffure, while the faded gray eyes studied him with a coolness bordering on disinterest.

"Will you greet me properly, or have your years on Earth dulled your manners?"

He scrambled up, swept her a bow, and dropped to one knee before her. Her long, dry fingers caged his face, drawing him close, and the withered lips pressed a kiss onto his forehead.

"You weren't always so silent. At home your chattering was held to be a flaw." He remained quiet, not wanting to lose position by asking the first question. "Sedjur says you've learned to fight. Has Earth also taught you to keep your own counsel?"

"Rabdan tried to kill me."

She was neither disconcerted by the bluntness of the statement, nor insulted by his flat, hostile tone. "Not everyone would welcome your return to Takis."

"And Zabb is on board."

"And from that you may draw your own conclusions."

"I see." He looked away, revulsion lying like a foul taste on the back of his tongue. "I'm not going back, and neither are the humans."

Her thin fingers closed like talons on his chin, and forced him to face her. "You sulky-faced boy. What about your duty and responsibility to the family?"

"And what about my pursuit of virtue?" he countered, throwing up to her the other equally important and utterly contradictory tenet of Takisian life.

"Time has not stood still at home while you have amused yourself on Earth. When you vanished, Shaklan suspected you had followed the ship to Earth.

"But you were not alone in your concern over the great experiment. Others watched, but rather than haring off to prevent the release, they struck at the source. L'gura, that motherless animal, welded a coalition of fifteen other families, and they came." She stared down at her hands, and suddenly she looked very old. "Many died in the attack. But for Zabb I think we *all* might have died." Tach caught his lower lip between his teeth, holding back the excuses for his absence. "Did you never wonder, as the years passed and still we did not come, what might have happened?"

A cold blade seemed to twist in his belly, and he forced out, "Father?"

"A head injury. The flesh lives, but the mind is gone." Numbness gripped him, and the remainder of her words seemed to come to him from a great distance. "With you gone Zabb agitated for the scepter, but many feared his ambition. In order to block his ascension your uncle Taj maintained a regency, but it was decided that you had to be found, for it is doubtful how much longer Shaklan's body can continue . . ."

Bitterly cold mornings, and his father pressing a paper cone filled with roasted nuts into his hand while a street vendor bobbed and beamed at the noble ones. . . . Swinging sadly on a door while Shaklan conducted business and forgot that he had promised to teach his small son to ride that day. The meeting ending, and the arms opening wide. Racing into that embrace, feeling safe as those powerful arms closed about him, the tickle of a lace cravat against his cheek, and the warm, man scent, overlaid with the spice of his cologne. . . . The indescribable pain when his father had shot him through the upper thigh during one of his psi training sessions. Their tears had mingled as Shaklan tried to explain why he had done it. That Tisianne had to be able to withstand anything this side of death without losing mental control. Someday his life might depend upon it. . . . The flicker of firelight on the etched planes of his face as they shared a bottle of wine, and wept, the night they learned of Jadlan's suicide.

Tach covered his face with his hands, and sobbed. Benaf'saj made no move, physical or mental, to ease his anguish, and he hated her. The storm wore itself out, and he mopped at his running eyes and nose with a handkerchief supplied by his many-times great-granddam. Their eyes met, and he saw in them . . . pain? He could scarcely credit it, and the moment passed before he could assure himself of the reality of what he had seen.

"We will be under way as soon as we have swept the area for swarmlings. We are not well enough armed to fight off an attack by one of the devourers, and our screens must be dropped before we can enter ghostflight. It is a shame," she continued to muse, "that we were able to save so few specimens. It is likely the T'zan-d'ran will destroy this world." His head moved in quick negation. "You disagree?"

"I think the humans might surprise you."

"I doubt it. But at least we have gathered our data." She pinned him with a cold, gray eye. "You will, of course, have the run of the ship; but, please, do not approach the humans. It will only agitate them, and make it harder for them to adjust to their new lives."

She gave a telepathic summons, and a slender woman entered the room. Tach realized, with a start, that the last time he had seen her she had been a roly-poly five-year-old, nursing a fine family of dolls, and making him promise to marry her when she grew up so they could have pretty babies. She would never marry now. The fact that she was on this ship, and not safely ensconced in the women's quarters, meant that she was *bitshuf'di*, one of the neutered ones who had been deemed to carry dangerous recessives, or to be of insufficient genetic worth to be permitted to breed.

Her eyes flicked (sadly? . . . it was difficult to gauge the emotion, so quickly had it passed) over him, and she made obeisance.

"Sire, if you will accompany me."

He swept Benaf'saj a final bow, and fell into step with Talli, debating how to break the silence. He decided small talk would be inappropriate—*of course she'd grown, it'd been decades!*

"No word of greeting, Talli?" The corridor curved before them, gleaming like polished mother-of-pearl as they spiraled deeper into the heart of the ship.

"You gave none in farewell."

"It was something I had to do."

"Others also live by that imperative." She glanced nervously about and switched to the tight, intimate telepathic mode. *Zabb means to have you dead. Eat or drink nothing that I have not brought, and watch your back.* She pressed a small sharp dagger into his hand, and he ran it quickly up his sleeve.

I suspected as much. But thank you for the warning and the weapon.

He'll kill me if he suspects.

He won't learn it from me. He was never my equal in

mentatics. But she looked doubtful, and he realized with embarrassment how lax were his shields. He strengthened them, and she nodded with relief.

Better.

No, terrible. This is a dreadful situation. He looked at her seriously. *I have no intention of returning to Takis.*

They had reached the door to the cabin, and the ship obligingly shuttered open for him.

She placed her hands on his shoulders, and urged him in. *You must. We need you.*

And as the door lensed shut he decided that maybe she wasn't much of an ally after all.

Tom Tudbury was having one of the worst days of his life. The very worst day had been March 8, when Barbara had married Steve Bruder, but this one was running a real close second. He had been on his way to Tachyon's clinic with the strange device he'd taken off the street punk when a strange ship, looking rather like a wentletrap seashell, had looped out of the clouds, pulled up beside him, and invited him aboard. Maybe *invited* wasn't the right word; *compelled* was closer to the mark. Icy talons seemed to settle about his mind, and he had calmly flown the shell through the yawning doors of a cargo bay. He didn't remember anything more until he had found himself standing in a gigantic room, his shell squatting behind him.

Several slender men in comic-opera gold and white uniforms stepped forward and searched him, while another darted into the shell, and emerged with the strange black ball and a half-drunk six-pack of beer. He gestured with the cans causing them to clunk dully together, and there was a burst of laughter. Next the device was examined amid a ripple of musical words filled with random and inexplicable pauses. With a shrug, the device was placed on a shelf which ran along one side of the curving room. One of his captors gestured politely toward a doorway. The courtesy of the gesture removed his worst fear—he clearly wasn't in the hands of the Swarm. Somehow politeness seemed out of place with monsters.

They exited into a long snaking corridor whose walls floor, and ceiling shone like polished abalone. As they proceeded, the arching ceiling would light before them and darken after they had passed. One wall held a tracery of rose colored lines like the petals of a flower. This section suddenly shuttered open, and Tom was urged into a luxurious cabin.

A burst of brittle, feminine laughter met his arrival, and he goggled at the beautiful woman curled up in the center of a large round bed.

"Well, you don't look like much," she said, her eyes raking over him. He sucked in his belly, and wished his tee shirt was cleaner. "I'm Asta Lenser. Who the hell are you?" He was scared, but the fear made him cautious. He shook his head. "Oh, fuck you! We're in this together."

"I'm an ace. I've gotta be careful."

"Well, big fuckin' deal! So am I."

"You are?"

"Yeah, I do the dance of the seven veils." Her long, graceful arms wove a pattern about her. "I out-Salome Salome." He looked puzzled. "Don't you ever go to the ballet?"

"No."

"Moron." She scrabbled in a large shapeless bag, and emerged with a packet of white powder, a mirror, and a straw. Her hands were trembling so much that it took her five tries to get the lines set. She sucked in the cocaine, and leaned back with a long sigh of relief. "Where were we? Oh yeah, my power. I can mesmerize people with my dancing. Particularly men. But it's a real dinky power when you've been kidnapped by aliens. Still, Himself sure appreciated it. I got him a lot of good information with my dinky power, and kept him . . . up." She made an obscene gesture between her legs.

Tom wondered who and what the hell she was talking about, but he frankly didn't care to puzzle it out. He staggered across the room, and collapsed on a low bench that seemed to be an extrusion of the ship itself. As he seated himself on the thick, embroidered cushion there was a crackle as of leaves or dried petals, and a rich spicy aroma filled the air.

He wasn't sure how long he huddled on the bench, agonizing over his situation—Takisians! Jesus Christ! What was going to happen to them? Tach? Could he help? Did he even know? Oh shit!"

"Hey," called Asta. "I'm sorry. Look, we're both aces, we ought to be able to do something to get out of this mess."

Tom just shook his head. How could he tell her that he had left his powers behind with his shell?

* * *

The rasp of the match was loud in the silent room. Tach watched with unnecessary attention as the candle flared to life. The light struck color from the ship wall, and shed the gentle scent of flowers. Pulling a quarter from his pocket he laid it on the altar. It looked incongruous among the gold Takisian coins. He hefted the tiny pearl-handled knife, murmured a quick prayer for the release of his father's spirit, and made a tiny cut on the pad of his forefinger. The blood welled slowly out, and he touched the gleaming drop to the coin. He sank down to sit cross-legged before the family altar, sucking at his cut finger, and flipping the tiny two-inch knife over and over in his hand.

"It won't make much of a weapon."

Zabb was leaning against the door, arms folded across his chest. He was close to six feet tall with a whip-lean body and the heavy chest and shoulders of the long-distance swimmer or martial artist. Wavy, silver gilt hair swept back from a high white forehead, and just brushed the collar of his white and gold tunic. Cold gray eyes added to the impression of metal and crystal. There was no warmth to the man. But there was power and command, and an overwhelming charisma.

"That wasn't what I was thinking about."

"You should be."

There was something in the moment, the set of Zabb's shoulders, or perhaps the indulgent cock to his head, that made Tach remember an earlier time . . . before family politics had intruded, before he understood the whispers linking Zabb's mother to the death of his mother, before . . . A time when a five-year-old Tach had adored his glamorous older cousin.

"I was remembering that you gave me my first puppy. From that litter old Tu'shula had."

"Don't, Tis. That's dead and past."

"Like I'm going to be?"

Their eyes met, gray to lilac. Tach's fell first.

"Yes." One fine, manicured hand was brushing nervously at his full mustache and sideburns. "I intend to kill you before we reach Takis." Zabb's tone was conversational.

"I don't want the family. I want to stay on Earth."

"That doesn't matter. As long as you live I can't have it."

"And the humans?"

"They're laboratory animals. Useful if we're to move to the second stage." He turned to leave.

"Zabb, what happened?"

His cousin's shoulders hunched, then relaxed back into their military erectness. "You lived to maturity." The door whispered closed behind him.

Tom and Asta started as the two men entered, dragging between them a sprawling, gangling form in a purple Uncle Sam suit. The younger man dropped to one knee, riffled quickly through the hippie's voluminous coat pockets, and pulled out a small vial filled with a silver-shot blue powder. The elder accepted the bottle, uncapped it, and sniffed curiously at the contents. One eyebrow quirked up.

"This one was with Tisianne?" he said in English.

"Yes, Rabdan."

"And they seemed friendly?" His pale eyes shot to Tom.

"Y—yes."

"This is a drug of some sort. And too much of a drug can cause terrible effects. I certainly hope my esteemed cousin is conversant with the treatment of an overdose. Otherwise his friend might die." Another secret, catlike glance to Tom.

His companion's fingers pressed quickly at his lips, then he hesitantly said, "Shouldn't we ask Zabb?"

"Nonsense, he won't care what happens to a human friend of Tisianne's."

Kneeling, he poured the contents of the vial between the hippie's slack lips. Tom half rose, a protest on his lips, but a look from Rabdan dropped him back onto the bench. Everyone's eyes fastened on the scraggy figure on the floor; Asta with excitement, the tip of her tongue just showing between her lips; Tom with horror; the young Takisian with worry; and Rabdan with jovial good humor.

The man writhed, shifted, and for an instant everyone gaped as a blue-glowing figure rose majestically from the floor. Within his cowled cloak of deep-space darkness, his eyes were slits of white fire, and the lining of the cloak glittered with glowing stars, nebulas, galactic whorls. The Takisians leaped forward, clutching at air, as the exotic form sank quickly and cleanly through the floor.

Tachyon returned to his cabin, and sprawled on his belly on the bed, chin propped in his hands, and tried to decide what to do. His brief conversation with Zabb had indicated not only his danger, but the danger to the humans. It was clear they were to be experimental guinea pigs, Benaf'saj's remarks notwithstanding.

It hadn't taken long to identify the ship as *Hellcat*, his cousin's favorite and much-beloved vessel. So an attempt to take over the ship would be fruitless. There was no way he was going to handle *this* ship. He could still remember the day when the ship growers had called to say that his cousin's newest vessel had better be thrown back, so they could start again. She was wild, arrogant, utterly untrainable. That had been enough for Zabb. Even among the other families, who were notoriously stingy with their praise, he was known as the most brilliant ship trainer on the planet. And he couldn't resist a challenge. Nine-year-old Tisianne had been present with his father on the orbital training center. Zabb had entered the ship, the powerful grappler beams had been released, and the ship had gone haring off in the general direction of galactic center. No one had ever expected to see Zabb again, but two weeks later ship and man had coming limping home, and nothing could be more docile than *Hellcat*'s demeanor when under the command of her conqueror. She was a one-man ship.

Rather the way Baby *is with me*, Tach thought defensively.

The point was, she couldn't be controlled by mere psi power alone. Still, she was a military vessel, which meant there were actual control consoles built into her hull so that if she should be badly injured, the crew might be able to nurse her home. But if he did attempt to take the ship using the consoles, she would merely disregard his orders, and yell for Zabb. And though he could handle Zabb in a one-on-one mental confrontation, there were nineteen other Takisians on this ship.

So what to do? Benaf'saj was clearly in command. And if she were to give the order to return Tachyon and the prisoners to Earth . . . He rolled off the bed and went in search of his *Kibr*.

She was on the bridge glaring at Andami while Sedjur frowned down at a readout which *Hellcat* had obligingly projected onto the floor. The younger man was squirming.

"Would you be so kind as to explain to me why you administered an unknown substance to a prisoner?"

"It was Rabdan who did it," Andami said sulkily.

"Then you are both lackwits—him for doing it, and you for

permitting it. Now we have an alien creature of unknown abilities loose in the ship."

"He's moving again," snapped Sedjur. "He's on level five. No, back to two. Now he's in your cabin."

Benaf'saj's mouth twisted in disapproval.

"I don't know why everyone's so upset. *Hellcat* can tell us where he is."

"Because he moves through walls and floors, and by the time we reach a place he has moved again," the old woman explained with careful patience, as if speaking to a retarded child.

Tach stepped forward, trying to avoid drawing the attention of the threesome by the main port, gripped the back of an acceleration chair, and sent out a tiny thread. He had a gift for insinuating himself past shields, but Benaf'saj had had more than two thousand years to perfect hers. His mouth was dry and he could feel the pulse hammering in his throat as he slipped past the first barrier.

Second level. Trickier here. Traps built for the unwary to throw the infiltrator into never-ending mental loops until Benaf'saj saw fit to release them.

He chipped one of the shields, and quickly wove a ward to cover his error. It sat like a dancing snowflake in the midst of his *Kibr's* mind, smoothing over the ragged edge he had left. Past one more. *How many levels did the old she-devil have?*

Brrrrrrang*********! He never even saw the blow coming. He tripped an alarm, a white-hot sheet rose up like a wave of fire, and crashed down. He felt like every synapse in his brain had been simultaneously fired, and his mind seemed to be rattling about in his skull like a rotting walnut in its shell. He realized he was sliding backward across the floor on his butt, his fingers scrabbling at *Hellcat's* pearly floor. He hit the wall, and the air went out of him in a rush.

Benaf'saj stared at him, amusement and irritation flicking across her face. He could feel the blood rushing into his thin cheeks.

"I had my shields up!" he announced throbbingly and irrationally. He was feeling terribly abused.

"Mind-control *me*, you silly boy. And you can't build a shield I can't break. I changed your diapers when you were a squalling brat! There's nothing I don't know about you!" She turned away, dismissal written in every line of her fragile body, and humiliation rose up to choke him. "Take him away," she threw over her shoulder to Sedjur. "And this time *lock* him in his cabin." The last command was directed to the ship.

Stony-faced, Sedjur offered him a hand up, and escorted him back to his cabin. He hurried ahead, head down, shoulders hunched, feeling five. The old man left, and Tach helped himself to several liberal pulls from his silver hip flask. The brandy helped to steady his jangled nerves, but did nothing to promote his mental processes. He paced round and round the luxurious cabin trying to think of a plan; panicking when *nothing* suggested itself. Wondering what was loose in the ship. Wondering.

He decided to determine precisely which humans were being held on the ship. He touched a familiar female mind. Asta Lenser, the prima ballerina with the American Ballet Theater. She was thinking about a man. A man who was having a great deal of difficulty performing. As his stocky, sweat slick body pounded down on hers, struggling for release, she was thinking how ironic it was that a man with his power couldn't get it up. *The most feared man in—*

Embarrassed by his intrusion and feeling like a voyeur, Tach withdrew and searched further. There was nothing that felt like the amiable lunatic who had accosted him outside the clinic, and he hoped that Trips hadn't been deemed useless and disposed of. There was something strange. A mind so heavily blocked as to be almost opaque. He would never have sensed it without a sudden flare of terror, but it was quickly suppressed, and he lost the source. Perhaps this was the intruder. He searched further and found . . .

"Turtle!" he ejected, surprise and worry bringing him bolt upright.

He narrowed and refined his probe, constructed a penumbra to give the illusion to any mental eavesdropper that he was sleeping, and made contact. It was harder than he expected. His first brief touch had shown him a Turtle that he did not know, and he didn't want to jar the man by suddenly appearing in his head. He began to search for ways to make the man gradually aware of his presence, becoming more depressed with each passing moment. Dark, heavy emotions rolled like sullen, viscous waves through Turtle's mind: fear, anger, loss, loneliness, and an overwhelming sense of hopelessness and futility.

Feeling like an interloper, and not wanting Turtle to think he was prying into private matters that did not concern him, he tapped firmly at the man's primitive shields until a spark of surprise and wary interest showed him he had attracted Turtle's attention.

Turtle.

Tacky, is that you?

Yes. He sensed distrust and suspicion. It hurt, and he again wondered what had happened to his oldest friend on Earth. *I'm a prisoner like you.*

Oh. One of those other families you're always talking about?

No, my family. Come to see the results of the experiment, and to find me. Turtle's doubt felt like a hard blade. *What can I do to convince you that I had no part in this?*

Maybe you can't.

My friend, you didn't used to be like this.

Yeah. Bitterness edged the thought. *And I didn't used to be on the wrong side of forty, and all alone, and going nowhere except toward death.*

Turtle, what is it? What's wrong? Let me help.

Like you and all the rest of your kind helped when you brought the virus to Earth? No thanks.

The old pain and guilt returned, stronger than it had been in years; years during which he had built the clinic, become famous rather than infamous, beloved by many of his "children." Years that had dulled the edge of his culpability. They were wide open to each other, and Tach thought he sensed in Turtle a perverse satisfaction at his pain.

How did they capture you?

It wasn't very hard. They must have used mind control, because I just flew right to them.

What were you doing out, anyway? Tach said irritably, irrationally trying to shift the blame to Turtle.

I was bringing you a fucking bowling ball, I thought maybe you'd want to roll a few games, what the fuck do you think I was doing?

I don't know, that's why I'm asking, snapped Tach, his mental tone as surly as Turtle's.

It was a fucking weird bowling ball, I took it off some street kids.

Where is it now?

They took it out of the shell, and placed it on a shelf in the room.

Which room, show me.

Turtle's exasperation was like acid against his mind, but he obliged. And Tach really didn't know why he was being so insistent about the device. Probably just something to divert him from their present predicament.

I'm debating about the feasibility of a breakout, he said after a long pause. *Between your teke, my mind control, and the dagger my great-great niece Talli gave me, I think we might be able to pull it off. I'm glad you did not attempt to free yourself earlier.*

I . . . . can't.

I beg your pardon?

I said, I can't.

The years rolled back, and suddenly it was he, not Turtle, saying those words. He had stood shivering and crying on the steps of Jetboy's tomb trying to explain that though he *wanted* to help, he just couldn't. Turtle had hit him; the ace's TK power lashing out like a great, invisible fist driving him down the stairs. But he didn't want to hit Turtle, he just wanted to understand.

Why Turtle? Why can't you?

I don't have my shell. The Great and Powerful Turtle could make chopped liver of these pukes, but not me. I'm just plain old Tom— He jerked back, but the rest of the thought came clearly through to Tachyon.

Tom Tudbury.

Fortunately the name meant nothing to Tachyon. So Turtle's secret identity was to all intents and purposes still intact.

It's all right, he soothed. *It probably wouldn't have worked anyway. The plan would depend on us taking them out one by one, and the minute you ripped open the door* Hellcat *would scream for Zabb, and they'd be all over us. And even if we did succeed I'd be right back to the original dilemma—how to handle* Hellcat.

Who?

The ship. She's sentient.

Then, she must be a little startled, because there's some guy floating around inside her.

You saw? What—

"YOU!" enunciated a voice, filling the word with all the throbbing outrage possible.

Tach's eyes flew open, the concentration necessary to maintain so private a telepathic link completely lost. An eerie blue-glowing figure stood in the center of the cabin. Swiftly he rolled off the bed, the blade sliding down his sleeve and into his hand. He dropped into a knife-fighting pose, the blade and his free hand weaving an intricate and confusing pattern before him. From behind the barrier of his mental shields he put out a telepathic probe, and met a powerful mindblock.

"Oh, do put that away, you dreadful little man! You cannot harm *me*."

"That's not what I'm concerned about. I'm a little more worried about *your* intentions toward *me*."

The creature drew itself up, its strange eyes glittering like sparklers in the featureless face. "This is all *your* fault. I tried to keep that drug-soaked hippie from this outrageous course, but he was intractable, utterly intractable! Father to the aces, indeed. He has a perfectly good father who would never encourage him in this type of juvenescent irresponsibility. The world would have gone on very nicely indeed without your interference.

"It's not enough that you should subject us to strange and unnatural alien substances, now you must needs bring your *family* in on us. A whole tribe of you! Our only hope is that they are as bumbling and ineffectual as you have shown yourself to be. First you lose the virus, then permit its release, help harry and harass your friends and lovers into prison, insane asylums, and—"

"SILENCE!" roared Tachyon. *Oh, Blythe,* he cried, and the thought acted like water on a fire, extinguishing his blazing anger, and leaving behind only a cold slimy mess of mud and ashes.

Still, his eruption seemed to have had an effect on his visitor. The man's mouth pinched tightly closed, and he was pulling in sharp little breaths through narrowed nostrils. Then with supreme dignity he began to sink through the floor. For an instant Tachyon goggled, but only for an instant. This man could be useful, and he had stupidly driven him away. He prided himself on his astuteness, and on his ability to read and handle people. Now was the moment to test out just how real that ability was.

He rushed forward. "No, wait, I pray you, good sir. Do allow me to apologize for my rudeness and lack of manners." The apparition paused, only his head and upper torso visible above the floor. "I haven't had the honor of making your acquaintance. I am Dr. Tachyon."

"Cosmic Traveler."

"You must excuse me. I . . . I've been under rather a great deal of stress today. I was unattentive when you arrived, or I would have been aware from the beginning of your puissance."

Traveler simpered, then an expression of Olympian calm and wisdom swept over his features. And Tachyon realized that he need not even struggle for subtlety. With this man even the most blatant of flattery would serve.

"Will you please stay? My mind is all in a whirl, and I feel certain that even a few moments of conversation with you would help." Traveler graciously floated back out of the floor, and settled onto a chair. As he did so, the lines of his body became firmer and more well defined.

So, he can become substantial, mused Tachyon.

"You've seen the other prisoners?"

"Yes. When that pathetic moron Trips was taken to the cabin, I noticed a tubby little man in blue jeans and tee shirt, and a most strikingly beautiful young woman." The tip of his tongue appeared from between his thin lips, moistened his upper lip, and disappeared.

"Where were you?"

"I was . . . present," he said cagily. "Fortunately I was able to get free. I shudder to think what might have happened if one of those other bumptious fools had appeared. They have not the slightest concern for my well-being." He glared at Tachyon, obviously including him in the statement.

Tach was rather at sea with all this talk of other persons, and drug-soaked hippies. Meadows perhaps? But at the moment he was less concerned with the metaphysical problems presented by Cosmic Traveler, and far more interested in his unique abilities.

"Traveler, I think with *your* help we can escape, and return to Earth."

"Oh?" Suspicion laced the word.

"Go back to the cabin where Turtle and the Captain and the woman are being held—"

"The Captain is no longer there."

"Eh?"

"*I'm* here."

"Oh . . . yes . . . well, whatever. Anyway, go to the cabin, and tell them to stand ready. Then lead Zabb and his goons to the far end of the ship." Tachyon cocked his head to the side, and contemplated his strange ally. "It would save time if you didn't have to return here to report. Would you be willing to drop your mental block so I could remain in telepathic contact with you?"

"No! Allow some alien Peeping Tom into my head? It's out of the question."

Tachyon stared at him in exasperation. "I'm not particularly interested in what's in your head. I'm interested in—"

The door lensed open, and Traveler went, sinking elegantly through the chair and the floor, still in a seated position. Zabb with five of his soldiers came tumbling into the room. Tach closed his mouth, and arranged his face into an expression of innocent interest.

"Where is he?" gritted Zabb.

Tach pointed a finger downward. "He went that way."

Things were becoming increasingly confusing. First the hippie had disappeared, then the blue-glowing apparition had vanished and the Takisians had pelted off in hot, if somewhat disorganized, pursuit; then Tachyon had contacted him, and now he had broken off abruptly in the midst of their telepathic conversation. Tom kept trying to regain the contact with his friend, even going so far as to murmur "Tach?" several times under his breath. He looked up, met Asta's wary look, and ran a self-conscious hand through his hair.

"I . . . I was trying to get in touch with Tach."

"Right." And the fact that she clearly thought he was a nut did nothing to bolster his already-sagging spirits.

If the Turtle were here she wouldn't be looking at him like that, he thought, torn between resentment and weariness. She would be scrabbling for safety atop his shell, while he burst from the cabin, scattering Takisians like ninepins, rescued Tach, and flew them triumphantly home. Or, rather, forced the Takisians to fly them home. There wasn't room in the shell for passengers, nor did he know how tightly sealed it was. He'd look like a real dork if they all suffocated. . . .

He jammed a fist into his thigh, cutting off the tantalizing but pointless thoughts. He wasn't Turtle; he was just Tom Tudbury, the New Jersey boy who in thirty years had managed to move two blocks. He closed his eyes, and watched the dark, ghostly images of ships passing down the Kill, running lights reflected in the dark, unseen waters. And he realized that he was finally about to go on a voyage, though not one of his own choosing.

A squeak from Asta brought his head up. The creature was back.

"I am Cosmic Traveler," he announced, and then paused as if awaiting a fanfare. Asta and Tom stared at him, fascinated. "That ridiculous little man has sent me here to ascertain the whereabouts of our captors, and to inform you that he is concocting some, no doubt utterly unworkable and highly dangerous, escape plan."

Asta wriggled forward on the bed, rising silkily onto her knees. "You can move at will through the ship," she whispered. "Can you also return to Earth?"

"Yes."

She stretched out her arms, the bones of her clavicle etched beneath the white skin. "Would you be willing to take me with you?" she purred.

Tom wanted to point out to her that first, what made her think the man was telling her the truth? and second, even if he could withstand the cold and vacuum of space, how was he going to take her?

She arched her swanlike neck, and lifted her hair with her hands. The gestures forced her small, upright bosoms against the leotard, the nipples hard knobs beneath the thin material. "I can be very generous to people who help me, and my employer might be able to make an interesting offer to a man of your unique abilities."

The total incongruity of the situation left Tom breathless. He wondered if this woman was really going to shuck it, and screw with this stranger right before his wondering eyes. Surely the man would realize that more pressing matters were facing them. But Cosmic Traveler was going for it in a big way. Asta's gyrations had set him to panting, and his fingers were working spasmodically at his sides. He shot a nervous glance over his shoulder toward the door, and Tom saw lust and fear battling it out on his smooth blue face. Lust won.

With a breathy "I agree" that was half groan and half words, he tottered to the edge of the bed. Asta was already stripping out of her blue jeans. Beneath them she wore pale pink tights. They and the leotard were quickly removed, and she held out her arms. Traveler collapsed with a moan onto her thin, white body, and they began frenzied foreplay.

Tom, embarrassed yet fascinated, noticed (with that

strange attention to detail that seems to arise whenever one is in an acutely uncomfortable position) that her feet were very ugly. The toes were covered with sores and calluses, and one big toe was bruised black from the constant pounding of the toe shoe.

Ten minutes later they were still at it, Asta, with increasing irritation, saying "Come on! Come on!" Harsh, grunting sounds periodically erupted from Traveler as his blue ass pumped virgorously, and with increasing desperation, up and down, up and down.

The ring of a boot heel pulled a gasp from Asta, followed by a wild shriek as Traveler sank *through* her prone body, and vanished into the depths of the bed. Tom, too, almost lost it, and he rushed to the bed to ascertain if Asta was still alive. She was lying deathly still, and he reached out and touched one bare shoulder. She shrieked again, and Tom, startled by the outburst, lost his balance and pitched headfirst onto the bed. The Takisian goggled at the bed, then yelled, "Captain, he was—" The closing of the door cut off the rest of his words.

Cosmic Traveler returned.

"Well! I sincerely hope you don't have to serve as a sex toy for Takisians. You're singularly lacking in the most rudimentary erotic skills."

"Me!" yelped Asta, shoving Tom away. "You're the one who couldn't get it—"

"And what are you sniggering at, you tubby little man," roared Traveler. Tom hadn't sniggered, not really, but the ludicrousness of the situation had drawn a sound from him.

"Do you know what they have planned for you?" Traveler continued, "Vivisection! Do you know what that means? I can't imagine why they seized you. You must be the most paltry of aces. Shaking like a bowl of Jell-O, and sniveling like a reluctant virgin." He shot a smoldering and resentful glance toward Asta, who threw him a bird.

Tom exploded. "Would you just get the fuck out of here! Fuck off! You think you're so fucking smart, but you're stuck too, just like the rest of us. You can't get off this ship. If you could, you would have. Now get out. Get out!" Tom charged at him, waving his arms wildly about like a man shooing chickens. Traveler went, his features looking decidedly curdled.

* * *

"Where the hell have you been?" Tachyon halted his nervous perambulations. "How long does it take to scout out a ship—" Traveler, halfway through the cabin wall, began to withdraw. Tachyon rushed forward. "No, please wait. I'm sorry. The stress . . . What did you find out?"

"Our captors are charging about the ship in pursuit of *me*. Though I can't imagine how they are tracking me. They'll no doubt be here soon—"

"And my *Kibr*? The old woman with the jewels in her hair," he explained at Traveler's blank look.

"I haven't a notion."

Tach held his tongue, deciding that Benaf'saj's whereabouts were perhaps not all that important.

"All right, never mind, we'll try it. To the left of the cabin doors there is a small protuberance on the wall. That is an override panel for the doors. Open mine, and then we'll—"

"No."

"I beg your . . ." he began politely, then stopped and rumbled, "What?"

"You heard me, I said no. I have not the slightest faith in your ability to successfully execute this escape plan, and I will not be a party to it. Besides, as I stand substantial and helpless outside your door, those thugs will come upon me, and harm me."

"It will only take an instant."

Traveler folded his arms across his chest, and stared majestically at the far wall. "No."

"Please?"

"No."

Tachyon folded his hands at his breast. "Please, please, please?"

"No."

"You whining, groveling coward!" bellowed Tach. "You're endangering all of us. You're the only one—"

But Traveler was leaving. Tachyon leaped for a wall niche, pulled down a beautiful Membres vase, and launched it at the rapidly departing ace. It passed through him, smashed into the wall, and Traveler gave him a look of withering contempt and loathing. The entire incident left Tach shaking; partly with anger, partly with despair over his violent reaction. He untied his lace cravat, and yanked open his collar, gasping for air. He had tried so hard over the years to put such responses behind him, to deal gently and kindly with all people. And he had lost it all. He was behaving like . . . He paused, searching for some appropriately disgusting comparison.

Like Zabb.

This brief indulgence in self-castigation felt good, but it didn't remove the primary problem. They were up a creek without the proverbial paddle.

And this too is my fault, thought Tach without pausing to consider whether any amount of bribery or cajoling might have moved the recalcitrant ace.

His hour was almost gone. Raging against the vagaries of an unkind and uncaring universe that had left him trapped within the body of man he considered little better than a vegetable, he wandered through the Takisian ship dodging increasingly hysterical search parties. But this could not last. If he delayed he would revert to that moron Meadows, and the aliens might *harm* him. And however much Traveler might despise his host body, he realized that without Mark there was no life. He had noticed that doorways left faint lines on the walls like the fossilized imprint of ancient flower petals. Some opened automatically, others seemed to require a telepathic command, and still others used the access panels that Tachyon had described. He went in search of one that would not open automatically. One that seemed firmly and soundly locked from the outside.

Mark returned to himself slowly. And blinked . . . and blinked again, because it was *dark*. His hands roamed fitfully over his face and head until he had fully assured himself of his consciousness. But it was still dark. He shuffled forward, and ran his long nose firmly into a wall. Holding his bumped nose with one hand he stared out into the stygian darkness. Slowly he stretched out his arms, exploring the dimensions of his prison. It was small. Closet-size. Coffin-sized.

That thought was depressing so he shook it off, and tried through the hazy filter of Traveler's memories to piece together what had happened.

"Aliens, man. Oh, bummer."

And Tachyon . . . a prisoner? Yes, that felt right. He had been angry, Traveler had done or failed to do . . . something. Mark sighed, and scrubbed at his face with his hands. Yeah, that sounded about right where Traveler was concerned.

For a moment he stood in morose contemplation of his alternate personae's social and emotional shortcomings.

He wondered what time it was. Sprout might be home from kindergarten by now. He could trust Susan to keep an eye on her for as long as the Pumpkin was open, but once the head shop closed who would watch her? Surely Susan wouldn't just leave her alone if Mark hadn't returned. He tried to pace his tiny prison, but kept misjudging in the inky blackness, and slamming into the walls.

"I gotta get out of here, and help Dr. Tachyon. He'll know what to do." He began fumbling around in his leather pouch, and emerged with a vial. He held it up before his eyes and peered, but to no avail. It was too dark to see the glass, much less the color of the powder it contained.

"Oh, bummer, man. If I get Flash he can burn down this door, but Starshine can't work in the dark. And Moonchild . . ." He poked at the unyielding wall. "I don't know if she could bust this or not."

He returned the vial to the pouch and fished out another one. And dithered. And returned it and tried another. And finally pulled out two. His head wove back and forth between the bottles like a puzzled stork. He put them away, and clutched his head.

"I gotta do something. I'm an ace, man. People are depending on me. This is like a test, and I gotta prove I'm worthy."

He went back to his fruitless pawing through the pouch. He imagined he could feel the ship moving, hurtling them out beyond the orbit of Neptune, carrying him away from Sprout. His beautiful, golden-haired daughter who would never be mentally more than four years old. His Alice-in-Wonderland darling who needed him. And he needed to be needed. His fingers closed convulsively about a vial, he yanked it out, muttering, "Ah, fuck it."

Unstopped the bottle, and tossed back the contents. Later he might know if his choice had been an appropriate one.

Talli had brought him a meal. Delicate meat- and fruit-filled crepes that had been his favorite back home. The first mouthful choked him, and he tossed the rest down the toilet. His restless pacings had accomplished nothing except to give him a cramp in his left calf, so he seized a brush from the

dressing table in the lavatory, and tried to soothe himself by
brushing his hair. The rasp of the bristles over his scalp felt
good, and some of the tension eased from his shoulders.

Then *Hellcat* gave a tiny shudder, and ringing through his
mind came a loud, aggrieved "OW!" Obviously this ship did
not believe in suffering in silence.

Traveler? he wondered. Had that puling coward finally
decided to do something? Or could it be Turtle, overcoming
his psychological block, ripping through the door, squashing
Zabb into jelly . . .

Hellcat was making such a psi racket that he didn't think
anyone would notice a nonshielded communication with
Turtle. The probe lanced out.

Oh shit!

Sorry, didn't mean to startle you.

There was no sense of danger in Turtle's mind, and Tach
sighed. *I take it you are not in the process of rescuing us.*

I can't, Turtle sullenly replied. *I told you that.*

Tom, he said gently, and remembered only when he heard
Turtle's gasp that he wasn't supposed to have revealed his
knowledge of the man's secret identity. He plunged on.
Couldn't you just try. I'm sure if you tried you could—

*I CAN'T! How many times do I have to tell you, I can't.
And I seem to remember a booze-soaked derelict who kept
whining about not being able to do it, and then felt hurt when
I wasn't very understanding. Well, the shoe's on the other foot,
Tachy. You be understanding.*

The slap hurt. He was fully aware of the debt he owed to
Turtle, but he didn't like to have his nose rubbed in his past
sins. They were just that . . . past. *The virus is encoded in
your very cells . . .*

*I know that. How can I ever forget it? It's ruined my
fucking life! You and Jetboy, and your goddamn fucking
Takisians. Just leave me the fuck alone.*

Turtle lacked the mental skills to actually block Tachyon,
but he could layer every meaningful thought beneath a thick
blanket of anger, making it very difficult to read or send. Tach
sucked in several sharp breaths through his nose, and reminded himself that this was his oldest friend on Earth. He
wondered if he could mind-control Turtle, and force him to
override his emotional block. But no, the trauma was too
deeply buried to reach by such a sledgehammer technique.
His father with his skills could . . . Tach hugged himself,

rocking back and forth as grief crashed down and bore him under yet again.

The sound of screams, crashes, and curses pulled him back. He frowned at the door, then began backing slowly toward the bed as he realized that the sounds were getting closer. A lot closer. Very close. A large gray fist slammed through the door. The spatulate fingers closing on the rough edges of the hole tensed and a large section of door came ripping loose. *Hellcat* screeched, and the clear, viscous fluid that served as blood in the sentient ship flowed from the wound. It had soon set into clear, frozen rivulets. Tach stared with dread fascination as section by section the door came down. And lumbering through the uneven hole came a huge, stocky man with glabrous grayish skin and a bald head with a bulging forehead. Takisians were hanging off him like ornaments on a Christmas tree.

"Mind-blast him!" screamed Zabb, slamming a fist into the creature's face. He danced back as the monster plucked a soldier from his back and pitched him toward Zabb.

One Takisian was not being dislodged even by the creature's great strength. A delicately drawn face set upon a mountainous body, and an expression of dogged ferocity. Durg at'Morakh bo Zabb. Zabb's pet monster. Revulsion and disgust clawed at the back of Tach's throat. He darted for the ruined doorway, thoughts tumbling wildly.

Not by those hands. Wash in my blood if you must, Zabb, but not—

And came up against three feet of tempered steel. Slowly he raised his eyes to his cousin's.

No, by my hand.

A regretful but predatory smile touched Zabb's lips, and he lunged. Tach, skittering backward, lost his footing on the slick floor and went down. It saved his life, for the blade passed only inches above his head. There were more thumpings and crashings as the grotesque gray apparition staggered about the room dislodging Takisians and clawing futilely at Durg. Benaf'saj strode into the room, and Zabb lowered his blade; apparently he was not yet prepared to do out-and-out murder in the presence of an *Ajayiz'et*. Tachyon had never been so glad to see anyone.

The old lady let loose with a blast of mental energy that rattled the synapses of everyone in the room, and the creature collapsed like a felled tree. Bruised and battered crew members swarmed over the prone form, binding him with tangler ropes.

She pinned her commander with a cold gray-eyed gaze. "Would you be so good as to explain this tumult?"

"We found the creature."

"Really?" The accents were freezing.

Zabb sucked at his cheeks, his eyes avoiding his grand-dam's. "Well, he does seem to have changed form again."

Benaf'saj pinned Rabdan with a look. "And may we assume that these vials have something to do with the changes?"

A nervous clearing of the throat. "That would seem logical."

"So, where are these vials?"

"I don't know, *Kibr*. Perhaps he has hidden them some-where about the ship."

"Or perhaps they are only present when he is in his human form." She eyed the ruined door. "It will take Che Chu-erh of Al Matraubi," she said, referring to the ship by its full pedigree name, "some time to repair this door. Post guards. They can watch both Tisianne and this creature, and if the human returns, search him for the vials. Then, I trust, we will have no more of these ill-bred commotions." She left with a rustle of brocaded skirts.

Tach pulled a handerchief from his pocket, and knelt beside the strange captive. "You are?" he asked as he gently wiped at the blood flowing sluggishly from a sword wound.

The man glared up at him then reluctantly growled, "Aquarius."

"How do you do. I am Tisianne brant Ts'ara sek Halima sek Ragnar sek Omian, otherwise known as Dr. Tachyon."

"I know." He stared coldly past Tachyon's left shoulder.

He bent in low and whispered. "Do you have any other tricks up your sleeve? Something that might help us take out—" he jerked his chin toward the door, and the two rigid guards, "them?"

Aquarius stared rancorously up at him. "I turn into a dolphin, and I swim real fast."

The expression, together with his harsh, angry tone, snapped the thin thread of patience to which Tachyon was still managing to cling.

"You will forgive my bluntness, but that does us very little good in our present predicament."

"I did not ask to be here, land-dweller." And closing his eyes Aquarius proceeded to ignore both his fellow prisoner and his captors.

Tach unlimbered his hip flask, and while he paced made substantial inroads on the brandy. Twenty minutes later he noticed that Aquarius's skin was starting to crack and peel.

"Are you all right?"

"No. I must remain moist, or I am damaged."

"Well, why didn't you say so fifteen minutes ago?" Aquarius did not answer, and with a snort of aggravation Tach went trotting into the lavatory, and emerged with a glass of water. It didn't make much of an impression on the large form on the floor.

"Andami, could you bring me a pitcher or a bucket?"

The younger man worried his lower lip between his teeth. "My orders are to stay here."

"There are two of you."

"You'll try something."

"Am I your prince?"

"Yes. But you'll still try something, and I'm not about to get another reprimand from Zabb."

"May your line wither," he gritted, and resumed his harried trotting.

The next thirty minutes passed slowly as Tach tried to keep ahead of the rapid drying of the merman's skin. He was pouring a glass of water onto Aquarius's face when suddenly the form wavered and shifted, and there was Captain Trips, coughing and sputtering as the water ran up his nose.

Startled by the abrupt transformation, Tach yelled, dropped the glass, and backed off.

Trips stared fuzzily about the cabin, then down at his long, lanky form still festooned with loosely wrapped tangler ropes. He had lost a lot of bulk with Aquarius's departure, and as he rose the ropes sloughed off him, landing in a tangled heap on the floor around his feet.

He removed his glasses, and furiously polished them, all the while blinking myopically at Tachyon. The glasses were replaced, and he muttered.

"Oh, bummer, man."

Andami hurried over, and quickly rifled through Trips's pockets. He located the leather pouch with three unused vials. Tachyon craned to see, but the brightly colored powders looked singularly innocuous. He itched to get his hands on the substances, and do a full analysis. Something that could transmute a human form . . . and then it hit him. Captain Trips was not a nut—he was an ace.

"Captain." He thrust out his hand. "I owe you an apology."

"Uh . . . me, man?"

"Yes." Tach seized the man's limp hand, and gave it a hearty shake. "I doubted your story. In fact, I thought you a harmless lunatic. But you *are* an ace. And a most unusual one at that. These potions?"

"Help me call my friends."

He stepped in close, and lowered his voice. "And I don't suppose you have any more . . ." He winked, and Trips stared blankly down at him. Tach sighed. Nice, the man might be, but he wasn't precisely quick on the uptake. "Have you any more secreted about your person?"

"Oh no, man. It takes a long time to make this stuff, and I didn't think I'd be running into aliens. I mean, we beat the Swarm, and I didn't expect . . . I'm really sorry, man. I didn't mean to let you down. . . ."

"No, no. You couldn't have known, and you did very well." The Captain beamed, and Tach realized, with an overwhelming sense of failure and unworthiness, that this man adored and admired him.

And I'm going to fail him.

Tach crossed to the bed, and slumped down, his hands hanging limply between his thighs. Trips, with a sensitivity that the alien hadn't expected, crossed to the other side of the room, and left him alone with his miserable thoughts. Sometime later there was a tentative touch on his shoulder.

"Excuse me, man, I'm sorry to bother you, but I was wondering, like, how much longer until you got us . . ." He broke off, and splotches of red suffused his long face. "See, I got this little girl, and she's probably home from school by now, and the shop will be closing, and I'm afraid Susan won't stay with her, and Sprout's, like, not able to take care of herself." His long fingers twisted desperately through each other.

"I'm sorry. I wish I could do something. I wish I was the leader everyone thinks I am. But I'm not. I'm a fraud, Trips, both among my own people and among yours." The gangling hippie laid an arm across Tach's shoulders, and he leaned his head against the bony support of Trips's shoulder.

Trips gave a mournful shake of his head. "It's not like it is in the comics. In the comics the good guys always win. They've always, like, got the right power at the right time."

"Unfortunately life doesn't work that way. I'm very tired."

"Why don't you sleep awhile. I'll keep watch."

Tach wanted to ask him "Against what?" but he appreciated the generosity that had sparked the offer, and remained quiet. He kicked off his shoes, and Trips tenderly pulled a coverlet up to his chin.

He realized muzzily, as sleep claimed him, that he had always used bed and booze as an escape, and today he had used both. *The right power at the right time.* The thought nagged at the edges of his consciousness. *The right power—*

"By the Ideal!" He shot bolt upright, and kicked away the coverlet.

"Hey, what, man?"

He clutched feverishly at the lapels of Trips's coat. "I'm an idiot. An idiot. The answer's been right in front of me, and I missed it."

"What?"

"The Network device."

"Huh?"

Andami was regarding him curiously, and Tach quickly dropped to a whisper. "It's not a bowling ball. It's a singularity shifter." He hurriedly slipped his feet into his pumps. "Years ago, before I left home, one of the Master Traders discussed the possibility of selling my clan a new experimental teleporting device. He demonstrated one, and said they might become readily available after a few more tests. This has to be one of those devices. And it's in the main hold."

Trips was completely bewildered by his babblings. He grabbed for the only remark he had understood. "Yeah, but we're, like, not in the main hold."

"How to get us all there?" Tach's fingers scrabbled in his hair. "If we're all together, I think I could trigger the device and send us home. The greater the telepathic ability, the greater accuracy, and the size of what can be carried. That was the theory. Of course the Master Trader could have just been puffing. Hard to tell with the Network. They have the souls of greedy tradesmen."

"Uh . . . what's the Network?"

"Another spacefaring race, actually a number of spacefaring races, but we don't have to concern ourselves with that. The point is that a singularity shifter is here, on this ship, and it can get us home. Of course if Turtle had the device, that means the Network is present on Earth, and that could mean trouble." He scrubbed at his face. "No, one problem at a time. How to get to the hold."

"Like, what goes on there?"

"Well, obviously it's used for cargo storage, and when there's no cargo—which is most of the time, on a ship of this class—it's used for recreation. Dances and so forth."

Trips looked dubious. "I don't suppose we can invite everybody to a dance."

Tach laughed. "No." His expression went flat. "But we can invite them to a duel."

"Huh?"

"Hush a moment. I must think on this."

And he finally did what he should have done from the beginning. He thought like a Takisian instead of like an Earthman.

"Got it?" Trips asked when he again opened his eyes.

"Yes."

He lay back down, and probed for a familiar mind.

Turtle. There's a way out of this.

Yeah? The mental tone was one of utter defeat and hopelessness.

The device you had, it can send you home.

Yeah, but it's—

Just shut up, and listen. We're all going to be in the cargo bay—

Why?

Would you stop! Because I'm going to get us there. The attention will be on me, and while it is you must get that device.

How?

You know how.

I can't!

Tom, you must! It's our only hope.

It's not possible. The Great and Powerful Turtle could do it, but I'm just—

Thomas Tudbury—the Great and Powerful Turtle.

No, I'm just an ordinary man who's on the wrong side of forty, drinks too much beer, doesn't eat right, and who works at a fucking electronics repair shop. I'm no fucking hero.

You are to me. You gave me back my sanity and probably my life.

That was the Turtle.

Tom, the Turtle is a conglomeration of iron plates, TV cameras, lights, and speakers. What makes Turtle, Turtle is the man inside. You're the ace, Tom, it's time to come out of the shell.

Terror was coming off the man's mind in powerful waves, battering at Tach's shields, making him doubt his own plan. *I can't. Leave me alone.*

No, I'm going through with this, and you're going to have to come up to scratch, because if you don't, I will have died for nothing.

Died! What do you—

He broke the telepathic link wondering if he might have put too much pressure on Turtle's fragile emotions. Too late to worry about it now.

Kibr?

What, boy?

We find your tone to be less than pleasing, Ajayiz'et Benaf'saj.

She moderated her tone, adding a formal overlay of respect, if not for him, at least for his position. *What is it you wish, clan head?*

Summon the crew, there is a ceremony of adoption to be observed.

What trick are you up to?

Wait and see, or deny me, and be forever curious, he said impudently.

Her laughter glittered in his mind. *A challenge. Very well, my little prince, we will see just what it is you are up to.*

They had all gathered in the bay. Tom looked about, and let out an anguished cry, "My shell!"

Zabb's lips skinned back in a harsh smile. "We jettisoned it. It was taking up far too much room."

Tach paid little attention to Turtle's distress. His eyes roved quickly about the room ascertaining that the singularity shifter was still in its place.

"It had infrared and zoom lenses, and tuck-and-roll upholstery, and—" Zabb laughed. "You puke!"

Zabb stepped forward, fist upraised.

"Zabb brant Sabina sek Shaza sek Risala, touch my *stirps*, and I will not give you the courtesy of facing me. I will kill you

like a cur in the street." Zabb froze, and turned slowly to face
his small cousin.

"What farce is this?"

"As a breeding member of the house of Ilkasam I exercise
my right to add, by blood and bone, to my line."

"You would embrace these humans?" asked Benaf'saj.

"I would."

She raked them with an imperious glance. "They will, I
think, add little to your consequence."

Tach stepped between Trips and Turtle, and gripped them
by their wrists. "I would rather have them bound and bonded
to me than many who can make a greater claim to that right."
His eyes slid to Zabb.

"Very well, it is your right." The old woman settled
herself on a stool that *Hellcat* obligingly extruded for her. "Do
you agree to this adoption, understanding the duties and
obligations of those so honored?"

Three pairs of eyes stared at Tach, and he nodded slightly.

"We do," Asta said firmly when the two men continued to
stand and dither.

"Know then that you, and all your heirs and assigns, are
forever bound to the house of Ilkazam, line of Sennari through
its son, Tisianne. In all matters be great, and bring glory and
service to this house."

"Are we, like, Takisians now, man?" asked Trips in a
penetrating whisper.

"This ritual is to bind the psi-blind to a house. You would
not be permitted to mate with any member of the mentat
class, but you are deserving of our aid and protection."

"So we're serfs," Tom rasped.

"No, more like equerries. Mere servants are never
formally adopted." He turned on his heel, and pinned Zabb
with a hard glance. "But by my fathers, you, cousin, have
given me insult, and shown both contempt and abuse toward
my *stirps*, and I will have satisfaction."

Before Zabb could move, Benaf'saj spoke up. "You need
not accept this challenge. Courtesy does not apply retroactive-
ly to the psi-blind."

The commander swept her a bow. "But, *Ajayiz'et*, it will
give me the greatest pleasure to meet my beloved cousin.
Rabdan, you will act for me?"

"Yes, Commander."

"And Sedjur, you will act for me?" Tachyon asked. The old man managed a nod.

The two men moved quickly to an arms locker, and Tach joined his friends. As he kicked off his shoes, stripped out of his coat and brocaded waistcoat, and began tucking up his ruffles, he said quietly, "Stay well together. Tom, you know what you must do, but for god's sake act quickly." He ignored the human's frantic head shakings. "Fortunately the small sword gives the advantage to the defense, but I will be hard-pressed to hold off Zabb. The attention of my family will be focused on me. No one should notice your actions, and once you have the device I will send you home."

"What about you?" muttered Tom.

Tachyon shrugged. "I stay here. It is, after all, a matter of honor. I won't run."

"I hate fucking heroes."

"Has someone something with which to tie back my hair?"

Asta dropped to one knee, and rummaged about in her capacious dance bag. Pulling out a toe shoe, she tore the pink ribbon from the shoe, and held it out to the Takisian. It clashed horribly with his metallic red curls.

"Sir," Sedjur said softly. He was holding out a chain-mail sleeve which covered the sword arm up to the elbow, and a beautifully etched and hammered sword. The hilt was inlaid with semiprecious stones, and the filigree work on the basket was so fine that it looked like lace.

"Don't look so depressed, old friend."

"How can I not? You're no match for him."

"Unkind of you to say so. Especially when you trained me."

"And him; and I say again, you are no match for him."

"It is necessary." His tone indicated that the subject was closed, and he stared autocratically over the old retainer's head while the armor was strapped to his right forearm.

Asta giggled hysterically when a resin box was brought over, and Tach carefully coated the soles of his stockinged feet. She clapped her hands over her mouth, and subsided.

Tach, moving to the center of the room, hefted his rapier several times to accustom himself to its weight, and to remind his muscles of old skills, long unused. He didn't blame Asta for tittering. To modern humans this archaic ritual fought with archaic weapons must seem strange, especially in a spacefaring race. But there were sound reasons for the Takisian devotion to bladed weapons. They had atomic and laser weapons, but for hand-to-hand combat inside the skin of one of the living ships, a weapon that did not exceed the reach of the arm was better. An indiscriminate firing of projectile or coherent light weapon could badly damage a ship, and then it wouldn't much matter if the crew had won or not. There was also the Takisian love of drama. Virtually any fool could learn to fire a gun. It took real skill to be a swordsman.

Zabb joined him, and said in an undertone, "I have been looking forward to this moment for years."

"Then, I am delighted to be able to oblige you. It doesn't do to be denied so fondly a wished-for occurrence."

Their swords flashed in a brief salute, and engaged with a scrape of steel on steel.

Tom was no expert on the niceties of fencing, but he could see that this fight bore little resemblance to the brief glimpses of Olympic fencing he had seen on television. The speed was the same, but there was a deadly intensity about the two men as they fought for their lives. Their eyes were locked on each other, and the shifting of their stockinged feet on the floor of the ship made a soft whispering counterpoint to Tach's gasping breaths.

His companions were staring at him, Trips with the look of a desperate basset hound, Asta the tip of her tongue just moistening her lips. Tom slowly turned his head, and stared at the black ball where it rested on the shelf only feet away. He reached out, struggling so hard that sweat popped out along his forehead and upper lip, and he found a great, yawning emptiness. The device didn't even quiver.

Trips moaned, and Tom looked back just in time to see the foible of Zabb's blade glance across Tach's upper arm. A trail of red followed its path. Tach withdrew with more haste than grace, and barely parried a vicious thrust from his cousin. Trips, his watery blue eyes wild behind the thick lenses of his glasses, flung himself forward, and landed on Zabb's shoulders. With a snarl the Takisian reached back, and flipped the hippie neatly across the room. Trips lay stunned on the luminous deck, gasping like a fish. Several of Zabb's guards dragged him back, and dumped him on the floor between the other humans.

"I can't, I just can't," Tom whispered frenziedly.

"You fucking wimp," Asta enunciated clearly, and turned her back on him, returning her attention to the duel which had begun again.

Tach blinked hard, trying to clear the stinging sweat from his eyes. Each breath burned, and tiny tongues of flame seemed to be licking at the muscles of his sword arm.

Watch, watch, he urged himself.

Blade, coming up so fast it was just a blur.

He parried with a sharp beat, the force of the blow vibrating down his already-overtaxed muscles.

A riposte . . . but not with the blade. With his mind. A section of shield flowed, wavered. He thrust, hit, and Zabb staggered under the mental attack. He charged back. *Corps a corps.* Zabb's breath hot on his face. The blades hopelessly tangled between them. Tach strained, trying to throw Zabb back, but he was overmatched. The mind, a gray, implacable wall. *No, not quite!*

Tach jerked his body to one side, avoiding a vicious knee to the groin, leaped back, and kicked Zabb's back leg out from under him. Envelopment, but his cousin was too fast for him. Zabb parried, and followed with a swift riposte, and a mind blast. It slid off Tach's shields.

His vision seemed to be blurring around the edges. No stamina. Wind almost gone. *Turtle!*

He tried a wild, desperate thrust in tierce. Zabb tapped it aside almost contemptuously. He was a demon. That smile, still in place, and only a few beads of sweat mingled in the curly sideburns. His lashes dropped, hooding his eyes, and he pressed the attack. Nausea lay thick on his tongue as Tach realized that Zabb had only been toying with him before.

"Would you like to call it quits, beloved cousin?" whispered his tormentor. "Of course you would. But it's not to be. As promised, I am going to kill you."

No breath to answer the taunt, he just shook his head, more to clear the sweat than to deny the statement. He lanced out with a desperate mental blow which was turned by Zabb's shields, and then, like a miracle, he saw an opening. He lunged, blade scraping along Zabb's. Zabb took his foible in a flashing parry, and passed on, his point searching for the heart.

Time thrust! Lure to the unwary. Death!

* * *

He was sure he was seeing it: the brief flaring of the nostrils, the sardonic half-grin. Steve Bruder, with the same mannerisms as he crushed Tom's hand. *Fuck you!* he flung at Zabb as the power washed through him, tingling in his extremities. He reached out, and . . .

The blade coming swift and true, then miraculously pulled off line. Not much room, but enough! Tachyon brought up his sword, parrying on the forte.

A plentitude of targets offered themselves. The heart, the belly, a shoulder cut? Tach caught his lower lip between his teeth, and for one wild, glorious moment considered driving the point deep, deep into that hated body. He lunged, and their eyes met for one eternal, frozen moment. The blade turned in his hand, the hilt taking Zabb neatly in the chin with a sound like an ax hitting wood. Zabb's sword clattered to the floor, and he pitched forward on his face. There was a gasp like a rising wind from the assembled watchers. For a moment Tach stared at his sword, then flung it aside, and knelt beside his cousin. Gently he rolled him over, and cradled the larger man in his arms.

"You see, I couldn't do it," he whispered, and he wondered why there were tears pricking at his eyelids. "I know you'd rather I killed you, but I couldn't. And despite our training, death is not preferable to dishonor."

Tom stood, his hands clenched at his sides, and reveled in the waves of excitement and joy that were washing through his body. He had *done* it. True, he had used enough concentration to shift a bulldozer, and the end result had been only a minute deflection. *But it had been enough!* Tach would live—indeed, had won—because of Tom's action. With a little swagger he faced the alien device. It flashed through the air, landing with a satisfying *smack* in Tom's hands.

"Come on, Tachy, time to go," he sang out, his round cheeks flushed with excitement.

Tach laid Zabb gently down, and leaped to his friends. Not a single relative made a move.

Tom handed over the device with an awkward little bow.

Tach returned the salute. "Well done, Turtle. I knew you could do it."

He looked to Benaf'saj, made an elegant leg, winked, and ordered them *home*.

* * *

It was like being in the center of a vortex of nothingness. Icy cold and utter darkness, and for Tachyon the feeling that his mind was being torn into tiny, tattered streamers by the stress of holding all four travelers within the envelope of the singularity shifter.

By the ancestors, he wailed. *At least let us land on dry land.*

Tachyon crumpled, the device rolling from his nerveless fingers. Trips was squatting in a gutter holding his head in his hands, and muttering over and over, "Oh wow!" Tom retched a few times as his abused stomach tried to decide just where in space and time it was currently residing. There was a growing commotion, people yelling, windows being flung open, horns blaring as cars rolled to a stop, their occupants gawking at the tableau on the sidewalk. Tom dug the heels of his hands into his eyes, looked down at Tach, and quickly dropped to his knees beside the Takisian. Blood was pumping sluggishly from the long gash on his arm, and was running from his nose, and he was alarmingly white. The alien seemed to be scarcely breathing, and Tom pressed his ear to his friend's chest. The heartbeat fluttered erratically.

"Is he gonna be all right, man?" mumbled Trips.

"I don't know." Tom threw back his head, and stared up at a ring of black faces. "Somebody get a doctor."

"Shit, man, they just popped in from nooowhere."

"Teleportin' honkies. You think they be aces, or what?"

"Doctor, git a doctor," bawled a burly man.

Asta backed slowly away from the circle of spectators, her eyes searching quickly for the black ball. A couple of kids were inspecting the device, and she stepped to them.

"I'll give you five dollars each for that."

"Five dollars! Shit! It just be a bowlin' ball with no holes in it. What good that gonna do you?"

"Oh, you'd be surprised," she said softly, and fished her billfold out of her dance bag. The exchange was quickly made, and she tucked away the alien device.

The howling of sirens presaged the arrival of the police and an ambulance. Tach was loaded in, and Tom started to climb in with him. "Hey, where's the gizmo?"

Asta opened her mouth, blinked several times, and closed

it. "Gee, I don't know." She peered about as if expecting it to materialize from the Harlem landscape. "Maybe somebody in the crowd took it."

"Hey, buddy, you want to get your friend to the hospital or not?" growled one of the ambulance attendants.

"Well . . . look for it," Tom ordered, and climbed in.

Asta gave an ironic wave to the departing ambulance. "Oh, I will."

And Kien is going to be so pleased with this.

She sauntered away, searching for a subway station to carry her to the waiting arms of her lover and commander.

The padlock opened with a grating snap, and Tach pushed open the small side door to the warehouse. Trips and Turtle followed him into the echoing gloom, and Trips muttered something unintelligible at the sight of the ship resting in the center of the vast, empty building. The amber and lavender lights on the points of her spines glimmered faintly in the gloom, and dust spiraled in from all sides as she quietly collected and synthesized the tiny particles into fuel. She was singing one of the many heroic ballads that made up such a large part of ship culture, but cut off when she perceived Tach's entrance. The music was, of course, inaudible to the two humans.

Baby, he telepathed to her.

Lordly one. Are we going out? she asked with pathetic eagerness.

No, not tonight. Open please.

There are humans with you. Do they also enter?

Yes. This is Captain Trips, and Turtle. They are as brothers to me. Honor them.

Yes, Tisianne. I am pleased to have your names.

They cannot hear you. Like most of their kind, they are mind-blind.

Sorrow.

There was the ache of another kind of sorrow in his chest as he led the way to his private salon. Memory—it could be so clear—the day his father had taken him to select this ship. *All gone now.*

He settled back among the cushions on the bed, and ordered, *Search and contact.*

There are lordly ones present?

Yes.

And one of my kin? Baby asked, again with that pathetic eagerness.

Yes.

Seconds stretched into minutes, Tach lounging at his ease on the bed, Trips perched like a nervous roosting bird on a settee, and Tom bouncing nervously on the balls of his feet.

The wall before Tachyon shimmered, and Benaf'saj's face appeared. The ship boosted his powerful telepathy, and the link was made.

Tisianne.

Kibr. You were expecting the call?

Of course. I've known you—

Since I was in diapers, yes, I know.

You have surprised me, Tisianne. I think Earth has had a beneficial effect upon you.

It has taught me many things, he corrected in a dry tone. *Some more pleasant than others.* He paused, and fiddled with the foaming lace beneath his chin. *So, does it continue to be dagger points between us?*

No, child. You may stay with your rustic humans. After the defeat you dealt him, Zabb has no hope of the scepter. You should have killed him, you know. Tach just shook his head. Benaf'saj frowned down at her hands, and straightened her rings. *So we part. It is disappointing that we have no specimens, but the success of the experiment cannot be denied, and it will delight Bakonur to have our data. This effort will be the salvation of the family yet.*

Yes, Tach replied hollowly.

I will send a ship every ten years or so to check on you. When you are ready to return to us we will welcome you. Farewell, Tis.

Farewell, he whispered.

"Well?" asked Tom.

"They'll leave us in peace."

"Like, I'm really glad you're not gonna leave."

"So am I," he said, but his tone lacked certainty, and he stared mournfully at the glowing wall as if trying to pull back the image of his granddam.

A warm, capable hand with its short, stubby fingers closed firmly over his shoulder. A moment later Trips had gripped his other arm, and he sat silent, basking in the wash of love and affection coming off both the men, driving back his homesickness.

He laid a hand over Tom's. "My dearest friends. What an adventure we have had."

"Yeah, life is, like, pretty neat, man."

"Why didn't you kill him?" Tom asked.

Tach shifted, and stared up into Tom's brown eyes. "Because I would like to believe in the possibility of redemption."

Tom's grip tightened. "Believe it."

WITH A LITTLE HELP FROM HIS FRIENDS

By Victor Milán

CONTROVERSIAL SCIENTIST BRUTALLY SLAIN IN LAB, the headline read.

"You should see what it says in the *Daily News*," she said.

"Young lady," Dr. Tachyon said, shoving the sheaf of *New York Times*es away with fastidious fingertips and settling back perilously far in his swivel chair, "a policeman I am not. A doctor I am."

She frowned at him across the meticulous rectangle of his desk, cleared her throat, a small, fussy sound. "You have a reputation as father and protector to Jokertown. If you don't act, an innocent joker is going to go down for murder."

It was his turn to frown. He ticked the high heel of one boot against the desk's metal lip. "Have you evidence? If so, the unfortunate fellow's legal counsel is the man to take it to."

"No. Nothing."

He plucked a yellow daffodil from a vase at his elbow, twirled its bell before his nose. "I wonder. You are perceptive enough to play on my sense of guilt, surely."

She smiled back, made a deprecating hand-wave, forest-animal quick and almost furtive, but slightly stiff. It was coming to him, irrelevantly, how acculturated he had become to this heavy world; his first reaction had been that she was scarcely this side of painfully thin, and only now did he appreciate how closely she approached the elfin pallid Takisian ideal of beauty. An albino almost, skin pale as paper, white-blond hair, eyes barely blue. To his eyes she was drably dressed, a peach-colored skirt suit, cut severely, worn over a

260

white blouse, a chain at her neck, as pale and fine as one of her hairs.

"It's my job, Doctor, as you're well aware. My paper expects me to know what goes on in Jokertown." Sara Morgenstern had been the *Washington Post's* expert on ace affairs since her coverage of the Jokertown riots ten years ago had gleaned her a nomination for the Pulitzer prize.

He made no response. She dropped her eyes. "Doughboy wouldn't do that, wouldn't kill anyone. He's gentle. He's retarded, you see."

"I know that."

"He lives with a joker they call the Shiner, down on Eldridge. Shiner looks after him."

"An innocent."

"Like a child. Oh, he was arrested in '76 for attacking a policeman. But that was . . . different. He—it was in the air." She seemed to want to say more, but her voice snagged.

"Indeed it was." He cocked his head. "You seem unusually involved."

"I can't stand to see Doughboy get hurt. He's bewildered, afraid. I just can't keep my journalist's objectivity."

"And the police? Why not go to them?"

"They have a suspect."

"But your paper? Surely the *Post* is not without influence."

She shook back icefall hair. "Oh, I can write a scathing exposé, Doctor. Perhaps the New York papers will pick it up. Maybe even *Sixty Minutes*. Maybe—oh, in a year or two—there'll be a public outcry, maybe justice will be done. In the meantime he's in the Tombs, Doctor. A child, lonely and afraid. Do you have any idea what it's like to be unjustly accused, to have your freedom wrongfully taken away?"

"Yes. I do."

She bit her lip. "I forgot. I'm sorry."

"It's nothing."

Tach leaned forward. "I'm a busy man, dear lady. I have a clinic to run. I keep trying to convince the authorities that the Swarm Mother won't necessarily go away simply because we defeated her first incursion, but instead may be preparing a new and even deadlier attack." He sighed. "Well. I suppose I must look into this."

"You'll help?"

"I will."

"Thank God."

He stood up and came around to stand by her. She tipped her head back, lips curiously slack, and he had the sense that she was trying to be alluring without quite knowing how to go about it.

What is this? he wondered. He was not normally one to pass up an invitation from so attractive a woman, but there was something hidden here, and the old Takisian blood-feud instincts made him sheer away. Not that he sensed a threat; just a mystery, and that in itself was threatening to one of his caste.

On a whim, half irritated that she was making an offer and making it impossible to accept, he reached out and snagged the chain at her throat. A plain silver locket emerged, engraved with the initials A. W. in copperplate. She reached for it quickly, but cat-nimble he flipped it open.

A picture of a girl, a child, no more than thirteen. Her hair was yellow, the features fuller, the grin haughtier, but she bore an unmistakable resemblance to Sara Morgenstern. "Your daughter?"

"My—my sister."

"'A. W.'?"

"Morgenstern was my married name, Doctor. I kept it after my divorce." She half-turned away, knees pressed together, shoulders hunched. "Andrea was her name. Andrea Whitman."

"Was?"

"She died." She stood up rapidly.

"I'm sorry."

"It was a long time ago."

"Uncle Tachy! Uncle Tachy!" A blond projectile hit him in the shin and wrapped about him like seaweed as he stepped up to the door of the Cosmic Pumpkin ("Food for Body, Mind, & Spirit") Head Shop and Delicatessen on Fitz-James O'Brien Street, near the border of Jokertown and the Village. Laughing, he bent down, scooped the little girl up and hugged her.

"What did you bring me, Uncle Tachy?"

He rooted in a pocket of his coat, produced a caramel cube. "Don't tell your father I gave you this." Wide-eyed solemn, she shook her head.

He carried her into amiable clutter. Inside he clenched. Hard to believe this beautiful child of nine was mentally retarded, like Doughboy, permanently consigned to four.

Doughboy had been easier, somehow. He was immense, over two meters tall, an almost-spherical mass of white flesh, hairless, faintly bluish, face bloated almost to featurelessness, raisin eyes staring out from fat and tears. He was in his late twenties. He could not remember ever being called by anything other than a cruel nickname from a bakery's registered trademark. He was frightened. He missed Mr. Shiner and Mr. Benson the newsdealer who lived below them, he wanted the Go-Bot Shiner had bought him shortly before the men came and took him away. He wanted to go home, to get away from strange harsh men who poked him with their fingers and called him mocking names. He was pathetically grateful to Tachyon for coming to see him; when Tach took leave, in the bile-green visitation room in the Tombs, he clung to his hand and wept.

Tach wept too, but afterward, when Doughboy couldn't see.

But Doughboy was obviously a joker, victim of the wild card virus Tach's own clan had brought this world. Sprout Meadows was physically a perfect child, exquisite even by the exacting standards of the lord-lines of Ilkazam or Alaa or Kalimantari, sweeter-tempered than any daughter of Takis. Yet she was no less deformed than Doughboy, no less a monster by the standards of Tach's homeworld—and like him would have been instantly destroyed.

He looked around. A couple of secretaries nibbled late lunch by the front window, under the weathered aegis of a cigar-store Indian. "Where's your daddy?"

Her mouth carameled shut, she nodded her head left toward the head shop.

"What are you staring at, buster?" a voice demanded.

He blinked, focused belatedly on a sturdy young woman in a soiled gray CUNY sweatshirt standing behind the glass deli display. "I beg your pardon?"

"Listen, you male chauvinist asshole, I know about you. Just watch yourself."

Belatedly Tach recalled Mark Meadows's interchangeable pair of clerks. "Al—Brenda, is it?" A pugnacious nod. "Very well, Brenda, let me assure you I had no intention of staring at you."

"Oh, I get it. I'm not a debutante type like Peregrine, not

your kind at all. I'm one of those women men like you don't
see." She ran a hand through a stiff brush of hair, reddish with
tea-colored roots, sniffed.

"Doc!" A familiar stork figure stood bent over in the
doorway to the head shop.

"Mark, I am so glad to see you," Tachyon said with
feeling. He kissed Sprout on the forehead, ruffled her pigtailed
hair, set her on the murky linoleum. "Run and play, dearest
child. I would speak with your father."

She scooted off. "Have you a moment, Mark?"

"Oh, sure, man. Always, for you."

A pair of kids with leather overcoats and dandelion-climax
hair lurked among the paraphernalia and vintage posters on
the other side, but Mark was not the suspicious type. He
nodded Tach toward a table by the far wall, collected a teapot
and a couple of mugs, and followed, loose-limbed, bobbing his
head slightly as he walked. He had on an ancient pink Brooks
Brothers shirt, a fringed leather vest, a pair of vast elephant
bells faded almost to the hue of the white firework bursts tie-
dyed into them. Shoulder-length blond hair was crimped at his
temples by a braided thong. Had Tachyon not seen him in the
full splendor of his secret identity, he'd have thought the man
had no sense of dress at all.

"So what can I do for you, man?" Mark asked, beaming
happily through the glass planchets of his wire-rims.

Tach set elbows on the tablecloth—also tie-dyed—pursed
his lips as Mark poured. "A joker named Doughboy has been
arrested for murder. A young woman reporter has come to me
maintaining that he's innocent."

He drew breath. "I myself believe it, too. He is a very
gentle individual, for all that he is huge and hideous and
possesses metahuman strength. He is . . . retarded."

He waited a moment, heart hanging in his throat, but
what Mark said was, "So it's a rip-off, man. Why do the pigs say
he did it?" The epithet was spoken without rancor.

"The murdered man is a Dr. Warner Fred Warren, a
popular astronomy—to use the term loosely—writer in the
tabloids. To give you some idea, he wrote an article last year
entitled, 'Did Comet Kohoutek Bring AIDS?'"

Mark grimaced. He was not your standard hippie,
disdaining/distrusting all science. Then again, he was a
latecomer to the faith, who had gotten into Flower Power at a

time when everyone else in the Bay Area was getting heavily into Stalin.

"Dr. Warren's latest prognostication is that an asteroid is about to strike the Earth and end all life, or at least civilization as you know it. It did create quite a bit of controversy; amazing what attention you Earthers lavish on such folly. The police theorize that Doughboy heard his friends talking about it, became frightened, and one night last week went into the doctor's lab and beat him to death."

Mark whistled softly. "Any evidence?"

"Three witnesses." Tach paused. "One of them positively identifies Doughboy as the man he saw leaving Warren's apartment building the night of the crime."

Mark waved a hand. "No problem. We'll get him free, man."

Tachyon opened his mouth, shut it. Finally he said, "We need to see what other information they have amassed in the case. The police are not proving cooperative. They tell me to mind my own business, almost!"

Mark's blue eyes drifted off Tach's sightline. Tach sipped his tea. It was stringent and crisp, some kind of mint. "I know how you can take care of that. Does Doughboy, like, have an attorney?"

"Legal Aid."

"Why don't you get in touch with him, offer to act as unpaid medical expert."

"Splendid." He looked quizzically at his friend, head tipped like a curious bird. "How do you know to do that?"

"I don't know, man. It just came to me. So, like, where do I come in?"

Tach studied the tabletop. In the background forks clove tofu and thunked against earthenware cushioned by soggy romaine lettuce. It had been as much for the tonic effect Mark had on his spirits that he'd come here from the Tombs. But still . . .

He was out of his depth; he was, as he'd assured Sara, no detective. Now, Mark Meadows, the Last Hippie, didn't on the surface appear a much more promising candidate for sleuth, but he happened also to be Marcus Aurelius Meadows, PhD, the most brilliant biochemist alive. Before dropping out he'd been responsible for a number of breakthroughs, laid the groundwork for many more. He was trained to observe and trained to think. He was a genius.

Also, Tach liked the cut of his coat, which in itself was about enough for a Takisian.

"You've already helped me, Mark. This is your world, after all. You understand its ways better than I." *Though I've been on it longer*, he realized. "And there are your friends. You do have, ah, others than the two we met on my cousin's ship?"

Mark nodded. "Three others, so far."

"Good. I hope these prove more tractable than the others." He hoped one or the other of the Captain's alter egos would have skills that might fall handy; fortunately he could imagine no purpose the surly were-porpoise Aquarius might serve, but the vainglorious coward Cosmic Traveler was another matter. And even to save poor Doughboy from death in life, he wasn't ready to endure the Traveler again so soon.

He scraped his chair back and rose. "Let us go play detective together, you and I."

The kid had cammie pants and a Rambo rag, standing there on the corner of Hester and the Bowery trying to hold down magazine pages against the wind's tugging. Tach glanced over his shoulder. The article was slugged, *"Dr. Death: Self-made Cyborg Soldier of Fortune Battles Commies in Salvo."*

The kid looked up as the two men took their places beside him at the newsstand, truculence tightening lean Puerto Rican features. His expression flowed like wax into awe.

He was looking at the center button of a yellow paisley vest. Out over his forehead an immense green bow tie with yellow polka dots blossomed from a pink shirt collar. To either side hung a purple tailcoat. A purple stovepipe hat, its green band embossed in gold peace signs, threatened the watered-milk overcast.

Yellow-gloved fingers flashed a V. "Peace," said the beaky *norteamericano* face hovering up there amid all that color.

The kid tossed the magazine at the proprietor and fled.

Captain Trips stood blinking after him, wounded. "What'd I *say*, man?"

"Never mind," chortled the being behind the counter. "He wouldn't have bought it anyway. What can I do you for, Doctor? And your colorful friend here?"

"Mm," said Mark, sniffing, nostrils wide, "fresh popcorn."

"That's me," Jube said. "That's how I smell." Tachyon winced.

"Far out!"

For a moment glass-bead eyes stared, blue-black skin rumpled up Jubal's forehead: orogenic surprise. Then he laughed.

"I get it! You're a hippie."

The Cap'n beamed. "That's right, man."

Blubber shook. "Goo-goo-goo-Jube," he bellowed. "I am the Walrus. Pleased to meetcha."

He *did* look like a walrus, five foot nothing, hanging fat, a big smooth skull with random hair-tufts sticking out from it here and there like rusty shaving brushes, flowing into the collar of his green and black and yellow Hawaiian shirt without the intervention of a neck. He had little white tusks stuck at either end of his grin. He pushed out a Warner Brothers cartoon hand, three fingers and a thumb, which the Captain eagerly shook.

"This is Captain Trips. An ace, a new associate of mine. Captain, meet Jubal Benson. Jube, we need from you some information."

"Shoot." He made a pistol gesture with his right hand, rolled his eyes at Trips.

"What do you know about the joker called Doughboy?"

Jube scowled tectonically. "That's a bum rap. Boy wouldn't hurt a fly. He even lives in the same rooming house I do. See him most every day—used to, before this came down."

"He didn't, like, hear people talking about an asteroid crashing into the Earth and get real worked up about it, did he?" Trips asked. A vagrant piece of newsprint had washed up against the backs of his calves on a wind that hadn't yet realized it was spring. He ignored it and the chill alike.

"If he'd heard anything like that, he'd hide under his cot and you'd never get him out till you convinced him it was a joke. Is *that* what they're claiming?"

Trips nodded.

"The one to talk to is Shiner. He rents the place, feeds Doughboy, and lets him stay there. He's got a shoeshine stand up Bowery almost to Delancey, up where Jokertown's more touristy."

"Would he be there now?" Tach asked.

Jube consulted a Mickey Mouse watch whose band all but vanished into his rubbery wrist. "Lunch hour's over, which means he's prob'ly knocking off himself to eat lunch right now. He should be home. Apartment Six."

Tachyon thanked him. Solemn, Trips tipped his hat. They started off.

"Doc."

"Yes, Jubal."

"Better get this cleared up quick. Things could get very heavy around here this summer if Doughboy gets a railroad job. They say Gimli's back on the streets."

An eyebrow rose. "Tom Miller? But I thought he was in Russia."

The Walrus laid a finger along his broad flat nose. "That's what I mean, Doc. That's what I mean."

"I found him, oh, fifteen, sixteen year ago it was." The man called Shiner sat on his cot in the single room of the apartment on Eldridge Street, rocking to and fro with his hands clasped between skinny knees. "Back in 1970. Wintertime it was. He was sitting there next to a dumpster in a alley behind this mask shop, bawling his eyes out. Mama just took him there and left him."

"That's terrible, man," said Trips. He and Tach were standing on the meticulously swept hardwood floor of the apartment. Shiner's cot and a big mattress with stained ticking were the only furniture.

"Oh, I guess maybe I can understand. He was eleven or twelve, already twice as big as me, stronger'n most men. Must have been powerful hard to take care of."

He was small for an Earther, shorter than Tach. From a distance he looked to be an unexceptional black man in his fifties, with gray-dusted hair and a gold right incisor. Up close you noticed that he shone with an unnatural luster, more like obsidian than skin. "I do my own advertisin', like," he'd explained to Trips when Tachyon introduced them. "Drum up business for my 'shine stand."

"How well could Doughboy find his way around the city unaided?" Tachyon asked.

"He couln'nt. Find his way around Jokertown all right, always be jokers looking out for him, you know, seeing he didn't wander off." For a moment he sat and stared at a spill of sunlight in which a tiny metal Ferrari lay on its side. "They say he killed this scientist dude up by the Park. He never even been to the Park but twice. He don't know nothin' about no astronomy."

He squeezed his eyes shut. Tears leaked through. "Oh,

Doctor, you got to do something. He's my boy, he's like my son, and he's hurtin'. And there nothing I can do."

Tachyon shifted weight from boot to boot. The Captain plucked a daisy, rather the worse for wear, from his lapel, squatted down and held it out to Shiner.

Sobbing, the black man opened his eyes. They narrowed at once, in suspicion, confusion. Trips just hunkered there with flower proffered. After a moment Shiner took it.

Trips squeezed his hand. A tear fell on his own. He and Tachyon quietly left.

"Dr. Warren was not just a scientist," Martha Quinlan said as she guided them back through the apartment, "he was a saint. The quest to get the truth before the people was never-ending for him. He is a martyr to man's quest for Knowledge."

"Oh, wow," Cap'n Trips said.

As far as Tachyon had been able to learn, the late Warner Fred Warren had had no next of kin. A legal battle was shaping up for possession of the trust fund which had enabled him to keep a penthouse apartment on Central Park and devote his life to science—his grandfather had been an Oklahoma oil millionaire who attributed his success to dowsing and died claiming he was Queen Victoria—but in her capacity as managing editor of the *National Informer* Ms. Quinlan seemed to be acting as executor for Warren's estate.

"It's so good of you to come pay your respects to a fallen colleague, Dr. Tachyon. It would have meant so much to dear Fred, to know our distinguished visitor from the stars had taken a personal interest in him."

"Dr. Warren's contribution to the cause of science was unparalleled," Tachyon said sonorously. . . . *since Trofim Lysenko*, he emended mentally. *Ah, Doughboy, may you never guess what I endure to gain you justice*. It was a reflexive bit of Takisian misdirection, the story Tachyon had given Quinlan when he called to see about looking over the murder scene.

"It's a terrible thing," Quinlan warbled, leading them along a hallway hung with framed prints of hunting dogs from 1920s magazines. She was a little taller than Tach, wearing a dress like a black sack from neck and elbows to thighs, scarlet tights, white shoes, and thick plastic bracelets. Her gray-blond hair was styled straight and cut at a bias. Her eyes were made up like Theda Bara's; she wore no lipstick. "A tragedy. So fortunate they caught the fellow who did it. Not right in the head, they say, and a joker to boot. Probably some kind of sex deviant. Our reporters are looking into this story *very* carefully, I can assure you."

Trips made a sound. Quinlan stopped at the end of the hall. "Here it is, géntlemen. Preserved as it was the day he died. We intend to make this a museum, against the day poor Fred's greatness is at last acknowledged by the scientific establishment which so persecuted him." She gestured them grandly in.

The door to Dr. Fred's lab had been wood, solid even for a ritzy New York apartment. It didn't seem to have slowed down his last visitor. Conscientious gnomes from the forensic lab in the brick tower at One Police Plaza had swept up most of the splinters, but a shattered stub of door still hung on bent brass hinges.

Tachyon still had a certain difficulty fitting his eyes around the utilitarian, rectilinear shapes of terrestrial scientific equipment. Science on Takis was the province of the few, even among the Psi Lords; their equipment was grown of gene-engineered organisms even as their ships were, or custom-built by craftsmen concerned to make each piece unique, significant. Here he didn't have much trouble. The gear that occupied the rubber-topped workbenches had been busted all to hell. Papers and shattered glass were strewn everywhere.

"Did he have, like, his observatory here?" Trips asked, craning around with his stupendous topper in hand.

"Oh, no. He had an observatory out on Long Island where he did most of his stargazing. He analyzed his results here, I suppose. There's a darkroom and everything." She rested a long fingernail on the line of her jaw. "What exactly was your name again? Captain . . . ?"

"Trips."

"Like in that Stephen King book? What was it? *The Stand*."

"Uh, no. It's like, they used to call Jerry Garcia that." When she showed no signs of enlightenment, he went on, "He was the leader of the Grateful Dead. He, uh, he still ·is. He didn't draw an ace, you know, like Jagger or Tom Douglas, and . . ." He noticed that her eyes had gone glassy and focused on oblivion, trailed his words away, and wandered off around the perimeter of the largish, cluttered, ruined room.

"Say, Doctor, what're these dark splashes all over the walls?"

Tach glanced up. "Oh, those? Dried blood, of course." Trips paled and his eyes bulged a bit. Tachyon realized he'd run roughshod yet again over Earther sensibilities. For a folk so robust, Terrestrials had such tender stomachs.

Still, even he was amazed at the savagery vented on the penthouse lab. There was a mindless quality to it, a palpable psychic emanation of fury and malice. Given the limited imagination of most police he'd encountered, Tachyon was no longer surprised they found Doughboy a plausible suspect; they thought him a demented freak, a caricature from a slasher flick, and that certainly described Dr. Warner Fred Warren's assailant. Yet Tach was more convinced than ever that vast gentle child was incapable of such an act, however provoked.

The *Informer* editor had vanished, overcome with emotion no doubt. "Hey, Doc, come look at this," Trips called. He was bending over a drafting table scattered with star-speckled photographs, peering intently at one edge.

Tach bent down beside him. There was a thin patch of gray, wrinkled, like a bit of tissue paper that had been wetted, stretched on the plastic surface, and left to dry. There was a curious membraneous quality to it that tickled the fringes of cognition.

"What is this stuff?" Trips asked.

"I do not know." His eyes skimmed curiously over the photographs. A date penciled on the edge of one caught his eye: 4/5/86, the day Warren was murdered.

From a pocket Cap'n Trips produced a little vial and a scalpel in a disposable plastic sheath. "Do you always carry such implements?" Tach asked as he began to scrape up a few flakes of the gray stuff.

"Thought they might come in handy, man. If I was gonna be a detective and all."

Shrugging, Tach turned his attention to the photograph that had caught his eye. It was the top of a small stack. Picking it up, he discovered a dozen or more photos which to his untrained eye all seemed to show the same star field.

"All right, Doc, Captain," an unfamiliar voice blared from behind. "Give us a big smile for posterity."

With a dexterity that surprised even himself, Tach half-rolled the photos and slipped them into one voluminous coat sleeve even as he spun to face the intruder. Martha Quinlan stood inside the door beaming while a young black man dropped to one knee and bombed them with a camera flash that could have driven a laser beam to Mars.

With a certain reluctance Tach let his fingers slip from the outsized wooden grips of the .357 magnum neatly concealed in a shoulder rig beneath his yellow coat. "I presume you've an explanation for this," he said with fine Takisian frost.

"Oh, this is Rick," Quinlan warbled. "He's one of our staff photographers. I simply *had* to have him come down and record this event."

"Madam, I'm afraid I do not do this for publicity," Tach said, alarmed.

Unfolding himself, Rick waved a reassuring hand. "Don't sweat it, man," he said. "It's just for our files. *Trust* me."

"Tezcatlipoca," Dr. Allan Berg said, tossing the print back on top of the mound of books, papers, and photos under which his desk putatively lurked.

"Say what?" Trips said.

"1954C–1100. It's a rock, gentlemen. Nothing more, nothing less."

The little office smelled strongly of sweat and pipe tobacco. Trips stared out the window at the afternoon Columbia campus, watching a gray squirrel halfway up a maple tree cussing out a black kid walking past with a scuffed French-horn case.

"A curious name," Tachyon said.

"It's an Aztec deity. A pretty surly one, I gather, but that's the way it goes: you find an asteroid, you get to name it." Berg grinned. "I've thought about hunting for one to name after me. What the hey—immortality of a sort." He looked like a good-natured Jewish kid, eager eyes, long oval face, big nose, except that his curly unkempt hair was gray. He had a blue shirt and brown tie under a sweater so loosely woven you could just about fish with it. His manner was infectious.

"It's big enough to, like, do some damage if it hits?" Trips asked. "Or is that more exaggeration?"

"No, ah, Captain, I can assure you it's not." He stumbled a little over the honorific. Norms, especially in the New York area, had pretty well had to accustom themselves to the ways of aces, especially those who chose to emulate the comic-book heroes of yore and don colorful costumes. And Cap'n Trips was weirder than most. "Tezcatlipoca's a nickel-iron oblong roughly a kilometer by a kilometer and a half, weighing a good many million metric tons. Depending on the angle at which it struck, it could create devastating tidal waves and earthquakes, it could produce effects such as those hypothesized for a nuclear winter, it could quite conceivably crack the crust or blow away much of the atmosphere. It would almost certainly be the greatest catastrophe in recorded history—I might give you a better estimate if I took time to work it all out on paper.

"But I won't. Because it's not going to hit the planet." He sipped coffee from a cracked mug. "Poor Fred."

"I admit I was rather startled that you spoke so sympathetically of him when I called you, Dr. Berg," Tachyon said.

Berg set the cup down, stared at the tepid black surface. "Fred and I went to MIT together, Doctor. We were roommates for a year."

"But I thought everybody said Dr. Warren was just some kind of crackpot," Trips said.

"That's what they say. And he was a crackpot, much as I hate to say it. But he was not just *any* crackpot."

"I fail to see how a trained scientist could espouse the theories for which Dr. Warren was so, ah—"

"Notorious, Doctor. Go ahead and say it. You sure you won't have any coffee?" They refused politely. Berg sighed.

"Fred had what you call a will of iron. And he had a romantic streak. He always felt there should be fantastic things out there—ancient astronauts, alien machines on the moon, creatures unknown to science. He wanted to be the first to go out and rigorously prove so many things respectable scientists scoffed at." His mouth slipped into a sad smile. "And who knows? When Fred and I were kids, people thought the idea of intelligent life on other planets was farfetched. Maybe he could have pulled it off.

"But Fred was impatient. When he didn't see the results he wanted—why, he started seeing them anyway, if you know what I mean."

"So it was as Dr. Sagan said in his article in the *Times*," Tachyon said, "Dr. Warren fastened upon a rock which falls by the Earth at regular intervals and embued it with menace."

Berg frowned. "With all due respect, Dr. Sagan got it wrong this time. Gentlemen, Dr. Warren had an infinite capacity for self-deception, but he wasn't just some fool the *Informer* dragged in off Seventh Avenue. He knew how to use an ephemeris, was surely cognizant of 1954C–1100's history.

He was a trained astronomer, and as far as technical and observational details go, a damned fine one." He shook his shaggy head. "How he could talk himself into believing this nonsense about Tezcatlipoca, God alone knows."

Trips was polishing his glasses on his fantastic bow tie. "Any chance he could've been right, man?"

Berg laughed. "Forgive me, Captain. But Tezcatlipoca's newest approach was spotted and plotted eight months ago by Japanese astronomers. It does in fact intersect the Earth's orbital path, but well clear of the planet itself."

He stood up, smoothed down his sweater, which had ridden up to the center of his stomach. "That's the pity, gentlemen. Oh, not this"—patting incipient paunch—"but the disservice Fred performed his fellow scientists. Our instruments are so much more sophisticated than they were even last time Tezcatlipoca passed, in 1970. And yet any astronomer who dares twitch his telescope in its direction will wind up lumped with von Däniken and Velikovsky forevermore."

The night was well advanced. Tach was sitting slumped in a chair in his apartment in a maroon smoking jacket and semidarkness, listening to Mozart in violins, bibbing brandy, and getting far gone in maudlin when the phone rang.

"Doc? It's me, Mark. I've found something."

The tone in his voice cut through brandy fog like a firehose. "Yes, Mark, what is it?"

"I think you better come see for yourself."

"I'm on my way."

Fifteen minutes later he was on the floor above the Cosmic Pumpkin, gaping around in stoned amazement. "Mark? You have a whole laboratory above your head shop?"

"It's not complete, man. I don't have any real big-scale stuff, no electron microscopes or anything. Just what I was able to piece together over the years."

It looked like a cross between Crick & Watson and a hippie crash pad circa 1967, shoehorned into a space barely larger than a broom closet. Diagrams of DNA strands and polysaccharides shared wall with posters of the Stones, Jimi, Janis, and, of course, Mark's hero Tom Marion Douglas, the Lizard King—a twinge here for Tach, who still blamed himself for Douglas's death in 1971. A Terrestrial biochemist's tools were more familiar to Tach than an astronomer's, so he recognized here a centrifuge, there a microtome, and so on. A lot of it had obviously seen hard use before passing into Trips's hands, some was jerry-rigged, but it all looked serviceable.

Mark was in a lab coat, looking grim. "'Course, I didn't need anything too fancy, once I saw the gas chromatography on that tissue sample."

Tach blinked and shook his head, realizing the large and convolute piece of equipment whose identity he'd been puzzling over the last half-minute was possibly the world's most intricate bong. "What did you find, then?" he demanded.

Mark passed him a slip of paper. "I don't, like, have enough data to confirm the structure of that protein chain. But the chemical composition, the proportions . . ."

Tachyon felt as if a coin were being dragged down the vertebrae in his neck. "Swarmling biomass," he breathed.

Mark gestured at a bale of papers stacked on a bench. "You can check the references on this, analyses from the Swarm invasion. I—"

"No, no. I trust your work, Mark, more than anyone's but mine." He shook his head. "So swarmlings murdered Dr. Warren. Why?"

"How about *how,* man? I thought swarmlings were great big things, like in some Japanese monster movie."

"At first, yes. But a Swarm culture—a Mother—how to say?— *evolves* in response to stimuli. Its first brute-force attack failed. Now it refines its approach—as I've been warning those fools in Washington it might, all along." His mouth tightened. "I suspect that it is now attempting to emulate the life-form that repulsed it before. Such is a common pattern for these monsters."

"So you've had a lot of experience with these things?"

"Not I. But my people, yes. They are, you might say, our bitterest enemies, these Swarm creatures. And we theirs."

"And now they're, like, infiltrating us?" Mark shuddered.

"I think they are a long way from being able to pass undetected. Yet something about this troubles me. Usually at this stage of a Swarm incursion they are not so discriminating."

"And why did they pick on poor Fred?"

"You begin to sound like that horrid woman, my friend." Tach grinned, clapped him on the shoulder. "I hope we'll find the answer to that question when we track these horrors down. Which is the next thing we must do."

"What about Doughboy?"

Tach sighed. "You're right. I will call the police, first thing in the morning, and tell them what we learned."

"They're never gonna buy it."

"I can but try. Get rest, my friend."

They didn't buy it.

"So you found swarmling tissue in Warren's lab," rasped the Homicide South lieutenant in charge of the case. By phone she sounded young, Puerto Rican, harassed, and as if she did not at the moment love Tisianne brant Ts'ara of House Ilkazam. "You are taking a very active interest in this case for a medical expert witness, Doctor."

"I am trying to perform my civic duty. To prevent an innocent man from suffering further. And, incidentally, to alert the proper authorities to a frightful danger which may threaten this entire world."

"I appreciate your concern, Doctor. But I'm a homicide investigator. Planetary defense is not in my jurisdiction. I have to get permission just to go into Queens."

"But I have solved a homicide for you!"

"Doctor, the Warren case is under investigation by the competent authorities, which is us. We have a witness who positively identifies Doughboy leaving the scene at the right time."

"But the tissue samples—"

"Maybe he was growing them in a petri jar. I don't know, Doctor. Nor do I know the credentials of whoever identified this alleged swarmling tissue—"

"I assure you I am an alien biochemistry expert—"

"In several senses." He jerked slightly back from the receiver; perversely, he was starting to like this woman. "I'm not saying I doubt you, Doctor. But I can't just wave my hand and let your man walk free. That's up to the DA. Whatever you have, take to Doughboy's attorney and have him present it. And if you've really found more swarmlings, I'd suggest you take that up with General Meadows at SPACECOM."

Who is Mark's father. "And one thing more, Doctor."

"What is that, Lt. Arrupe?"

"Get off this case or I'll chuck your ass in the joint. I don't need amateurs muddying the water."

Chrysalis looked at him with a face glass-clear and china bone. "Anything strange happening in Jokertown?" she drawled in that hermaphrodite British accent of hers. "Whatever makes you think anything strange might happen here?"

He sat at one end of the bar, well away from the morning regulars. He wasn't exactly a stranger at the Crystal Palace. He never quite relaxed here, just the same.

"Not just Jokertown. This part of Manhattan, from Midtown south."

She set down a glass she was polishing. "You're serious?"

"When I say strange, I mean strange for Jokertown. Not the latest outrage at Jokers Wild. Not Black Shadow dangling some mugger from a streetlamp by his foot. Not even another bow-and-arrow murder by that maniac with his playing cards. Something out of what passes for the ordinary hereabouts."

"Gimli's back."

Tach sipped his brandy and soda. "So they say."

"What are you paying?"

He raised a brow.

"Dammit, I'm not just a back-fence gossip! I pay for my information."

"And are well paid. I've contributed my share, Chrysalis."

"Yes. But there's so much you don't tell me. Things that go on at the clinic . . . confidential things."

"Which shall remain confidential."

"All right. Goodwill in this mutant community is my stock in trade too, and you don't have to remind me how influential you are. But someday you'll go too far, you metal-haired little alien fox."

He grinned at her. And was gone.

Tring. Tach winched one eye open. The world was dark but for the usual Manhattan light-haze and perhaps a little moonlight oozing in through open curtains, silvering the bare female rump upturned beside him on the maroon coverlet of his water bed. He blinked, gummily, and tried to remember the name of the person to whom the buttocks belonged. They were really outstanding buttocks.

Tring. More exigent this time. One of this world's most satanic inventions, the telephone. Beside him the glorious buttocks shifted slightly and a pair of shoulders came into view from behind a ridge of comforter.

Trrrr- He picked up the phone. "Tachyon."

"It's Chrysalis."

"Delighted to hear from you. Do you have any idea what hour of the night it is?"

"One-thirty, which is more than you knew. I've got something for you, Doctor darling."

"Whozat, Tach?" mumbled the woman at his side. He patted her rump abstractedly, trying to remember her name. Janet? Elaine? *Blast.*

"What is it?" Cathy? Candi? Sue?

Chrysalis hummed a tune.

"What in the name of the Ideal was that?" he demanded. Mary? *Confound Chrysalis and her damned humming!*

"A song we used to sing, back when I was at camp. 'Johnny Rebeck.'"

"You called at one-thirty in the morning to sing me a campfire song?" Belinda? This was getting to be too much.

"'And all the neighbors' cats and dogs will nevermore be seen/They've all been ground to sausages in Johnny Rebeck's machine.'"

Tach sat up. "What is it?" the woman beside him demanded, petulant now, turning toward him a face masked with sleep and dark hair.

"You've got something."

"Like I told you, luv. Not Jokertown, but nearby. Around Division, next to Chinatown. Dogs and cats disappearing— strays, pets; people in these parts aren't too concerned with leash laws. And pigeons. And rats. And squirrels. Several blocks are just devoid of the usual urban wildlife. Jokes about oriental cuisine aside, I thought this might qualify as your strange event."

"It does." *Ancestors, how it does!*

She purred. "You owe me, Tachyon."

He was swinging his legs out of bed, wishing for courtesy's sake he could remember this young woman's name to send her packing. "I do."

"And by the way," Chrysalis said, "her name's Karen."

"Doctor," Trips said through a cloud of his own breath, "do you have any idea what Brenda *called* me when I phoned her to come look after Sprout at this hour of the night?"

In the weeks he'd known Mark, it was the first time he had heard him voice a complaint of any sort. He sympathized. "I don't want to even imagine, dear Mark. But this is crucial. And I feel we have no time to waste."

Mark crumpled. "Yeah. You're right. Doughboy's got it a whole lot worse than anything I've ever known. I'm sorry, Doc."

Tachyon looked at this man, a brilliant scientist whom personal demons had driven to batter himself into little more than a derelict, and honestly wondered. He stroked his arm. "No harm done, Mark."

Not far away the cars hissed over the Manhattan Bridge. They had here a dark side street in a none-too-prepossessing part of town, small shops and shadows and loan sharks and derelict manors, gray cramped buildings winking here and there with broken windows in the glow of a single fading streetlight. Not an hour to be abroad here, even without the prospect of otherworldy menace.

"This may just be a false alarm," Tach said. "When Chrysalis told me about the animal disappearances, it occurred to me that swarmlings need food, and unless this culture advances more quickly than any I've heard of, they could scarcely buy it at the A&P."

He stopped, faced his friend, gripped him by the biceps. "Understand this now, Mark. There may be nothing here. But if we've found what we are looking for, we are going to be confronting a monster like something from a horror movie. But it's real. It's the enemy of every living organism on this planet, and it is utterly without compunction."

Mildly, Mark gestured up the block. "Does it look anything like that, man?"

Tach stared at him a moment. Slowly he swiveled his head right.

A figure stood on the corner at the end of the block nearer the overpass. A coat was stretched around it, a hat pulled low, but even muffled as it was there was no hiding that its proportions were never those of a normal human being.

"Excuse me a moment, man," Trips said. He pulled away, and holding hat on head ran from the apparition, rounding the corner with knee-swinging sole-slapping strides.

Coward! blazed up nova in Tach's breast, and then, *But no, I cannot be so hard on him, for he is no fighter and this is a menace strange to his kind.* He squared his shoulders, straightened his cravat, and turned to face the creature.

It took a swaying step forward, another. One foot made a sucking sound as it came off the asphalt. From the darkness behind it another figure lurched, clothed the same way, its outline different but clearly kindred. *Ah, Benaf'saj, you were right to doubt me. I never imagined there might be two.* He readied his spirit for death.

"Doctor."

His head snapped round. A young woman stood beside him, dressed from throat to soles in black broken only by the sideways commas of a *yin-yang* design on her chest. The emblem was matched by a black mask which curved up from her left cheekbone across the right side of her forehead, leaving half her face bare. She was taller than he. Her hair was black and lustrous. What he could see of her face looked Oriental and breathtakingly beautiful.

He performed a courtly if abbreviated bow. "I don't believe I've had the pleasure."

"I am Moonchild, Doctor. And I have the honor of knowing you—if not exactly at first hand."

It was beginning to seep through his blood-brain barrier. "You're one of the Captain's friends."

"I am."

Danger always made his blood run high. At least that was his subsequent excuse for the lechery that gripped him now. "Dearest child," he breathed, grabbing her hands, "you are the loveliest sight these eyes have beheld in ages . . ."

Even in the diffuse glow he saw her blush. "I will do my poor best to aid you, Doctor," she said, misunderstanding . . . maybe.

She whirled from him and glided down the street, relaxed and poised and deadly-seeming as a stalking leopard. He marveled at her aura of strength, her liquid grace, the play of buttocks beneath her tight black suit—buttocks were much with him, tonight. He trotted after her, Takisian-unwilling to let a woman face danger.

When she was twenty meters from the nearer swarmling she flowed into a charge, at ten launched herself clear of the street with panache that made him gasp. She pirouetted in flight, snapped her right heel around behind her, pivoting, driving a perfect spinning back kick into the shoulder of the beast. There was a dry squelch, dropped-pumpkin sound. The thing gave back. Still spinning, Moonchild rebounded, touched lightly down, recovered into battle stance.

The monster's arm fell off. Dropped right out of its sleeve. She freaked.

All at once she was all over the street without even

moving. Screaming, wailing, thrashing like a three-way cat-fight, sinking to the pavement all the while. Tachyon stared. *But she made such a strong start*, he thought plaintively.

For a moment the swarmlings seemed to stare at her too. Then as one they turned back to face Tachyon, the chemoreceptors that had alerted them to his nearness guiding them inexorably toward the hated, dreaded Takisian. An empty sleeve flapped grotesquely against the first one's side.

Tach reached for its mind. It was like clutching fog. His thought passed ineffectually through the diffusion of electrochemical signals that made up the thing's mind.

Unsurprised, he pulled out the snub-nosed Smith & Wesson, leaned into an isosceles stance, gun gripped both-handed, sights lined up on the center of that unlovely mass, inhaled, held it, squeezed twice. The pistol produced a very satisfactory amount of flame and recoil and noise. No other results.

Shocked, he lowered the pistol. The beast was twenty meters away; he couldn't have missed. Then he saw the two small holes, right where they should have been, one on either side of the buttoned coat-front. Mental attacks weren't the only things that passed right through a swarmling.

"I'm in trouble," he announced. He aimed for the shadow beneath the hat-brim, fired twice more. The hat flew off. So did great chunks of the diseased-potato mass within that served the being as a head. It came on.

Moonchild had quit screaming and beating at herself, and sat with hands between knees, watching intently. "Bullets don't hurt them," she said, voice raw from screaming. "They—they're not human."

"Very observant." He fired off the last two, started backing away, groping in a pocket for a speed reloader, hoping he had one.

"I thought I had mutilated a human being, a joker," she said. She was on her feet. She raced toward a building to Tach's right, crossing behind the lumbering swarmlings, launching herself again, this time on a trajectory Tach would have sworn would take her to the third floor of the structure. But he didn't see, because when she entered the building's shadow she vanished.

To reappear seconds later, feetfirst right through the middle of the second swarmling. Cloth tore, biomass gave, and the being just generally came apart as she hit pavement and rolled.

A moment and she was up again, sprinting forward, dropping low to support herself on one hand while her leg swept before her in a scything kick. The first swarmling's legs simply snapped out from beneath it at the knees. It landed on the stumps, plodded imperturbably on. Grimly, Moonchild closed.

Sirens were chasing each other up the sky when she finished. Tachyon applauded softly as she walked up to him. "I owe you an apology, lovely lady, for what I was thinking about you."

She started to smooth back her hair, looked at her fingers, used her wrist instead. "You need never apologize to me, Doctor. You had reason to think as you did. But I must never use my arts to permanently harm a thinking being. And I thought I had."

He gathered her into his arms. She laid her head on his shoulder. *Indeed,* he thought. He was not sure how he was going to explain this to Mark. . . .

She pushed herself away. "It won't do for me to be found here. Too many questions."

"But wait. Don't go—there's so much to say!"

"But no time to say it." She kissed him on the cheek. "Be careful, Father," she said, and once more disappeared.

"So you really did turn up swarmlings, Doctor," said Lieutenant Pilar Arrupe, taking a plastic-tipped black cigarillo out of her mouth. "You are definitely the most active expert witness I ever saw."

'*Father,*' he was thinking. *An honorific, nothing more.* "Sure did a number on those mothers," observed a patrolman who clutched a riot gun like a talisman.

"With a little help from his friends, Dr. Smith and Dr. Wesson," somebody else offered.

The street was full of flashing blue lights and uniforms and camera crews. "Guns don't do much against those Swarm fuckers," the first cop said.

"So how did you overcome these creatures, Doctor?" asked a reporter, thrusting the foam phallus of a mike under his nose.

"Mystic fighting arts."

"Get these jerks out of here," Arrupe said. To Tach's

disappointment she wasn't pretty. She was stumpy and thick-legged, with a bulldog face and stiff short hair, like Brenda's at the Pumpkin. She had dark freckles liberally smeared across her pug nose. But her eyes were sharp as glass shards.

"Well, Lieutenant," he said. "Will you let Doughboy go now?"

"You have got alleged swarmling stuff in the victim's lab, and you got a whole street full of unmistakable swarmling parts, except where they used to look like Godzilla's baby they now look like derelicts, which may or may not be an improvement. It's a hell of a state of affairs."

"You won't."

"I have a witness, Doctor."

"Burning Sky, woman, have you no compassion? Don't you care for justice?"

"Do you think I'm just off the boat from San Juan? This is a solid citizen, doesn't know Doughboy from the Pope, has no grudge against jokers, and he walks in and describes him personally. And don't tell me witnesses are unreliable. They are. But this one's *solid*."

Tach combed back his hair with clutching fingers. "Let me talk to him." She rolled her eyes. "It's important. Something is happening, not just Doughboy. I know it."

"You have some kind of damned alien *brujería* in mind."

Lothario grin: "But of course."

She slumped. "You made yourself a hero with these swarmlings, Doctor. And you know more about this kind of thing than I do." Sidelong: "But you fuck me up with a civil-liberty beef on this, *'manito*, I'm just simply gonna shoot you."

As soon as he touched the mind, he knew.

He was a dentist, a short, athletic, ruddy man in his fifties who lived in the building next door to Warren's. He'd been out walking the dog around the block—a daring act at that time of the night—and seen a peculiar-looking man emerge from the alleyway that ran behind the apartments. The man stopped for a moment, not ten feet away, looked the intrepid dentist straight in the eye, and shambled off into the Park.

The story jibed with that of the other two witnesses, one of whom was the super of Warren's building, who had been investigating a broken-in back door when he was clubbed down from behind, the other a woman who had for reasons best known to herself been looking down into the alley from the apartments across. They had both glimpsed a large, pallid, manlike shape coming out the back door and lurching down the alley. But neither could offer anything but the most general description.

Tachyon had only to brush the dentist's mind to know his story was untrue. Not a lie; he believed it implicitly. Because it had been implanted.

Reluctantly, Tach dug deeper. The old pain of Blythe had receded, he no longer went clammy inside at the mere thought of using his mental powers; it wasn't that. The nature of the implant clearly revealed what sort of being had made it. All that remained was to uncover which individual from among a very few possibilities. He had a good idea.

In a way it didn't matter. The implications were already inescapable.

And monstrous beyond anything Tach had imagined.

"I mislike that place," grumbled Durg at'Morakh bo Zabb Vayawand-sa as they mounted the rickety back stair to their flat in a less than fashionable corner of the Village.

Rabdan sneered back over a gold shoulder-board. "How can you cavil? You never went inside."

"The Gatekeeper, the one with the strange dead face, he wouldn't let me."

"Ha! What would the Vayawand say, if they knew one of their precious Morakh sports permitted a groundling to say him nay? Truly, their sperm runs thin."

Durg flexed a hand that could powder granite. The tough white twill of his uniform sleeve parted at his biceps with a sound like a pistol shot. "Zabb brant Sabina sek Shaza sek Risala commands I fight only as needful to the mission," he grated. "Even as he commands me to serve one as unworthy as you, to test my devotion. But I warn you: some day your incompetence will lose you the master's pleasure. And on that day I pluck your limbs off, little man, and squash your head like a pimple."

Rabdan tried to laugh. It stumbled, so he tried again. "So hostile. Such a pity you could not have seen: a woman flayed, a maid dismayed; quite stylish entertainment. When the groundlings are destroyed some rare talents shall be lost, I must admit."

They came to the top landing and their door. Rabdan paused outside, furrowed his brow as his mind probed within.

It would not do to be ambushed by groundling burglars. Durg stood silently a few steps below. His kindred were of the Psi Lord class, but like most Morakh he was virtually mind-blind. If Rabdan detected danger, then he would fulfill his function.

Satisfied, Rabdan unlocked the door and stepped inside. Durg followed, closed it behind him. From the hallway to the bedrooms stepped a figure.

"Tisianne! But I searched—"

"You of all my cousin's people could never drive a probe I could not deflect," said Tachyon. "It bodes ill for us all that I find you here. Indeed, perhaps for all of Takis."

"But worst for you," Rabdan said. He stepped to one side. "Durg, dismember him."

"Zabb's monster!" Tach hissed, despite himself.

"The little prince," Durg said. "This will be sweet."

A second figure appeared at Tachyon's side. "Doctor, who is this?" Moonchild asked, squinting a little in the bright light of the single lamp on the low table.

She saw a small man—even to her, unmistakably Takisian—with fine sharp features, metallic blond hair, pale eyes that bulged and rapidly blinked. The being lumbering across the threadbare carpet of the little living room she found harder to classify. He was short, barely above five feet, but terrifically muscled, literally almost as broad as tall. Yet his head was a Takisian elf-lord's, long and thin, austere of feature: beautiful. The contrast was jarring.

"My cousin's toady Rabdan," Tach said, "and his monster, Durg." For all that he had lived four decades among jokers Tach could scarcely stomach sight of the Morakh killer. This was not a near-Takisian Earther twisted into a grotesque misshape; this was the sight most abhorrent to Tach's people, a perversion of the Takisian form itself. Part of what made Morakh so terrible in war was the revulsion they instilled in their foes.

"He's a creature bred by a family hostile to mine. An organic killing machine, powerful as an elephant, trained to perfection." Durg had halted, perfect brow furrowed at this new arrival. "Even by our standards they're almost indestructible. Zabb took this one in a raid when he was a pup; he transferred his loyalty to him."

"Doctor, how can you speak of a human being that way?"

"He's not a human," he gritted, "and *watch him.*"

Squat as a troll, Durg lunged with a speed no human

could match. But Moonchild wasn't strictly human; whatever she was, wherever she came from, she was an ace. She caught gold-braided sleeve behind the hand that grabbed for her, tugged, pivoted her hips. Durg shot past to slam into the wall in an explosion of plaster.

"How did you find us?" Rabdan asked, leaning against the doorjamb.

"Once we found that man whose mind you tampered with, I knew Takisians were still on Earth," Tach said, sidling away from Durg, "and from the ineptness of technique I deduced it could be none but you. Once we knew what to look for, you weren't that hard to trace. Your appearance is distinctive, and you would hardly cower in an abandoned warehouse and subsist off rats and stray cats like the swarmlings.

"Of course—" he nodded at Rabdan's white-and-gold outfit, "I never guessed even you'd be fool enough to venture out in Zabb's own livery."

"The groundlings find us the height of fashion. And would you have swans go about in the guise of geese?"

"When the swans' mission—" Durg came up from the depression he'd made in the plasterboard, moaning, shaking off plaster powder like water— "is to pass for geese, then yes."

Durg's hand lashed out in a vicious knifehand that caught Moonchild in the ribs and threw her into the bar that separated living room from kitchen. Wood splintered. Tach started forward with a cry. Grinning, Durg came for him.

Moonchild lunged from the wrecked bar, took two mincing steps forward, kicked Durg in the side of the knee. His leg buckled. She slammed a second kick into the side of his jaw. He groaned—his hand flashed up, caught her ankle, yanked her forward into reach of his other arm.

He grappled for a backbreaking hold. Tach started forward again. Rabdan's hand came out of his tunic with the flat black glint of an arrester. "Go for him and I'll finish you now, Tis."

Moonchild slammed an elbow down on top of Durg's head. Tach heard teeth slam together like a trap. She swung cupped palms viciously inward against his ears. He groaned, shook his head, and she writhed free.

. . . Durg was on his feet facing her. She kicked for his chest. He blocked without effort. She flew at him with *bolas* fury, kicking for head, knee, groin. He gave back several steps, then as she struck again leapt up and lashed out with both feet, kicking Moonchild across the room to smash against the outside wall.

Tachyon hesitated. He could attempt to seize Durg's mind, but that ran him up against the sole psionic ability the Morakh possessed, an all-but-insurmountable resistance to mental compulsion. While he concentrated on Durg, Rabdan would kill him . . . if he tried to fight down Rabdan's rather feeble screens, Durg would kill Moonchild. He reached for his pistol, hoping the girl would not think too harshly of him—

She stirred. Durg was shocked; when he kicked someone that hard, they stayed down. He hurled himself forward, heedless.

She met him halfway. Grabbing his tunic front she fell backward with her boot in his belly, projected him over her. The combined force of his leap and her thrust drove him like a rivet through the wall, four stories above the street.

"Oh, dear," she said, standing, "I hope I didn't hurt him." She ran to the hole. "He's still moving." She clambered out without hesitation.

Guessing she could take care of herself Tach let her go, still all aback. Durg was as strong as some powerhouse human aces. Moonchild, though she had metahuman strength, was nowhere his match—she had mastered him with skill alone, Durg the master slayer.

Rabdan came out of freeze and threw open the door. Tachyon's mind grabbed his like a mailed fist. And squeezed.

"And now, friend Rabdan," he remarked, "we are going to talk."

It was bad. Rabdan was an incompetent and more than something of a coward. Yet he was a Psi Lord, and at the last he behaved as one, the worse for him. No normal shield he might erect could keep the subtle Tisianne from prying the last crumb of information from his brain. But Rabdan *in extremis* went heroic, put the deathlock on, laid his name upon it. *All that he was* opposed Tachyon, and no subtlety, no artifice, no force, could get past such an opposition and leave anything of Rabdan intact.

Perhaps that was Rabdan's final cunning; knowing his distant cousin's softness of heart, he gambled that Tisianne would turn away from the awful finality of unraveling his mind skein by skein.

Rabdan's judgment was never the best.

Joy, joy, joy. My master comes again so soon. Or is something wrong, that he has so much time for me of a sudden?

Knock it off, Baby.

"Hi, Baby. What's happenin'?" She twinkled her lights in happy greeting and sphinctered open a lock in her side.

The damned rock was headed for Earth, of course. Zabb's people had deflected it months ago. Not much; it would take tremendous amounts of power to change the moment of such a mass by any appreciable amount. A sliver of a degree, scarcely perceptible—but over time, enough.

It was a rock familiar to the groundlings, its reappearance unremarkable. Nonetheless Rabdan and Durg had been sent down to make sure its intended recipients didn't realize its itinerary had changed. What luck, then, when the alteration in course had been noted by the one man absolutely no one in authority would listen to—whose having claimed the rock for his own, as it were, would mean every other scientist on the planet would shun it like offal. The Takisians could have asked for nothing better to seal the planet's fate. No one would realize what was happening until the asteroid was so close its path was unmistakable. And that would be too late, not all the thermonuclear weapons in all the planet's stockpiles could forestall the wrath to come.

But their ally had panicked. Zab's ally. Much as he hated his cousin, Tachyon could barely bring himself to believe it.

The vast lump of malignance which was the Swarm Mother had detected *Hellcat* as she floated in orbit around the world it intended, in its dim, insistent way, to make its own, and had attacked. And somehow, for his own mad reasons, once the attack was repulsed, the warhound of the Ilkazam had made alliance with the greatest enemy of his house—of all Takisians.

Together they had made a plan. Semisentient, the Mother had perceived only that the plan was detected when Dr. Warren made his announcement. It acted in haste—leaving Rabdan something less than leisure to try to undo the damage it had wrought.

It had seemed fabulous fortune to spot on the Jokertown

streets a being who might be mistaken for a swarmling. So Rabdan and Durg went up to Central Park and made themselves a witness. *How can it fail?* Rabdan had gloated to his comrade.

Tach had given Rabdan the final mercy no Takisian could deny another. Moonchild accepted that his heart gave out unexpectedly under mind probe, and Tach felt soiled at having lied to her. Tach took the pictures purloined from Warren's lab to *Baby*. Her astrogational analysis confirmed Rabdan's story. A hasty planning session, a night spent trying to sleep.

Now Trips and Tachyon were ready to launch a genuinely harebrained scheme to Save the World. There was no time to come up with a better one. It might already be too late.

And out there Zabb waited. Zabb. Who'd killed Tach's *Kibr*. And betrayed all Takis. In his warship: Zabb.

Jake was trucking down the street with his bottle of La Copita in its paper bag in hand. On the waterfront, in Jokertown, and him a nat, and it was no damned thing to do at this hour of the night, especially if you were this shitfaced. But Jake wasn't sure where he'd wandered since the big fuck with the head like an iguana threw him out of his bar for messing on the floor. A good thing he'd thought to carry a spare in his coat pocket.

A rumbling took his ear. He stopped and watched as the top came off a building right in front of him—not exploding, not collapsing, but coming off in a piece, neatly as you please, like the lid off a box. It set down gently on the roof next door, and then this gigantic seashell covered all over with tiny specks of light came floating up out of the building. Nary a sound was made. It hovered against the dull-orange sky while the roof floated back into place. Then it angled upward and was gone, lining out for the Long Black.

Very deliberately, Jake walked to the nearest storm drain, and with precise aim dropped his half-full La Copita bottle down it. Then he walked very rapidly out of Jokertown.

"I never thought of, like, flying a starship from your bedroom, man," Captain Trips said, clearly enchanted.

"I think your people would call this a stateroom, yes?" As a matter of fact, it looked like a cross between an Ottoman harem and Carlsbad Caverns. In the midst of it all was a huge canopied bed piled with fat cushions, and in a dressing gown in the midst of that lay Tach. He had long ago sworn to die in bed; Takisian biotechnology made it possible to achieve that goal and a heroic demise at the same time, if you were so inclined.

"There is no formal command center—bridge?—on a ship such as this. On most warships, such as my cousin's vessel *Hellcat*, there is, but on a yacht, no." He felt a sizzle of fury from *Baby* at the mention of *Hellcat*'s name. They were rivals of long standing.

"A Takisian symbiont-ship is psionically controlled. The pilot can receive information directly, mentally, or visually. For example . . ." Tach gestured and an image of Earth sprang into being on a curve of membranous bulkhead next to the bed. A yellow line reached away from it, describing their orbit. Then like a computer animation the globe spun away, dwindled, until an out-of-scale image of their entire projected flight path from Earth to 1954C–1100 was displayed.

Trips applauded. "That's fantastic, man. Groovy."

"Yes, it is. You Earthers are attempting to create sentience in your computers; we have grown sophonts who are capable of performing computer functions. And much more."

"How does *Baby* feel about all this?"

The picture vanished. Words appeared: *I am honored to convey lords such as Master Tis and yourself—though I'm afraid you may poke me with that hat, it's so tall.*

Trips jumped. "I didn't know she could do that."

"Neither did I. She's stealing knowledge of written English from me with a very low-powered drain—which is mildly naughty. However, she knows I am indulgent, and will forgive her."

Trips shook his head in amazement. He was sitting on a chair that had thrust itself from the floor for him and adjusted to his frame when Tach finally convinced him to sit on it. "Not that I don't have faith in *Baby*," he said, "but isn't your cousin's vessel, like, a warship?"

"Yes. And you don't have to ask the question you're hoping not to have to. Under normal circumstances *Baby* would have no chance against *Hellcat*—and don't go static in my head like that, Baby, or I'll spank you! It's true.

"But *Baby* is fast, even with her ghostdrive gone, none faster. And maneuverable. And, frankly, smarter than *Hellcat*. But the important factor is that *Hellcat* was badly injured by the Swarm attack. A Swarm Mother as ancient and vast as this one generally will have developed biological weapons—

antibodies, almost—against Takisians and their ghostships. We use similar weapons against them, since only a full war fleet can carry enough firepower to harm even a small one, whereas infection can spread of itself. Zabb fought off a boarding attack, with sword and pistol and bioweapons, and was able to drive off the swarmlings. But *Hellcat* was infected and damaged, and though they arrested the sickness she will be a long time healing."

Softly: "And Zabb felt each of her wounds as his own, whatever you may say of him." His eyes stung.

Mournfully Trips shook his head. "Talking about fighting bums me out, man."

"This must be hard for you, given your pacifist convictions. But your role in what lies ahead is not martial, and I'll fight only if attacked."

"But Moonchild fought. Most of the others would too. I've never fought in my life. I only hit one person, and *he* hauled off and busted my nose, and then one day I'm in, like, someone else's body while she throws some muscle-bound alien through a wall."

"It was a glorious spectacle," said Tach, chuckling despite himself.

"Being an ace is turning out to be a pretty heavy trip."

Tisianne, I feel her! Hellcat *comes.*

Tach rumpled his hair and sighed. "I fear it's time, my friend." He swung his legs out of bed and rose. "I'll see you to the lock."

Luminance paced them down a curving corridor. "You're sure you—he—can find the rock?" Tachyon said.

"It's not like there're going to be many others in the vicinity, Doc."

The bitch is shaping interception orbit. Max weapons range in twenty minutes.

Head her off, Baby.

They stopped by the inner sphincter of the crewlock. Tach and Trips embraced, both weeping, both trying not to show it. "Good luck, Mark."

"Same to you, Doc. Say, this whole ship is *Baby*, isn't it?"

"That's right."

Self-consciously, Trips leaned over and lightly kissed a brace whose form flowed like a stalagmite. "Bye, Baby. Peace."

"Good-bye, Captain. Godspeed."

Pandering to primitive superstitions, Tach chided as they withdrew politely around a bend.

Amusement. *What will the new person be like, Tis?*

I don't know. I'm eager to see. Another Moonchild was too much to hope for. Fortuitous enough that they had access to an ace with a combination of powers that gave them some small chance of success.

"Doctor?" The voice rolled around to them like liquid amber, deep and rich. Tachyon walked forward.

The visual impact stopped him in his tracks. Ace as Greek god: tall, elaborately muscled, a jaw like a bridge abutment, a clear green gaze, a nimbus of curly blond hair, all wrapped in a skintight yellow suit with a sunburst blazing on the chest.

"I," the vision said, "am Starshine."

"The honor is entirely mine," Tach said reflexively.

"Quite correct. You are a militarist, representative of a decadent and repressive civilization. I am about to attempt to avert a horror brought upon my world by your unbridled technology, while you engage in combat with another faction of the same technocratic gang that afflicted Earth with your satanic virus in the first place. Under the circumstances I find it difficult to wish you success, Doctor. Nonetheless, I do so."

Tachyon's voice seemed to have vanished, and *Baby* was making little staticky phosphene pops in his head. "I'm so grateful," he managed at last.

"Yes." Starshine stroked his heroic jaw. "Perhaps I shall compose a poem, about the moral dilemma I face—"

"Hadn't you better go face the asteroid first?" Tach almost screamed.

Starshine scowled like Zeus caught by Hera, but he said, "I suppose so."

The lock dilated. "Farewell," Tach said.

"Thank you." He stepped through.

As the outer lock cycled open, *Baby* transmitted the view from outside—every square centimeter of her skin was photosensitive at need—to Tach's mind. Starshine floated out into vacuum, turned his face into the full glare of the sun, now more or less astern, and appeared to take a deep breath. Then he pushed off from the ship, arms and body straightened to a line, and he became a single brilliant yellow beam bisecting eternal night.

"Photon transformation," Tach said, impressed. "Like the tachyon transformation of our ghostdrive, but allowing only lightspeed. Incredible." For a moment he felt almost proud of the wild card.

He shook the sensation off. "I'm going to find it hard," he remarked, "to like that one."

He's sure a prick. I liked the Captain ever so much better. Tis, they're coming.

Floating, timeless. Pure release, nonexistence/coexistence with all the universe. The final consummation: satori in a laser beam.

But duration must be. Resolution, downward to ego. To matter.

The asteroid awaited. An unlovely lumpish mass of slag, seeming to fall toward Starshine, though his line of sight ran perpendicular to its path.

He rubbed his jaw and frowned. He had a lot more to say to that alien doctor, about the evil his kind had brought the world, about his own culpability in luring that pathetic burnout Trips into wild dangers. But it would have to wait; time passed.

He wondered how much time he had. From the memories he shared with Mark and the rest, he knew the drug lasted an hour. He hoped he could do what had to be done in that time.

He held out a hand. A beam of light leapt from it to Tezcatlipoca's pockmarked surface, dazzling white-hot. A circle of rock raced the spectrum and boiled from the surface in a glowing jet.

He was fabulously strong. But all his strength would not divert the evil mass. Nor did he have the power to destroy the rock. What he could do was use his sunbeam to heat a spot on its flank, so that the stuff of the asteroid flared away like a rocket exhaust at right angles to its orbit. Even now, a million miles from Earth, a tiny deflection would make all the difference.

But even the tiniest deviation in the asteroid's course would require fantastic amounts of energy. And an unknown amount of time.

By increments Starshine increased his output. He felt alive, and huge, and full of power; he could not fail, here before the holy Sun's naked eye, with her energy to sustain him.

At stake was a planet, his planet, Earth, green and gravid.

And, incidentally, his own life, and that of Mark Meadows and the other entities whose existence was somehow locked in his.

At detection's instant Tach knew *Hellcat's* deadliest weapon was out. The coherent tachyons of her ghost lance would have strewn *Baby's* component atoms—and his—across a dozen dimensions in an attosecond if it still functioned, and with *Baby's* ghostdrive gland had also gone her tachyon sense, so they would have had no warning. But Tach gambled that the Swarm attack had disabled the tachyon beam. It would have been the Mother's most urgent target; the planetoid-beings feared the lance, even small ones such as Courser-class ships like *Hellcat* carried.

Zabb's ship was far from helpless, though. As *Baby* thrust on a course tangent to hers, crossing outsystem from the path Starshine had taken, a pulse of purple light flashed by to port. *I was expecting that,* Baby said smugly as she threw herself into an evasive dance, intricate as a minuet, which kept her crossing *Hellcat's* bows as the other vessel rounded on her.

Together they sent forth a probe, Tach directing *Baby's* greater raw psionic power to scan the other craft. He sensed damage that brought bile to his throat, raw wounds with edges burned or withered gaping in *Hellcat's* flanks. *She seeks our lives,* he thought, *but no faithful ship of Takis deserves the taint of swarmling contagion.*

Before he could gain a sharper vision he was cut off by mental force like a guillotine blade. No matter; *Baby* had sensed enough to evaluate what capacity her rival still possessed. Still, he was surprised.

Spavined slut, consort of barges! Tach felt *Hellcat's* anger stab *Baby* like a spear. *This jaundiced sun shall taste thee and thy weakling lord.*

Brave talk, thou who cannot waddle fast enough to catch me!

Your mental powers have grown, cousin, he projected.

A dry chuckle came into his mind. *Adversity forces growth. You've come, Tisianne. I take it you found my emissaries on Earth?*

Baby was reporting *Hellcat's* status: *Tegument weakened in several sections; a lesion in her main drive organ . . .*

I have, thought Tach.

Rabdan was a fool. You've disposed of him? I perceive you have. And Durg? His death was clean, I trust.

He lives, cousin. With malice: *He's transferred his loyalty to the groundling who bested him. Your former captive, Captain Trips.*

White-hot anger spike: *You lie!* A moment. *But no. Perhaps you begin to understand why I've taken the steps I have, then, Tis.*

According to plan, *Baby* shaped a curving orbit on constant boost. Despite her best efforts *Hellcat* could not close the range. Her fire control had suffered as well; at this distance the overwhelming superiority of her firepower was cancelled by the more precise aim of *Baby's* single heavy laser—picking at her, forcing her to trade pursuit for evasion.

I understand you've betrayed our clan and our people, Tach thought.

It seems so, Tis. But consider: this virus you loosed on that hot, heavy world threatens our existence far more surely than the mindless Swarm.

The experiment was a success.

Therein lies the danger. These altered groundlings, these aces, aided you to escape against all our strength. Now you tell me a gangling weakling bested the deadliest bare-hand fighter Takis has produced. Do you not in this see the eclipse of our kind, Tisianne?

Perhaps the fall of the Psi Lords is overdue.

And you call me traitor. The thought felt more wearily amused than outraged.

You would've destroyed the entire species.

Of course. They're groundlings.

Agony splashed Tach's brain like acid. He was thrown half out of bed as *Baby's* acceleration compensator slipped. *Baby! Are you all right?*

A grazing wound, Lord Tis. I'm fine. But there was a tentative note; she'd never been injured in battle before.

He caressed her with a brief, healing mind-touch, drove fiercely at Zabb, *So you made common cause with the filthy Swarm?*

You've seen what they did to poor Hellcat. *This Mother's encountered Takisians before, or shared plasm with another who had, and survived—which ought to tell you much, cousin mine. A pod seeded swarmlings in orbit on the far side of this adoptive world of yours, where they remained inert until we drifted in among them. Then they were upon us, with acid, quick-acting pathogens, and brute force.*

We drove them off. Tach's mind filled with images stolen from Rabdan's, of battle in wavering light against amorphous beings whose touch might mean death by irreversible dissolution. Of swordblades glinting, and screams, and the most desperate defense of all, laser pistols flaring in the corridors while peristaltic spasms racked *Hellcat's* whole fabric. *We lost four, your old weapons-master among them. The next attack would have finished us. So I chose negotiation.*

Violet eyes clenched shut. *Sedjur.*

After we repulsed the assault, Zabb continued, *I managed to touch the swollen dimness that is the Mother's consciousness even as we tended our wounded and flushed the passageways with antibiotic emulsion, to impress on her that I wished to deal. She understood but vaguely; I believe she felt something akin to curiosity at my temerity, wanted to examine me at closer range. I traveled to her in a single lifeboat, passed within.*

Baby was back in control of herself; her violent high-gee maneuvering no longer so much as rippled the surface of the brandy remaining in the goblet by the bed. Sweat stood out in cool domes on Tach's forehead. Despite himself he felt awe of his cousin—even admiration. To journey alone and unarmed into the colossal body of the Mother, ancient enemy, bogey of a million cradle stories—that took courage from the epic songs.

And this above all was why Zabb had done it, Tach knew: he had suffered humiliation at Tach's hands, he who had never known defeat. He had to perform some fabulous deed or have his significance, his *virtu*, drain from him like water from a broken vessel. And to a Takisian even treason was glorious, if grand enough in scale.

Inside a great cavern I stepped from my craft and stood upon the very substance of our oldest foe. The walls around seemed festooned with strands of black moss, illuminated by witchlights in half a hundred pallid covers; the stink was such my vision dimmed. But I made contact with a mind as huge and diffuse as a nebula. After a fashion, we communicated.

The monster and I alike had interest in destroying life on this Earth of yours. So we came to an accommodation.

Bile bubbled into Tach's mouth in shocked reflex. *We came to an accommodation.* With what insouciance his cousin passed the thought, as if it did not at once describe the greatest treason and the greatest act of courage their kind had known.

I honor you, Zabb. I must. If you win this day, they'll sing your song for a thousand generations. But . . . I despise you.

I'll try to bear up.

Tach shuddered in a breath. *And you murdered Benaf'saj.*

I had to do so. She would never have consented to taking action against you and your precious Earth, to say nothing of treating with the Swarm. To all appearances she died in the swarmling assault; Rabdan saw to it, you'll be pleased to know.

A tear fell to the silk coverlet.

Zabb. I'm coming to kill you.

Perhaps you even can, so weakened is Hellcat. *Or it may be I'll kill you.* A weary chuckle. *Either outcome is satisfactory, from my point of view.*

Baby screamed.

Suddenly Tach was bouncing around the organiform opulence of his stateroom. He smelled hot silicone; his mind reverberated to his vessel's anguish.

Now, bitch, came *Hellcat's* thought, sizzling with hatred, *thou canst flee no longer.* A blue-white flare unfolded as *Hellcat* threw her drive into terminal triumphant overdrive, closing for the kill.

Baby, Baby! Her mind was white-noise terror and pain. Symbiont-ships had advantages over nonliving craft, could think for themselves, could heal themselves of damage. But they had wills of their own, and those could be broken.

Tach grabbed a projection, clung, spread his mind to encompass his tormented ship. Air rushed from a two-meter gash in her hull, tumbling her through space. *Oh, Baby, get control of yourself!*

He felt the demon breath of a laser pass her by. *Daddy, Daddy, I can't, I can't!*

Light pulsed from the walls in random splashes of color. He summoned all his healing strength, all his love and empathy for his ship, poured his whole being on the terrified flames within her. *I love you, Baby. But you must let me help you.*

No!

Our lives lie at stake. A whole world's at stake.

Slowly terror ebbed. The ship's wild gyration damped, and Tach felt her compensator TK field enfold him once again. He breathed once more.

Hellcat had shape now without magnification, a spiked darkness alive with tiny lights, riding a tidal wave of fire. Her triumph filled Tach's head as a laser spiked forth and one of *Baby's* sponsors evanesced in a flash. *Scream for mercy, coward! Thou'll float forever friendless!*

DAMN YOU! Baby's internal lights dimmed as she channeled all power to her laser. A scarlet spike impaled *Hellcat* just ahead of her drive. She shrieked—then again, louder, a tumult of agony that went on and on until Tach thought his brain would burst.

1954C–1100 was vomiting its own substance into space. For a moment Starshine almost wished he'd brought some sort of instrument, to measure his progress. Time was fast running out, and no sign of that treacherous alien technocrat returning. It would be good to know if his sacrifice was going to be in vain.

He firmly squelched the thought. He would at least die free of the subtle chains of technology. And the green Earth would live a while longer, until the land-rapers and techno-freaks burned her out. But he would have done his part.

He began composing his final poem; a poignant piece, the more so since there were none to hear it above the asteroid's silent photonic scream but the other entities who made up the composite which was Captain Trips.

When he could think again: *Baby, are you all right?*

We won! Lord Tis, I beat her!—An image of *Hellcat*, lightless and torn, tumbling away on a cometary path, away from the world her master had sought to devastate.

Zabb! Zabb, do you still live? No reply, and he wondered why his pulse quickened anxiously.

And then, *I do. Damn you. Can you do nothing right? What of our people?*

Three died when your shot blew the drive: Aliura, Zovar S'ang, that servant wench you were so fond of. All vanished in a gout of flame. Are you then proud, Tisianne?

He sat dead still, cold emptiness within. He had murdered his own kinsman, first Rabdan, then these others. And Talli, his playmate, who'd warned him of Zabb's intentions when he and Turtle and Trips were kidnapped. All for a good cause, of course. Yet could not Zabb claim the same?

You've won. Take your vengeance, Tisianne.

Baby, match vectors with Hellcat. *This must be quickly done.*

But, Master . . .

What?

Starshine—he's about to revert to Captain Trips.

What are you waiting for? A rising note. *Do you gloat, Tisianne? It isn't like you.* Finish it.

Tach stared blankly at the membrane-wall ahead, where *Baby* formed an image of her stricken foe. His pride demanded consummation. And practicality: as long as Zabb lived, Tachyon was in mortal peril, and Earth besides.

Tis: when my mother cast that mongrel bitch who pupped you down the stairs, I watched. I stood by the balustrade and laughed. The way her head lolled on her neck—

But Tachyon laughed. *Enough. Save your venom for the Void, Zabb.*

Shoot, then. Damn you, shoot.

No. Repair your ship if you can, limp back to Takis, fly to Network space and live as a renegade. Live in the knowledge that I've bested you again. That you betrayed your lineage—and failed.

He threw up a wall against a surge of fury. *Baby, find the Captain quickly!* She sheered away, her own drives a yellow coma.

. . . destroy you, Tisianne, I swear . . . he sensed. Then Zabb was gone out of range, tumbling into the infinite hole of night.

The shine of his hands winked out. As they did, Starshine felt a sickness, a shifting of the very fabric of his being. *At least I died in the Sun's embrace . . .*

Three hundred seconds later *Baby* braked to match velocity with a form hanging apparently lifeless above a still-glowing crater in the asteroid's flank. Gently she reached out with her grappler field, caught up the purple-clad form with blood dried in rings about mouth and ears, the silk hat which followed it like a purple satellite, drew them within her. As her master bent weeping over his friend she set her prow toward the world which had become their home.

"Mark, Mark old man!" Dr. Tachyon exploded through the door of the Cosmic Pumpkin, arms full of bouquets and bottles of wine in paper bags.

Mark wheeled his chair in from the head shop. "Doc! It's, like, far out to see you. What's the occasion?" His face had an unnaturally ruddy cast where vacuum had burst capillaries beneath the skin, and until his eardrums healed he was hearing by a little bone-conduction unit taped to the mastoid process beside his left ear, but on the whole he didn't look too bad for what he'd survived.

"What's the occasion? What's the occasion? Doughboy is cleared of all charges, he comes home today. You're a hero—that is, your friend the Captain is. And I, of course. There's a celebration at the Crystal Palace, and the drinks are on the house."

"What about those bottles?"

"These?" A smile. "I might be having a private celebration of my own, after the festivities at Chrysalis's."

He stuck out a bouquet. "These are for you. Let me be the first to congratulate you, Mark."

Mark sniffled. "Uh, thanks, Doc."

"Shall we away? Why don't you slip into—you know—more formal clothing?"

Mark glanced away. "I, uh, like, I think I better stay here. I got the store and Sprout to look after, and I'm not getting around too well."

"Nonsense. You *must* come. You've earned adulation, Mark. *You*. You're a hero."

His friend evaded his eye. "Brenda will be more than happy to look after the shop and Sprout for you."

"Not so fast, buster," said the woman behind the counter. "And I'm Susan."

Tach fixed her with a penetrant stare. After a moment she crumpled. "I, I guess I could."

"But this *chair*," Mark whined.

"Do you require assistance, Mistress Isis?" a voice asked from the rear of the store, deep and resonant like an alien gong. Durg at'Morakh bo-Isis Vayawand-sa emerged into the deli, a collector's-item Steppenwolf tee shirt stretched to near explosion across his giant chest. He was limping, his cheeks puffy and bruised, but otherwise little the worse for wear. "I can carry you wherever you wish to go, Mistress."

Mark's drunkard's flush deepened. "I wish you'd quit calling me that, man. My name's *Mark*."

Durg nodded. "As you wish, Mistress. If you wish to conceal your name from the envy of your weaker fellows as you conceal your form, I shall use your nom de guerre when there are groundlings present."

"Jesus," Mark said. For his part Tach was annoyed that the Morakh had managed to learn that Moonchild's real name (whatever that meant) was Isis Moon, which was more than he knew. He was also more than slightly amused.

"Splendid," he said, shifting his grip on his burdens. "You run upstairs and change, and I'll meet you at the Palace."

"Where'll you be?"

"I've an appointment first." Durg picked Mark up, wheelchair and all, and carried him up the stairs.

Sara Morgenstern's face was flushed almost as deeply as Mark's, here in the late-afternoon gloom of Tach's office. "So you did it," she breathed.

He was aware of the scent of her, sensed her excitement. He could barely contain his own. "It was simple," he lied.

"Tell me. How was the crime committed?"

He told her, with a minimum of embellishment, since concupiscence enjoyed a higher priority even than inflating his ego. And when he finished he saw to his amazement that her eager expression had collapsed on itself like a fallen soufflé.

"Aliens? It was aliens?" She could barely force the words out; her disappointment beat at his frontal lobes like surf.

"Why yes, new-stage swarmlings in league with my cousin Zabb. And that's an important part of this story you will write, the danger posed by this new manifestation by the Swarm. Because this means the Mother's not been content to go and leave this world in peace."

The bouquet he'd given her dropped to the floor. A dozen roses lay around her feet like trees flattened by an air-bursting bomb. "*Andi*," she sobbed, face distorted, shellacked with tears. Then she was gone, heels ticking heedlessly down the corridor.

As they receded Tach knelt, tenderly picked up a single blood-red bud. *I will never understand these Earthers*, he thought.

Tucking the flower into the buttonhole of his sky-blue coat, he stepped delicately over the other flowers, shut the door, locked it, and went out whistling to join the celebration.

JUBE: SIX

Subways were a human perversion that Jube had never quite grown accustomed to. They were suffocatingly hot, the smell of urine in the tunnels was sometimes overwhelming, and he hated the way the lights flickered on and off as the cars rattled along. The long ride on the A train up to 190th Street was worse than most. In Jokertown, Jube felt comfortable. He was part of the community, someone familiar and accepted. In Midtown and Harlem and points beyond, he was a freak, something that little children stared at and their parents studiously failed to notice. It made him feel almost, well, *alien*.

But there was no avoiding it. It would never do for the newsboy called Walrus to arrive at the Cloisters in a taxi.

These past few months it had sometimes seemed as though his life was in ruins, but his business was doing better than ever. Jube had discovered that Masons read newspapers too, so he brought a large armful to each meeting, and read them on the A train (when the lights were on) to take his mind off the smells, the noise, and the looks of distaste on the faces of the riders around him.

The lead story in the *Times* announced the formation of a special federal task force to deal with the Swarm menace. The ongoing jurisdictional squabbles between NASA, the Joint Chiefs, SCARE, and the secretary of defense—all of whom had claimed the Swarm as their own—would finally be ended, it was hoped, and henceforth all anti-Swarm activities would be coordinated. The task force would be headed by a man named Lankester, a career diplomat from State, who promised to begin hearings immediately. The task force hoped to requisition the exclusive use of the VLA radio telescopes in

New Mexico to locate the Swarm Mother, but that idea was drawing heavy flak from the scientific community.

The *Post* highlighted the latest ace-of-spades murder with pictures of the victim, who had taken an arrow through his left eye. The dead man had been a joker with a record as long as his prehensile tail, and ties to a Chinatown street gang variously known as the Snowbirds, the Snowboys, and the Immaculate Egrets. The *Daily News*—which featured the same murder, minus the art—speculated that the bow-and-arrow killer was a Mafia hit man, since it was known that the Immaculate Egrets of Chinatown and the Demon Princes of Jokertown had been moving in on Gambione operations, and Frederico "the Butcher" Macellaio was not one to take kindly to such interference. The theory failed to explain why the killer used a bow and arrow, why he dropped a laminated ace of spades on each body, and why he had left untouched the kilo of angel dust his latest victim had been carrying.

The *National Informer* had a front-page color photograph of Dr. Tachyon standing in a laboratory with a gawky, bewhiskered companion in a purple Uncle Sam suit. It was a very unflattering picture. The cutline read *Dr. Tachyon and Captain Zipp pay tribute to Dr. Warner Fred Warren. 'His contribution to science unparalleled,' says psychic alien genius.* The accompanying article suggested that Dr. Warren had saved the world, and urged that his laboratory be declared a national monument, a suggestion it attributed to Dr. Tachyon. The tabloid's centerfold was devoted to the testimony of a Bronx cleaning lady, who claimed that a swarmling had attempted to rape her on the PATH tubes, until a passing transit worker transformed himself into a twelve-foot-long alligator and ate the creature. That story made Jube uneasy. He glanced up and studied the others in the A train, hoping that none of them were swarmlings or were alligators.

He had the new issue of *Aces* magazine too, with its cover story on Jumpin' Jack Flash, "The Big Apple's Hottest New Ace." Flash had been utterly unknown until two weeks ago, when he'd suddenly appeared—in an orange jumpsuit slit to his navel—to extinguish a warehouse fire on South Street that was threatening to engulf the nearby Jokertown clinic, by drawing the flames in on himself and somehow absorbing them. Since then, he'd been everywhere—booming along through the Manhattan sky on a roaring column of fire, shooting flame blasts from his fingertips, giving sardonic and cryptic interviews, and escorting beautiful women to Aces High, where his penchant for flambéing his own steaks was giving Hiram fits. *Aces* was the first magazine to plaster his foxy grin on its cover, but it wouldn't be the last.

At the 59th Street station a slender, balding man in a three-piece suit got on the train and sat across the car from Jube. He worked for the Internal Revenue Service, and was known in the Order as Vest. At 125th Street, they were joined by a hefty, gray-haired black woman in a pink waitress uniform. Jube knew her too. They were ordinary people, both of them. They had neither ace powers nor joker deformities. The Masons had turned out to be full of such people: construction workers and accountants, college students and moving men, sewer workers and bus drivers, housewives and hookers. At the meetings Jube had met a well-known lawyer, a TV weatherman, and a professional exterminator who loved to talk shop and kept giving him cards ("Lots of roaches in Jokertown, I'll bet"). Some were rich, a few very poor, most just worked hard for their living. None of them seemed to be very happy.

The leaders were of a more extraordinary cut, but every group needs its rank and file, every army its privates. That was where Jube fit in.

Jay Ackroyd would never know where he had made his mistake. He was a professional private investigator, shrewd and experienced, and he had been painstakingly careful once he had realized what he was dealing with. If only he had been a little less talented, if only Chrysalis had sent a more common sort of man, they might have gotten away with it. It was his ability that had tripped him up, the hidden ace power. Popinjay, that was the street name he loathed: he was a projecting teleport who could point a finger and *pop* people somewhere else. He had done his best to stay inconspicious, had failed to *pop* a single Mason, but Judas had sensed the power nonetheless, and that had been enough. Now Ackroyd had no more memory of the Masons than did Chrysalis or Devil John Darlingfoot. Only Jube's obvious jokerhood and conspicuous lack of power had spared his mind and his life . . . that, and the machine in his living room.

It was dark by the time the A train pulled into 190th Street. Spoons and Vest walked briskly from the subway while Jube trudged after them, newspapers under his arm. The harness chafed under his shirt, and he felt desperately alone.

He had no allies. Chrysalis and Popinjay had forgotten
everything. Croyd had woken as a bloated gray-green thing
with flesh like a jellyfish and had promptly gone to sleep again,
sweating blood. The Takisians had come and gone, doing
nothing, caring less. The singularity shifter, if it was still intact
and functional, was lost somewhere in the city, and his tachyon
transmitter was useless without it. He could not go to any
human authorities. The Masons were everywhere; they had
penetrated the police, the fire department, the IRS, the transit
authority, the media. At one meeting, Jube had even spotted a
nurse who worked at the Jokertown clinic.

That one had troubled him deeply. He had spent several
sleepness nights floating in his cold tub, wondering if he ought
to say something to somebody. But who? He could whisper
Nurse Gresham's name to Troll, he could report Harry
Matthias to his captain, he could spill the whole story to
Crabcakes at the *Cry*. But what if Troll was a Mason himself?
Or Captain Black, or Crabcakes? The ordinary Masons saw
their leaders only at a distance, and frequently in masks, and
there were rumors of other high-degree initiates who never
came to meetings, aces and power brokers and others in
positions of authority. The only one he could really trust was
himself.

So he had gone to their meetings, listening, learning. He
had watched with fascination when they donned their masks
and acted out their pageants and rituals, had researched the
attributes of the mythological gods they aped, had told his
jokes and laughed at theirs, had made friends with those who
would befriend a joker and observed the others who would
not. And he had begun to suspect something, something
monstrous and troubling.

He wondered, not for the first time, why he was doing
this. And found himself remembering a time long ago, aboard
the great Network starship *Opportunity*. The Master Trader
had come to his cabin in the guise of an ancient Glabberan, his
bristling hair gone black with age, and Jhubben had asked why
he was being honored with this assignment. "You are like
them," the Master Trader had said. "Your form is different, but
among those warped and twisted by Takisian bioscience, you
will be lost, another faceless victim. Your thought patterns,
your culture, your values, your moralities—these are closer to
the human norms than those of anyone else I might select. In
time, as you dwell among them, you will become still more

alike, and so you will come to understand them, and be of great value on our return."

It had been true, all true; Jube was more human than he would ever have guessed. But the Master Trader had left one thing out. He had not told Jhubben that he would come to love these humans, and to feel responsible for them.

In the shadow of the Cloisters, two youths in gang colors stepped out to confront him. One of them had a switchblade. They knew him by now, but still he had to show them the shiny red penny he carried in his pocket. Those were the rules. They nodded to him silently, and Jube passed within, to the great hall where they were waiting with their tabards and masks, with their ritual words and the secrets he was terrified to learn, where they were waiting for him to arrive, to conduct his initiation.

BY LOST WAYS

By Pat Cadigan

It was unseasonably hot for May, a fast preview of deep summer, and the children gathered at the fire hydrant made a timeless scene. The only thing missing was expertise—no one knew how to release the water from the hydrant. Never mind that such a thing would result in a precipitous drop in the local water pressure, seriously impairing fire fighting, which was why arsonists were always willing to accommodate a gaggle of sweaty kids on a hot day. But there was never an arsonist around when you needed one.

The man in the mom-and-pop convenience store was not watching the kids; he was watching the young woman with the shoulder-length auburn hair and the wide green eyes who was watching the kids. He'd been tracking her since she'd gotten off the bus three days before, usually from the shelter of one of his favorite tabloids, like the one he was holding now. The headline read: WOMAN TURNS INTO JOKER, EATS MATE ON WEDDING NIGHT!! Harry Matthias had always had a taste for the lurid.

The girl across the street, however, was anything but lurid. *Girl* suited her better than *young woman*, even though he was reasonably sure she was over twenty-one. Her heart-shaped face was unmarked, unlined; unfinished. Unsophisticated, very attractive if you looked twice and he imagined most people did. You'd never think that she was anything other than one more innocent morsel throwing herself into the jaws of the big city. But Harry, more often referred to as Judas, knew differently. The Astronomer would reward him handsomely for this one.

Or rather, the Astronomer's people would. The Astrono-

mer himself didn't bother with you, not if you were lucky, and
Judas had been very lucky, almost too lucky to live. He'd gone
from being a joker groupie, what they'd called a jokee (and
laughing at him, too, when they said it) to being an ace
himself. A very subtle ace, to be sure, but very useful with his
ability to detect another ace and the power involved. His
power had come out that night in that crazy cabaret, the Jokers
Wild. Saved his life; they'd been about to serve him up proper
when the spore had turned and he'd exposed that shape-shifter
woman. What changes they'd put her through, to coin a
phrase. He didn't like to think about it but better her than
him. Better anyone than him, even the girl across the street,
though it would have pained him; she *was* attractive. But he
was only delivering her to the Masons, where she wouldn't be
wasted. What a talent she had; they'd probably pin a medal on
him when he brought her in. Well, they'd pay him, anyway,
enough to take the sting out of being called Judas. If he'd felt
any sting, which he didn't.

The girl smiled and he felt himself smiling in response.
He could sense her power gathering itself. Absently, he tossed
a few coins at the cashier for the tabloid and stepped out onto
the sidewalk with the paper under his arm. Once again he
found himself marveling; even though he knew it took a special
power all its own to detect an ace, he was still amazed that
people never knew when they stood before something greater
than themselves, whether it was an ace, TIAMAT, or the One
True God. He glanced at the sky. God was on coffee break and
TIAMAT had yet to arrive; right now it was just him and the
girl, and that was company enough.

He alone felt it when she let fly. The power surged out of
her both like a wave and like a fusillade of particles. The
magnitude was frightening. This was a power primeval,
something that felt old in spite of the relative newness of the
wild card virus, as though the virus had activated some ability
native but dormant for centuries.

Could be, he thought suddenly—didn't every primitive
people have some kind of rite meant to call down the rain?

Without warning, the fire hydrant popped and water
gushed out onto the street. The kids waded in cheering and
laughing, and she was enjoying them so much, she never
noticed his approach.

"Police, miss. Come along quietly." The complete surprise on her face as she stared at the badge he held under her

nose made her seem younger still. "You didn't really think you were going to get away with this, did you? And don't play innocent—you're not the only ace we've ever had in this town, you know."

She nodded meekly and let him lead her away.

The Cloisters were completely wasted on her. She didn't bother to look up at the soaring French Gothic architecture or even the ornately carved wooden door where he delivered her like so much goods into the waiting hands of Kim Toy O'Toole and Red. He resisted the urge to kiss her. For a guy named Judas, kissing would be pouring it on too thick. Hey, little girl; she hadn't even noticed the absense of police uniforms.

Red had been mildly florid until the wild card virus had bitten him. Now he was completely red all over and hairless as well. He thought of it as a comparatively tolerable condition. "Maybe I've got some red Indian in me," he would say from time to time. He didn't. His wife, Kim Toy, was the offspring of an Irish career Army man and the true love he had met while on R&R in Hong Kong. Sean O'Toole had been a Mason, but he would barely have recognized the organization his daughter had turned to after her own spore had bloomed and she had discovered that the combination of mental power and pheromones could dazzle men far more greatly than was usual for a reasonably attractive woman. Red hadn't needed that kind of dazzling. Good thing; sometimes she couldn't help making it fatal.

They took the fresh piece Judas had brought them and stuck her in one of the old downstairs offices where interrogations (*interviews*, Roman would always correct them) could take place in privacy. Then they sat down outside in the hall for an unscheduled break. Roman would be along at any moment, after which they would have to dispose of the girl however the Astronomer thought best.

"Little creep," Red muttered, accepting an already-lit cigarette from Kim Toy. *Little creep* was a term that always referred to the Astronomer. "Sometimes I think we ought to stomp his ass and run."

"He's going to own the world," Kim Toy said mildly. "And give us a piece. I think that's worth keeping him around for."

"He *says* he's going to give us a piece. Like he was a feudal lord. But we're not all samurai, wife o' mine."

"Neither am I. I'm Chinese, fool. Remember?" Kim Toy looked past her husband. "Here comes Roman. *And* Kafka." She and Red sat up and tried to look impassive. Roman was one of the Astronomer's high-level flunkies, someone who could visit those segments of society that would have been considered above most of the questionable types the Astronomer had recruited. His blond good looks and flawless grooming gave him entrée almost anywhere. It was whispered that he was one of the rare "reverse jokers," someone the spore had made over from a hideously deformed wreck into his present state of masculine beauty. Roman himself wasn't saying.

Following along behind him was his antithesis, the one they called Kafka or the Roach (though not to his face), for he looked like nothing so much as a roach's idea of a human. No one made fun of him, however; the Shakti device that the Astronomer had said would be their salvation was mostly Kafka's doing. He'd figured out the alien instrument that had been in the Masons' custody for centuries and he had single-handedly designed and constructed the machine that completed its power. Nobody bothered him; nobody wanted to.

Roman gave Red and Kim Toy a minuscule nod as he headed for the office door and then stopped abruptly, almost causing Kafka to bump into him. Kafka leaped back, clutching his skinny arms to himself, panicked at the prospect of any contact with someone who washed less than twelve or thirteen times a day.

"Where do you think you're going?" Roman's smile was flat.

Kafka took a brave step forward. "We've found six aliens passing as humans in the last three weeks. I just want to make sure she's human."

"*You* want to make sure she's human." Roman gave him an up-and-down. "Judas brought her in. The ones Judas brings us are always human. And the Astronomer doesn't want us scaring off the good ones, which is why *I* interview them when they first get here. You'll pardon me for saying so, Kafka old thing, but I don't think your appearance will be any too reassuring."

Kafka's exoskeleton rasped as he turned away and went back down the hall. Kim Toy and Red watched him go, neither of them caring to break the silence by so much as letting out a breath.

"He was watching the monitors when she came in," Roman said, straightening his expensive, tasteful tweed jacket. "Pity. I mean, the man obviously wouldn't mind getting next to such a nice female but the way he is . . ."

"How's your wife, Roman?" Red asked suddenly.

Roman froze in the middle of brushing an imaginary piece of lint off his sleeve. There was a long pause. One of the incongruous overhead fluorescents began to hum.

"Fine," Roman said at last, slowly lowering his arm. "I'll tell her you asked after her."

Kim Toy elbowed her husband in the ribs as Roman went into the office. "What the *hell* did you have to do that for? What was the point?"

Red shrugged. "Roman's a bastard."

"*Kafka's* a bastard! They're *all* bastards! And *you're* a fool. Next time you want to hit that man, get up and break his nose. Ellie Roman never did anything to you."

"First you're telling me how you want to own the world— excuse me, a piece of it—and then you're chewing me out for throwing Roman's wife up to him. Wife o' mine, you're a real Chinese puzzle sometimes."

Kim Toy frowned up at the buzzing light, which was now flickering as well. "It's a Chinese-puzzle world, husband o' mine."

Red groaned. "Samurai bullshit."

"State your name, please. In full." ·

He was arguably the best-looking man she had ever met in person. "Jane Lillian Dow," she said. In the big cities, they had everything, including handsome men to interrogate you. *I heart New York*, she thought, and suppressed the hysteria that wanted to come bubbling up as laughter.

"And how old are you, Ms. Dow?"

"Twenty-one. Born April first, 19—"

"I can subtract, thank you. *Where* were you born?"

She was terrified. What would Sal have thought? *Oh, Sal, I wish you could save me now.* It was more a prayer than a thought, cast out into the void with the dim hope that perhaps the wild card virus could have affected the afterlife as well as this one and the late Salvatore Carbone might come trucking back from the hereafter like ectoplasmic cavalry. So far, reality still wasn't taking requests.

She answered all the man's questions. The office was not

especially furnished—bare walls, a few chairs, and the desk with the computer terminal. The man had her records in under a minute, checking the facts against her answers. He had access to her whole life with that computer, one reason why she'd been so reluctant to register with the police after her wild card spore had turned itself out in high school five years before. The law had been enacted in her hometown long before she'd been born, and never taken off the books when the political climate had changed somewhat. But, then, not much had changed in the small Massachusetts town where she'd grown up. "I'll be licensed and numbered like a dog," she'd said to Sal. "Maybe even taken to the pound and gassed like a dog, too." Sal had talked her into complying, saying she'd draw less attention to herself if she obeyed their laws. When they could account for you, they left you alone. "Yeah," she'd said. "I'd noticed how well that kind of thing worked in Nazi Germany." Sal had just shaken his head and promised that things would work out.

But what about this, Sal? They're not leaving me alone, it's not working out. New York was the last place she had expected to be picked up by the police as an ace and, when a break came in the questioning, she said so.

"But we're not the police," the handsome man told her pleasantly, making her heart sink even lower.

"Y-you're not? But that guy showed me a badge . . ."

"Who did? Oh, him." The man—he'd told her to call him Roman—chuckled. "Judas *is* a cop. But I'm not. And this is hardly a police station. Couldn't you tell?"

Jane scowled into his slightly incredulous smile. "I'm not from here. And I saw what happened a few months ago on the news. I figured after that the police would just set up anywhere they needed to or had to." She looked down at her lap where her hands were twisting together like two separate creatures in silent combat. "I wouldn't have told you about Sal if I'd known you weren't the police."

"What difference does that make, Ms. Dow? Or can I call you Jane, since you don't like to be called Water Lily?"

"Do what you want," she said unhappily. "You will anyway."

He surprised her by getting up and telling the people in the hall to bring in some coffee and something to eat. "It occurs to me we've kept you here far too long without refreshment.

The police wouldn't do that for you, Jane. At least, not the New York City police."

She took a deep breath and let it out slowly. "Sure. Then, I guess I'll have some coffee and be on my way."

The man never stopped smiling. "Where have you got to go?"

"I came here—here to New York, I mean—looking for Jumpin' Jack Flash. I saw him on the news . . ."

"Forget it." The smile was still there but the eyes were cold. "You can't do anything for each other."

"But—"

"I said, *forget it*."

She looked down at her lap again.

"Come on, Jane." His voice softened. "I'm just trying to protect you. You need it. I can just imagine what a hot dog like that would do to an innocent little morsel like yourself. Whereas the Astronomer has a use for you."

She lifted her head again. "A *use*?"

"A use for your power, I should have said. Forgive me."

Jane's laugh was brief and bitter. "A use for my power is a use for me. Maybe I *am* innocent next to you but I'm not stupid. Sal used to warn me about that."

"Yes, but Sal wasn't an ace, was he? He was just a pathetic little swish, one of that very early kind of joker we've always had in the world. One of nature's mistakes."

"Don't you talk that way about him!" she flared, moisture suddenly beading on her face and running down her arms and legs. The man stared at her wonderingly.

"Are you doing that on purpose? Or is it just a stress reaction?"

Before she could answer, the red man and the Oriental woman came in with a platter of small, neatly made sandwiches. Jane subsided and watched as the couple laid everything out on the desk, even pouring the coffee.

"Fresh from the Cloisters' own kitchens," Roman said, gesturing at the platter. "An ace has to keep her strength up."

"No, thanks."

He jerked his head at the couple, who took positions on either side of the door. More water ran down Jane's face and dripped from the ends of her hair. Her clothes were becoming saturated.

"It's water pulled out of the air around me," she said to

Roman, who was beginning to look alarmed. "It happens
sometimes when I'm under pressure or—or whatever."

"Fight or flight," he said. "Adrenaline produces sweat to
make you more slippery, harder to hold onto. Probably the
same principle at work."

She looked at him with new respect. Even Sal hadn't
thought of that and he'd been pretty smart, coming up with all
those experiments to test the depth and range of her power. It
was only because of Sal that she knew her power was effective
on things no more than half a mile away from her. He had also
figured out that she could cause atoms to combine to make
water as well as call already-existing water out of things, and
he'd been the one to calculate it would take her forty-eight
hours to recharge after exhausting the power, and coached her
on how to stretch her energy out so she wouldn't spend herself
all at once. "No good being completely defenseless," he'd said.
"Don't ever let it happen." And since that one time back home
in Massachusetts, she hadn't and never would again. Sal had
watched over her for those two days when she'd been half
afraid and half hopeful that the power was gone for good. But
Sal had been right about its return; she'd been prepared to
hand herself over to him completely.

He'd refused her. Once again, she'd offered herself and
he'd turned her down. He couldn't be her lover, he'd said, and
he wouldn't be her father. She would have to be responsible
for herself, just like anyone else. And then, as though to drive
the point home, he'd gone back to his apartment and drowned
in the bathtub.

Like some sadist's idea of the cruelest joke in the world.
Sal Carbone, her one real friend, had fallen and struck his
head and breathed soapy water till he died. Only five weeks
ago.

"Sal, you're my soulmate," she'd told him over and over
and he'd allowed it was true. They had a rare friendship, a
meeting of minds, hearts, and spirits. Perfect for each other
except for the fact that he'd been gay. The second-cruelest joke
in the world.

"Water Lily."

The name snapped her back to the present. "I told you
not to call me that. Only Sal called me Water Lily."

"Sal's exclusive option expired with him." The man
suddenly softened again. "Never mind, dear. Tell me, just how

how much do you know about what's been happening over the last few months?"

"As much as anybody else." She reached forward shyly and picked up the cup of coffee nearest her. "I watch the news. I guess I mentioned that."

"Well, it isn't over. In the next month, this town—this country, the entire world—will see something that made what happened a few months ago look like a Bible-class picnic. Only the people we recruit stand a chance of ending up on the right side of the graveyard."

More water appeared on her face. "If you're not the police, who are you?"

The man smiled approvingly as she sipped at her coffee. "What do you know about the Masons, Jane?"

"Masons? *Masons?*" In spite of everything, she burst into laughter. "My *father's* a Mason!" She forced her giggles to subside before they became hysterics. "What do *Masons* have to do with anything?"

"Scottish rite."

"Pardon?" Jane's laughter wound down and faded away. The flat cold quality was back in the man's smile.

"Your father's affiliation was probably Scottish-rite. We're Egyptian. Egyptian is quite different."

Her giggles threatened to come back. "That's funny, you don't look Egyptian."

"Don't get nervy, it doesn't become you."

She glanced at the man and woman by the door. "You're the one who knows everything. I just got here." More moisture sprang out on her face and ran down her neck. "And I can't leave, can I?"

"We need you, Jane." He sounded almost kind now. She pulled a napkin off the desk and blotted her face with it. "We need you very badly. Your power could make all the difference."

"My power," she echoed thoughtfully, remembering the boy in the cafeteria five years before, tears pouring from his eyes while he screamed. He hadn't cried a bit at the news of Debbie's suicide (exsanguination from self-inflicted lacerations—medicalese for *she slashed her wrists and bled to death*—and, oh, yes, victim had been thirteen weeks pregnant). She'd always wondered what Debbie would have thought about what she'd done to her faithless boyfriend. Debbie had been her best friend before Sal but she never prayed to Debbie the way she prayed to Sal, as though Debbie belonged to some other universe. Maybe that was so. And maybe there was still another universe where Debbie hadn't taken her own life when the father of her baby had rejected her, and so no need for Jane to have forced the tears out of the boy's eyes, no wild card virus to have shown itself. And then maybe there was even another universe where Sal hadn't had to drown in his own bathtub, leaving her alone and so in need of someone, anyone, to trust. Maybe . . .

She looked at the man sitting in front of her. Maybe if pigs had wings, they could soar like eagles. "We need you," he'd said. Whoever *we* were. Egyptian Masons, whatever. How good it would be to give herself over to someone's care and know that she'd be looked after and protected.

Can you understand that, Sal? she thought at the great void. *Can you understand what it's like to be completely alone with a power too big for you? They need me, Sal, that's what they say. I don't like them—and you'd hate them—but they'll look after me and I need someone to do that right now. I'm all alone, Sal, no matter where I am, and I've come here by lost ways and there's nowhere else to go. You know, Sal?*

There was no answer from the great void. She found herself nodding at the handsome man. "All right. I'll stay. I mean, I know you won't let me go but I'll stay willingly."

His answering smile almost soothed her heart. "We understand the difference. Red and Kim Toy will take you to your room." He stood up and reached across the desk to take her hand. "Welcome, Jane. You're one of us now."

She drew back, putting both hands up as though she were at gunpoint. "No, I'm not," she said firmly. "I'm staying here of my own will but that's all. I'm not one of you."

That frightening coldness returned to his eyes. He let his hand drop. "All right. You're staying but you're not one of us. We understand the difference there, too."

The room they gave her was the corner of some larger area of dismal, cold stone converted into a warren of smaller rooms with prefab, plasterboard walls. Thoughtfully, they fetched her few worldly goods from the tiny efficiency she'd rented and, also thoughtfully, they provided her with a television as well as a bed. She watched the news, looking for more footage of Jumpin' Jack Flash. Otherwise, she occupied herself by producing small droplets of water from her finger-tips and watching them distend and fall.

"Is she pretty?" asked the Astronomer, sitting in his wheelchair by the tomb of Jean d'Alluye. There was still some blood on the stone figure; the Astronomer had lately felt the need to recharge his power.

"Quite pretty." Roman took a perfunctory sip from the glass of wine and set it aside on the preacher's table nearby. The Astronomer was always offering him things—booze, drugs, women. He would take a taste out of courtesy and then set whatever it was aside. Exactly how much longer the Astronomer would allow that to go on was anyone's guess. Sooner or later he was bound to make some bizarre demand involving Roman's debasement. No one came out of association with the Astronomer unscathed. Roman's attention wandered to a shadowy area under a brick arch where the skinny blasted ruin called Demise slouched brooding, his bottomless gaze fixed on something no one else could see. In another part of the room, near one of the lantern poles, Kafka was rustling impatiently. He couldn't help rustling with that damned exoskeleton. It sounded like a multitude of cockroaches going wingcase to wingcase. Roman didn't bother trying to hide his disgust at Kafka's appearance. And Demise—well, he was beyond disgusting. Sometimes Roman thought that even the Astronomer was ginger about Demise. But both Demise and Kafka had been through their allotted humiliations courtesy of the wild card virus, while he could only wait and see what the Astronomer had in mind for him. He hoped there'd be enough time to know which way to jump. And then there was Ellie. . . . The thought of his wife was a fist in his stomach. No, please, no more for Ellie. He looked at the glass of wine and refused for the millionth time to succumb to the desire for anesthesia. *If I go down—no, when I go down, I will go down in full possession of my faculties. . . .*

The Astronomer laughed suddenly. "Melodrama becomes you, Roman. It's your good looks. I could see you in some other life rescuing widows and orphans from blizzards." The laughter faded, leaving a malicious smile. "Watch yourself around that girl. You could end up a little prematurely as the dust we all are."

"I could." Roman's gaze went to the upper gallery. The

Italian wood sculptures were gone now; he couldn't remember what they'd looked like. "But I won't."

"And what makes you so sure?"

"She's a white-hat. A good guy. She's a twenty-one-year-old innocent, she doesn't have murder in her soul." Belatedly, he looked at Demise, who was staring at him the way you never wanted Demise to stare at you.

Roman braced himself against a broken-off pedestal. It would be horrible but it wouldn't last long, not really. The eternity of a few seconds. At least it would put him beyond the Astronomer's reach for all time. But it also meant he wouldn't be able to help Ellie, either. *I'm sorry, darling*, he thought, and waited for the darkness.

A quarter of a second later, the Astronomer lifted one finger. Demise sank back into himself and resumed staring at nothing. Roman forced himself not to sigh.

"Twenty-one," mused the Astronomer, as though one of his people had not just narrowly escaped being killed by his pet murder machine. "Such a fine age. Plenty of life and strength. Not the most level-headed age. An impulsive age. You're sure you're not just a little bit afraid of her impulses, Roman?"

Roman couldn't resist sneaking a glance at Demise, who was no longer paying any attention. "I don't mind staking my life on someone whose heart is in the right place."

"Your life." The Astronomer chuckled. "How about something of value?"

Roman allowed himself an answering smile. "Excuse me, sir, but if my life didn't have some value to you, you'd have let Demise do me a long time ago."

The Astronomer burst into surprisingly hearty laughter. "Brains *and* good looks. They're what make you so damned useful to all of us. Must be what attracted your wife to you. You think?"

Roman kept smiling. "Very likely."

Her dreams were full of strange pictures, things she'd never seen before. They troubled her sleep, passing through her head with an urgency that felt directed and reminded her of Roman's impassioned pleas for her to join them. Whoever *they* were. Egyptian Masons. Her dreams told her all about them. And the Astronomer.

The Astronomer. A little man, shorter than she was, bone-thin, head too large. What Sal would have called bad-ass eyes while making that sign with his hand, the index and little fingers thrust out like horns, the middle two curled over his palm, some kind of Italian thing. Sal's face floated through her dreams briefly and was swept away.

She saw the entrance of some kind of church—no, a temple, definitely not a church. She saw it but she wasn't there, couldn't have been there; this was a time before she'd been born. Her disembodied presence scanned a nighttime street and then floated up the temple steps past the man on the door who seemed to be frozen. She had a glimpse of a great room aglow with candles, two columns, and a man on a platform, wearing some kind of gaudy red and white thing over his front, just before the screams began.

Not just screams but *screams*, SCREAMS, ripped from the throat of a soul gone forfeit. The sound stabbed into her. There was time for her point of view to swing around cameralike so she could see it was the little man screaming, the Astronomer, staggering into the hall. Then there was a fast jumble of pictures, a jackal face, a hawk's head, another man, his wide face pale; light glinting off the little man's glasses and then some kind of a thing, a creature-thing-slime-mass-damned-thing-thing-thing—

She found herself sitting up in bed, her arms thrown up in front of her face.

"TIAMAT." Unbidden, the word came to her, and unwanted it hung there in the darkness. She rubbed her face with both hands and lay down again.

The dream returned immediately, dragging her under with horrible strength. The little man with the enormous head was smiling at her—no, not at her, she wasn't there and she was glad; she didn't ever want anyone to smile at her that way. Her point of view drew back and she saw that he was now standing on the platform, and around him she saw several figures—Roman, the red man, and the oriental woman, a thin wreck of a man with the feel of death about him, a woman with regret so etched into her features that it hurt to look at her (somehow she knew the woman was a nurse), a young albino man with a prematurely old face, a creature—male, she thought—that might have been an anthropomorphic cockroach. There but for the grace of God, she thought.

God is still out on coffee break, little girl. She was looking into the face of the man who had brought her here, the one they called Judas. He was the only one who could see her. *It's just the luck of the draw, babe, and you were lucky. And so was I. Blackjack!*

Everything went dark. There was a sensation of incredibly fast movement. Something was propelling her toward a tiny point of light far ahead in the blackness.

And then suddenly she was there; the light swelled from a pinpoint to a fiery mass and she hit going full-out at the speed of thought. The light shattered and she was tumbling softly on the mossy floor of a forest. She rolled over once and came to rest gently at the base of a large tree.

Well, she thought, *this is more like it. I must have missed the White Rabbit, but the Mad Hatter ought to be around here somewhere.* She shifted position and found she had to grab hold of a large root to keep from floating away.

Look, whispered a voice very close to her ear. She turned her head, her hair floating around her as though she were underwater, but she saw no one. *Look. Look! Look and you'll see them!*

A puff of mist blew between two larches in front of her and disintegrated, leaving behind a man dressed in the height of eighteenth-century finery. His face was aristocratic, his eyes so piercing that she caught her breath as his gaze rested on her. But she had nothing to fear. He turned; the air beside him shimmered and a strange machine melted into existence. She blinked several times, trying to see it clearly, but the angles refused to resolve themselves. Try as she would, she couldn't tell whether it was large and sharp-cornered or small and molded, sculpted in marble or nailed together with wood and rags. Something glimmered and detached itself from the machine. She marveled; a part of it had just gotten up and walked away.

No. What she thought was part of the machine was a living being. She wanted to pull her gaze away just for a moment but she couldn't. It wouldn't let her. Alien. Reminiscent of certain other aliens she'd seen on the news in the attack. *Jumpin' Jack Flash.* The thought was neatly shoved aside.

The alien turned to the man and stretched out an arm, or some appendage. Now it began to look more like living matter than part of a machine. The alien smoothed into something roughly bipedal though it seemed to be holding the form only by sheer will—the ergotic hypothesis (where had *that* come from?). The appendage touched the machine and melted into it. A moment later something protruded from the side near the man. He took hold of it and very carefully removed it. The alien sank a little, diminished. She realized it had expended a great deal of its life-force to give the man—what?

The man held the thing to his lips, his forehead, and then lifted it high overhead. Briefly, it took on the form of a human bone, a club, a gun, then something else.

Shakti, whispered the voice. *Remember this. The Shakti device.*

I'll never forget it, she thought. The floating feeling was starting to leave her and she grew afraid.

Now, look. Look up.

Unwillingly, she raised her head and looked up at the sky. Her vision shot up, racing through the sunlight, through the blue, through clouds, until it left the Earth entirely and she was looking at the naked stars. The stars dispersed before her until she was staring into the blackness of space, and still her vision was traveling.

Something was there ahead of her, invisible in the blackness. Something . . . it was so far away she could not begin to conceive of the distance. It was on its way to Earth. It had been this far away in 1777, when that man (*Cagliostro,* said her mind and she didn't wonder how she knew) had accepted the thing—Shakti—from the alien and then—and then—*went on to perform many feats seen as miraculous including mind reading, levitation, transubstantiation, amazing all those in the courts of Europe while passionately recruiting for the Egyptian Freemasons . . .*

She struggled to absorb the information pouring into her from the dream. Not that it mattered, because when she woke up she wouldn't remember any of it. That was the way it was with dreams. Wasn't it?

. . . because he wanted an organization that would keep the Shakti device safe and hand it down from generation to generation, to only the most trusted people, until its mysteries could be unlocked and completed, when it would be needed for the arrival on Earth of—

Something writhed in the darkness ahead of her. Or perhaps the darkness itself was writhing in agony at having to contain this thing, this—

—for the arrival on Earth of—

It burst upon her without warning or mercy, far worse

than it had been when she touched it in the Astronomer's mind. It was the gathering, the congealing, of the highest, lowest, most developed, polished, and refined forms of evil in the universe, evil that made the greatest human atrocities seem petty by comparison, evil she could not understand except with her gut, evil that had been rushing toward this world for thousands of years, swallowing anything in its path, evil that would be arriving any day now, any day—

TIAMAT.

She woke up screaming. Hands were on her and she fought them, twisting, striking out. Water poured over her, thickening the air, soaking the bed and the rug.

"Sh, sh, it's all right," said a voice. Not the voice from her dream but a female voice. The oriental woman Kim Toy was there, trying to soothe her as though she were a delirious child. A light went on; Kim Toy enfolded her in a calming embrace. She let herself be held and willed the water flowing over both of them to stop.

"I'm okay," she said when she could speak. Her wet hair dripped into her eyes, mixing with her tears. The whole bed was drenched, but she saw with a little relief that she had spared the rest of the room.

"You were screaming," Kim Toy said. "I thought someone was killing you."

TIAMAT. "I had a nightmare."

Kim Toy stroked her wet hair gently. "A nightmare?"

"I dreamt someone threw a bucket of worms in my face."

The Astronomer roared with laughter. "Oh, she's excellent, she really is excellent!"

The albino sitting on the floor next to the wheelchair looked up at him imploringly.

"Was it a good dream, then?"

"Oh, yes, the dream was excellent, too." The Astronomer petted the white hair. "You did it just right, Revenant."

The man smiled, the prematurely aged skin around his pink eyes crinkling with pathetic joy.

"Roman."

Across the shadowy room, Roman looked up from the computer display terminal.

"We'll give her just a little more time for the horror to sink in before you introduce her to the rest of our little confederation. And keep Kim Toy mothering her."

Roman nodded, glancing surreptitiously at the computer terminal.

"Tomorrow night again, Revenant," the Astronomer said to the albino. "You'll do it once more. I want her to wake up screaming for the next two nights."

The pink eyes lowered with shame.

"Now, now. You know you're better off than before, when you were selling perverts wet dreams at ten bucks a crack. If you'll pardon the expression." The Astronomer chuckled. "You're one of my most useful aces. Now, go get some rest yourself."

As soon as the albino disappeared down a darkened gallery, the Astronomer sagged in his wheelchair. "Demise."

Demise was at his side instantly.

"Yes, Demise. We both need it now, don't we? Call for the car."

Roman remained at the computer terminal as Demise wheeled the Astronomer out. Going out to find some poor streetwalking scumbag who didn't know this would be her last date. He refused to think about it. He would not feel sorry for any of them, he would *not*. All of them—Revenant, Kim Toy, Red, Judas, John F. X. Black, Coleman Hubbard (oh, hadn't that been a piece of work, the Astronomer's big ace in the hole, one-zero-zero-one), even that little piece of innocence Jane Water Lily—they were all the same, every one of them. Pawns in the Astronomer's game. Himself, too, but only for Ellie's sake, to try to protect her.

ELLIE, he typed, the letters glowing on the monitor. I LOVE YOU.

The words I LOVE YOU, TOO flashed briefly on the screen before they were replaced by INVALID ENTRY, NULL PROGRAM.

Somewhere else in town, Fortunato woke, shuddering, his face covered with cold sweat.

"Easy. Easy, baby." Michelle's voice was gentle, her hands soft and warm. "Michelle's got you. I'm here, honey, I'm here."

Fortunato allowed her to gather him into her arms and press his face to her perfect breasts.

"It's those dreams again, isn't it? Don't worry. I'm here."

He nuzzled her, stroking the warm flesh and willing her to sleep. Then he slipped out of her embrace and locked himself in the elegant bathroom.

Once you were in, you were in. What was learned could

not be unlearned. Knowledge was power, and power could trap.

He would have to call Tachyon; better, go down to the Village and wake him up.

Eileen.

Fortunato clenched his eyes shut until the thought of her had passed. He should have let Tachyon give him something for that, some kind of forgetfulness drug so he wouldn't keep stumbling over her in his mind, but somehow he couldn't bring himself to do it. Because then she really would be gone.

He splashed water on his face and paused in the act of blotting it with a towel, staring at himself in the mirror. For half a second, he had seen another face covered with water; young, female, wide green eyes, dark reddish hair, very pretty, a stranger to him, calling for help. Not calling to him, specifically, but calling without a hope in hell of answer. Praying. Then the face was gone and he was alone with his reflection.

He pressed his face into the towel. One of a soft, luxurious set that Michelle had bought. When she'd brought them home, they had rubbed them all over each other and made love.

Kundalini. Feel the power.

(Lenore. Erika. Eileen. All lost to him.)

He went out to Michelle.

Jane accepted the steaming cup of green tea from Kim Toy and sipped at it delicately. "Here's to the second night in a row of no nightmares," she said with a weak smile. "I hope."

Kim Toy's answering smile was less than hearty. The girl should have been a quivering mound of jelly after the dreams the Astronomer had sent her, and that was barely a taste of TIAMAT. Real contact would have driven her permanently mad. But here she was, the fragile little innocent, drinking tea and getting her color back. She was made of sterner stuff than any of them had given her credit for. It was always the innocent ones you had to watch, Kim Toy thought wryly. Their strength was as the strength of ten because their hearts were pure and their sincerity made them lethal. She wondered if twisted-up old pervos like the Astronomer had any inkling or whether he was so far removed from anything even remotely resembling innocence that he couldn't even conceive of such a thing. When she thought about the way the Astronomer recharged his power, yeah, she could allow that was entirely possible. What would a sick old fuck like that know about innocence?

And he was going to own the world. Sure.

But she *did* believe that. She was unshakable on that. Had been unshakable on that. No, still was. Wasn't she? And who was she calling a sick old fuck, anyway? What was it when you scrambled a man's brains to make him fall in love with you, and then, when he'd served his purpose, you turned it up from scramble to liquify, and the same people who dumped the bodies for the Astronomer dumped that one, too. She looked at Jane. It was no wonder she preferred the company of women if she couldn't be with Red.

Jane reached over and pressed the On button of the remote control. The TV screen flickered to life. "I watched *Peregrine's Perch* last night and I didn't have the dreams," she said, a bit sheepishly. "Now it's made me superstitious. I feel like I have to watch it to keep the nightmares away. Even if it's a re-run."

Kim Toy nodded. "You and about a billion other people."

"Sal adored talk shows. Especially *Peregrine's Perch*. He said he watched because he was dying to see how they'd work around those wings each night." She paused as a commercial gave way to the stunning features of Peregrine herself. "Sal said they never disappointed him."

"Who?"

"Her wardrobe department."

"Oh." Kim Toy fell silent and dutifully watched the program with the girl. Half an hour into the show, a picture of a handsome red-haired man with russet eyes and a lean, sculpted face appeared on the screen, causing Jane to leap out of her chair.

"There he is!" She knelt down close to the TV. "Jumpin' Jack Flash. I followed all the news stories about him. He's one of my heroes."

Kim Toy turned up the sound. The man's face vanished and was replaced by the talk-show set where Peregrine was interviewing an expensively dressed woman holding an even more-expensive-looking camera.

"I think you've captured the spirit of Jumpin' Jack Flash exactly," Peregrine was saying. "That couldn't have been easy."

"Well, it was all the more difficult because it was a candid shot," the other woman said. "Believe it or not, I was just lucky, being in the right place at the right time. J.J. didn't know I was taking that picture, although he later gave permission for its use."

"J.J.?" said Peregrine.

The photographer looked down demurely. "That's what his intimates call him."

"I'll bet," Kim Toy muttered.

"What?" said Jane.

"His 'intimates.' Gimme a break. He probably tells all the women he sleeps with to call him J.J., just so he can keep track. It's easier than remembering their names, and far less trouble than notching their ears, or having them all rounded up and branded."

Jane looked a little hurt. One of her heroes, right. Kim Toy shook her head. At her age, the girl was overdue to learn that certain heroes had—well, not dicks of clay, but certainly hyperactive ones.

Like your heroes, madam? Like the Astronomer, maybe?

Kim Toy shoved the thought away and forced herself to concentrate on the interview. The photographer apparently specialized in photographing aces. More pictures flashed on the screen; to Jane's delight, Jumpin' Jack Flash reappeared several times in between shots of Modular Man, Dr. Tachyon, the shell of the Great and Powerful Turtle, Starshine, and Peregrine herself.

"Too bad she can't take your picture," Kim Toy said as the segment ended and the show went to another commercial.

Jane shrugged. "I'm a joker."

"You're starting to get on my nerves."

"But the joke's on me. One of the two people who meant the most to me drowned; the other bled to death." She turned away from the TV. "Yeah, the joke's definitely on me and it isn't a bit funny."

Kim Toy was about to answer when something shimmered in the air to the right of the TV set. Both women were very still as the image of the Astronomer congealed out of the shadows. "Kim Toy. Jane. I wish to see you."

There was no need to answer. Kim Toy remained at a sort of attention, hoping her annoyance didn't show. Cheap theatrics for Jane's benefit. The Astronomer must have thought she was one hell of a hot ticket to go this far to impress her. He could have conserved his energy and sent Red to fetch them.

* * *

Dr. Tachyon still looked his stylish best, even on the downside of midnight. "I knew he had some aces up there. But the machine you describe from the dreams—well, it does exist and it's very old by your standards." His eyes narrowed as he studied Fortunato's swollen forehead. "Rather unusual for you to have an out-of-body experience spontaneously, isn't it?"

Fortunato turned away from Tachyon (*goddamn faggot, just what we need, faggots from space*) and stared out the window in the direction of the Cloisters. "I just came here to tell you. There's a hell of a lot of power massing up there. It called me. Power calls to power."

"Indeed," murmured Tachyon. Faggots from space. Fortunato would never love him, but he had never seen the tall, exotic Earthman in such an openly emotional state before.

"They're calling to that thing out there. TIAMAT. The whole organization has existed for centuries just for the purpose of bringing that horror down on us."

Tachyon's sigh was heavy. Suddenly he felt very tired. Forty years of one horror and another, he was entitled to feel fatigued. He knew Fortunato, standing in his elegant living room with his bulging forehead and the power practically crackling in the air, wouldn't have agreed with him.

Power calls to power? Oh, what he could have told them about *that*, Tachyon thought. And if he could have stepped back far enough to see the grand design of the universe, what he might have learned himself about his own people and the Wild Card Day and the approach of TIAMAT or the Swarm or whatever it was. Maybe there was a true grand design to the universe; or maybe it was just the wild card powers calling the Swarm. Of course, that would mean the virus had called the Swarm before the virus had even existed, but Tachyon was accustomed to dealing with the absurdities of space and time.

Not that any of it mattered anyway. He looked at Fortunato, who was energized with kundalini and impatience. The time for agonizing was long, long past; now was the time for doing, for doing as much as he could and not a bit less. To atone, perhaps, for a time when he might have done more, but had failed.

When he had failed Blythe.

After so many years, the sense of loss had not abated. It wouldn't stay hidden at the bottom of a bottle, it couldn't be obscured by an unending parade of the finest lovers. Only the work he did at the clinic ever seemed to give him some kind of comfort, inadequate but better than nothing at all.

His gaze met Fortunato's and he recognized the look in the other man's eyes. "Power calls to power and sorrow to sorrow." He gave Fortunato the barest of smiles. "We have all lost something precious to us in this battle against horror. But still we must go on, go on and turn back the darkness. If we can."

Fortunato didn't return the smile. Everything seemed to call for one of his goddamn fucking faggot speeches. "Yeah, sure," he said roughly, turning away. "Go up there and kick some ass, you and me and what army?"

Tachyon reached for the telephone. "We'll have to call them out."

The cop actually threw a net over him. It was so startling that he reverted to human form, bruising elbows and knees and scraping his flesh as he rolled over and over on the sidewalk. The cop was laughing even as he pulled his gun out and stuck it through the net.

"Don't get any ideas about changing back," said the cop, "or I'll have to put you out of your misery. Jesus, wait till they check your action up to the Cloisters. I can hardly believe it myself."

He shivered in the net, unable to take his eyes off the barrel of the pistol. The cop really would shoot him, he didn't doubt it. Silently, he cursed himself for not being content with simply sailing over the city enjoying the lights and scaring the piss out of the occasional rooftop couple. How many people could say they'd been buzzed by a pterodactyl—lately?

The cop bundled him into the back of his car and drove through town, still snickering. "I don't know what the Astronomer'll want to do about you, but you'll probably amuse the hell out of him. You make the smallest tyrannosaurus that ever was."

"Ornithosuchus," he murmured, swallowing hard. Another dinosaur-illiterate with a gun. He wasn't sure what to be more afraid of—the gun, this Astronomer guy, or his own father, who would shortly discover he wasn't up in his room asleep. He was only thirteen and he wasn't supposed to be out this late on a school night, especially in the form of a fast-running flesh-eater of the Triassic period.

* * *

"Come here, my dear. So I can see you better."

Jane hesitated. The aura of evil that her dreams had hinted at was too definitely present around the old man in the wheelchair. Moisture began to bead lightly on her face and neck. She looked to Kim Toy but the woman's attention was on the Astronomer, just like everyone else's in the great hall. Whoever they all were. Masons. She recognized the man who'd brought her in—Judas, Roman had called him. Roman was seated at a computer terminal off to one side, near a low brick wall that seemed to have been attacked with a pickax. Spray-painted on it in metallic gold was the legend EAT ME.

"You have a great power, my dear," the old man said. "One that would be greatly useful for the visitor bearing down on us from the stars. TIAMAT." He paused, waiting for her reaction. She stood uncomfortably under his gaze. The extra illumination they had brought in and tacked up so carelessly had only made the shadows at the far corners that much darker. She had a sense of horrible things waiting there for a signal from this Astronomer to crawl out and devour her. EAT ME. She put one elbow in her fist, pressing the other hand against her mouth so she wouldn't start laughing and never stop.

"Are you familiar with that name? TIAMAT?" prodded the Astronomer. Jane pressed her hand tighter against her mouth and shrugged awkwardly.

"Well." The old man leaned forward slightly. "It would be helpful if we could have a demonstration of your power. Aside from what you did on the street with the fire hydrant." He squinted at her. "Or are you doing it now, my dear?"

"Oh, really subtle," said the bleakly thin man standing at the Astronomer's right. His eyes made Jane think of tombstones. "Just what we need, an ace whose big power is heavy sweating. World domination, here we come."

The Astronomer chuckled here and Jane thought it was the most evil sound she'd ever heard. "Now, now. We all know she's capable of much greater feats. Aren't you. Yes. For instance, you could conceivably remove all the water from a body, leaving—well, not much." He gestured at the rest of the people and chuckled again at the look on her face. "No, I thought not. The only one you might care to use it on right now is myself, and I'm immune." He nodded to Red, who vanished under one of the brick arches. A few moments later, he reappeared, guiding two men who were pushing a cage on wheels into the middle of the room. Jane blinked several times, unable to believe her eyes in the bad light.

There was a dinosaur in the cage. A *Tyrannosaurus rex*, all of three feet high.

As she watched, it bared its ferocious-looking teeth and ran back and forth behind the bars, its little forearms cuddled up close to its scaly body. One dark reptilian eye regarded Jane with a glitter of intelligence.

"Vicious creature," said the Astronomer. "If I were to let it out, it could snap your leg off in one bite. Kill it. Withdraw all the water from its body."

Jane lowered her arms, her hands still curled into fists.

"Oh, come now." Another of those evil chuckles. "Don't tell me your heart is touched by every stray dinosaur that comes along."

"There's someone in there," she said. "You want a sample of my power? Here's a close-up!"

Something *almost* happened. She had focused on an area just in front of the Astronomer's face, intending to dash a gallon of water into his eyes. The air blurred momentarily and then cleared. The old man threw back his head and roared with laughter. "You were right, Roman, she breaks out with bravado at the oddest moments! I told you, my excellent dear, that your power won't work if I don't want it to. No matter how much power *you* have, I have *more*. Isn't that right, Demise?"

The skinny man stepped forward, ready to obey some order. The Astronomer shook his head. "There's another waiting for us, much more receptive. She won't try to throw a bucket of water in our faces."

Jane wiped her own face without effect. Water was beginning to pool around her feet. The Astronomer watched her, unmoved. "To have real power is to be able to use it, to be able to do certain things, no matter how awful you may find them. There is more power than you can imagine in being able to do such things, or in being able to make someone do them." He gestured at the cage. Jane followed the movement and then had to clap both hands over her mouth to keep from crying out.

The tyrannosaur had been replaced by a boy no more than twelve or thirteen years old, with sandy brown hair, gray-blue eyes, and a small pink birthmark on his forehead. He would have been startling enough, except that he was also completely naked. He crouched at the bars, doing his best to cover himself.

"There is no more time to try to court you, my dear," said the Astronomer, and all pretense of kindliness was gone from his voice. "TIAMAT is very close now and I cannot waste even a moment trying to lure you in with us. It's too bad; your killing a child even in the guise of a dangerous dinosaur would have bound you over to us, traumatically but completely. If I had but a few more weeks, you would have been ours painlessly. Now it's a matter of choosing between your life and your brave little ethics. You have as much time to decide as it takes for me to cross this room. I have no doubt which you'll choose. May your ethics sustain you in the next life. If there is one." He gestured at the skinny man. "Demise—"

Several things happened at once. The cockroach-man stepped forward with a loud rustling sound and shouted *"No!"* just as water splashed into Demise's face forcefully enough to knock him over and then another voice, incredibly loud, bellowed, "THIS IS THE GREAT AND POWERFUL TURTLE! YOU WILL ALL COME OUT PEACEFULLY, WE HAVE THIS PLACE SURROUNDED AND NO ONE NEEDS TO GET HURT!" And then, impossibly, Jane thought she heard something that sounded like the old theme from the Mighty Mouse cartoons: *Here I come to save the daaaaaaaay!* This was followed by an ungodly caterwauling that went from extreme bass to an earsplitting high, shaking the entire building. There was a crash as the cage topped to the floor, spilling the boy out. Jane fought to keep her balance and reach the boy in the general chaos of people trying to run in every direction. He turned into another dinosaur barely two feet high, this one very slender and agile-looking, with slim, clawed fingers. She forced herself to grab the fingers as it scuttled over to her.

"We've got to get out of here!" she said breathlessly and more than a little unnecessarily, and looked around. Demise and the Astronomer had vanished. The little dinosaur pulled her across the room and into a shadowy gallery under the archways. Holding hands with a dinosaur, she thought as they fled down the gallery. Only in New York.

She didn't notice Kafka struggling after them.

It was really a hell of a beautiful sight, the Great and Powerful Turtle said later. Aces of every variety rising up out of the trees around the Cloisters, swooping down on the Masons that spilled out of the building onto the brick paths and into the ruined gardens. He had seen just about everything during the battle. One of the things he missed, however, was Jane and the boy-dinosaur creeping along part of a columned arcade surrounding an outdoor area now overgrown with weeds. They saw the Turtle sailing overhead with several colorfully costumed aces clinging to his shell. One of the aces pointed down at something; in the next moment, he was floating gently to earth, lowered by the Turtle's power. Jane heard the little dinosaur hiss alarmingly. When she turned to see what was the matter, he had changed back into a boy, his nudity covered by shadows.

"That's the Turtle!" he whispered to Jane. "If we could just get his attention, he could get you out of here!"

"What about you?"

For answer, he reverted to dinosaur again, this one well-muscled and almost as ferocious-looking as the tyrannosaur. It looked vaguely familiar to Jane, who couldn't tell a crocodile from an alligator. She tried to remember the name. An Alice-something-or-other. Alice or perhaps *alas*, for as mean-looking as it was, it was also no bigger than a German shepherd. It growled and pushed her along with its three-clawed hands, hustling her onto the stone path surrounding the weed-choked garden. There was another one of those grotesque howls; Jane felt it shudder clear through her and the little dinosaur— *allosaurus*, she remembered suddenly, for no reason—roared in response, clawing at its head painfully. She bent, meaning to embrace it or comfort it, when there was a flurry of feathers, a glint of metal, and then an extraordinarily beautiful woman lit on a low marble wall.

"Peregrine!" Jane breathed.

The allosaurus made a small, excited sound, looking the winged woman over with wild eyes.

"Better get out," Peregrine said good-naturedly. "The Howler is going to shout this place down. Can you manage, you and your, uh, pet lizard there?"

"It's a boy. I mean, he's really a little boy, an ace—"

The allosaurus bellowed, either in agreement or in protest at being called a little boy.

"Vicious, really vicious." Peregrine smiled at Jane as she launched herself upward, her great wings beating the air.

"Best you get out now. I mean it," she called and soared away, the famed titanium talons up and ready.

Jane and the allosaurus ran around the ruined garden and tore down another arcade. She heard the little dinosaur fall behind, and paused, squinting in the darkness. "What's wrong?"

She could just make out a human silhouette. "Gotta change. Need a fast runner, I'm getting tired. Hypsilophodon's better than an allosaurus for running."

A moment later she felt long claws grab her gently and tug her along. This one was about the size of a large kangaroo.

"I don't think we're going the right way to get out of here," she huffed as they came to a dimly lit area and a staircase leading down. The dinosaur melted into boy briefly before he reshaped as a pterodactyl and glided down the stairs. Jane could only gallop after him. At the foot of the stairs, the pterodactyl suddenly swooped around and came back toward her. Reflexively, she ducked, stumbled, and hit the bottom just in time to come face to face with a man even handsomer than Roman. He wore a navy-blue jumpsuit and a tight-fitting skullcap and there were guns seemingly attached directly to his shoulders.

"Hi," he said. "Didn't I see you at the ape-escape?"

Jane blinked, shaking her head dazedly. "What—I don't—" And then, as the man's guns swung up to track the pterodactyl circling around them, "No! He's just a little boy, he's a *good guy!*"

"Oh, all right, then," said the man, smiling at her. "You two better get going." Jane ran past him, the pterodactyl gliding over her head. "Are you *sure* I didn't see you at the ape-escape?" he called after her.

She wouldn't have had the breath to answer him even if she'd wanted to. The pterodactyl sailed ahead of her as she felt her legs beginning to weaken. Panting, she stumbled along, watching as the gap between herself and the pterodactyl began to widen.

The pterodactyl banked sharply to round a corner in the hall and disappeared. Half a moment later there was a flash of blue light, a screech, and a thump. Jane thudded to a stop, hanging onto the stone wall. *Please*, she prayed. *Not the little boy. Don't let them hurt the little boy and they can do anything they want with me.* She forced herself to move forward, holding the wall for support, and peeked around the corner.

He had changed back into a boy again when he'd hit the floor, but she could see his bare chest rising and falling as he breathed. The roach-man was standing over him with a nasty-looking weapon that looked like a stinger.

"I had to stop him," the roach-man said, looking up at her. "He's not really hurt, though. He'll come out of it in a few minutes. Honest. I need your help." He held out his free hand to Jane. She took a step forward. The face was inhuman but the eyes were not. Just before she would have taken his hand, he snatched it back.

"I meant that just as a gesture. Don't touch me. Rouse him and come with me."

Jane knelt beside the unconscious boy.

Judas stood by the tomb with his hands over his ears, unable to clear his head long enough to decide what he should do. Every time he tried to think, another one of those awful howls would shiver through him. He swore his ears were bleeding.

The chaos was beyond believable. The Astronomer's people had been running in and out of the large room like the bunch of chickenshit losers they all really were. He'd known they were all chickenshits in the beginning, he'd been a cop long enough to recognize the breed. It was enough to make a person want to change sides and start wiping them out himself, and maybe that wasn't such a bad idea, what with aces storming the place; sure, he had his badge, he had his gun, he could claim he'd been undercover, who would bother checking, at least for tonight. Sure.

He looked around and saw Red and Kim Toy making their way toward one of the darkened galleries, searching for a way out. Might as well start with them as anyone else, he thought, and drew his gun.

"Halt! Halt or I'll shoot!"

Kim Toy's head snapped around, her long straight dark hair flying with the movement.

Judas switched his aim from her face to Red's. "I told you not to move!"

Red threw a hand up in front of his head as Judas was about to pull the trigger and then, suddenly, he was in love. Birds were singing, making nests in his brain, and the whole world was beautiful, especially Kim Toy, most exciting and exotic of women. He flung his gun away and staggered toward her, loving her too much to feel hurt when she fled from him with Red.

His ears really were bleeding now but he no longer cared enough to notice.

Like all the rooms in this place, this one reminded her of a chapel. She could see where an altar or a baptismal font might have stood; that place was now occupied by a machine.

"You've seen this in a dream," Kafka said to Jane, putting a hand on one of the machine's impossible angles. Jane had to look away—the craziness of the outline was threatening to tie her vision in knots. She stared at the more-prosaic form of a nearby computer housing with a large monitor sitting dark and silent on top of it.

"The Shakti device," she said.

"Yes. The Shakti device." He winced as another one of those awful howls tore through the building. "Tonight we may all die, but this must be protected."

Jane's mouth twisted with distaste. "That TIAMAT creature—"

"Our only chance . . ."

There was a rustle as the dinosaur-boy—Kid Dinosaur, he'd told her—wrapped a sheet from Kafka's cot more tightly around himself. She'd asked him to stay in human form so she could talk with him and reluctantly he'd agreed, provided the roach-man would give him something to cover himself with. "I don't know how much you think you can trust this guy," the boy said, "but I sure wouldn't."

Steps thudded in the hall outside and Roman raced in, wild-eyed. "The computer housing—is it all right?" Without waiting for an answer, he shoved Kafka aside, scrambling madly for the computer. "Ellie! I'm here, Ellie, I'm here!"

Kafka went to him. "Where's the Astronomer?"

"Fuck him," Roman said and pushed Kafka away. "Fuck him and fuck all of you!" Another howl shook the building and they both fell against the computer together. One of the panels came off in Roman's hands, exposing part of the computer's circuitry.

"Holy shit!" said the boy. "Gross me out!"

Even in the bad light, Jane could see the circuitry pulsing, could see the texture of the boards and the moistness there, the living flesh mixed with the hard, dead machinery.

Or had the flesh itself hardened?—Jane put a hand over her eyes, feeling sick.

"Water Lily!"

Kafka's warning came just as she felt the hands on her from behind. They spun her around and she was staring into the tombstone gaze of Demise. She put her hands on his shoulders, and for one absurd moment it was as though they were embracing.

"Are you afraid to die?" he asked her.

In such extremity, she did not find his question out of place. "Yes," she said simply.

Something in his face changed and his grip loosened slowly.

"Water Lily!" Kafka cried again, his voice filled with despair. But she remained standing, remained alive, putting one hand on Demise's gaunt face. He recoiled from her touch.

"It hurts, doesn't it?"

"Everything hurts," he said roughly and shoved her away from him. She sprawled on the floor near Kafka's machine and started to get up again just as a thick, stained-glass window exploded inward, spraying the room with multicolored shards. She covered her head with both arms, diving for the floor; a long flame roared across the room, scorching wood and stone. She heard someone scream. There was a rustling sound as Kafka crawled across the floor to her and tried to urge her closer to the machine.

"The only thing," he panted. Another howl shook them like an earthquake. ". . . TIAMAT . . . protect . . . need your help for TIAMAT's—"

He was torn away from her; she heard him shriek at the contact. Then someone pulled her to her feet and she saw Kafka fall backward from a kick to the head.

"Nooooo!" she screamed. "Don't hurt him, *don't!*—" She had seen those russet eyes a thousand times, most recently tonight. Her mouth worked but she couldn't make a sound. The russet eyes crinkled with a quick smile before they thrust her to one side.

"Stand back, honey, I don't want to mix you up with the french fries." He turned and began to point at Kafka and the Shakti device and the boy, who had turned back into a dinosaur, a stegosaurus this time, and was all too obviously in the line of fire. Jane fought for her voice and the right words and came up with possibly the only thing that could have stopped him from making one big cinder of them all.

"J.J., *don't!*"

Jumpin' Jack Flash turned back to her, his mouth dropping open with surprise.

A moment later, he was even more surprised to see that she was covered with water.

Fortunato had been running in and out of every room and gallery and alcove he could find, searching for aces or anyone else, the faggot from space hot on his heels. So far, they'd only found some clown crawling around on a stone floor with blood running out his ears. The space faggot had wanted to stop and examine him but Fortunato had fixed that. This wasn't the clinic at noon, he'd said, and had dragged the space faggot away by the fancy collar of his faggot coat—faggot, yeah, sure, man, let's talk faggot, call your man Crowley a faggot, and while we're at it, how was it you raised that boy from the dead, speaking of faggots—he shut the flow of thoughts off firmly as he ran down a narrow hall.

"Fortunato—where—what are you—trying to do?" huffed Tachyon.

"I feel him," Fortunato said over his shoulder.

"Feel who?"

"He did Eileen. And Balsam. And a lot of others—" he staggered as the Howler gave another one of those long, horrible screams. Tachyon stumbled into him and the two of them nearly fell. "Shit, I wish he'd shut the fuck up," Fortunato muttered. He stopped suddenly and grabbed Tachyon by his faggot coat-front. "Listen, you stand back. He's all mine, understand that?"

Tachyon looked up at Fortunato's swollen forehead, his dark, angry eyes. Then he pried Fortunato's hands off himself. "I've never seen you like this before."

"Yeah, well, you ain't seen shit yet," Fortunato growled, and kept going, with the space faggot tagging after him.

For several long moments, it seemed as though nobody knew what to do. Roman had gotten to his feet and was shielding the exposed computer with his body. Kafka had scuttled over to the Shakti machine; the little stegosaurus was looking from side to side. Even Jumpin' Jack Flash seemed to be frozen, looking from Jane to the strange machine and Kafka, to Roman and back to Jane.

Then he turned away from her and time started again and he was stretching an arm out toward Kafka's machine.

"Not him," Jane said desperately, and reached for him just as Demise said, almost too soft to hear, "Hey. You."

Before Jumpin' Jack Flash could react, the stegosaurus twinkled to the form of a naked boy and then to a tyrannosaur, and launched himself across the room to bury his teeth in Demise's thigh. Demise screamed and fell backward, wrestling with the tyrannosaur. Kafka started to shout; there was a swirl of light, a glimmering, and the Astronomer was standing in the middle of the room. His head was something out of a nightmare now—he had a strange curved snout, rectangular ears, and slanting eyes, but Jane knew it was the Astronomer. She heard Kafka say "The god Setekh!" with either fear or relief. The Astronomer smiled at Jane and she saw blood smeared on his teeth and lips. No wheelchair now; he seemed to be filled with vitality and strength. As though to confirm her thoughts, he suddenly rose five feet in the air.

Jumpin' Jack Flash took a step back, lifted both hands, and then looked puzzled. The Astronomer wagged a finger at him as though he were a naughty child, and turned his attention to Demise, who was still rolling around on the floor with the tyrannosaur. A moment later, the tyrannosaur was a naked boy again.

"Aw, shit!" the boy yelled, and squirmed out of Demise's grasp, fighting to get to the door. Just as he reached it, a tall black man with a bulging forehead appeared at the threshold. Jane gasped, not at his appearance but at the sense of power around him; she could feel the unreleased forces charging the air.

"I've sensed you," said the Astronomer, "stirring around the edges, here and there."

"More than stirring, motherfucker." The man drew himself up so that he seemed even taller, and reached out toward the Astronomer as though to embrace him. The Astronomer descended slightly, still smiling.

"I would enjoy putting you through your paces . . ." said the Astronomer, and suddenly drew back, floating across the room to Kafka's machine. He twisted his fists sharply upward. The tall man staggered forward several steps, stopped, and braced himself with his feet wide apart.

"Don't be coy, Fortunato. Come closer." The pull on Fortunato seemed to grow stronger. Jumpin' Jack Flash looked at Jane.

"If you know any other tricks besides drowning yourself, honey," he said in a low voice, "you better use them."

Another man suddenly appeared in the doorway. Jane had just enough time to notice the improbable red hair and the flashy clothing before there was even more red, a whole body's worth of red, knocking the man over. The two forms rolled over and over on the floor, Red fighting to pin the smaller man. Then Kim Toy was there, pulling at her husband, telling him to forget it, just forget it and let's get out of here.

Near Kafka's machine, the Astronomer and Fortunato were still balanced against each other. Jane had the feeling the Astronomer was gaining slightly. The strain on Fortunato's face intensified with the strange glow around him and now horns projected from his bulging forehead. In response, the Astronomer's body was assuming an animal shape, like a greyhound, with a huge forked tail rising up like something poisonous. Her fear began to crescendo and there was no one to hold onto, no one who offered shelter or comfort or escape.

The boy-dinosaur, thin and long-tailed now, whipped back into the room and landed on Red, knocking him off the man in fancy dress. Kim Toy jumped back and then a fourth person was confusing things, throwing himself on Kim Toy. With a shock, Jane saw it was Judas. Blood was trickling from his ears but he seemed not to notice as he knelt on Kim Toy's legs, pinned her chest with one hand, and then, absurdly, began to undo his pants.

Jane shook her head incredulously. It was some weird vision of hell, the Astronomer, Roman, that obscene computer, Kafka, the Shakti machine, the dinosaur and Red and the black man and his horns and the other man—Tachyon, she recognized him now, he seemed to be dazed—and Jumpin' Jack Flash, unable to do a thing, and that sleazy scumbag who had brought her here—whom she had allowed to bring her here, she corrected herself, like somebody's dog on a short leash—the scumbag trying to rape Kim Toy in the middle of a fight for all their lives.

All this ran through her mind in a second and the power gathered itself effortlessly and poured out of her.

This time Judas was the only one who was oblivious to what she was doing. He never knew, even when it hit him, that all she had meant to do was blind him by drawing a flood of tears to his eyes, but the power had been building up without proper release for too long and she was too scared and too strong in her fear. He never knew, even as he raised up. Then he was *not*, and in his place was a form made of powder that hung briefly in the air for an impossible moment before it disintegrated. Wetness splattered the walls, the floor, and Kim Toy.

Jane tried to scream but only a faint sighing came out. Everything stopped; even the struggle between the Astronomer and Fortunato seemed to diminish slightly. Then Jumpin' Jack Flash yelled, "Don't anybody move or she'll do it again!"

Jane burst into tears.

The whole room burst into tears; suddenly there was a rainstorm in the room, water spraying from every direction. Jumpin' Jack Flash flung himself out the window and hung suspended in midair. "Drown 'em or turn it off!" he shouted.

And then it *was* turned off, with a gesture from the Astronomer. He favored Jane with another hideous smile. "Do it again. For me."

She felt herself being turned by an invisible hand and power gathered itself within her again, aiming itself for the black man, Fortunato—

Who was no longer there but behind the Astronomer, standing over Kafka's Shakti machine with both arms raised—

And Kafka hollered, *"NO!"* and the word echoed in Jane's mind as the power flew from her against her will, deflected at the final moment with her last shred of strength, so that it bypassed everyone, even the Astronomer, and hit the computer just as the Shakti machine collapsed with a sound too much like a human scream.

The force from Fortunato struck the machine again and there was another scream, this time very human, as the computer's awful living circuitry crumpled to powder that flowed over Roman's arms and chest.

Fortunato turned to the Astronomer, reaching out for him. The animal form melted away, leaving the Astronomer human again and very small. He wavered in the air for a moment and the light around him began to dim.

"Fool," he whispered, but the whisper penetrated the whole room and everyone in it. "Stupid blind nigger fool." He looked around at all of them. "You will all die screaming."

And then, like smoke, he vanished.

"Wait! Wait, goddamn you!" Demise struggled to his feet, clutching his already-healing leg. "You promised me, goddamn you, *you promised me!*" Underneath his enraged shrieks, Roman's sobs made a bizarre counterpoint.

Jane felt her knees start to give. She had nothing left. Even with her power, she had no more strength. Tachyon was beside her, holding her up. "Come," he said gently, pulling her toward the door. She felt something flow over the incipient hysteria in her mind, as comforting as a warm blanket. Half in trance, she let him take her out of the room. With another part of her mind, she heard Kafka call to her, and distantly, she was sad that she could not answer him.

From the shelter of a stand of trees, she watched the last of what became known as the Great Cloisters Raid. Occasionally she caught a glimpse of Peregrine swooping around the tower or flying rings around the Turtle's shell, sometimes accompanied by a graceful, if rather small (to her eyes), pteranodon. Columns of fire shot up into the night, exploding through rooftops, scorching stone. Vainly, she searched for a glimpse of Kafka or Demise in the groups of people—Masons, she thought, shaking her head at the absurdity, *Masons*— gathered neatly up and removed from harm by the Turtle's power.

"In the end, I tried to take care of someone. I tried to take care of the little boy," she murmured, uncaring if Tachyon beside her knew what she was talking about or not. But he did. She could feel his presence sorting through her thoughts, touching her memories of Debbie and Sal and how Judas had found her. And wherever he touched, he left the warmth of comfort and understanding.

The Howler let loose with another one of those awful wails, but it was a short one.

She might have cried, except she seemed to have no tears left for the time being.

A little later, familiar voices brought her back to awareness. Jumpin' Jack Flash was there with the boy-dinosaur, who had chosen another odd form she didn't know. ("Iguanodon," Tachyon whispered to her. "Look appreciative." And, somehow, she did.) Fortunato emerged from an entrance that flickered with dying fire; he stepped over glowing fragments and found his way to them, looking even more tired than Jane felt.

"Lost them," he said to Tachyon. "The cockroach, the death freak, the other one. That red guy and his woman. Got away, unless the Turtle's picked them up." He jerked his chin at Jane. "What's her story?"

She looked past him to the burning Cloisters, pulled herself together, felt for the power. There was a surprising amount still left, enough for what she wanted to do.

Water splashed down on the worst of the flames, helping a little, not much. There *was* an arsonist around when you needed one after all, she thought, glancing at Jumpin' Jack Flash.

"Don't waste your energy," he said, and as though to back him up, she heard the sound of fire engines approaching.

"I was born in a fire station," she said. "My mother didn't get to the hospital in time."

"Fascinating," he said, "but I've got to leave pretty soon." He looked at Tachyon. "I, uh, I would like to know how you knew—uh, *why* you called me J.J."

She shrugged. "J.J. Jumpin' Jack. It was faster to say." She managed a tiny smile. "That's all. We've never met before. Honest."

Relief was large on his face. "Ah. Well, listen, sometime soon we could get acquainted and—"

"Sixty minutes," Tachyon said. "I'd say you're just about out of time. What we could call the Cinderella factor. When someone *trips*."

Jumpin' Jack Flash gave him a dirty look before he lifted into the air. A halo of flame ignited itself around him as he roared off into the darkness.

Jane stared after him for a moment and then looked down sadly. "I almost hurt him back there. I *did* hurt someone— I . . ."

Tachyon put his arms around her. "Lean on me. It's all right."

Gently, she removed his arms from her. "Thank you. But I'm done leaning." *Okay, Sal?*

She turned back to the burning Cloisters and continued to pour water on the worst of the flames.

Curled up in an alleyway, Demise shuddered. His leg was bad enough that it wasn't completely healed yet, but it would heal; he knew it the way he knew how much he hated the Astronomer for abandoning him, for ever pulling him in with his promises and favors in the first place. TIAMAT, hell. He'd get that twisted-up old fuck before TIAMAT ever got here and that was a promise. He'd put that old fuck through a dance he'd take to hell with him.

He drifted in semidelirium. Not far away, but unknown to him, Kafka watched the destruction of the Cloisters. When the water poured down into the flames from thin air he turned away, willing the cold deadness of hatred to stay in him.

MR. KOYAMA'S COMET

By Walter Jon Williams

Part One: March 1983

In June of 1981 a third-generation Mitsubishi executive, Koyama Eido, took his retirement amid the extravagant praise and well-earned respect of his peers and underlings. He got extravagantly drunk, paid off his mistress, and the very next day put into operation a plan he had been working on for almost forty years. He moved with his wife to a house he had built on the island of Shikoku. The house was in rugged terrain on the southern part of the island and was difficult to access; it cost Mr. Koyama an extraordinary amount of money to get the telephone and utilities put in; and the house was built in an unusual style, with a flat roof that would not weather well—but to Mr. Koyama none of that mattered. What mattered was that the house was so remote there was little light pollution, that it looked east to the Pacific and southwest to the Bungo Channel, and that the *seeing* was better over water.

In a hutch built on his flat roof, Mr. Koyama installed a fourteen-inch reflective telescope that he had built with his own hands. During good weather he would trundle this out onto the platform and gaze into the sky, at stars and planets and distant galaxies, and he would take careful, studied photographs of them which he would develop in his darkroom and later hang on his walls. But simply watching the sky wasn't quite enough: Mr. Koyama wanted more. He wanted something up there to bear his name.

Every day, therefore, just after sunset and just before dawn, Mr. Koyama would go onto his roof with a pair of Fujinan naval binoculars that he had purchased in Chiba from a starving ex-submarine captain in 1946. Patiently, wrapped in a warm wool overcoat, he would focus their five-inch objective lenses on the sky and inspect it carefully. He was looking for comets.

In December of 1982 he found one, but unfortunately had to share the credit with Seki, a comet-finder of some reputation who had discovered the comet some days previous. Mr. Koyama was chagrined by missing Seki-Koyama 1982P by some seventy-two hours but kept looking, vowing increased dedication and vigilance. He wanted one all to himself.

March of 1983 opened cold and drizzly: Mr. Koyama shivered under his hat and overcoat as he scanned the sky night after night. A bout of influenza kept him off the roof till the twenty-second, and he was annoyed to discover that Seki and Ikeya had together discovered a new comet while he was laid up. Increased dedication and vigilance, he vowed again.

The morning of the twenty-third, Mr. Koyama finally found his comet. There, near the not-yet-risen sun, he saw a fuzzy ball of light. He sneezed, gripped the Fujinans tightly, and gazed up again to confirm the sighting. Nothing else should be in that part of the sky.

His heart pounding, Mr. Koyama descended to his study and picked up the telephone. He called the telegraph office and sent a wire to the International Astronomical Union. (Telegrams are de rigueur with the IAU; a telephone call would be considered vulgar.) Offering vague prayers to a host of gods in which he did not profess actual belief, Mr. Koyama returned to the roof with the strange feeling that his comet would have disappeared while he wasn't looking. He breathed a sigh of relief.

The comet was still there.

The confirmation from the IAU came two days later, and confirmed as well what Mr. Koyama already knew from his own observations: Koyama 1983D was a real whizzer. It was flying from the sun like a bat out of hell.

Further reports indicated all sorts of anomalies. A routine spectrographic analysis showed that Koyama 1983D was a decidedly odd duck indeed: instead of the normal hydroxyls and carbon, Mr. Koyama's comet registered large amounts of oxygen, nitrogen, hydrogen, carbon, silicon, and various mineral salts. In short, all that was necessary for organic life.

A storm of controversy immediately arose over Koyama's comet. How anomalous was it, and was organic life possible in the cold and dusty ranges of the Oort Cloud? Mr. Koyama was interviewed by teams from the BBC, NBC, and Soviet television. He was profiled in *Time* magazine. He offered modest statements about his amateur status and his astonishment as to all the fuss; but he was inwardly more pleased than he had been over anything, even the birth of his eldest son. His wife observed him walking about the house with the strut of a twenty-year-old and the broad grin of a clown.

Every night and morning, Mr. Koyama was on the roof. It was going to be hard to top this, but he was going to try.

Part Two: October 1985

Astronomy was getting more attention these days, what with the reappearance of P/Halley 1982I, but Mr. Koyama maintained his equilibrium in the face of the turmoil. He was an old hand now. He had discovered four additional comets since Koyama 1983D, and was assured of a prominent place in cometary history. Each of his comets had been the so-called "Koyama-type" comets with their weird spectrography and their bat-out-of-hell speed. Koyama-type comets were being discovered by all manner of amateurs, always hugging the sun.

The controversy had not died down; had in fact intensified. Was it possible that the solar system was passing through a storm of comets containing organic elements, or was this a fairly ordinary occurrence that somehow hadn't been noticed till now? Fred Hoyle smiled and issued an I-told-you-so statement reiterating his theory of cosmic seedlings containing organic life; and even his bitterest opponents conceded that the annoying old Yorkshireman might have won this round.

Mr. Koyama received many invitations to speak; he

declined them all. Time speaking meant time away from his rooftop observatory. Currently the record number of comet discoveries was nine, held by an Australian minister. Mr. Koyama was going to win the honor for Japan or die trying.

Part Three: Late June 1986

There: another comet, barely visible, chasing the sun about the sky. That made six altogether. Mr. Koyama descended to his study and called the telegraph office. His heartbeat increased. He needed confirmation on this one desperately—not confirmation of the sighting, but of the spectrography.

Mr. Koyama was climbing the charts of comet-sighters, and this was in a period of a nervous, increased watching of the sky: people were looking up a lot these days, hoping to find the dark nonreflective Swarm parent that was presumably lurking nearby. But the prospect of number six wasn't what excited Mr. Koyama—he was getting fairly blasé about finding new comets these days. What he needed was confirmation of his new theory.

Mr. Koyama accepted the congratulations of the telegrapher and put down the telephone. He gazed with a frown at the chart he had on his desktop. It suggested something that he suspected he was the only one to notice. It was the kind of thing that was only noticed by people who spent their nights on rooftops, counting the hours and days, shrugging off the dew, and staring at bits of the night through long refractive lenses.

The Koyama-style comets seemed to possess not only weird organics and uncommon velocity, but an even stranger periodicity. Every three months, more or less, a new Koyama-type comet appeared near the sun. It was as if the Oort Cloud were shrugging off a ball of organic compounds to mark each new Terran season.

Smiling, Mr. Koyama savored the idea of the sensation his observation would cause, the panic among cosmographers trying to work out new formulas for explaining it. His place in astronomy would be assured. Koyama comets were proving as regular as planets. In a way, he thought, it was lucky the Swarm had landed, because otherwise the observation might have been made earlier . . .

The thought echoed slowly in his mind. Mr. Koyama's smile turned to a frown. He looked at his chart and performed some mathematics in his head. His frown deepened. He took out a pocket calculator and confirmed his calculations. His heart lurched. He sat down quickly.

The Swarm: a tough kilometers-long shell protecting vast quantities of biomass. Something like that would be vulnerable to changes in temperature. If it got near the sun it would have to bleed off excess heat somehow. The result would be a fluorescence not unlike that of a comet.

Suppose the Swarm were in a fast orbit with the sun at one focus and the Earth at the other. With the Earth in motion relative to the sun, the orbit would be complicated, but not impossible. But with all the sightings of Koyama-type comets, it should be possible to pinpoint the approximate location of the Swarm. A few hundred hydrogen-tipped missiles would then end the War of the Worlds in bang-up style.

"*Muthafucka*," breathed Mr. Koyama, a strong word he had learned from GIs during the occupation. Who the hell should he tell about this? he wondered. The IAU was the wrong forum. The Prime Minister? The Jieitai?

No. They would have no reason to believe an obscure retired businessman who called up raving about the Swarm. No doubt they got enough of those calls as it was.

He would call up his comrades from Mitsubishi. They had enough clout to see that he got heard.

As he reached for the phone and began to dial, Mr. Koyama felt his heart begin to sink. His place in astronomical history was assured, he knew, but not as he wanted. Instead of six comets, all he had discovered was a damned lump of yeast.

HALF PAST DEAD

By John J. Miller

i.

Brennan followed the Mercedes full of Immaculate Egrets to the gate of the cemetery in a gray BMW he had stolen from the gang three days before.

He stopped a hundred yards behind them, his headlights off, while one of the Egrets got out of the Mercedes and swung open the graveyard's sagging wrought-iron gate. He waited until they went on into the cemetery, then he slid out of the BMW, took his bow and quiver of arrows from the back seat, slipped his hood over his head, and crossed the street after them.

The six-foot-high brick fence around the graveyard was stained with city grime and crumbling with age. He pulled himself over it easily and dropped down inside without a sound.

The Mercedes was somewhere near the center of the cemetery. The driver killed the engine and turned the headlights off as Brennan watched. Car doors opened and slammed shut. He could hear or see nothing significant from where he stood. He had to get closer to the Egrets.

It was a dark night, the full moon often hidden by thick, shifting clouds. The trees growing wild inside the cemetery screened most of what city light there was. He moved slowly in the darkness, the sounds of his passing covered by the wind blowing with a hundred whispering voices through the branches overhead.

A shadow shifting among shadows, he moved behind an

old slab tombstone canted like a crooked tooth in the mouth of
an unkempt giant. He watched three of the Egrets enter a
mausoleum that had once been the crowning glory of the
cemetery. The monument of a once rich, now forgotten family,
it had been allowed to sink into decay like the rest of the
graveyard. Its marble stonework had been eaten away by acid
rain and bird droppings, its giltwork had flaked away over
years of neglect. One of the Egrets stayed behind as the others
went through the wrought-iron door into the interior of the
mausoleum. He closed the door behind the others, and leaned
against the front wall of the sepulcher. He lit a cigarette and his
face shone briefly in the flame of the match. It was Chen, the
Egret lieutenant Brennan had been following for the last two
weeks.

Brennan crouched behind the tombstone, frowning. He
had known since Vietnam that Kien was channeling heroin to
the States through a Chinatown street gang called the
Immaculate Egrets. He had scouted the gang and latched onto
Chen, who appeared to rank fairly high in the organization,
with the hope of finding hard evidence to link the Egrets to
Kien. He had witnessed a dozen felonies over the last few
weeks, but had uncovered nothing concerning Kien.

There was one inexplicable thing. The past several weeks
had seen an incredible influx of heroin into the city. It was so
plentiful that the street price had plummeted and there had
been a record number of o.d.'s. The Immaculate Egrets,
through whom the drug flowed, were selling it at cut-rate
prices, stealing customers right and left from the Mafia and
Sweet William's Harlem crowd. But Brennan had been unable
to discover how they were getting their scag so cheaply and
plentifully.

Skulking behind a tombstone was getting him nowhere.
The answers, if the graveyard had any, would be in the
mausoleum.

His mind made up, he drew an arrow from the quiver
velcroed to his belt and nocked it to the string of his bow. He
breathed deeply, smoothly, once, twice, caught his breath, and
stood. As he did he glimpsed the name pecked into the
weathered rock of the tombstone. Archer. He hoped it wasn't
an omen.

It wasn't a difficult shot, but he still called on his Zen
training to clear his mind and steady his muscles. He aimed a
foot lower and a little to the left of the glowing cigarette tip,

and, when the time was right, let the string slip from his fingers.

His bow was a four-wheel compound with elliptical cams that, once the tension point was reached, reduced the initial pull of one hundred and twenty pounds to sixty. The nylon bowstring thrummed, sending the shaft through the night like a hawk swooping on an unsuspecting target. He heard a thud and a strangled groan as the arrow struck home. He slipped out of the shadows like a cautious animal, and ran to where Chen lay slumped against the mausoleum wall.

He tarried long enough to make sure that Chen was dead and to leave one of his cards, a plastic-laminated ace of spades, stuck on the arrowtip protruding from Chen's back.

He nocked another arrow to his bowstring and creaked open the wrought-iron door that closed off the interior of the tomb. Inside, a stairway led down a dozen steps to another door haloed by a dim, steady light that burned in a chamber beyond. He waited for a moment, listening, then went down the stairs silently. He stopped at the door of the inner chamber to listen again. Someone was moving around inside. He counted to twenty, slowly, but heard only quiet, scuffling footsteps. He'd come this far. There was no sense in turning back now.

Brennan dove through the door, and came up on one knee, bowstring drawn back to his ear. One man wearing the colors of the Immaculate Egrets was in the room. He was counting plastic bags of white powder and marking the tally on a sheet of paper on a clipboard. He opened his mouth wide in astonishment just as Brennan released the arrow. It struck him high in the chest and knocked him backward over the knee-high pile of keys.

Brennan leaped across the chamber, but the Egret was as dead as everyone else in the boneyard by the time Brennan reached him. Brennan looked up from the body and glanced around.

What had happened to the other two Snow Birds who had gone into the sepulcher? They had vanished into thin air. Or, more likely, Brennan thought, through a door concealed in one of the walls.

He slung the bow across his back and checked the walls, running his hands over them, looking for hidden seams or cracks, rapping and listening for a hollow sound. He had finished one wall without finding anything, and was starting on the next when he heard a muffled whoosh of air at his back and felt a warm, humid breeze.

He whirled around. The look of astonishment on his face matched that of the two men who had appeared from nowhere into the middle of the mausoleum. One, who wore the colors of the Egrets, had saddlebags draped over each shoulder. The other, a thin, reptilian-looking joker, was carrying what looked like a bowling ball. They had, Brennan realized with some astonishment, vanished into thin air. And now they were back.

The Egret carrying the bulging saddlebags was closest to him. Brennan unslung his bow, swung it like a baseball bat, and connected with the side of the Egret's head. The man dropped with a groan, collapsing next to the pallet loaded with heroin.

The joker reared back, hissing sibilantly. He was taller than Brennan and thin to the point of emaciation. His skull was hairless, his nose a slight bump with a pair of flaring nostril pits. Overlong incisors protruded from his upper jaw. He stared unblinkingly at Brennan. When he opened his lipless mouth and hissed, he exposed a lolling forked tongue that flicked frantically in Brennan's direction. He clutched his bowling ball tighter.

Only, Brennan realized, it wasn't a bowling ball that the joker held. It was the proper size and shape, but it had no finger holes and, as Brennan watched, the air around it started to pulsate with flickering bits of coruscating energy. It was some kind of device that had enabled the joker and his companion to materialize into the mausoleum. They were using it to bring heroin in from—somewhere. And the joker was starting to activate it again.

Brennan swung his bow at the joker, who dodged with easy, fluid grace. The halo around the artifact grew brighter. Brennan dropped his bow and closed in, determined to take the device from the joker before he could escape or turn the thing's energies on him.

He grappled the joker easily, but found that his opponent was unexpectedly strong. The joker twisted and heaved in Brennan's grasp in an oddly fluid manner, as if his bones were utterly flexible. They tugged against each other for a moment and then Brennan found himself staring at the joker, their faces inches apart.

The joker's long, grotesque tongue flicked out, caressing Brennan's face in a lingering, almost sensual manner. Brennan flinched backward involuntarily, exposing his neck and throat to the taller joker. The reptiloid lunged forward, relinquishing his grip on the strange device, and fastened his mouth on the side of Brennan's throat where it curved into his shoulder.

Brennan felt the joker's teeth pierce his flesh. The joker worked his mouth, pumping saliva into the wound. The area around the bite went numb almost immediately and Brennan panicked.

A surge of horror-induced strength enabled him to pull free from the joker's embrace. He felt his flesh tear, and blood ran down his throat and chest. The numbness spread rapidly over his right side.

The joker let Brennan pull away with the device. He smiled cruelly and licked Brennan's blood from his chin with his lolling forked tongue.

He's poisoned me, Brennan thought, recognizing the symptoms of a fast-acting neurotoxin. He knew that he was in trouble. He wasn't an ace. He had no special protection or defenses, no armor or fortified constitution. The joker was confident in the efficacy of his poison. He stood back to watch Brennan die. Brennan knew he needed help fast. There was only one person who might be able to reverse the damage the poison was already wreaking on his body. She'd be at Tachyon's Jokertown clinic now, but there was no way to reach her. Already he was finding it hard to stand as his heart pumped poison to every cell of his body.

Mai could help him, if he could get to her.

Brennan silently screamed her name with a surge of desperate energy.

Mai!

He was aware, dimly, of the corresponding pulsation of energy in the device that he cradled to his chest. It felt warm and comforting as he hugged it. The joker's smile turned into a frown. He hissed and sprung forward. Brennan couldn't move, but that didn't matter.

There was an instant of gut-wrenching disorientation that his numbed mind and body only half-felt and then he was in a well-lit, softly painted corridor. Mai was standing there, talking to a small, slight, foppishly dressed man who had long curly red hair.

They turned and stared at him in astonishment. Brennan, himself, was beyond such a feeling.

"Poison," he croaked through stiff, heavy lips, and

collapsed, dropping the artifact and plunging into deep darkness.

It was a swirly, starry darkness, redolent with musky jungle smells. The pinpricks of light scattered across his consciousness were the ends of his men's cigarettes and the faraway stars scattered across the Vietnamese night. There was silence all around him, broken only by the sounds of soft breathing and the noises made by the animals deep within the jungle. He glanced at the luminous dial of his wristwatch. Four A.M.

Gulgowski, his top sergeant, squatted next to him in the underbrush.

"It's late," Gulgowski hissed.

Brennan shrugged. "Choppers are always late. It'll get here."

The sergeant grunted noncommittally. Brennan smiled into the night. Gulgowski was always the pessimist, always the one to see the gloomy side of things. But that never stopped him from doing his damndest when the going got rough, never stopped him from picking up the others when they felt everything was hopeless.

From faraway came the *whupping* sound of a chopper. Brennan turned to him, grinned. Gulgowski spat silently onto the jungle floor.

"Get the men ready. And hang onto that briefcase. It cost a lot to get it."

Mendoza, Johnstone, Big Al . . . three of the ten-man picked squad that Brennan had led on a raid on regional VC headquarters were dead. But they had achieved their objective. They had captured documents proving what Brennan had suspected for a long time. There were men in both the Vietnamese Army and the United States Army who were dirty, who were working with the enemy. He'd only had a chance to glance at the papers before stuffing them in the briefcase, but they had confirmed his suspicions that the biggest thief, the vilest traitor, was the ARVN general Kien. These papers would hang him.

The chopper landed in the clearing and Gulgowski, clutching the evidence that would damn a score of men as traitors, chivied the others to their ride home. Brennan waited in the underbrush, staring down the trail from which he expected pursuing VC to come at any moment. Finally satisfied that they had shaken the pursuit, he backed into the clearing as a withering hail of bullets burst unexpectedly into the night.

He heard the screams of his men, half-turned, and felt a searing flash of pain as a slug creased his forehead. He went down and his rifle spun away from him into the darkness. The shots had come from the clearing. From the chopper.

He flopped silently on the ground, staring into the clearing with pain-misted eyes. His men lay sprawled in the starlight. All of them were down. Other men walked among them, searching. He blinked blood out his eyes as one of the searchers, dressed in ARVN-style fatigues, shot Gulgowski in the head with a pistol as the sergeant tried to stand.

A flashlight beam picked out the killer's face. It was Kien. Brennan bit back curses as he saw one of his henchmen pry the briefcase from Gulgowski's death-grip and hand it to him. Kien rifled through it, nodded in satisfaction, and then methodically burned its contents. As the papers burned, Kien stared out into the jungle, looking, Brennan knew, for him. He cursed the paralytic shock that gripped his body, making him shake like he had a fever. The last thing he remembered was Kien striding toward the chopper, and then shock drove him into unconsciousness.

There were no lights in this darkness, but sudden hands of cool fire on his cheeks. They burned with a soothing touch. He felt all his pain and grief and anger drawn outward through them bit by slow bit, taken away from him like a worn-out cloak. He sighed deeply, content to remain in the healing darkness, as a sea of ineffable serenity washed over him. He was done, he thought, with strife, with killing. None of the killing had ever done any good anyway. Evil lived. Evil and Kien. He killed my father, but I can not, should not, harm him. It is wrong to bring harm to another sentient being, wrong . . .

Confused, Brennan forced open his eyes. He wasn't in Vietnam. He was in a hospital. No, the Jokertown clinic of Dr. Tachyon. A face was pressed close to his, eyes closed, mouth screwed up tightly. Young, feminine, beautiful in a serene way, though now touched by extreme pain. Mai. Her long glossy hair enveloped his face like bird's wings. Her hands were pressed against his cheeks. Blood trickled down their backs from between the spread fingers.

She was using her wild card power to take his damaged

body to herself, make repairs, and order Brennan's body to do the same. They had mingled minds and beings and he, for a moment, became something of her while she became something of him. In a confused meld of memories, he experienced Mai's grief at the death of her father at the hands of Kien's men.

She opened her eyes and smiled with the serenity of a madonna.

"Hello, Captain Brennan," she said in a voice so low that only he could hear it. "You are well again."

She took her palms from his cheeks and the mingling of minds ended with the breaking of physical contact. He sighed, missing her touch already, missing the serenity that he could never in a thousand years find again on his own.

The man who had been with Mai in the corridor came to his bedside. It was Dr. Tachyon.

"It was touch and go there for a moment," Tachyon said, a look of concern on his face. "Thank the Ideal for Mai . . ." He let his voice trail off, regarding Brennan closely. "What happened? How did you come to possess the singularity shifter?"

Brennan sat up gingerly. The numbness was gone from his body, but he still felt light-headed and disoriented from Mai's treatment.

"Is that what it's called?" he asked. Tachyon nodded. "What is it?"

"A teleporting device. One of the rarest artifacts in the galaxy. I thought it was gone, lost forever."

"It's yours, then?"

"I had it for a while." Tachyon told Brennan the story of the peripatetic singularity shifter, at least what he knew of it.

"How did the Egrets get it?"

"Eh?" Tachyon glanced from Brennan to Mai. "Egrets?"

"A Chinatown street gang. The Immaculate Egrets. They're also known as the Snow Birds because they control a good deal of the city's hard-drug trade. They were apparently using this shifter device to smuggle heroin. I took it away from them, but was wounded by one of their more . . . extraordinary operatives."

"It vanished when we landed in Harlem," Tachyon said. "Perhaps an Egret was in the crowd that gathered around us?"

"And took it, realizing what it was? Not likely," Brennan said softly, his gaze turned inward. "Not likely at all. Besides,

Harlem isn't Egret turf. They have agents there, but not many of them."

"Well, however it turned up, I'm glad it did," Tachyon said. "It provides the possibility of a splendid alternative to Lankester's foolish plan of attacking the Swarm in space."

"The Swarm?" Brennan had been aware of the semi-sentient alien invaders that had been trying to get a toehold on the Earth for the past several months, but the fight against them had so far bypassed him. "What use could this, this shifting thing be against the Swarm?"

"It's a long story." Tachyon sighed and ran a hand across his face. "A man from the State Department named Lankester is in charge of the Anti-Swarm Task Force. He's been pestering me for weeks now to use my influence with the aces to convince them to attack the Swarm Mother—the source of the Swarm attacks—that's in an eccentric orbit around the sun. It's a nonsensical idea, of course. It would be suicide for even the most powerful aces to go up against that thing. It would be like gnats flinging themselves against an elephant. The singularity shifter, however, presents some interesting possibilities."

"It can teleport a man that far?" Brennan asked, seeing some of them himself.

"Someone totally unfamiliar with it, as, say, yourself," Tachyon said, "could use the shifter to teleport short distances. It would take a powerful telepath to reach the Swarm Mother. But it could be done. A man could shift himself into the interior of the thing. A man armed with, say, a tactical nuclear device."

Brennan nodded. "I see."

"I was sure you would. I'm explaining all this to you because, pragmatically speaking, the singularity shifter is yours."

Brennan looked from Tachyon, to Mai standing silently at the side of his bed, back to Tachyon again. He had the feeling that Mai had told Tachyon something about him, but he knew Mai would tell the doctor only what she had to. And only because she trusted him.

"I'm in your debt," Brennan said. "It's yours."

Tachyon gripped Brennan's forearm in a warm, friendly manner.

"Thank you," he said. He glanced at Mai, looked at Brennan again. "I know that you're involved in some sort of vendetta with people here in the city. Mai told me something of it in explaining her own background and abilities. No details. None were necessary." He paused. "I know all too well about debts of honor."

Brennan nodded. He believed Tachyon, and, up to a point, trusted him. Tachyon probably wasn't connected with Kien, but one of the aces who had been with him—Turtle, Fantasy, or Trips—was. One of them must have stolen the shifter and given it to Kien. And Brennan, someday, somehow, would discover which ace it was.

ii.

Brennan left the clinic a little before midnight and went home to the one-room apartment on the fringes of Jokertown that was his base of operations. There was a sense of organized clutter about the apartment, which consisted of a bathroom, kitchen area, and living area with a sofa-bed, ancient rocking chair, and an obviously handmade workbench overflowing with equipment any bowyer would recognize. And some that a bowyer wouldn't.

He pulled the bed out of the sofa, stripped, and flopped down with a bone-weary sigh. He slept for twenty-four hours, completing the healing process that Mai had begun. He was ravenously hungry when he awoke and was fixing himself a meal when there came a light knock on the door. He peered out of the peephole. It was, as he had expected, Mai, the only person who knew where he lived.

"Trouble?" Brennan asked, seeing the worry on her usually-placid features. He stepped aside to let her into the room.

"I don't know. I think so."

"Tell me about it." He went behind the counter that divided the kitchen area from the rest of the apartment and poured water from the pot whistling on the stove into two small, handleless teacups. They were porcelain, hand-painted with the colors of a dream. They were older than the United States and the most precious things Brennan owned. He handed one to Mai in the rocking chair, and sat down on the rumpled bed opposite her.

"It's Dr. Tachyon." She sipped the hot, aromatic tea, gathering her thoughts. "He's been acting . . . strange."

"In what way?"

"He's been brusque, demanding. And he's neglecting his patients."

"Since when?"

"Yesterday, since coming back from his meeting with the man from the State Department. There's something else."

She balanced the precious teacup on her lap and took a folded newspaper from the purse that she had set beside the rocker.

"Have you seen this?"

Brennan shook his head.

The headlines screamed TACHYON TO LEAD ACE ASSAULT AGAINST SPACE MENACE. A picture below the bold letters showed Tachyon standing with a man identified as Alexander Lankester, head of the Anti-Swarm Task Force. The accompanying article stated that Tachyon was recruiting aces to follow him in an assault against the Swarm Mother orbiting the Earth beyond ballistic missile range. Captain Trips and Modular Man had already agreed to go along.

Something was wrong, Brennan thought. Tachyon had hoped the singularity shifter would end the request for such a useless assault. Instead, it seemed as if the opposite were happening.

"Do you think the government is blackmailing him into doing this?" Brennan asked. "Or is controlling his mind somehow?"

"It is possible," Mai shrugged. "I only know that he may need help."

He looked at her for a long moment and she calmly returned his gaze.

"He has no friends?"

"Many of his friends are poor, helpless jokers. Others are hard to reach. Or may not be inclined to act swiftly if the government is somehow involved."

Brennan stood up and turned his back to her while carrying his teacup back to the counter. The network of human relationships was reaching out, ensnaring him in its sticky grip once again. He dumped the dregs of his tea into the sink and gazed into the bottom of the teacup. It was the blue of a perfect, depthless pool, the blue of an empty, endless sky. Looking into it was like contemplating the void. It was pleasurable in its utter peacefulness, but not, Brennan realized, his particular pathway to enlightenment.

He turned around to face Mai again, his mind made up.

"All right. I'll check it out. But I don't know anything about things like mind control. I'll need some help."

He reached for the phone and dialed a number.

Brennan had rarely been in the public rooms of the Crystal Palace, though he had spent more than one night in the rooms on the third floor. Elmo nodded as he came in, without commenting on the case he carried. The dwarf gestured to the corner table where Chrysalis sat with a man wearing black jeans and a brown leather jacket. He had handsome, regular features, except for his bulging forehead.

"You," Fortunato said as Brennan came up to their table. He looked from Brennan to Chrysalis. She regarded him with a level gaze, the blood pulsing steadily through the arteries of her glass-clear throat. She looked at Brennan and nodded coolly, showing no sign of the passion that Brennan knew from the time he spent on the Palace's third floor.

"This is Yeoman," she said as Brennan took the third seat at the table. "I believe that he has some information you might find interesting."

Fortunato frowned. Their last meeting hadn't exactly been cordial, though there was no actual animosity between the two.

"Word has it that you're looking for a way to get at the Swarm. I know something that could help."

"I'll listen."

Brennan told him about the singularity shifter. He told no lies, but he shaded things skillfully, having been coached by Chrysalis as to the approach that would most likely sway Fortunato to help him investigate Tachyon's strange behavior.

"What can you do beside making your mind go away?" Fortunato asked when Brennan was done with his story.

"I can take care of myself. And most others who might try to interfere with us."

"You that crazed killer the papers been speculating about lately?"

Brennan reached into his back pants pocket and withdrew

a card. He dropped it face up on the table in front of Fortunato. The sorcerer-pimp looked at it, nodded.

"Me and the Black Shadow are the only aces of spades I know of." He looked up at Brennan. "But I guess there's room for one more. The only thing I don't understand is what you get out of this," he said, turning to Chrysalis.

"If this works out, whatever I want. From both of you. . . ."

Fortunato grunted. He stood up.

"Yeah. You always do. Well, come along. We'd best be checking if that alien Beau Brummell's still got all his brains."

Brennan drove them through the early-morning darkness to Tachyon's apartment. Out of the corner of his eye he occasionally caught Fortunato studying him, but the ace chose not to ask any questions. Fortunato hadn't accepted him yet, Brennan realized, and he was still wary and watchful, if not openly distrustful. But that was all right. He wasn't sure of Fortunato yet, either.

He parked the BMW in the alley beside Tachyon's apartment building. He and Fortunato got out and looked up at the building.

"We go in by the front door," Fortunato asked, "or the back door?"

"When there's been a choice, it's always been my policy to go in by the back."

"Smart man," Fortunato murmured, "smart man."

Fortunato watched with a dubious expression, but said nothing as Brennan took his case from the BMW's trunk, opened it, slung his compound bow over his back, then attached the quiver of arrows to his belt.

"Let's go."

They made their way to the rear of the apartment building, and Fortunato burned a bit of his psychic energy in bringing down the fire-escape ladder. They cat-footed along the fire escape until they came to the window of Tachyon's apartment, and peered inside his bedroom.

The room, lit by the light from an overturned bedside lamp, was a shambles. It had been tossed by an impatient searcher who hadn't bothered to set things right again. Brennan and Fortunato glanced at each other.

"Something weird is happening," Fortunato muttered.

The window was locked, but that wasn't an obstacle to Brennan. He removed a circle of glass from the lower pane with his glass cutter, reached a hand in, unlatched the window, and silently slid it up. He put out an arm, stopping Fortunato from entering, and laid a finger across his lips. They listened for a moment, but heard nothing.

Brennan went in first, leaping down from the windowsill as silently as a cat, his strung bow in his left hand, his right hand hovering near the quiver velcroed to his belt. Fortunato followed, making enough noise to cause Brennan to stare at him accusingly. The ace shrugged and Brennan led the way through the room. In the hallway that led to the kitchen, living area, and guest bedroom, they heard a series of crashes, hollow thumps, and occasional shattering sounds, as if a careless or uncaring searcher were rummaging through the rooms deeper in the apartment.

They went quietly down the hall, passing a closed door to a guest bedroom. The hall opened out into the apartment's living room, which looked as devastated as a trailer park after a tornado. A slight, short man with long curly red hair was methodically pulling books off their shelves, looking behind them.

"Tachyon," Brennan said aloud.

He turned and looked at the two in the hallway, totally calm, utterly unstartled. He started toward them, no expression at all on his face.

Fortunato suddenly put a hand in the small of Brennan's back and pushed, sending him sprawling to the carpet.

"That's not Tachyon!" he shouted.

The next few seconds seemed to Brennan as if he were viewing a videotape on fast forward. Fortunato was doing something to time. He became a blur rocketing through the air toward the Tachyon look-alike, but was just as quickly thrown aside as soon as the two of them touched.

Brennan drew an arrow and snapped off a shot from a kneeling position.

The arrow was fletched with color-coded red and black feathers. Its shaft was hollow aluminum, packed with plastic explosives. Its tip was a pressure-sensitive detonator. The arrow was too heavy to be aerodynamically stable over long distances, but the thing masquerading as Tachyon was less than twenty-five feet away.

Brennan's arrow struck it high on the chest and exploded, sending a shower of flesh and green ooze over the room. The thing was flung backward by the impact. Its upper half disappeared, leaving a twitching pair of legs attached to a trunk that spilled inhuman organs and oozed a thick green ichor. It was some moments before the legs ceased their attempts to walk.

"What was that thing?" Brennan shouted over the roaring in his ears.

"Damned if I know," Fortunato said, getting up from where it had flung him. "I tried to scan its mind, but it had no mind. Nothing human, anyway."

"It looked like Tachyon," Brennan said in a lower voice, his hearing returning to normal. "Down to the last detail." He frowned, looked at Fortunato. "Tachyon's mind wasn't taken over. He was replaced."

"When was the last time you saw what you're certain was the real Tachyon?"

"Yesterday. At the clinic. Before he went to a meeting at the Olympia Hotel with that Lankester fellow from the State Department."

"Let's check in."

The frail, white-haired old man in the bellhop uniform lifted Brennan over his head and slammed him against the wall. Brennan hit the wall hard and slid down to the carpet, panting like a dog for breath. He was in trouble.

The bellhop loomed over him, no expression at all on his lined face. Brennan surged to his knees, his lungs on fire, and saw the bellhop's eyes roll up in his head. The bellhop tottered backward, windmilling his limbs as if he were caught in a hurricane wind. He did a crazy staggering dance and crashed through the window at the end of the hall. It was a long way to the street below.

Brennan pulled himself upright while Fortunato flexed his fingers. He took Brennan's arm and said, "No brains to control, but you can push them around."

"Someone probably heard that," Brennan gasped, the breath returning to his lungs.

"I could have let it smash you flat."

"There's that." He took a deep, grateful breath. "We need to lie low for awhile."

They stopped in front of one of the rooms.

"How about this one?" Fortunato asked. Brennan shrugged silently. Fortunato put his hand on the knob and reached out with his mind. Tumblers clicked and bolts lifted and the door opened.

"It'll take them some time to track us down," the ace said as they entered the dark hotel room. "How many agents you think they have?"

"No telling," Brennan said, stretching his aching back carefully. "More than I suspected, for sure."

"I thought you were surreptitious as shit."

Brennan shook his head. The plan had been for him to scout the floor where Lankester's suite was located, gathering what intelligence he could, while Fortunato used his mental powers to monitor his progress from the stairwell. The false bellhop had spotted and attacked him almost immediately. It was all Brennan could do to hang on until Fortunato arrived.

"We'd better try our alternate plan," Brennan said.

"It may take some time."

Fortunato settled himself on one of the double beds, legs crossed in front of him, back straight, hands dangling in his lap. He stared ahead at nothing. Brennan stood between him and the door, listening for sounds in the corridor outside, as he removed his bow and quiver of arrows from the case Fortunato had kept for him while he scouted the hotel.

Fortunato seemed to sink deep into a trance, not unlike, Brennan thought, a student of Zen descended into zazen, the state of meditation. After a moment, a set of ram's horns materialized from Fortunato's bulging forehead, shimmering and indistinct in the darkness.

Brennan watched with pursed lips. His Zen training had taught him that there was no such thing as magic, but here was evidence to the contrary, right before his eyes. What was magic, perhaps, but unexplained science?

Brennan filed the question away for later meditation as Fortunato abruptly opened his eyes. They were pools of darkness, his pupils dilated so much that they almost swallowed the irises. His voice was husky, a little shaken.

"They're all around us, those things," he said. "At least twenty. Maybe more. They're not human, not even of this Earth. Their minds, if you could call them that, are alien, utterly beyond my experience."

"Are they Swarm creatures?"

Fortunato rose with easy, fluid grace, shrugged.

"Could be. I thought the best they could do was hulks that

looked like the Pillsbury doughboy. I thought bellboys and shit like that was beyond them."

"Maybe they've refined their technique." Brennan held up a hand, pressed his ear to the door. The footsteps in the corridor beyond passed by their room as he and Fortunato waited quietly. "What about Tachyon?"

Fortunato frowned. "I contacted one human mind. A maid. She didn't realize anything unusual was going on. A little pissed off that the guests on this floor weren't tipping too well. Weren't tipping at all, in fact. There was also something I touched by the elevators. Could've been Tachyon's mind, but there was a blanket on it, a fence around it. I could catch only vague, filtered notions. They were full of weariness. And pain."

"It could be Tachyon?"

"It could."

Brennan took a deep breath. "Any plans?"

"All out of 'em."

The two looked at each other. Brennan touched the quiver at his side.

"I wish you had a weapon," he said.

"I do. Several." He tapped his forehead. "And they're all in here."

They waited until it was quiet in the corridor outside, then opened the door and moved fast. They ran as quietly as they could down the hotel corridor, hung a right as it turned to a T, and found themselves by the bank of elevators. In a niche, off to one side, was something that looked like a linen closet. Brennan notched an arrow and drew it back while Fortunato gestured the door open.

Brennan lowered the bow.

"Sweet Christ in heaven," he murmured. Fortunato glanced from him to the closet, and froze.

Tachyon was inside. His hair, drenched with sweat, fell over his face in limp curls. His eyes stared through the tangle of hair. They were puffy and bloodshot, and glazed with pain and weariness. The shelves and linens had been removed from the closet, making room for Tachyon and the thing that embraced him. Tachyon was pressed against a vast, purplish couch of biomass that bound him with a score of ropy tendrils across his neck, chest, arms, and legs. The thing pulsed rhythmically, rippling like a fat lady bouncing on a water bed.

Tachyon was set into a hollow in its surface that cupped him securely, perfectly following his contours and dimensions.

His eyes focused upon Fortunato, flicked to Brennan.

"Help," he croaked, his lips working for several moments before any sound came out.

Brennan reached down, drew the knife he carried in an ankle sheath, and slashed at the tendrils binding Tachyon to the thing. It was like cutting through hard, stretchy rubber, but he sawed away grimly, ignoring the increasing pulsations of the thing and the greenish ichor that splattered himself and Tachyon.

It took a minute to saw through all the tendrils, but even then it still clung to Tachyon. It was then that Brennan noticed the suckers fastened to the sides and back of Tachyon's neck.

"How do we get you out?" he asked.

"Just pull," Tachyon whispered.

Brennan did, and Tachyon began to scream.

The doctor finally came free. He collapsed into Brennan's arms, stinking of sweat and fear and alien secretions. He was deathly pale and bleeding profusely from the points where the suckers had fastened. The wounds didn't look serious, but there was, Brennan realized, no telling how damaging they actually might be.

"Look out," Fortunato said, "we've got company."

Brennan looked up the corridor. A dozen of the human simulacra were approaching, dressed as bellhops, maids, and ordinary men and women in dresses and three-piece suits. In the middle of them was Lankester of the State Department.

Brennan dragged Tachyon over to the elevator as the creatures advanced at a steady pace, their faces composed and utterly unemotional. Fortunato joined him, a worried look on his face.

"What do we do now?"

"Punch for an elevator."

The things were twenty feet away when they heard the chime of an arriving elevator.

"Take him," Brennan said, thrusting the limp, barely conscious form of Tachyon into Fortunato's arms. He drew an arrow from his quiver as the elevator door swished open. Inside were three middle-aged men dressed in conservative business suits with Shriner's hats on their heads. They stared wide-eyed as Fortunato dragged Tachyon inside. Fortunato looked at them.

"Basement, please," he said. The one standing by the panel of buttons punched it automatically as Fortunato stopped the door from closing with his foot. Brennan placed three explosive arrows in the midst of the advancing creatures. The first one hit Lankester in the chest. The second and third exploded to the left and right of him, blowing gore and protoplasm all over the hotel corridor. He fell back into the elevator and Fortunato let the door close.

Brennan leaned on his bow, took a deep, relieved breath. The Shriners huddled together fearfully in the corner of the elevator.

Fortunato looked at them.

"First time in town?"

iii.

"So Lankester had been replaced by one of these new-generation swarmlings some time ago?" Brennan asked.

Tachyon nodded and took a long pull from the mug Mai handed him. It was full of thick black coffee, laced generously with brandy.

"Before I ever met him—it. That's why it was pushing for that insane attack plan. It knew we wouldn't be able to really harm the Swarm Mother, yet such an attack would make everyone think something concrete was being done to fight the menace." He paused, took another long pull from the mug. "And there's another thing. The Swarm Mother might want specimens of aces."

Brennan looked at him quizzically. "Specimens?"

"To take apart and replicate from her own biomass."

"Shit," Fortunato murmured. "It wants to grow its own aces."

They were in Tachyon's office at the clinic. Tachyon had cleaned up, but was still pale and shaky from the ordeal he had undergone. There was a bandage around his neck where the Swarm creature had attached its suckers.

"What happens now?" Brennan asked.

Tachyon sighed, set the mug aside.

"We attack the Swarm Mother."

"What?" Fortunato said. "That Swarm thing scramble your brains? You just said it was insane to attack the Mother."

"It was. It is. But it's the best option open to us." He looked from Fortunato, who was openly incredulous, to Brennan, who looked blankly noncommittal. "Look, the Swarm has started a new wave of attack which is much more sophisticated than its previous ones. There's no telling how far they've managed to penetrate into the government."

"If they could replace Lankester," Brennan murmured, "who else might they have gotten?"

"Exactly. Whom does it have?" Tachyon shuddered. "The possibilities are mind-boggling. If it could replace enough key personnel to carry it off, it'd think nothing of starting a worldwide nuclear exchange and simply waiting the necessary millenia until the surface of the planet is inhabitable once again.

"It's obvious that we can't trust anyone from the government to help us attack the Swarm Mother. We have to do it ourselves."

"How do we do that?" Fortunato asked in a tone that indicated he wasn't won over by Tachyon's arguments.

"We have the singularity shifter," Tachyon said, his voice rising eagerly. "We need a weapon, though. Takisians have successfully used biological weapons against Swarm Mothers in the past, but your biological sciences aren't sophisticated enough to produce a suitable weapon. Perhaps I can come up with something . . ."

"There is a weapon," a quiet voice said. The three men turned and looked at Mai, who had been silently listening to their conversation.

Tachyon stared at her, and then sat upright in his chair, sloshing the brandy-laced coffee over the front of his brocaded dressing gown.

"Don't talk nonsense," he said sharply.

Fortunato looked from Tachyon to Mai. "What is this shit?"

"Nothing," Tachyon said. "Mai works with me at the clinic. She's used her power to help some of my patients, but it would be out of the question for her to get involved in this."

"What power?"

Mai lifted her hands, palms facing outward. "I can touch a person's soul," she said. "We become one and I find the sickness in it. I take the sickness to myself and soothe it, smoothing the curves of the life pattern and mending the breaks. We can then both become well again."

"Meaning, in English?" Fortunato asked.

"She manipulates genetic material," Tachyon said with a sigh. "She can mold it in near any way she visualizes. I suppose she could use her power on the Swarm Mother in a reverse manner to cause cellular disruption on a massive scale."

"She can give the Mother cancer?" Fortunato asked.

"She probably could," Tachyon conceded. "If I allowed her to get involved, which I'm not. It would be insanely dangerous for a woman."

"It's insanely dangerous for anyone," Fortunato said sharply. "If she's the best bet against that Mother and she's willing to try, I say let her do it."

"And I forbid it!" Tachyon said, sloshing coffee from his mug as he slammed it against the arm of his chair.

"It is not for you to forbid," Mai said. "I must do it. It is my karma."

Tachyon turned to Brennan. "Can't you talk some sense into her?"

Brennan shook his head. "It's her decision," he said slowly. He wished he could agree with Tachyon, but Brennan knew he couldn't interfere with Mai's karma, her chosen path to enlightenment. But, Brennan resolved, she wouldn't walk her path alone.

"That's settled, then," Fortunato said flatly. "We get Mai up to the Swarm Mother and she sticks it with a fatal dose of cancer. I'm going too. I want a piece of that motherfucker myself."

Tachyon looked from Fortunato to Mai to Brennan and saw that nothing he could say would change their minds. "All right," he sighed. He turned to Fortunato. "You'll have to power the singularity shifter," Tachyon said. "I can't do it myself." He dragged his fingers through his curly hair. "The swarmling temporarily burned out some of my powers in trying to suck out my memories for the duplicate Tachyon. We can't afford to wait until they come back.

"I can, however, ferry a boarding party close to the Swarm Mother in *Baby*. Fortunato can shift the party inside the Swarm Mother. Speed and stealth will be necessary, but the boarders will need some protection. Modular Man perhaps, or maybe one of Trips's friends . . ."

Brennan shook his head. "You said speed and stealth would be necessary. If you sent Modular Man in there blazing away, he'd bring down the defenses of the Swarm Mother in an instant."

Tachyon massaged his forehead wearily. "You're right. Any suggestions?"

"Of course." Brennan took a deep breath. This was getting far from his original reasons for coming to the city, but he couldn't let Mai face the Swarm without him. He wouldn't. "Me."

"You?" Tachyon said hesitantly. "Are you up for it?"

"He was up for rescuing you from the blob," Fortunato broke in. He looked at Brennan, the doubt in his eyes replaced by certainty. "I've seen him in action. He can handle himself."

Tachyon nodded decisively. "It's settled, then." He turned to Mai. "I don't like sending a woman into danger, but you're right. You're the only one who has a chance of destroying the Swarm Mother."

"I'll do what I have to," she said quietly.

Tachyon nodded gravely and took her hand in his, but a cold chill passed through Brennan at her words. He was sure that Tachyon had heard an entirely different meaning in them than he had.

Lift-off was something Brennan filed away as an interesting experience. He would not willingly seek it out again, but the sight of the Earth in *Baby's* viewscreens was a scene of awesome beauty that he would carry for the rest of his life. He felt almost unworthy of the sight and wished that Ishida, his roshi, could view it.

There were three others in the Arabian Nights fantasy that was Tachyon's control room. Tachyon guided his ship in silence. He was still hurting from his mistreatment by the Swarm. Brennan could see that he kept himself going by willpower alone. His face was lined with weariness and uncharacteristic tenseness.

Fortunato virtually crackled with impatient, nervous energy. He had spent the time before lift-off charging his batteries, as he had put it. He was now ready, and impatient for action.

Only Mai seemed calm and unmoved. She sat quietly on the control room's couch, her hands in her lap, watching everything with unworried interest. Brennan watched her watch. She had agreed readily to Tachyon's plan. How she would carry it out, though, was a different matter. That thought worried him.

After a time, Tachyon spoke, tension and weariness cracking his voice.

"There it is."

Brennan peered over Tachyon's shoulder at the globular monstrosity that filled *Baby's* forward viewscreens.

"It's immense," he said. "How do we find our way around it?"

Tachyon turned to Fortunato. "Instruct the singularity shifter to take you to the middle of the thing. You should end up pretty close to where you want to be. You can find the nerve center by tracking its mind." Tachyon felt the mind of his ship tug at his brain. *What is it, Baby?*

We're approaching the Swarm Mother's detector range.

Thank you. He turned to the others. "You'd better get ready. It's almost time."

Fortunato took out the singularity shifter from the backpack in which Tachyon had hidden it in the spare bedroom of his apartment. In the bottom of the pack was a .45 automatic in a shoulder rig.

"What's this?" Fortunato said. He looked at Tachyon.

"You may need it," the doctor said. "It's going to take more out of you than you know, to power this jump."

Fortunato touched the butt of the gun, looked at Tachyon. He shrugged. "What the hell," he said, and strapped it on. He hefted the singularity shifter, and he and Brennan and Mai formed a circle. All helped hold the shifter. Brennan glanced at Mai. She looked back steadily. Out of the corner of his eye he saw in a viewscreen a brilliant flash of light wink out from the Swarm Mother. *Baby* rocked as the organically generated particle beam struck her, but her defensive screens held. Brennan felt a soft whisper in his brain.

Remember. You must not allow Mai or Fortunato to be captured by the Swarm Mother.

He looked up at Tachyon, who stared at him steadily for a moment, then turned back to his viewscreen.

"Go!" Tachyon shouted.

Fortunato's eyes closed, his brow furrowed in concentration. Spectral ram's horns glimmered from the sides of his head. Brennan felt a sudden wrenching, a tearing as if every cell of his body were being hurled apart. He couldn't breathe with lungs that were no more, he couldn't relax muscles that were torn into their constituent molecules and hurled across hundreds of miles of empty vacuum. He stifled a scream and his consciousness slammed up against a wall of nausea. The trip was worse than his jaunt to the clinic, for it seemed to last forever, though Tachyon had said a journey by singularity shifter lasted no time at all.

Then, suddenly, he was whole again. He and Mai and Fortunato were in a corridor that was dimly lit by large blue and green phosphorescent cells in the translucent ceiling and walls. Ropy tendrils ran below their feet, presumably conduits for whatever was used as blood and nutrients in the thing. The air was hot and wetly humid and smelled like a greenhouse gone bad. Its oxygen content was enough to make Brennan giddy until he adjusted his breathing. He felt light on his feet, though there was a definite gravitational pull. The Swarm Mother, he realized, must be spinning, producing artificial gravity that was necessary for directed organic growth.

"Are you all right?" he asked his companions.

Mai nodded, but Fortunato was breathing harshly. His face was an ashen mask.

"The . . . space faggot was right . . ." he panted. "That was a bitch." His hands were shaking as he fumbled the shifter back into the backpack.

"Relax—" Brennan began, and fell silent.

Somewhere ahead in the twisting, rolling passageway was a vast sucking sound.

"Which way do we have to go?" Brennan asked quietly.

Fortunato concentrated mightily. "I can sense some kind of mind up ahead." He pointed in the direction of the sucking sound. "If you could call it a mind . . ."

"Great," Brennan muttered. He unslung his bow.

"Listen," Fortunato grabbed Mai's arm. "You could help me out . . ."

"No time for that," Brennan said. "Besides, Mai will need all her own energy to get through this thing. And so will I."

Fortunato began to say something, but the sucking sound, which was getting louder and louder, was suddenly right upon them when a grotesque green and yellow mass of protoplasm rolled down a bend in the tubular corridor toward them. It had a score of suckers placed randomly over a globular body that nearly filled the passageway.

"Christ!" Fortunato swore. "What is that thing?"

It was plastered to the side of the corridor, scouring the wall and floor with myriad suckerlike mouths that were ringed by hundreds of foot-long cilia.

"I don't know, and I don't want to find out," Brennan said. "Let's get going."

He selected an arrow and laid it loosely on the string of his bow, and started to edge past the thing. Mai and Fortunato followed warily. The thing continued to scour away. The cilia of the mouths facing them quivered eagerly as they passed, but the creature made no move toward them.

Brennan sighed in relief.

The blue phosphorescent twilight tinged their surroundings with a sense of soft-focus unreality as they followed the passageway deeper into the Swarm Mother. The unmoving air was so thick with the scents of living things that it reminded Brennan of the jungles of Vietnam. He kept glancing around, twitching with nervousness, feeling as if he were in the crosshairs of a sniper's rifle. He couldn't shake the ominous, oppressive sensation of being watched.

They followed the undulating passageway for half an hour in tense silence, always expecting, but never actually facing, a deadly attack from the Swarm Mother's killing machines. They stopped when the corridor branched into a Y-shaped fork. Both tines of the Y seemed to be leading in the direction they needed to go.

"Which way?" Brennan asked.

Fortunato rubbed his swollen forehead tiredly.

"I can hear a thousand little twitterings. Not real minds, at least not sentient minds, but their noise is driving me crazy. The big one is still up ahead, somewhere."

Brennan glanced at Mai. She looked at him placidly, as if willing to let him make all the decisions. Brennan tossed a coin in his mind and it came up heads.

"This way," he said, taking the right fork.

They hadn't gone a hundred yards before Brennan realized that something was different in this passageway. The air smelled sweet, almost cloying. It was difficult to breathe, yet at the same time almost intoxicating. The odor grew stronger as they advanced.

"I'm not sure I like this," Brennan said.

"Do we have a choice?" Mai asked.

Brennan looked at her and shrugged. They went on,

turned a sharp bend in the passageway, and stopped, staring at the scene before them.

The passageway widened to forty feet across. On both sides of it, hanging near the ceiling, were scores of grotesque swarmlings with shriveled limbs and huge, swollen abdomens. They were nursing from what looked like swollen nipples jutting from the walls of the passageway.

In turn, Swarm creatures of every size and description crowded around each of the hanging swarmlings, jostling for a place at one of the hollow tubes dangling from their swollen abdomens. The Swarm creatures ranged in size from tiny, insectlike entities to tentacular monstrosities that must have weighed several tons. There were hundreds of them.

"It looks like they're feeding," Fortunato whispered.

Brennan nodded. "We can't go through there. We'll have to go back and try the other branch."

They started back down the passageway, and suddenly stopped when they heard a quiet buzzing, as if from a multitude of small wings, drift down toward them from the way they had come.

"Shit," Fortunato said in disbelief. "We're caught in the middle of a damn shift change."

"The first Swarm creature we ran into ignored us," Brennan said. "Maybe these will too."

They hugged the wall of the passageway—it was warm, Brennan found, and pliable to the touch—and were as quiet and unobtrusive as they could be. They waited.

A swarm of the insectoid creatures buzzed down the corridor. They were four to six inches long with segmented bodies and large, membranous wings. The first few passed them by and went straight to the feeding chamber, and Brennan thought they were safe. But then one stopped and landed on Mai. Another joined it, then another and another. She looked down at them calmly. One landed on Brennan's shoulder. He stared at it. Its mouth parts consisted of multiple mandibular arrangements. One set of mandibles began tearing at the fabric of Brennan's shirt while another stuffed fragments of cloth into its little mouth.

Brennan brushed the thing aside distastefully and stepped on it. It crunched loudly under his foot, like a cockroach, but two had already taken its place on Brennan's body. He heard Fortunato swear and knew they were crawling over him, as well.

"Let's try to move away from them," he said quietly, but that did no good. The bugs followed and landed on the three in increasing numbers.

"Run for it," Brennan called, and they took off down the corridor.

Some of the swarm continued on to the feeding chamber, but more followed them down the passageway in an angrily buzzing cloud. Brennan batted at them as he ran, knocking some out of the air. He slapped at the ones crawling on him, but there were many to take the place of those he knocked down or crushed. They landed on his face and arms and he could feel their thousand little feet crawl all over him. They seemed to be most interested in his clothes, and, more importantly, his bow and arrows. It was as if they were scavengers programmed to dispose of nonliving matter. But that didn't make them harmless. Brennan felt their sharp mandibles tear into his flesh nearly as often as not. The buzzing of their wings and the clacking sounds of their mandibles were loud in Brennan's ears. They had to get away from them.

They reached the point where the passageway divided into the Y, looking desperately for something, anything, that would enable them to shake the little scavengers. Fortunato ran down the other branch of the passageway and Brennan and Mai followed. The floor was slick with moisture. Its surface was uneven. The moisture caught in shallow pools that set off a fine spray of liquid as they slogged through them. The liquid was warm and clear, though murky. They splashed down the corridor and the swarm of insectoids seemed to pull back. Fortunato flopped down into a shallow pool that had gathered in one of the deeper hollows, and rolled around and around, dislodging and crushing the insectoids that were crawling all over him. Brennan and Mai joined him. Brennan kept his lips shut tightly, but the murky liquid drenched him from head to toe. It looked, and smelled, like tepid water with fine particles suspended in it. Brennan was not particularly eager to ingest any of it.

Brennan glanced at his companions as they crouched in the shallow pool. Their clothes looked like they had been attacked by a legion of moths, and they had numerous cuts and gouges, but no one seemed badly injured. The swarm of persistent insectoids hovered over their heads, buzzing, it seemed to Brennan somewhat angrily.

"How do we get rid of them?" he asked, irritated himself.

"I may have enough left to send those little mothers somewhere," Fortunato ground out.

"I don't know—" Brennan began, and never got a chance to finish.

The surface below their feet fell away as a sphincter opened. All the liquid in the passageway gushed downward and they went with it. Brennan had time to take a deep breath and a tight grip on his bow. He reached out and grabbed Mai by an ankle as she was sucked down into darkness and he swirled down after her, cursing as he lost half the arrows in his quiver.

There was more liquid in the passageway than he had realized. They were caught in a rushing vortex with no air to breathe and no light to see by. Brennan held tight to his Mai's ankle, remembering Tachyon's silent warning.

They splashed down into a large chamber, totally submerged in a pool of liquid the size of an Olympic swimming pool. Brennan and Mai bobbed to the surface and treaded water, glancing about. Fortunately, this chamber was lit by the same blue phosphorescence as the passageway above. Fortunato swam over to join them, fighting against a current that was drawing them to the other end of the pool.

"What the hell is this?" Fortunato asked.

Brennan found that it was hard to shrug while treading water. "I don't know. Maybe a reservoir? All living things need water to survive."

"At least those bugs are gone," Fortunato said. He struck out for the side of the chamber, and Brennan and Mai followed.

They scrabbled up the slope, going slowly and cautiously because the surface was wet and slippery. They finally flung themselves down, panting, for a moment's rest. Brennan patched up the worst bug-bites with bandages from the small first-aid kit he carried on his belt.

"Which way now?"

Fortunato took a moment to orient himself, and then pointed. "There."

They went on through the belly of the beast. It was a nightmarish trek through a strange realm of organic monstrosities. The passageway they followed opened up into vast halls where menlike creatures mewling in half-formed idiocy hung by umbilical cords from pulsating ceilings, led through galleries where sacks of undifferentiated biomass quivered like loathsome jellies while awaiting sculpting by the will of the Swarm Mother, passed by chambers where monsters of a hundred alien forms were being manufactured for what purpose the Swarm Mother alone knew. Some of these last were developed enough to be aware of the interlopers, but they were all still attached to the body of the Mother by protoplasmic umbilical cords. They snapped and snarled and hissed as Brennan and the others passed by, and he was forced to put arrows through the brains of a few of the more persistent creatures.

Not all had the inhuman forms of swarmlings. Some were manlike in shape and appearance, with human faces. Recognizable human faces. There was Ronald Reagan with slicked-back hair and a twinkle in his eye. There was Maggie Thatcher, looking stern and unyielding. And there was Gorbachev's head, strawberry-colored birthmark and all, set upon a mass of quivering protoplasm that was as soft and puffy as a human body sculpted from bread dough.

"Sweet Jesus," Fortunato said. "It looks like we got here just in time."

"I hope so," Brennan murmured.

The passageway began to narrow and they had to stoop, and finally get down on hands and knees and crawl. Brennan looked back at Fortunato and the ace nodded them on.

"It's ahead. I can feel it pulsing: feed and grow, feed and grow."

The flesh of the tunnel wall was rubbery and warm. Brennan disliked touching it, but he pushed himself forward. The tunnel narrowed until it was so cramped that Brennan realized he couldn't bring his bow to bear. They were helpless, and traveling into the most dangerous area in the Swarm Mother, her nerve center. He shoved on through a crawlway of living flesh for a hundred yards or more, Mai and Fortunato following him, until at last he popped out into an open space. Fortunato followed and they both helped Mai down.

They looked around. It was a small chamber. There was hardly room in it for the three of them and the large, tri-lobed, gray-pink organ suspended in the middle of the chamber by a network of fibrous tendrils that penetrated into the floor, ceiling, and walls.

"This is it," Fortunato muttered in an exhausted voice.

"The nerve center of the Swarm Mother. Its brain or core or whatever you want to call it."

He and Brennan turned to Mai. She stepped forward and Brennan took her arm.

"Kill it," he urged. "Kill it and let's get out of here."

She looked at him calmly. He could see his reflection in her large, dark eyes. "You know I've sworn to never harm another sentient being," she said quietly.

"Are you crazy?" Fortunato cried. "What did we come here for?"

Brennan released her arm and she walked toward the organ suspended in the net of nerve fibers. Fortunato looked at Brennan. "Is the bitch crazy?"

Brennan shook his head, unable to speak, knowing that he was losing another. No matter which way this turned out, he was losing another.

Mai slipped around the tendrils and placed her palms against the flesh of the Swarm Mother. Her blood began to flow down the organ of the alien creature.

"What's she doing?" Fortunato asked, caught between fear and anger and wonder.

"Merging."

The narrow tunnel that led to the Swarm Mother's sanctum began to dilate. Brennan turned to face the opening.

"What's happening?"

Brennan nocked an arrow to his bowstring. "The Swarm Mother's resisting," he said, and shut his surroundings, shut Fortunato, shut Mai even, from his mind. He narrowed the focus of his being until the mouth of the tunnel was his universe. He drew the bowstring to his cheek and stood as taut and ready as the arrow itself, ready to shoot himself into the heart of their enemy.

The fanged and taloned killing-machines of the Swarm Mother poured through the opening. Brennan fired. His hands moved without conscious direction, drawing, pulling, loosing. Bodies piled up by the mouth of the tunnel and were cleared away by the creatures trying to push their way inside and by the blasts of the explosive arrows. Time ceased to flow. Nothing mattered but perfect coordination between mind and body and target, born from the union of flesh and spirit.

It seemed like forever, but the resources of the Swarm Mother were not inexhaustible. The creatures stopped coming when Brennan had three arrows left. He stared down the corridor for over a minute before he realized that no more targets were in sight and he lowered his bow.

His back ached and his arms burned like they were on fire. He looked at Fortunato. The ace stared at him, shook his head wordlessly. Brennan's consciousness returned from the pool where his Zen training had sunk it.

A sudden movement caught his eye and he turned. His hand dropped to the quiver at his belt, but stopped before it drew an arrow. There were three forms, man-sized, man-shaped, at the mouth of the tunnel. A sense of dislocation swept through Brennan like a cold wind and he lowered his bow. He recognized them.

"Gulgowski? Mendoza? Minh?"

He went forward as if in a dream as they stepped over and around the blasted bodies of the swarmlings, coming to meet him. Brennan was numb, caught between joy and disbelief.

"I knew you would come," Minh, Mai's father, said. "I knew you would rescue us from Kien."

Brennan nodded. A feeling of vast weariness swept over him. He felt as if his brain were isolated from the rest of his body, as if somehow it had been wrapped in layers of cotton batting. He should have known all along that Kien was behind the Swarm. He should have known.

Gulgowski hefted the briefcase he carried. "We've got the evidence here to nail the bastard, Cap'n. Come here'n take a look."

Brennan dropped his bow, stepped forward to look into the briefcase Gulgowski proffered, ignoring the shouts behind him, ignoring the blasting roar that reverberated through the corridor.

Gulgowski, holding out the briefcase toward him, staggered. Brennan looked at him. It was odd. He had only one eye now. The other had been shot out and thick green fluid was running sluggishly down his cheek. But that was all right. Brennan seemed to remember that Gulgowski had been shot in the head before, and lived. He was here, after all. He looked at the briefcase. The handle melted into the flesh of Gulgowski's hand. They were one thing. The mouth of the briefcase was lined with rows of sharp teeth. It jerked at him, the teeth snapping.

He felt a sudden shock as something hurled itself at his knees from behind. He went down and lay with his cheek pressed against the floor of the chamber, feeling its pulsating warmth, and glanced back in annoyance.

Fortunato had tackled him. The ace released his hold on Brennan, kneeled, and drew the .45 again. Brennan looked up at his men. Fortunato shot pieces of them away, part of a face here, a bit of an arm there. Fortunato cursed in a steady stream as he fired the .45 and Brennan's men died again.

Brennan felt a surge of tremendous anger. He half-stood and closed his eyes. The roar of gunfire stopped as Fortunato ejected an empty clip, but the stench of powder was in the air, the thunder of gunfire was in his ears, and the hot, humid smell of the jungle was in his nose. He opened his eyes again.

Ghastly caricatures of men, faces and body parts shot away, dripping green slime, were shambling toward him. They weren't his men. Mendoza had died in the raid on VC headquarters. Gulgowski had been killed by Kien later that night. And Minh had been killed years later by Kien's men in New York City.

Although his brain was still foggy, Brennan picked up his bow, and shot his last explosive arrow at the simulacra. It hit the caricature of Minh and exploded, sending gobbets of biomass everywhere. The backblast knocked Brennan down and took out the other two simulacra as well.

Brennan took a deep breath, and wiped slime and crushed protoplasm from his face.

"The Swarm Mother took their images from your mind," Fortunato said. "The other things were just buying time so it could prepare those walking wax-dummies."

Brennan nodded, his face hard and set. He turned from Fortunato and looked at Mai.

She was almost gone, nearly covered by the gray-pink flesh of the alien being. Her cheek rested against the pulsating organ and the half of her face that Brennan could see was untouched. Her eye was open and clear.

"Mai?"

The eye turned, tracking the sound of his voice, and focused on him. Her lips moved.

"So vast," she whispered. "So wondrous and vast."

The light in the chamber dimmed for a moment, then came back.

"No," Mai murmured. "We shall not do that. There is a sentient being in the ship. And the ship itself is also a living entity."

The floor of the chamber shook, but the light remained on. Mai spoke again, more to herself than Brennan or Fortunato.

"To have lived so long without thought . . . to have wielded so much power without consequence . . . to have traveled so far and seen so much without realization . . . this shall change . . . all change . . ."

The eye focused again upon Brennan. There was recognition in it that faded as she spoke.

"Don't mourn, Captain. One of us has given herself to save her planet. The other has given up her race to save . . . who knows what? Perhaps some day the universe. Don't be sad. Remember us when you look to the night sky, and know we are among the stars, probing, pondering, discovering, thinking innumerable wondrous things."

Brennan blinked back tears as the eye in Mai's face closed.

"Good-bye, Captain."

The singularity shifter began to throw off sparks. Fortunato slung the pack off his back. He looked down at it, startled. "I'm not doing that. She . . . it . . ."

They were back on the bridge of Tachyon's ship. The three men stared at each other.

"You succeeded?" Tachyon asked after a moment.

"Oh yeah, man," Fortunato said, collapsing on a nearby hassock. "Oh yeah."

"Where's Mai?"

Brennan felt a stab of anger cut into him like a knife.

"You let her go," he cursed, taking a step toward Tachyon, his hands clenched into quivering fists. But his eyes told who he really blamed for Mai's loss. He shuddered all over like a dog throwing off water, then abruptly turned away. Tachyon stared at him, then turned to Fortunato.

"Let's go home," Fortunato said.

After a while, Brennan would remember Mai's words, and wonder what philosophies, what realms of thought, the spirit of a gentle Buddhist girl melded with the mind and body of a creature of nearly unimaginable power would spin down through the centuries. After a while, he'd remember. But now, with a sense of pain and loss as familiar to him as his own name, he felt none of that. He just felt half past dead.

JUBE: SEVEN

There was a knock on the door. Dressed in a pair of plaid Bermuda shorts and a Brooklyn Dodgers tee shirt, Jube padded across the basement and peered through the spyhole.

Dr. Tachyon stood on the stoop, wearing a white summer suit with wide notched lapels over a kelly-green shirt. His orange ascot matched the silk handkerchief in his pocket and the foot-long feather in his white fedora. He was holding a bowling ball.

Jube pulled back the police bolt, undid the chain, lifted the hook from the eye, turned the key in the deadlock, and popped the button in the middle of the doorknob. The door swung open. Dr. Tachyon stepped jauntily into the apartment, flipping the bowling ball from hand to hand. Then he bowled it across the living-room floor. It came to rest against the leg of the tachyon transmitter. Tachyon jumped in the air and clicked the heels of his boots together.

Jube shut the door, pressed the button, turned the key, dropped the hook, latched the chain, and slid shut the police bolt before turning.

The red-haired man swept off his hat and bowed. "Dr. Tachyon, at your service," he said.

Jube made a gurgling sound of dismay. "Takisian princes are never at anyone's service," he said. "And white isn't his color. Too, uh, colorless. Did you have any trouble?"

The man sat down on the couch. "It's freezing in here," he complained. "And what's that smell? You're not trying to *save* that body I got you, are you?"

"No," said Jube. "Just, uh, a little meat that went bad."

The man's outlines began to waver and blur. In the blink of an eye, he'd grown eight inches and gained fifty pounds, the red hair had turned long and gray, the lilac eyes had gone black, and a scraggly beard had sprouted from a square-cut jaw.

He locked his hands around his knee. "No trouble at all," he reported in a voice much deeper than Tachyon's. "I came in looking like a spider with a human head, and told them I had athlete's feet. Eight of them. Nobody but Tachyon would touch a case like that, so they stuck me behind a curtain and went for him. I turned into Big Nurse and ducked into the ladies' room down from his lab. When they paged him, he went south and I went north, wearing his face. If anyone was looking at the security monitors, they saw Dr. Tachyon entering his lab, that's all." He held his hands up appraisingly, turning them up and down. "It was the strangest feeling. I mean, I could see my hands as I walked, swollen knuckles, hair on the back of my fingers, dirty nails. Obviously there wasn't any kind of physical transformation involved. But whenever I passed a mirror I saw whoever I was supposed to be, just like everyone else." He shrugged. "The bowling ball was behind a glass partition. He'd been examining it with scanners, waldoes, X rays, stuff like that. I tucked it under my arm and strolled out."

"They let you just *walk out?*" Jube couldn't believe it.

"Well, not precisely. I thought I was home free when Troll walked past and said good afternoon as nice as you please. I even pinched a nurse and acted guilty about stuff that wasn't my fault, which I figured would cinch things for sure." He cleared his throat. "Then the elevator hit the first floor, and as I was getting off, the real Tachyon got on. Gave me quite a start."

Jube scratched at a tusk. "What did you do?"

Croyd shrugged. "What *could* I do? He was right in front of me, and my power didn't fool him for an instant. I turned into Teddy Roosevelt, hoping that might throw him, and devoutly wished to be somewhere else. All of a sudden I was."

"Where?" Jube wasn't sure he really wanted to know.

"My old school," Croyd said sheepishly. "Ninth-grade algebra class. The same desk I was sitting at when Jetboy blew up over Manhattan in '46. I have to say, I don't remember any of the girls looking like that when I was in ninth grade." He sounded a little sad. "I would have stayed for the lecture, but it caused quite a commotion when Teddy Roosevelt suddenly appeared in class clutching a bowling ball. So I left, and here I am. Don't worry, I changed subways twice and bodies four times." He got to his feet, stretched. "Walrus, I've got to give it to you, it's never dull working for you."

"I don't exactly pay minimum wage either," Jube said.

"There is that," Croyd admitted. "And now that you mention it . . . have you ever met Veronica? One of Fortunato's ladies. I had a notion to take her to Aces High and see if I could talk Hiram into serving his rack of lamb."

Jube had the stones in his pocket. He counted them out into the Sleeper's hand. "You know," Jube said when Croyd's fingers closed over his wages, "you could have kept the device for yourself. Maybe gotten a lot more from someone else."

"This is plenty," Croyd said. "Besides, I don't bowl. Never learned to keep score. I think they do it with algebra." His outline shimmered briefly, and suddenly Jimmy Cagney was standing there, dressed in a snappy light-blue suit with a flower in his lapel. As he climbed the steps to the street, he began to whistle the theme song to an old musical called *Never Steal Anything Small*.

Jube shut the door, pressed the button, turned the key, dropped the hook, and latched the chain. As he slid the police bolt shut, he heard a soft footstep behind him, and turned.

Red was shivering in a green-and-yellow Hawaiian shirt filched from Jube's closet. He'd lost all of his own clothing in the raid on the Cloisters. The shirt was so big he looked like a deflated balloon. "That the gizmo?" he asked.

"Yeah," Jube replied. He crossed the room and lifted the black sphere with careful reverence. It was warm to the touch.

Jube had watched the televised press conference when Dr. Tachyon returned from space to announce that the Swarm Mother was no longer a threat. Tachyon spoke eloquently and at length about his young colleague Mai and her great sacrifice, her courage within the Mother, her selfless humanity. Jhubben found himself more interested by what the Takisian left unsaid. He downplayed his own role in the affair, and made no mention of how Mai had gotten inside the Swarm Mother to effect the merging he spoke of so movingly. The reporters seemed to assume that Tachyon had simply flown *Baby* to the Mother and docked. Jube knew better.

When the Sleeper woke, he had decided to play his hunch.

"Hate to tell you, but it looks like a bowling ball to me," Red said amiably.

"With this, I could send the complete works of Shakespeare to the galaxy you call Andromeda," Jube told him.

"Pal o' mine," said Red, "they'd only send it back, and tell you it wasn't suitable to their current needs." He was in much better shape now than when he'd first turned up on Jube's doorstep three weeks after the aces had smashed the new temple, wearing a hideous moth-eaten poncho, work gloves, a full-face ski mask, and mirrorshades. Jube hadn't recognized him until he'd lifted his shades to show the red skin around his eyes. "Help me," he'd said. And then he'd collapsed.

Jube had dragged him inside and locked the door. Red had been gaunt and feverish. After fleeing the Cloisters (Jube had missed the whole thing, for which he was profoundly grateful), Red had put Kim Toy on a Greyhound to San Francisco, where she had old friends in Chinatown who would hide her. But there was no question of his going with her. His skin made him too conspicuous; only in Jokertown could he hope to find anonymity. He'd run out of money after ten days on the street, and had been eating out of the trash cans behind Hairy's ever since. With Roman under arrest and Matthias dead (freeze-dried by some new ace whose name had been carefully kept from the press), the rest of the inner circle were the objects of a citywide manhunt.

Jube might have turned him in. Instead he fed him, cleaned him up, nursed him back to health. Doubts and misgivings gnawed at him. Some of what he had learned about the Masons appalled him, and the greater secrets they hinted at were far, far worse. Perhaps he should call the police. Captain Black had been aghast at the involvement of one of his own men in the conspiracy, and had publicly sworn to nail every Mason in Jokertown. If Red was found here, it would go badly for Jube.

But Jube remembered the night that he and twelve others had been initiated at the Cloisters, remembered the ceremony, the masks of hawk and jackal and the cold brightness of Lord Amun as he towered over them, austere and terrible. He remembered the sound of TIAMAT as the initiates spoke the word for the first time, and remembered the tale the Worshipful Master told them of the sacred origins of the order, of Guiseppe Balsamo, called Cagliostro, and the secret entrusted him by the Shining Brother in an English wood.

No more secrets had been forthcoming on that night of nights. Jube was only a first-degree initiate, and the higher truths were reserved for the inner circle. Yet it had been enough. His suspicions had been confirmed, and when Red in his delerium had stared across Jube's living room and cried out, "*Shakti!*" he had known for a certainty.

He could not abandon the Mason to the fate he deserved. Parents did not abandon children, no matter how depraved and corrupt they might grow with the passage of years. Twisted and confused and ignorant the children might be, but they remained blood of your blood, the tree grown from your seed. The teacher did not abandon the pupil. There was no one else; the responsibility was his.

"We going to stand here all day?" Red asked as the singularity shifter tingled against the palms of Jube's hands. "Or are we going to see if it works?"

"Pardon," Jube said. Lifting a curved panel on the tachyon transmitter, he slid the shifter into the matrix field. He began the feed from his fusion cell, and watched as the power flux enveloped the shifter. Saint Elmo's fire ran up and down the strange geometries of the machine. Readouts swam across shining metal surfaces in a spiky script that Jube had half forgotten, and vanished into angles that seemed to bend the wrong way.

Red lapsed back into Irish Catholicism and made the sign of the cross. "Jesus, Mary, and Joseph," he said.

It works, Jhubben thought. He should have been triumphant. Instead he felt weak and confused.

"I need a drink," Red said.

"There's a bottle of dark rum under the sink."

Red found the bottle and filled two tumblers with rum and crushed ice. He drank his down straightaway. Jube sat on the couch, glass in hand, and stared at the tachyon transmitter, its high, thin sound barely audible above the air conditioner.

"Walrus," Red said when he had refilled his tumbler, "I had you figured for a lunatic. An amiable lunatic, sure, and I'm grateful to you for taking me in and all, with the police after me the way they are. But when I saw you'd built your own Shakti machine, well, who'd blame me for thinking you were a little short on the gray matter." He downed a slug of rum. "Yours is four times as big as Kafka's," he said. "Looks like a bad model. But I never saw the roach's light up that way."

"It's larger than it needs to be because I built it with primitive electronics," Jube told him. He spread his hands, three thick fingers and blunt curved thumb. "And these hands are incapable of delicate work. The device at the Cloisters would have lit up had it ever been powered." He looked at Red. "How did the Worshipful Master plan to accomplish that?"

Red shook his head. "I can't tell you. Sure, and you're a prince to save my sweet red ass, but you're still a first-degree prince, if you get my meaning."

"Could a first-degree initiate construct a Shakti machine?" Jube asked him. "How many degrees had you passed before they even told you the device existed?" He shook his head. "Never mind, I know the punch line. How many jokers does it take to turn on a light bulb? One, as long as his nose is AC. The Astronomer was going to power the machine himself."

The look on Red's face was all the confirmation Jube needed. "Kafka's Shakti was supposed to give the Order dominion over the Earth," the Mason said.

"Yeah," Jube said. The Shining Brother in the wood gave the secret to Cagliostro, and told him to keep it safe, to hand it down from generation to generation until the coming of the Dark Sister. Probably the Shining Brother had given Cagliostro other artifacts; without a doubt he had given him a power source, there being no way the Takisian wild card could have been anticipated two centuries ago.

"Clever," Jube said aloud, "yeah, but still a man of his times. Primitive, superstitious, greedy. He used the things he had been given for selfish personal gain."

"Who?" Red asked, confused.

"Balsamo," Jube replied. Balsamo had invented the rest himself, the Egyptian mythos, the degrees, the rituals. He took the things he had been told and twisted them to his own use. "The Shining Brother was a Ly'bahr," he announced.

"What?" Red said.

"A Ly'bahr," Jube told him. "They're cyborgs, Red, more machine than flesh, awesomely powerful. The jokers of space, no two look alike, but you wouldn't want to meet one in the alley. Some of my best friends are Ly'bahr." He was babbling, he realized, but he was helpless to stop. "Oh, yeah, it could have been some other species, maybe a Kreg, or even one of my people in a liquid-metal spacesuit. But I think it was a Ly'bahr. Do you know why? TIAMAT."

Red just stared at him.

"TIAMAT," Jhubben repeated, the newsboy gone from his voice and manner, speaking as a Network scientist might speak. "An Assyrian deity. I looked that up. Yet why call the Dark Sister by that name? Why not Baal, or Dagon, or one of the other nightmarish godlings you humans have invented? Why is the ultimate power word *Assyrian* when the rest of the mythology Cagliostro chose was Egyptian?"

"I don't know," Red said.

"I do. Because TIAMAT sounds vaguely like something the Shining Brother said. *Thyat M'hruh*. Darkness-for-the-race. The Ly'bahr term for the Swarm." Jube laughed. He had been telling jokes for thirty-odd years, but no one had ever heard his *real* laugh before. It sounded like the bark of a seal. "The Master Trader would never have *given* you world dominion. We don't give anything away for free. But we would have sold it to you. You would have been an elite of high priests, with 'gods' who actually listened and produced miracles on demand."

"You are crazy, pal o' mine," Red said with forced jocularity. "The Shakti device was going to—"

"*Shakti* just means power," Jhubben said. "It's a tachyon transmitter, and that's all it ever was." He rose from the couch and thumped over to stand by the machine. "Setekh saw it and spared me. He thought I was a stray, a leftover from some offshoot branch. Probably he felt it would be wise to keep me around in case anything happened to Kafka. He'd be here now, but when TIAMAT headed back toward the stars, the Shakti device must have seemed somewhat irrelevant."

"Sure, and isn't it?"

"No. The transmitter has been calibrated. If I send the call, it will be heard on the nearest Network outpost in a matter of weeks. A few months later, the *Opportunity* will come."

"What opportunity is that, brother?" Red asked.

"The Shining Brother will come," Jhubben told him. "His chariot is the size of Manhattan Island, and armies of angels and demons and gods fight at his beck and call. They had better. They've got binding contracts, all of them."

Red's eyes narrowed in a squint. "You're telling me it's not over," he said. "It can still happen, even without the Dark Sister."

"It could, but it won't," Jube said.

"Why not?"

"I don't intend to send the call." He wanted to make Red understand. "I thought we were the cavalry. The Takisians

used your race as experimental animals. I thought we were
better than that. We're not. Don't you see, Red? *We knew she
was coming*. But there would have been no *profit* if she never
arrived, and the Network gives nothing away for free."

"I think I'm getting it," Red said. He picked up the bottle,
but the rum was gone. "I need another drink," he said. "How
about you?"

"No," Jube said.

Red went into the kitchen. Jube heard him opening and
closing drawers. When he came out, he had a large carving
knife in his hands. "Send the message," he said.

"I went to see the Dodgers once," Jube told him. He was
tired and disappointed. "Three strikes and you're out at the old
ball game, isn't that what they say? The Takisians, my own
culture, and now humanity. Is there anyone who cares for
anything beyond themselves?"

"I'm not kidding, Walrus," Red said. "Don't want to do
this, pal o' mine, but us Irish are a stubborn bunch of cusses.
Hey, the cops are *hunting us down* out there. What kind of life
is that for me and Kim Toy, I ask you? If it's a choice between
eating out of garbage cans and ruling the world, I'll take the
world every time." He waved the carving knife. "Send the
message. Then I'll put this away and we can order up a pizza
and swap a few jokes, okay? You can have rotten meat on your
half."

Jube reached under his shirt and produced a pistol. It was
a deep translucent red-black, its lines smooth and sensual yet
somehow disquieting, its barrel pencil-thin. Points of light
flickered deep inside it, and it fit Jube's hand perfectly. "Stop
it, Red," he said. "It won't be you ruling the world. It will be
the Astronomer, and Demise, or guys just like them. They're
bastards, you told me so yourself."

"We're all bastards," Red told him. "And the Irish aren't
as thick as they say. That's a toy ray-gun, pal o' mine."

"I gave it to the boy upstairs for Christmas," Jube said.
"His guardian gave it back. It wouldn't break, you see, but the
metal was so hard that Doughboy was breaking everything else
in the house when he played with it. I put the power cell back
in, and wore the harness whenever I went to the Cloisters. It
made me feel a little braver."

"I don't want to do this," Red said.

"Neither do I," Jhubben replied.

Red took a step forward.

* * *

The phone rang a long time. Finally someone picked it up at the other end. "Hello?"

"Croyd," Jube said, "sorry to bother you. It's about this body . . ."

Available now from Titan Books

WILD CARDS

Into a world hungry for peace, comes a spaceship
ferrying chaos…

An alien bomb is detonated above the planet,
shedding an indiscriminate gene virus on an Earth
barely recovered from the horrors of World War II.

The result: Wild Cards. Aces blessed with
superhuman powers and Jokers cursed with physical
and mental disfigurements.

This is their story.

Coming soon from Titan Books

JOKERS WILD

For forty years the survivors of the 'Wild Cards' virus have struggled to cope with its legacy: the creation of superpowered ACES and disfigured JOKERS.

Now, from the subterranean depths of New York, one such survivor, embittered by deformity, hungry for control, unleashes the powers of darkness upon an unsuspecting populace...

Wild Cards Day brings twenty four hours of death, when ACES and JOKERS alike must fight for their lives!

Coming soon from Titan Books

ACES ABROAD

As the nations struggled through four turbulent decades, from the end of World War II through to the sleek New Wave '80s, the bizarre metahumans created by the Wild Cards shape the course of history.

Now an investigative committee of Wild Card victims, fueled by a new political awareness, sets out on a world tour to learn how Aces and Jokers are treated in other countries around the globe.

If you have any difficulty obtaining any of
the Titan range of books, you can order
direct from Titan Books Mail Order,
71 New Oxford Street, London, WC1A 1DG.
Tel: (01) 497 2150

Star Trek novels	£2.95 each
Star Trek: The Next Generation novels	£2.95 each
Star Trek Giant novels	£3.95 each
The Star Trek Compendium	£7.95
Mr Scott's Guide to the Enterprise	£6.95
The Star Trek Interview Book	£5.95
Star Trek V: Movie Calendar 1990	£4.95
Worlds of the Federation	£8.95
Thieves' World novels	£3.99 each
Wild Cards novels	£3.95 each
Thunderbirds novels	£2.95 each
Captain Scarlet novels	£2.95 each

For postage and packing:
on orders up to £5 add £1.20; orders up to £10 add £2;
orders up to £15 add £2.50; orders up to £20 add £2.70;
orders over £20 add £3.
Make cheques or postal orders payable to Titan Books.
NB. UK customers only.

While every effort is made to keep prices steady, Titan
Books reserves the right to change cover prices at short
notice from those listed here.